WICKED
LUCIDITY

Mandy M. Roth

Erotic Paranormal Romance

New Concepts   Georgia

Be sure to check out our website for the very best in fiction at fantastic prices!

When you visit our webpage, you can:
* Read excerpts of currently available books
* View cover art of upcoming books and current releases
* Find out more about the talented artists who capture the magic of the writer's imagination on the covers
* Order books from our backlist
* Find out the latest NCP and author news--including any upcoming book signings by your favorite NCP author
* Read author bios and reviews of our books
* Get NCP submission guidelines
* And so much more!

We offer a 20% discount on all new Trade Paperback releases ordered from our website!

Be sure to visit our webpage to find the best deals in e-books and paperbacks! To find out about our new releases as soon as they are available, please be sure to sign up for our newsletter (http://www.newconceptspublishing.com/newsletter.htm) or join our reader group (http://groups.yahoo.com/group/new_concepts_pub/join)!

The newsletter is available by double opt in only and our customer information is *never* shared!

Visit our webpage at:
www.newconceptspublishing.com

New Concepts Publishing, Inc.
5202 Humphreys Rd.
Lake Park, GA 31636

ISBN 1-58608-785-1
August 2005 © Mandy M. Roth
Cover art (c) copyright 2005 Eliza Black

NCP books are available at special quantity discounts for bulk purchases for sales promotions, premiums, fund raising, or educational use. For details, write, email, or phone New Concepts Publishing, Inc., 5202 Humphreys Rd., Lake Park, GA 31636; Ph. 229-257-0367, Fax 229-219-1097; orders@newconceptspublishing.com.

First NCP Trade Paperback Printing: April 2006

Dedication:

To my childhood friends, you know who you are, for still playing with me after it was painfully clear that I had a rather colorful imagination. Thanks for giving in and joining me in my own private insanity.

Prologue

"Do you hear me, Dark Angel? You cannot defeat us all."

I snickered as I stared up at the vampire that had me pinned to the hard pavement. He looked down at me with eyes that weren't even strong enough to decide between pale yellow and orange. Neither of which were found in nature but then again, vampires weren't exactly run of the mill. Well, unless you lived my life. In my reality, they were staples.

His rank breath moved over me as he practically spat in my face. "Have you nothing to offer, Dark Angel?"

He pushed down harder, using his forearm to press against my throat. My eyes widened as I stared up at him. I could feel him trying to force his power, his dark magik into my mind. Had I been human, it would have worked. He'd have been able to turn my mind with ease, bend my will to suit him.

For once, I was thankful that I was anything but human. I let my body go limp, pretending to succumb to the death he offered. Smugness radiated off him. I lay there, careful to use my own power to mask my life signs.

The vampire laughed, the sound so full of evil that I had to fight not to cringe. I remained still as he climbed off me. "Let all know that I have slain the great Dark Angel! She died at my hands! She took her last breath before my eyes! She..."

Blah, blah, blah.

I struck out fast, ramming the heel of my boot into his groin. "She is sick of hearing you babble, asshole." I rolled, following him as he backed up cupping himself. Quickly, I delivered another blow to his mid-section, catching him off guard and sending him tumbling to the ground.

I got to my feet fast and towered over him. Grinning, I stared down at him as I put my hand out. My magik rose to the occasion. "Stake," I said, conjuring one instantly. I glanced at it and then the not so smug looking vampire on the ground.

He hissed. "No. You were dead."

"Technically, you're dead so do we even need to get into a debate or do you want me to get this over with?"

"Boss?" Seger, my second in command, called out from around

the other side of the large building. "You back here?"

The ugly vampire seized the momentary distraction to sweep my legs out from under me. Never one to take the easy route, I flipped high into the air, tucked my long legs into my body and used my power to stop myself. Redirecting my momentum, I flipped back towards him.

He gasped as I extended my body, striking him back to the ground. I slammed the stake down, scoring a direct chest hit. A puff of dust surrounded me and I held my breath until it cleared.

A strong hand fell upon my shoulder. "Boss? Karri, you okay?"

Glancing down at the partially shifted, clawed hand, I smiled. "I take it that you guys ran into some more bad guys."

Seger chuckled, allowing his bloodied, lycan claws to slide back under his skin. The light layer of fur there began to recede quickly, leaving only a human hand in its place. "Yeah, you can say that. If you add in the dead bodies I see lying around you, I'd say our count for the night is up to forty-three. That's a hell of a lot higher than it should be. Any word from the powers on what's going on--why the bad guys seem to be coming in droves?"

The idea of the powers, the men and women sworn to over see and protect the innocents, giving a damn about a surge of evil in the tiny Midwestern town we had only just arrived in, made me laugh. We, various teams of four soldiers, dedicated our lives to serving them, righting wrongs and keeping humans safe from things they could only dream about. The only thanks we got was to be double-crossed or flat out ignored. "They don't care, but I do."

"I hate to admit it but you were right to want to warn the team based here, Karri. These demons we fought tonight aren't just piss-ant nothings. They were strong. Strong enough to take all four of us to beat."

"Yeah," I whispered, looking around at the carnage. Sighing, I lifted my arms high into the air. "Tell the others to hold on. I'm about to play clean up."

Seger grinned and pressed his hand to his walkie-talkie. "Karri's playin' housekeepin'. Watch your asses or you'll end up dusted too."

I rolled my eyes and shook my head as I let my power ride out and over the dead bodies. A second before I let it loose, I felt another presence, a familiar one. Gasping, I stared around at the darkness, trying to locate the source but finding nothing.

"Karri?" Seger asked, pressing up against me.

"Do you sense that?"

"Sense what?"

I shifted a bit, still feeling a familiar presence. "Someone I know is close."

He chuckled. "Not to point out the obvious, Karri-Lynn but Amber, your best friend lives a few blocks down."

"I know that. Not her, idiot. Someone else. Someone powerful."

"I don't feel anything, boss. But I believe you do." He put his arm around me and pulled me into the warmth of his body. "Come on, let's get rid of these bodies before a human wanders in and finds out that their shiny happy world isn't so sparkly. And then we need to get you moved into your new place."

I looked around at the bodies and snickered. "Somehow, I thought it would be different here, Seger."

"Different how?"

I shrugged. "I don't know. Less violent."

He laughed, deep and from the gut. "Oh, darlin' you'd be bored to tears if you didn't get to chop at least one demon's head off a night."

As sick as that sounded, he had a point. "Suburbia, here I come."

Chapter One

I stared at the large Victorian home in front of me. What was I thinking? The place was huge. Too big for just one person and certainly too much work for me. Calling it a fixer-upper was a far cry from the truth. My need to start a new life and protect the lives of others had outweighed my better judgment. I was hardly a master craftsman and I'd just taken on the project of a lifetime.

Pulling a box out of the trunk of my car, I glanced around at the rest of the neighborhood. It was even better than Amber had described. My house was one of three on the cul-de-sac. The one to my left had caught my eye the moment I'd arrived. The white home with green shutters looked as though it had been meticulously tended. Of course it would be my luck to move next door to someone who was picky. I could already see the feuds over my unkempt lawn. Maybe, if I were lucky, the neighbors would get mad enough to clean my yard because they were sick of looking at it.

"Karri, get your butt up here. You have got to see this!" Amber, my best friend, shouted from the fourth-story window.

I headed in, carrying the box of cleaning supplies as far as the front porch before I ran up the stairs. Walking into the large, full attic, I found Amber digging through two large chests I had specifically told the "movers" to put in the far back corner of the basement.

Yeah, they listened well.

The movers, also known as "my men," were currently out to lunch. They'd spent the morning setting up my home office. Since they worked for me in the fight against evil, it was in their best interests to get me up and running as soon as possible. Livelihoods and actual lives depended on me. They'd already banished me from the room because I was hovering too much. They told Amber that she could stay, but from the way they were all staring at her breasts, I was scared to leave her without a chaperone.

Amber dug through the contents of the chest, her long auburn hair falling in and over it. She looked like a curious nymph all tucked in on a secret she couldn't wait to reveal. She held up an object with a long silver handle and a pickaxe-like top. Her blue eyes grew with fascination. "What is all this stuff?"

"Weapons. They're all from my father's collection. I finally took them out of storage."

"Wow," she whispered.

I went to her quickly, removing the war pick from her hand, convinced she'd put an eye out if she wasn't careful. "Let's leave it be. Our luck we'll chop our fingers off or something."

"Pfft, you're like Karri Lee, fighting queen. Hey, did you see the thing in there that looks like brass knuckles but it has claws on it instead? That's wicked cool."

I chuckled. "Yeah, it is wicked all right."

Amber had a flare for dramatics. Not that it came even close to meeting mine, but still. The coffee shop she owned was set up more like a psychic reader's home base but the locals seemed to flock there for the coffee all the same. In truth, she was very sensitive to most people and places so it made sense that she'd naturally lean towards the Psychics R Us look. Had she not been battling sickness, her skills and gifts could have developed more and she would've made one hell of a psychic.

As far as I knew, or rather, as far as Amber let on, she'd been doing well for the greater part of a year now. I hoped that was true. The idea of losing my closest friend terrified me. The idea of losing her to a cancer-like illness that human doctors didn't understand and continually mislabeled sickened me. Amber's sickness came from not using her powers. It was that simple. Since she was unaware she even had powers it wasn't an easy fix and telling her to use what she'd been burying since birth wasn't as cut-and-dry as it sounded.

One had to come into one's powers on one's own. It was just the way things were. Trust me, if I could have fixed her by shouting "use your magik" I, of all people, would have. It would have saved me a lot of pain and several deals with the devil.

Amber laughed. "Have you looked in the mirror?"

"No. I don't have one hung up yet, so unless I can find a really reflective puddle then I'm not getting to see myself anytime soon. Why?"

Amber shook her head. "You look like an erotic cowgirl housekeeper."

"Excuse me?"

"You heard me." She pulled her long hair back at the base and fastened it with the tie she kept on her wrist. "I can't ever remember seeing you with a do-rag on your head. Don't get me wrong, the whole big brown eyes, white-blonde hair hanging in loose strands from that rather sad bun thing is hot. But the red handkerchief, barely there, tiny top you've got tied over those borderline obscene breasts might be a bit too much. That looks like a bikini top gone horribly wrong."

I snickered. So did Amber.

"Sort of like a cowgirl's version of a day at the beach, Karri. Oh, I do love the dirt on your nose and cheek though. And the jean cut-offs thing you've got going is all the rage. The topper is the brown work boots. Nice."

Glancing down, I bit my lip as I checked myself over. "I wasn't aware I was being judged in the housecleaning portion of the pageant. If I say that I want to end world hunger for my question and answer time with the panel judges, will I still have a sporting chance of winning? I really want to be Ms. Bitch of the Universe."

Amber shook her head and started down the wooden steps. "You are such a smartass."

"Thanks. Can I get some points on that as well? Have they wised up and added that category yet?" I answered, following behind her. She went towards the front door and I went for the fridge. "Pick your poison," I called out.

"Beer."

"Beer it is. I should have known. You're all cute and dainty looking, right up until I see you chugging on a cold one. Sorry I was a bad influence on you." Grabbing two, I headed out and found Amber sitting on the front porch steps with her head down. Immediately, I worried that she was lying about being in remission. I'd seen her at her worst with it and had no desire to see her go through it again. If I could head it off, I would. "Hey, you feeling okay? We can take a break. In fact, we can call it quits for the day. I don't win a turkey or turn into a pumpkin if I don't finish unpacking by midnight. And since I have no prince, I'm in no hurry. Should I leave behind a work boot for any possibilities to find me later?"

Laughing, she shook her head. "I'm fine. Don't start worrying for no reason."

I sat down next to her and handed her a beer. "I earned my worry badge, honey. Take it or leave it."

She nudged me and giggled. "I'm glad you finally moved out here. I hated knowing you were alone in New York."

"I wasn't alone, Amber. I had Chester." I grinned from ear to ear as she moaned.

"Karri, a parakeet, which has since died, doesn't count."

Taking a sip of my beer, I winked as I aimlessly fiddled with the triple knot, silver charm necklace I wore all the time. "Now you're discriminating against non-humans. What happened to you? We didn't graduate that long ago."

Amber snorted. "You know it's bad when I start thinking seven years is a lifetime."

To Amber, seven years was a long time. As sick as she'd been, it was a miracle that she was here at all. I wrapped my arm around her and gave her a good squeeze. "This is a music moment if I ever felt one coming on."

"Oh no, you aren't going to get me dancing around in public again. My days for that are long gone."

Ignoring her, I hopped to my feet and rushed to find my portable CD player. I'd last seen it in the dining room but that didn't mean much in the middle of a move. With the endless heaps of boxes scattered about my house, it could be buried anywhere. "Tony, Tony, look around." I smiled as I did my slight homage chant to the patron, Saint Anthony, who was supposed to help me find lost things. Or, at least that's what I think he was good at helping with. My luck he was the one you asked for help when you wanted to lose something.

I let my power up just enough to find what I was looking for. The second I zeroed in on the CD player, I dropped the power.

As I picked the player up, I found a box marked dresses and costumes. Setting the CD player on it, I picked it up and took it out with me, happy that I'd propped the screen door open with a brick. Trying to carry it all would have been impossible otherwise.

I set it down next to Amber and wagged my brows. Opening the box, I couldn't hide my excitement as I saw all the things I still had. I grabbed the long white wedding dress and its sister, a floor-length emerald green maid of honor dress. "Look what I found." I held the dresses up. The green one had been tailor made for Amber with the idea she'd be my maid of honor. Yeah, that's right. I was supposed to be the bride. I bit back a laugh. Too bad it didn't work out that way.

Amber shook her head. "No way."

"Hey, we might as well get our use out of them." Tossing the green dress to Amber, I laughed as she caught it and pulled it over her head quickly.

I stepped into the sleeveless wedding dress and pulled it up my body. Its large, bell-like bottom flared out all around me. I zipped it as best I could and bent down to the CD player. "I thought one of these moments might come about so I made a CD for the occasion."

Amber covered her eyes and peeked out from between her fingertips. "Please tell me that you didn't do what I think you did."

I pushed play and stood before her. One of the seventies disco songs that I'd played to death when we lived together came on and Amber squealed. "No, you still have this? You were too young to like it in college. I'll dig a hole so you can bury it. Dump the wedding stuff in it too. I'm sure I can even find you a sparkling silver shovel to bury it with."

Putting my hand out, I waited for her to take it. She refused it. I didn't give up. I swayed my hips back and forth, reenacted every seventies dance I could think of and was on the verge of singing. Amber stared out from under her hands, laughing hysterically.

"Hey, are you suggesting I dance like a court jester?"

"Yeah, if court jesters should be in a thong on a pole, then you sure do. Only you could pull it off in that get-up." She dropped her head down and snorted. "Heaven help the children of the neighborhood.

"Come on, Strawberry Field. Get out here."

"Don't go calling me that again, Karri."

I kept dancing. Seeing Amber happy made me not care who thought what of me. Not that I'd ever cared much in that department anyway. "I'll keep hitting repeat on the playing of the funky music if you don't join me."

Amber stood slowly and sighed. "Know that I do this only to spare your neighbors any further torture."

"*Mmmhmm.*" I put my hand out to her and pulled her gently to me. We did a fake bump of hips. I concentrated hard on paying attention to my strength with her. It wouldn't take much power on my part to inflict damage to her and that wasn't something I'd allow to happen.

The second Amber began moving her head to the beat, I couldn't help but smile wide. "I knew you still had it in you. And I would like to point out that even considering all of his flaws, *he,* note that I'm not naming names, did a wonderful job of selecting a dress that looks hot on you." Every piece of me wanted to shout exactly who had had the dresses made. Somehow, the very whisper of Jean-Paul's name could bring him and I wasn't really up to seeing him. Not that he'd venture out in broad daylight, but still. I held my tongue.

"Gee, I'll have to send him a thank you."

I laughed. "Umm, please don't." We moved to the beat, just like old times. "Whoohoo, it's still there. I was afraid you might have either lost your love for our private disco revival moments or did your best to forget them."

The faint sound of a screen door opening filled the air. It made the idea of being in a real neighborhood all that much more exciting. There wasn't, as yet, any demon shouting out how I was the Dark Angel sent to destroy them all. No. There was the sound of a screen door. As mundane as that may be to anyone else, to me, it was heaven.

The feeling of being watched came over me then passed quickly. I didn't obsess about it. In fact, having an audience for my theatrics was always kind of fun. At the moment, Amber laughing and smiling was the most important thing to me.

"How could I ever forget those revivals?" she asked, spinning into my arms and then back out again. "You worked your magik over me and left me a closet fan of music that people run from. Sorry, but that includes the '80's."

"Hey, I say we start a petition to get leg warmers, ripped up sweatshirts and spandex back on the market. Think jumpsuits and front men of bands. Though, unless they're a lycan or shifter of some sort, they aren't allowed to have chest hair."

"Oh, we're making exceptions now?" Amber mused, as we danced in close to one another shaking our upper bodies and laughing. "Are you now dating blondes too?"

I gasped. "Bite your tongue. That's blasphemy! Blondes--ugg. My hair is blonde enough. I don't want to be staring at another head of it. Besides, doesn't every little girl dream of growing up to find that tall, dark and deadly man of her fantasies?"

"You mean tall, dark and handsome."

I shrugged. "That too, but really, what's the fun of a pretty face? If the guy is that worried about what he looks like, he'd hate me. There have been days when I have to think about whether or not I brushed my teeth. It's gross. I know. But I don't care." I shook my hips a bit to the music and laughed. "And if he can't hold his own, that leaves me protecting two people. No thanks."

Amber laughed. "Oh, right. I always forget about the demons that want your head on a stick." She winked at me, clearly still not believing any of it. "Are any of them cute?"

"The sad thing is yes, most of them are cute. If it wasn't for that pesky   wanting-to-wipe-humans-off-the-face-of-the-earth   thing they've got going, they'd be the perfect catches." I winked. "When you're ready, I'll let some of my men shift for you. I will have to have a video recorder there, though, to see your face and catch your apology on film. I've earned it, sugar."

She snorted. "I will never get used to hearing you say that. Your men? You sound like you own an escort service. But if those guys who helped you move," she motioned toward the house, "are any indication of what the rest look like, then I won't complain a bit if you are."

"At times, it feels like I do run one. I go on more fake dates than anyone I know. And yes, the men who helped move me are like the rest."

Amber changed positions and stood next to me. We did one of our famous at-the-bar, giving-into-not-caring, personalized line dances. I laughed so hard my sides hurt. The sweet sound of Amber giggling was music to my ears. Turning to face the opposite direction, I spotted a little girl with long, dark brown pigtails staring up at us with big green eyes. She looked so familiar to me, but I was positive I didn't know her. I smiled.

"Hi Amber," she said, showing off her missing front teeth.

Amber kept dancing. "Hilary," she said, sounding very happy to see the child. "How was shopping?"

Hilary put her hand on her hip. "Next time I want you to take me. Daddy and Uncle Riston argued the whole time. They didn't know what size I wear. Uncle Riston told daddy to look at my tag. Daddy said that the reason we were there was to get the next size up. It was too big." She put her hands in the air and sighed, appearing so much older than her age. "*Men.*"

I snorted. "A girl after my own heart."

Amber laughed. "Uncle Riston was right. I got you that dress last week so it's the right size. Do you want me to take you this weekend?" Amber bumped my hip. "We can take Karri with us. She's very, umm, interesting to take shopping. She once made me try on every dress in the store."

"Every one of them?"

I nodded. "Yes, every one. Amber said that she'd never find a dress that looked good on her. I then made her find one that didn't. I even got a group of people to sit and eat popcorn with me while we waited for her to show us every last one."

Hilary giggled. "They must have been nice ladies to sit there that long."

Amber gave me a droll look. "Yeah, they were real nice guys that had really nice scorecards that Karri made out of napkins."

"You didn't get below an eight on any of the outfits. Told ya you looked great in anything you put on." I blew her a kiss and kept dancing. "You did get quite a few numbers after that if I remember right."

Amber ignored me and focused on Hilary. "Would you like to join us?"

"Really?" Her eyes widened.

I moved quickly to the porch and pulled the fairy princess dress, that had been intended to be the flower girl's dress at my "didn't happen" wedding, out of the costume box. "Would you like to wear this one?"

"I get to wear a dress too?" she asked, in a sweet little singsong voice.

Nodding, I brought it out and eased it over her head. Her pigtails bounced wildly about before settling back into place. "There. You look beautiful."

"I do?"

"Drop dead sexy," I said. Amber nudged me hard. I cleared my throat. "Umm, you look very, very pretty."

Hilary's brows rose. "I can't be drop dead sexy?"

I laughed. Amber nudged me again.

"I won't get it dirty," Hilary said, glancing nervously at the ground.

"Pfft, roll in the mud. It's fine by me," I said, touching the tip of her button nose.

Hilary gave me a cautious look. "Really? You won't be mad and go away."

I didn't really understand where she was going with this but I shook my head all the same. "Nope. You can do whatever you want in it. Want me to spray paint peace signs on it? You could draw on mine too."

"Are you sure I can get it dirty?"

"Yep." I dropped down on the slightly damp grass before her and grinned. "You can have the dress, Hilary. I'll even have it cleaned for you when you're done playing if you want. I promise that I can get any stain out of it. So, let's start by making ourselves unbeautiful brides."

Her tiny brow furrowed. "Hmm?"

Pushing my hands through the grass, I felt the slightly moist dirt beneath it. I took a handful of it and rubbed it on my dress, leaving a big mud streak. Hilary gasped and took a tiny step back. I picked up some more dirt and took her hand in mine. The minute our hands touched, I felt a spark of her power leap up and recognize mine. She gasped.

"Oh," she said, staring into my eyes. "You're special."

Amber choked on air as she touched my shoulder. "Aww, even children are staring to think you're crazy. Normally, they're your biggest fans."

I winked at Hilary, knowing we shared a secret that Amber didn't understand. "You're special too."

"She is not crazy," Amber said defensively. I chanced a glance at her, wondering why it was okay for her to refer to me like so many others had over the years but me being truthful to Hilary was not acceptable.

Hurt, I pushed a smile onto my face. "Relax, Amber. I meant it in the special-person kind of way. Not the *me* kind of way."

She exhaled deeply. "Oh, good."

I stiffened and instantly felt another energy in the air around me. It was soothing yet probing me, getting a sense of my intentions. Unsure of where it was coming from, I stood eerily still until it passed. "Okay, that was odd. Any one else feel like they just had little green men examining them from the inside out?"

Hilary raised her hand and giggled. "Me."

"Stop encouraging her," Amber said, glaring at me. "I don't need her stuck in some fantasy land her entire life, too. It's enough dealing with you."

I forced another smile onto my face and nodded. "Well, good thing for you that I gave you a seven-year reprieve. And if I should become a bother, oh mighty sane one, please write it backwards so that when I'm searching for life on Mars in my review mirror, I can decode it." I didn't bother to hide the hurt I felt.

Amber dropped down fast, touching my shoulder and licking her lower lip. The worry on her face told me that she cared about hurting me. That meant something to me. "I didn't mean it like that. I don't think you're crazy for real, Sweets. I just tend to… grr… I don't know. I'm shutting up now."

Hilary grabbed my face and pulled it close to hers. "My mommy told me once that crazy is sometimes beautiful, especially when it comes bearing sunshine." She lifted a stray strand of my blonde hair and smiled. "See, sunshine. I think she was right."

Tipping my head, I smiled. "Why do you think she was right?"

"Because I think you're beautiful and if you're crazy too, then she was right."

The feeling of being watched suddenly took on a new feel. Not a bad thing--just so much as more intense. I would have looked behind me but my gut told me Hilary would sense my unease. I held back.

"Why thank you, Ms. Hilary." I winked at her again. "I think you're beautiful too. In fact, you remind me a lot of someone I was very close to once. In my eyes, she was an angel."

"I remind you of an angel?" she asked, her mouth opening wide.

"Yes, you do." I stood slowly and put my hand out to her. "Want to dance with us?"

Amber touched my arm lightly. "Karri, I didn't mean all that the way it came out. I just… umm… gawd, I didn't mean it. I should think before I speak. It's not like I haven't had to explain to others that you're sane and here I go hitting below the belt."

Leaning over towards her, I wagged my brows. "I prefer eccentric but I think the state may agree with you." I kissed her cheek quickly. "I could use the down time. Do you think if I begged extra that they'd sedate me? Numb me from myself? I could go for that."

"Don't even talk like that, Karri."

"Amber doesn't like it when I talk about some things," Hilary said, softly. "I guess she doesn't like it when you talk about some stuff too."

"Really? What doesn't she like you to talk about?" I put my finger on my lips and pretended to be thinking extra hard. "Let me guess. Amber doesn't like it when you talk about the temper redheads have?"

Hilary giggled. "No, she doesn't like it when my daddy talks about that."

Really? That was interesting. I glanced at Amber.

She shot me a panicked look. "Karri, don't add fuel to the fire. We're having enough issues."

I gave her a puzzled look. "We?"

Hilary yanked on my skirt. "I heard you say lycans and vampires before. Do you believe in them?"

"Of course Karri doesn't, honey. She's silly like that sometimes. She pretend plays a lot."

I cleared my throat. "And she's standing right here." I smiled at Amber before looking down at Hilary. "Please know that Amber's going to pinch me for this, but do you believe in them?"

"Karri!" True to my guess, Amber pinched my arm.

Hilary smiled wide and nodded. "I do. I told Amber that there are nice ones, too. She doesn't believe in them and said so. "

"Oh, there are. I know. And just between you and me, most of them are very handsome."

She giggled and nodded her head madly. "Have you ever kissed one?"

"Hilary!"

I looked at Amber with wide eyes and tipped to the side. She arched a brow. "Why are you leaning like that, Karri?"

"Well, when your head explodes, I don't want to wear it. Brain tissue wouldn't go well with my dress." Had I not actually had the displeasure of wearing brain matter several times in my line of work, I'd have only meant it as a joke. It did tend to stain. I didn't point that out though.

"Ha, ha. Now tell Hilary you're joking and be very clear that you have never kissed one."

"Nope." Glancing down at Hilary, I nodded. "I have kissed a few in my time. The first one was my daddy." I pointed at her cheek. "I kissed him right there every night before I went to bed."

Her eyes lit. "I kiss my daddy there too. And I kiss my uncle there too."

"Please don't call your uncle a werewolf again."

Hilary and I sighed and spoke at the same time. "Lycan."

Amber stared at us and took a step back, covering her eyes and laughing so hard I thought she'd fall over. "Of course. I should have known the two of you would get along perfectly."

"Mrs. Karri, can you change into a wolf?"

Amber laughed even harder, snorting as she went.

Ignoring her, I shook my head. "No, Hilary. I can't. My dad didn't pass that on to me. I don't think many little girls get that from their daddies. I think it's more of a boy thing. But," I put my hand up, "I did get the same color eyes as him."

"Me too."

"And, Hilary. Just call me Karri. No *Mrs.* anything. I'm not married nor do I like being reminded that I'm technically a grown up. I'm only an adult when I'm working. Any other time I'm anything I want to be. Now, I feel like being a bride covered in mud, who spent the morning cleaning and who wants to dance instead of unpacking one more box. Sound good?"

She nodded and moved in quick, shaking her hips to the music. It was so cute that Amber and I stopped what we were doing and followed her lead for a minute. She giggled and laid it on even thicker. We mimicked her. "You two are silly."

"No, sweetie," Amber said. "I'm silly. Karri's crazy in the best way possible. She's crazy beautiful."

Hilary glanced at me. "Neat."

Amber huffed. "You get a cult following wherever you go."

Putting my arms out, I looked up to the sky and laughed. "It's good to be me. Oh, come my adoring fans. Gather around me. I want cabana boys with loincloths on."

"Watch what you say," Amber said, shaking her head, spilling various curls of red from her hair tie.

"What? Is it so wrong to want minions? I'll happily take them if they come about six-five, with dark hair and blue eyes. I'll even accept green eyes. I'm a very giving person. Ooo, and they have got to have a bigger butt than me."

Hilary giggled.

Amber snorted. "That shouldn't be hard since you're built like a supermodel."

"Right," I laughed hard, "I looked like a bean pole until I was sixteen. I woke up one day with a suddenly filled out body. It scared the heck out of me."

"You mean you got *hellos*," Hilary said, shaking her upper body.

"Hellos?" I asked, not following.

She pointed at my chest and giggled. "You know, chunga-chungas."

I thought Amber might actually pass out. "Hilary, who taught you that?"

"Well, Thatch and Seaton always point at women with them and call 'em chunga-chungas. Uncle Riston goes to yell at them, sees the lady and says 'hello.'"

"Does he now?" I did my best to fill the awkward silence while Amber began to hyperventilate. "Does your daddy have a name for them?"

She nodded. "I asked him what they were really called and he said 'something that he hopes I never get'."

I bent down and put my arms out. "Oh, honey. They're called breasts and someday, a long time from now, you will get them."

Her eyes widened. "Will it hurt?"

"No."

She wiped her forehead. "Whew. Those look like they'd hurt. Amber's especially look like they'd hurt coming in."

I did my best not to laugh. "Oh, yeah, hers just finally stopped growing."

Amber pinched me again.

"Could you pick a new spot? I'm going to have a bruise there."

Hilary touched my cheek. "My friend Mindy has a big sister who told us that we'll start to bleed once a month and won't ever stop soon. Is that true? I asked daddy and he got sick to his stomach. I tried to ask my uncle but he put his hand up and told me that he didn't want to talk about it."

"Amber?" I asked, suddenly needing a little back-up. The very idea of discussing menstruation with a child that I barely knew who came just below my hip level didn't appeal to me. Come to think of it, the idea of discussing it with a child of any age made my stomach turn. I was not a 'get to know your body functions' professor by far.

"Oh, no. You got yourself into it. You get yourself out of it."

I panicked and did the only thing I could think of doing--I tried to distract her. I snapped my fingers and the CD player stopped playing the CD I'd made and started playing the first song that popped into my head, *Like a Virgin*.

"Oh my God, Karri, I can't believe you..."Amber stopped yelling at me and covered Hilary's ears. "Go advance this. You should have warned me that you had this sort of stuff on there."

I shrugged. "I panicked. This was the first song that came to my head."

"Oh, like I'm supposed to believe you just made it come on out of thin air." She shook her head. "Get rid of it. Now!"

I grinned. "Party pooper."

She growled.

"You suck the fun out of everything." I jogged over to the CD player and thought about something that would be Hilary appropriate. I drew a blank. "Any suggestions?" I turned down Madonna and waited. Getting no help from Amber, I closed my eyes and relied on instinct. When *Wishin' and Hopin'* began to play, I sighed and turned it up.

Hilary's face lit. "My mommy used to sing this." She began to sing along and stopped. "You two need to sing too." A defiant little look passed over her face and the song instantly started over. I knew that Hilary had used her own power to cause that to happen. Amber didn't. Her brows arched.

"Uhh, CD must be scratched."

"I am not singing anything," Amber said, shaking her head.

Feeling bad for Hilary, I rolled my eyes and gave in. The moment I began to sing her little face lit up. I wrapped my arms around myself and spun in a circle, making the bottom of the wedding dress fan out. Hilary did the same thing as me as she began to sing too. I put my hands out and she came to me instantly.

I spun her in a circle fast, still singing as her little legs went out in the air. I wrapped her in my magik, assuring myself that she couldn't get hurt and felt another magik, the strange one I'd felt before move to encircle her as well. It bumped into mine and backed away quickly.

Setting Hilary down, I kept singing as she giggled and walked lopsided. I playfully danced my way to Amber who had her hands in the air while she shook her head no. Ignoring her, I took her hand and pulled her towards me. I rocked our bodies and reached back fast, grabbing Hilary and pulling her to me before she fell from being dizzy. She laughed harder.

I followed suit and backed up a bit, bumping into something solid when I knew that nothing was there. My entire body began to burn in the best way possible and for a split second I was convinced that a large hand touched my cheek. Knowing my imagination was off the charts when it came to overactive, I didn't dwell on the sensation. Instead, I finished the song and spun Hilary again. This time I crumbled onto the ground next to her and laughed as the song ended. I nodded my head in the direction of the CD player, assuring myself that only songs that were appropriate would play.

"I think you're wonderful!" Hilary beamed as she stared over at me. "You're not crazy. You're perfect."

"Can I get that in writing?" I asked, laughing softly.

"Sure but you might have to help me spell wonderful."

Amber and I both laughed. I bumped my elbow against Hilary's and winked. "I think we're off to a great start here. What do you think?"

"I think you should marry my uncle. He's very nice and very tall and very handsome and very staring at your..."

"Hilary!"

My eyes widened and I thought I might have to smack Amber's back to get her to quit coughing and choking on her own laughs. "Excuse me, but I think we already went over the 'I'm not getting...'"

"I heard you just fine," Hilary said, smiling wide. "That's how I know you can marry him, 'cause you aren't married now. You're free for the pickin'. He would like you. I know it." She glanced behind me and winked.

I couldn't help but follow her gaze. Nothing was there. "You wouldn't happen to have an imaginary friend standing behind me, would you?"

"Nope. He's real." She smiled so wide that I thought I might be able to see right through her dimples and out the other side of her head. "I think he likes your *hellos* and I think he likes your butt, too."

"Hilary!" Amber said, laughing under her breath and ultimately losing any credibility in the correction department she might have had.

"Sweetheart, I don't think you should try to play matchmaker for your uncle or for your--" I glanced behind me again and could have sworn I sensed something there, just briefly, "imaginary friend."

"No," Amber said, still snickering. "She really should. The guy could use a good woman. Now, I wouldn't wish you on him in a million years and there is no way you'd go for his personality. His looks, yeah. His personality, no."

"Gee, now I feel compelled to ask why."

Hilary gave me a toothless grin. "See, I knew you'd want to know more about him. All the ladies who come around do but he doesn't let me tell them. He'll let me tell you though." She wiggled her hips and nodded her head. "Yep. I can tell you all about him. Did I tell you he was tall already? I think I did. He's like daddy. He has big muscles. I think he can pick up my house but I can't get him to try it. Maybe you can."

"Hmm," I mused. "I'll have to see about that. An entire house is awfully big. How about we ask him to pick up a car instead. That would be fun to watch."

"Want me to have him take his shirt off? Ladies seem to like it when he does it. They all make funny noises. Well, all except Amber," she said, with nothing short of a serious look on her face. Her need to see me happy was suddenly opening a whole new world of hunkiness to me. I seriously considered taking her up on her offer, but held back.

That wasn't wrong, was it?

My gaze went to Amber who was actually holding her lips together to keep from laughing. "Can I ask where you got the idea to try to marry your uncle off?"

"I dunno." Hilary gave an awe shucks look. "I saw you dancing with Amber and it just popped into my head. I think you're his match."

"His match?" This, I had to hear more of. "What? We look alike?"

"No, silly. You know--a match. Someone you were made for. Umm ... err, mate. That's what it's called."

As Amber giggled, I narrowed my gaze on Hilary and thought hard about what she was saying. It was almost too much to believe that a little girl could come up with that on her own.

"You should really think about marrying him. He's really nice and he used to be very fun to play with."

Used to be? I held my question in.

"Amber, get the mini-you and do something with it. It's scaring me."

"Oh, that little girl is almost a carbon copy of you personality-wise, Sweets."

"Stop calling me that. I hate it."

"I know. But it's so cute. I give you a piece of candy and you sleep for a day. Your mom must have loved that. Anyone else ends up with a hyper kid. She got a tired one." She waved at me and I thought about zapping her in the butt with power. I held back. "Karri, you're lucky that I luv ya like a sister. I have a billion other things I could call you in place of Sweets."

"Great, since you know me so well, explain to Hilary that I don't date nice men much."

"Why don't you date nice men?" Hilary asked.

I winced. "Can we change the topic?"

"Want to tell me if I'll start bleeding and never stop?" she asked.

I gulped. "I do date nice men, sometimes. I just lose interest in them rather quickly."

"I see, you chose the easy way out," Amber said, putting her hand on her hip and winking at me. "Coward."

"Yeah, please remember that before I arrived she thought 'the girls' were called 'hellos' and 'chunga-chungas'."

"You can call them *the girls*, too?" Hilary beamed.

Groaning, I rolled over in the grass and began to bang my forehead against the ground lightly. "Example-A as to why I do not and am never going to have children. I've scarred her for life and she's not even mine."

"Uh-huh."

Taking a deep breath in, I prepared to hear the answer to a question I couldn't help but ask. "Okay, uh-huh what?"

"Uh-huh, you will have kids because I want a cousin. No. I want lots of cousins and I'm planning on marrying you off to my uncle so I get some."

I ignored the last comment. "Ohmygods, was I this persistent when I was her age?" When I thought hard about it and got a yes, I wanted to bang my head even harder. "Crap, now I feel like I need to write out apology letters to anyone who had to deal with me."

Hilary giggled and got her feet. I followed suit, noticing the feeling of being watched again. I wasn't sure it had ever really gone away.

"Look what I can do," Hilary said. She instantly did a summersault, popped up fast and immediately examined the dress she had on carefully, even going as far as smoothing the little yellow dress she wore beneath it.

"Very good. You know what you're doing, don't you?" I went and stood next to Amber.

The smile that spread over Hilary's face was adorable.

"Hilary, Sweets can do that too," Amber offered, giving me a smug look.

"Really?" She looked me up and down. "My mommy could do them too before she died."

Died? I glanced at Amber. She nodded and my heart broke for Hilary. "Did she teach you?"

"Yep, want to see?" She didn't wait for my answer. Instead she took off running and did a round off back handspring. She went high into the air after her ending, telling me she'd built up a good deal of speed. Amber and I clapped wildly for her as she finished.

"Did I do good?" she asked, running up to me.

"You rocked."

"I did?" she asked, with a shocked expression on her face. "Rocking is good, right?"

"You betcha." Bending down to her level, I grinned. "I think you did so good that you might be able to add one more back handspring to that. You still had a lot of momentum when you finished."

"Momentum?"

"You went real fast and real high." It was moments like this that made it clear why I had no children of my own. Speaking to them seemed to be a flip of coin, one moment I got it right, the next I was fucked, or rather, they were staring at me with confused looks on their faces. Yep, they were foreign little beings to me. That much was for sure.

"Oh. Okay, show me how," Hilary said, glancing behind me at something and smiling wide. She winked, and I wasn't sure if it was directed at me or the nothingness behind me.

Biting my lip, I glanced at Amber. "Do I get to play too or am I going to embarrass you more? I have a pink straightjacket around here somewhere. You could make me wear it and tie me out on a dog lead if it will make you feel better."

Amber snorted and crossed her arms over her chest. "Like you have ever cared if you embarrassed me or not. I can't believe you still have the straightjacket. I'm ashamed to admit it but I like it-- even though it was pink."

As I adjusted the wedding dress, I gasped. Looking down, I saw how loose the portion over my breasts was. "*Hello*, I think the girls are shrinking."

"Huh?"

Leaning to the side, I wiggled the front of the dress, showing her exactly how loose it was. She covered her mouth as a squeal came out. I growled. "Show a little support here, it's clear I need it." I cupped my breasts and realized Hilary was staring at me with wide eyes. "Don't be in a hurry to grow up, kiddo. Suddenly, things matter that shouldn't."

She nodded. "Like 'the girls.' I know. Being a woman is hard work. Men have no idea."

I was too shocked to laugh. Amber did it for me.

Something tugged on the back of the wedding dress lightly. As I heard the tell-tale sound of a zipper, the front portion of the dress tightened, conforming to my breasts perfectly. I glanced at Amber who had a rather wide, pleased expression on her face.

"Thanks, I didn't think of that. See! I need you for the details, Amber. I'm always leaving those out. I have horrible visions of tripping on *the girls* when I'm eighty. Couple that with my newfound fear of deflating and I'm going to need that jacket really soon." I took a deep breath and cupped my chunga-chungas once more. "You'd tell me if my butt took a trip south, wouldn't you? That's it. First thing I'm doing after I'm done unpacking the kitchen is going running with a tight sports bra on of course."

"Umm, Sweets…err… I didn't zip..."

Tipping my head, I wrinkled my nose. "It's okay to tell me that without you I'd either forget my own head or walk into yet another doorway. I swear that I only shut off mentally when I'm not working." As I stared at her it hit me what we were doing. "You do realize that we're traipsing around in designer wedding apparel."

She nodded nervously and turned slightly red. "Maybe we should take them off. *People* might see us."

"Pfft, you lived with me for how many years? Did you miss the days I went to the market for us? Remember when I wore that black bikini with the sheer mesh dress over it because that lovely lady there told me I couldn't come in that one time because I had on shorts and a bathing suit top?"

Amber burst out in laugher. "I liked the day she tried to tell you that you couldn't wear the mesh thing either. You made me check to be sure that no one was looking and untied the bikini top. The second that thing fell to the floor, old Mr. Parthron dropped his milk and clutched his chest. You felt bad for weeks because he ended up having to be rushed to the hospital."

I covered my eyes and chuckled. "I did visit him everyday but I don't think he knew."

"How could he not know?"

I glanced down at my chest. "He wasn't looking at my face. He was staring at my *hellos*."

Amber's jaw dropped. "He was like ninety!"

"You and I knew that. He didn't seem to care. Besides, I know men who are five hundred years plus and they still look. They look a lot. Immortals are the horniest..." I covered my own mouth to stop the rest of that from coming out.

Amber shifted awkwardly. "We should stop. We … umm … might ruin the dresses."

I narrowed my eyes on her. "Amber, you hated Jean-Paul. You're the one who sent him the cake topper with the groom's head missing and a tiny toothpick glued to where his heart would be. Nice vampire joke by the way. Didn't you?"

"Yes, I sent it. I didn't hate him. I just thought he was too pushy when it came to you. Most of the time he seemed all romantic and perfect for you but the way he watched you." She shivered. "It wasn't right. It was like he was ready and willing to eliminate anything that dared to step between him and you. I thought he seemed dangerous."

"He was and still is."

"Tell me he's not still in your life." She put her hand up. "Not that I think he'd really ever hurt you or that he's not one of the most gorgeous men I've ever laid eyes on, even if he does have black hair."

I let out a soft laugh. "I'd lie to you but he'll be here a lot, so I think you'll catch on."

She grabbed my arm. "Do you love him?"

I tried to answer but found myself laughing too hard to do much of anything.

"I'll take that as a no."

I snickered. "Good guess. But I should point out that I now consider him a friend. Granted, he seems to always have an ulterior motive but in the end he does the right thing."

"You spent years trying to keep him at arm's length. You kept insisting that he was a business associate yet the man did his best to try to lavish you with expensive gifts and French charm."

"Hmm, he still does that too."

"Yeah, well does he still come across like he's the leader of some deadly band of thugs? The men that would show up at our house with him to see you were huge, sexy and looked like they could rip the heads off anyone who got on their nerves. As if that wasn't weird enough, Jean-Paul did think he owned you."

Shaking my head, I sighed. "Amber, after you left I went to work for him. Well, not for him--but it's complicated. I'm my own boss now, but he's still in my life because he's not quite the man we thought he was."

"What? He's gotten even more suave?" She rolled her eyes, stood tall, cleared her throat and did her best to impersonate Jean-Paul's mannerisms. Putting her hand out, she touched my check. "*Ma chérie*, why can you not see what is right before your face? You wait for a man who does not care to come. A man who is not man enough to claim what is rightfully his. Any man who leaves you to never return is no man for you. He is no man at all. Allow me to love you as you were meant to be loved."

I instantly burst out into laughter. "He's not that bad anymore. But that was a dead-on impersonation."

"Not that bad? Has he stopped filling your car with so many roses you can't open the door without having an avalanche?" She rolled her eyes in disgust. "Or are you coming home with only one black eye now?"

That stopped my laughter. "Jean-Paul has never hurt me. He's saved my life more times than I can count. I told you what I do for a living. Coming home a little battered and bruised is an occupational hazard. Now, lighten this conversation so we can all go back to having fun."

Hilary pulled on the bottom of my dress. "What do you do for a living?"

"I, umm, it's hard to explain, sweetheart."

"Is it important and dangerous?"

Of course it was dangerous. I killed demons and bad things for a living. I was one of the men and woman who protected mankind from the evils that sprang forth from hell on a fairly regular basis. Without people like us, demons would roam free, take over the earth and slaughter everyone in its path. Somehow, important and dangerous didn't seem to really cut it but I wasn't about to stop and point that out to her. "You could say that."

"But you get pretty dresses to do it in."

Amber rolled her eyes and pointed at my dress. "When Jean-Paul showed up on the front lawn with all of this, dressed in a tux with an orchestra and a justice of the peace I knew he'd lost his mind. I thought the claiming to be a vampire was bad enough."

Hilary tugged on my dress. "You had a vampire show up with a wedding?"

"No, she had an as..." I slammed my hand over Amber's mouth and smiled down at Hilary.

"Yep, I had a guy show up with a wedding. I never really thought about it like that but that's exactly what he did."

"What did you do?" she asked, her eyes the size of half-dollars.

Amber bit my hand and I let go fast. "She kicked him in the head and threatened to stick the justice of peace up his..."

I glared at her.

"Up his jacket sleeve. Yes, sleeve," she added, keeping it as kid friendly as possible.

Hilary moved in closer to me. "Did you really kick him in the head?"

"See, there was this…umm…bee, yes a bee by him and I thought I'd help him out and keep him from getting stung. His head accidentally got in the way of my foot."

"Oh," she said nodding. "Did the bee live?"

"Yes."

"Good."

I laughed. "I like the way you think, kid."

She instantly mimicked my moves. "I like the way you think too, not kid. Will you still show me how to do the extra flip?"

"I don't know. I think I'm going to need to see you smile again first."

She beamed, showing off her missing teeth.

"That'll work." Lifting the dress, I kicked my boots off and rolled my shoulders. "I need to back up more and you need to move. I'm a little bit taller than you and need more space."

Hilary laughed. "You're a giant."

"Told ya so," Amber teased.

"Five-ten is not a giant. Six-five is. Remember when I took that poll?"

Amber's eyes widened. "Yeah, too bad the rest of what you took size preferences on is X-rated or we could have a trip down memory lane."

Pointing at her, I gave her a shit-ass grin. "Remind me later. I still have the pictures that I made them all pose for."

"No way!"

"Hey that was *hard* work. We now have over five hundred pictures to prove it. I've seen 'em all--big and sadly enough, small."

Amber snorted and then stopped, instantly glancing behind me. My supernatural senses didn't pick up anything unusual. I gave her a questioning look. She smiled sweetly.

"Okay, Hilary. If I break my leg you have kiss it and bring me ice water for two whole days until it's better."

She giggled as I took my running start. I did a round off, launched myself backwards into my first flip, hit the ground and quickly did another. The long dress fell in long waves over me. Pulling it down, I huffed as I struggled with it. "Hilary, I think the dress tried to eat me. Warn me not to do that again."

She giggled. "Well, just think, at least the dress isn't the vampire."

Wiping my face, I laughed. "I really do like the way you think, kid. You remind me of someone very special."

"Teach me that!"

Hilary didn't really give me much of a choice, she backed up a bit and launched into the same routine. I ran next to her, using my magik to spot her and nodded.

"Snap both legs together. Good. Okay, again." She landed and put her hands in the air like a pro. "You rock, kiddo."

"I did it! Amber, did you see me? I did it."

"Great job, baby." Amber clapped madly for Hilary while I received a hug that almost knocked me over.

"Daddy, did you see that?" she asked, letting go of me slowly.

I looked up and found two men standing behind Amber. Both seemed familiar in some way but I couldn't place them.

One had chin-length blond hair with green eyes. His gaze was locked on Hilary. The look he had was one of unconditional love, a father's look if I'd ever seen it. Amber seemed drawn to him and that piqued my interest.

When I glanced at the other man, my breath caught. Stunning didn't begin to cover it. His short chestnut-brown hair was just the way I liked my men to wear their hair, close on the sides and back but a bit longer on top. And he had the bluest eyes I'd seen a very long time. Tiny wire-framed circular glasses seemed to draw more attention to them, holding my gaze longer than they should have. I did my best to remember to breathe but my body wasn't cooperating very well.

As my gaze raked over his clean-shaven square jaw line and down his thick neck, I had to fight to keep from drooling as cords of muscle popped in it. It was a neck I could easily picture myself licking, nibbling on while laying him out before me and exploring every last inch of him.

The snug black tee shirt he wore left the muscles in his broad chest showing, allowing me to visually outline each and every one. His was certainly a body I could see myself staring at endlessly. I bit back a sigh. The light, faded loose-fitting jeans he wore managed to conform in all the right spots. He certainly was all man and if my calculations were correct, more man than I'd be able to fully take.

A girl can dream.

When I caught sight of the black military-style combat boots, I couldn't help but smile. He was like a mail-order man. He couldn't have been more on the mark for my wish list if he tried. Suddenly, suburban living was looking better and better.

"Mmm."

"What?" Hilary asked.

I kept my eyes locked on the brunette but bent down a bit. "It was the equivalent of yummy. And I do mean yummy."

Her green eyes widened. "Yummy?" She seemed to think about it a minute and formed a tiny 'O' with her mouth. "It's like a girl's way of saying *hellos*?"

"Sounds better than chunga-chungas don't you think? That makes me think of two cantaloupes strapped down with…err, forget what I was going to say there. Let's just go with a "men are yummy"."

Amber cleared her throat and I shrugged. "Oh, did you think I'd be able to stare at that," I nodded towards the walking version of my male wish list, "and not comment. You're so lucky it was G-rated."

The man's lips curled slightly, as though he was doing his best not to laugh. It only turned me on more. I did my best to think of a time when I'd been so drawn to a man the instant I laid eyes on him but couldn't come up with anything. "Do I know you two?"

They exchanged glances and the blond seemed to wait for the brunette's response before answering. That wasn't something one found in normal life much. Thankfully, my life wasn't normal. The brunette shrugged and lifted a dark brow as a rather sexy, smug look moved over his face. It didn't fool me. He was skeptical of me. I could almost feel it. I couldn't blame him. I got the sense that he was concerned for Hilary as well.

The music changed and the minute The Beatles came on, Amber groaned. "Here she goes."

I put my hands in the air and began to shake my hips slowly, working into the beat of *I Am The Walrus*. Amber laughed. I pointed at her. "Rule number one in my bizarre reality: If The Beatles come on, everything else stops."

The blond nudged the brunette. "Hmm, right up your alley. In fact, you do make us all stop what we're doing when The Beatles come on."

"Really?" I asked, impressed. I didn't wait for his response. Instead, I took hold of his hand and gasped as heat seemed to pour into me. "Come on."

Hilary giggled and ran at my feet. "Amber says this song doesn't make any sense."

I smiled. "I know and that's the beauty of it."

"You won't get him to dance with you, Sweets," Amber called out.

"Want to bet?" I pulled the tall brunette to me, turned into his body and took hold of his hands, placing them on my hips. He gave a tiny squeeze and I realized that his hands were so large that they almost touched around me. I began to move, slowly at first but working into the beat fast.

Hilary spun in tiny circles with her arms in the air like a ballerina while the sex god behind me gave in and moved with me. I couldn't help but to glance over my shoulder and smile. When he smiled back, I thought my heart would melt.

"Come on, Eric." Amber pulled the blond guy out into the yard and forced him to dance, too. She shook her head and her ass. It was great. "You're crazy!" she shouted at me.

"Crazy beautiful," the man dancing with me said under his breath. My supernatural hearing allowed me to pick up on it.

"I cannot believe you got him to do that and he's smiling nonetheless," Amber said, staring up at the hunk I was dancing with while she continued dancing next to us with a hunk of her own. We, surprisingly, didn't bump into each other and considering the close proximity we were dancing in, that was amazing.

Part of me couldn't believe the man was doing it too, but I didn't let on to that. Instead, I savored the feel of his large, muscular body pressing to me. Hilary began to sing and pretend to be a bird. I laughed. "Ohmygods, I used to do the same thing when I was your age."

"You did?" Hilary asked, her eyes wide and a huge smile across her face.

"Yep. And when the song was done, I would beg the person with me to play it again. I think I made him nuts with it."

"I make my uncle nuts with it. It's fun."

"Isn't it though?" The song neared the end and I realized that I was actually disappointed. Apparently, Hilary shared my opinion. It continued to play long after it should have been done and I knew I didn't do it. I cast her a sideways glance and found her doing her best to appear to be innocent.

I snorted. "I ain't buying it, sister. Keep working on the puppy dog eyes. You're oh, so close. Stick the lip out a bit more. Oh, and be sure to tilt your head down."

"Lots of cousins," she said, blinking in an overdone fashion. "Lots and lots."

"Do not make me cast a spell on you. I'll do it. You'll wake up tomorrow with..."

"*Hellos*?" she asked, sounding hopeful.

Looking up, I shook my head. "I surrender. She has done me in. Thank you for the whole no-kids thing. I'm surprisingly fine with it."

"Oh come on," Amber said, smiling as the tall blond spun her slowly. "As much as I make fun of you, you would be a fabulous mother."

I stumbled a bit and ended up stepping on the brunette's foot. "Oh, umm, sorry. The thought of reproducing scares the--" I glanced down at Hilary, "--umm, it scares the heck out of me."

"Lots of cousins," Hilary said, folding her arms over her chest.

The man holding me chuckled and the sound ran over me. I sighed and leaned into him. That made Hilary grin from ear to ear. "Lots and lots."

"Then I'll find your uncle a brood mare."

Amber coughed hard and I stilled.

"Are you okay?"

"I'm fine. Stop worrying about me all the time." She winked. "I'll live."

"You better," the blond said, tipping her chin up a bit. It was an intimate thing to do and I had to wonder at just how close she and this blond guy, Eric, really were. It wasn't like Amber to keep secrets from me but in her defense, I'd been absent from her life a long time and had no real clue what was going on in it. All I could do was hope that whatever was between them was mutual and made Amber happy.

Amber smiled and batted her eyes every so slightly that if I hadn't been looking at her to gage her reaction to Eric, I'd have missed it. Seeing how fixated she was on him, I knew then that something was at the very least, brewing between them. "Eric, you worry too much."

"I don't know, Riston, do I worry too much?" Eric asked.

The man holding me let out a slight laugh. "Just a little."

I was about to comment but stopped when I sensed the pressing feel of evil nearing at an alarming rate. It pushed in on me, seeming to run over my skin as it often did. My senses were set to pick up on negativity, on evil--they were trained for this sort of thing.

My heart began to beat wildly in my chest. I could feel the evil energy, reaching out, scanning the area for something. Riston, the hunk holding me, stiffened. I ran my hand over his doing something I never thought I'd do--seeking comfort.

The sounds of an ice cream truck approaching filled the air. My mind didn't want to register what it sensed to be true. The stench and feel of evil that surrounded me increased ten fold. It was radiating from the ice cream truck. The very demons I'd spent my younger years terrified of and my adult years fighting were trying to find Hilary. They must have sensed her gifts. It was a common thing with the shortage of females in the supernatural race. The bad guys liked to just steal theirs. Age didn't really matter.

Hilary's eyes lit. "Daddy, it's the ice cream man."

Eric pulled Amber behind him and the protective movement wasn't lost on me. He put his hand out to Hilary. "Not today, honey."

"But, daddy."

Amber sighed. "Eric, just let her have..."

We didn't have time for this. I stepped in. "Hilary."

"Are you going to tell me no, too?"

"Nope, I was going to ask what your favorite kind of ice cream is."

She smiled wide. "I like the kind with cookie dough in it but the ice cream man never has that."

This one has a hell of a lot more than that. A big scoop full of evil. No thanks.

"Amber, take Hilary in and get her a great big cone full of cookie dough ice cream."

Amber's brow furrowed. "But, you don't eat..."

"You have that kind?" Hilary asked, wide-eyed and happy, just the way I wanted to keep her.

Nodding, I put my hand on her shoulder. "I sure do. Now, take Amber's hand and make her do her silly ice cream dance. I'm sure you've seen it."

Giggling, Hilary grabbed Amber's hand. "Please?"

Amber looked to Eric and he nodded. She sighed. "Okay, come on."

I watched as they went into the house and thrust my power out, assuring that cookie dough ice cream and cones were now available in my kitchen. I leaned a bit towards Eric but directed my attention at the approaching ice cream truck. "I'm sorry about that. I hope I didn't spoil lunch for her."

"No. It's fine," he said, a bit fast. Did he sense the danger too?

As the truck neared, Riston pulled on my arm, trying to put me behind him. I wasn't having any of that. The truck pulled to a stop across the street from us and the driver, a man who looked to be about twenty-five but was more like three-hundred stepped out of the truck. He looked around the neighborhood slowly. If it was a magikal girl he'd been sent for, it was a magikal girl he was going to get.

"Excuse me, gentlemen." I ran, barefoot, across the street, lifting the wedding dress to keep from tripping on it. I knew I looked like a nut. I was aiming for that.

The man spotted me and raked his gaze over me slowly, looking amused. "Can I get you something?"

I nodded eagerly, almost child-like. "Oh, yes. I wanna marry you. I love ice cream men and my brother said I could. He's the blond back in the other yard. He said that if I wanted you I could take you." Seizing hold of him I began to dance in a circle to the music from the ice cream truck. Had I not been pretending to be off my rocker even more so than normal, I'm not sure I could have pulled that off. Though, if I didn't have witnesses, I would have just pulled the demon's head off and saved time.

"Mmm, marry me, huh?"

Oh, he sounded too enthused about that. I let my magik rise up fast, taking hold of him and spinning him hard into his truck. His forehead made an odd thumping sound as it bounced off the truck.

"Hey, what the... "

Grabbing his arm, I hugged him tight to me, applying enough pressure to let him know that I wasn't human either. "I'm so glad you came. I've been waiting in the attic for years and years and years and years for you."

He did his best to try to break my grasp but I wasn't having any of it. "Shit, you're fucking crazy, lady."

And deadly, asshole.

I began a nice little dance number that left me slamming his head into the truck again right before I kneed him in the groin. He cupped himself and fell to the ground. I tackled him fast, pinning him to the street. "I'm in my dress. Let's go. We can have lots and lots of babies. So many that we run out of names. I love babies, don't you?"

The man looked terrified. "No, I…off…what are you?"

"I'm the one you've all been looking for." I let my magik hold him tight. "I felt you all coming. Each one of you. Now I've finally found The One. I want to hug you forever. Can I hug you forever? Oh, you should meet my brother." Rolling off the demon masquerading as a man, I yanked him up and hugged him tight. "Eric, look it's the ice cream man."

I glanced up to find Eric and Riston standing side by side watching me with equally shocked looks. I waved and then picked the supposed ice cream man's hand up. I made him wave too. He tried to pull away and I pulled him back to me. "I wanna go now."

"Go?"

"Get married."

His eyes widened. "You're a crazy witch."

I'd given him exactly what he was looking for, a female with magikal powers. Granted, I added a hefty does of crazy to keep him from coming back but still. I danced around him poking and jabbing, knowing I was hurting him. Leaning in close, I let out a maniacal laugh. One I'd learned from years of going undercover. "Tsk, tsk, now it's not very nice to call me a witch. Especially when I'm anything but."

Spinning him one last time, I rammed him into his truck with glee, careful to make it look as though I was the world's clumsiest dancer. I was aware of just how insane I most likely looked to everyone but I didn't have much of a choice. The demon needed its ass kicked and I needed to keep the fact that demons were prowling the streets for children as low key as possible. Being labeled crazy seemed a small price to pay for the greater good. "Let's go. Hurry before my brother tries to stop us."

Riston and Eric made a move to come for me and I drew upon my power fast, thrusting the compulsion for them to remain where they were out and at them. I also made sure to lace my power with a calming energy. I didn't need any of them getting worked up about the situation. No. That was my job. The very idea of this asshole having come to collect Hilary to do gods only knew what with her sickened me. I'd have killed him if I thought I could get away with it without Hilary witnessing it. No child needed to see that kind of horror and no child needed to be hunted.

The man fought me off. I pretended to try to cling to him as he rushed into his truck. Forcing a smile to my face, I let my eyes go hard, hoping he got my point--I can be crazy and no one here can stop me. Want to play? "But I thought we were going to live happily ever after?"

"Uhh, I gotta go."

I stood, watching him speed away. When I knew he was gone I dusted my hands off and danced in a tiny circle, no longer looking like a crazed love-sick loon. Now I just looked crazy. That was fine because it meant Hilary was safe and so was the knowledge that things that go bump in the night also go bump in the day light. Again, small price to pay for a child's safely.

I laughed and froze when I found Amber staring at me. Hilary stood next to her licking a double scoop ice cream and grinning.

My gaze went to Riston and Eric. They both stood there with identical blank looks on their faces. Hilary giggled. "You got to dance with the ice cream man. Hey, I thought you said you didn't want to get married? How come you told him you did?"

Lowering my gaze, I smiled. "You and I know that," I pointed in the direction the man had sped off in, "he didn't. Plus, he could not dance. Rule number two in my world: If the man can't dance, then he's not a keeper."

A rather serious look came over her face. "What's rule number three?"

"That I'll never remember all my rules and make them up as I go."

"Oh," she said, laughing.

I crossed the street and Amber reached up. She put her hand on my forehead and then shrugged. "Well, I can rule out a fever. Try not to keep anymore ice cream men, please. Your pet collection of men is scarily big as it is."

"But my brother said..."

"You're an only child."

I licked my lips and let a smug look settle over me. "I know that."

Hilary pointed down the road in the direction the ice truck had disappeared in. "He doesn't. *Men.*"

"I really like you, kid."

"Thanks, I like you too. You remind me of my mommy." Hilary patted my upper thigh. "She would have really liked you. Want to come over and see her picture? She was pretty like you too. But she wasn't a giant."

Eric and Riston gasped. I looked at them, hoping to figure out what had shocked them. The blond's brow furrowed as he took a step up and stood close to Amber. "Amber?"

Amber glanced at me and winked. "Yeah, Eric, Hilary's been very open about Paula since she got here. She took instantly to my friend."

I sensed Hilary's anger the instant it came over her. It radiated off her in tiny waves. She was powerful. Too powerful to be left unchecked. Touching her shoulder, I ushered her several feet away from the group and I bent down fast. "Want to tell me what's making you so mad?"

She crossed her arm and turned her nose up. "No."

"Great then, we won't talk about you not talking about mommy ever and getting everyone all worked up about it."

Amber's eyes widened. I knew she didn't like the comment I'd made. What else was new?

Hilary nodded, still in her defiant stance. She gave me a good look over. "You make me think of her. She was fun too. But I'm not going to talk about her and you can't make me."

Putting my hand up, I bit my lower lip and shrugged. "Fine. We won't bring her up."

"Good."

"Did she like to dance too? I'm only asking because you are a very good dancer." I did my best to look like I had an attitude too as I waited for her to take the bait.

Hilary's eyes widened. "Oh, yes. She loved to dance. She could even dance so daddy turned really, really red. I think it had something to do with her 'hellos' but I'm not talking about her anymore."

I sat down on the grass and Hilary instantly dropped down in front of me. "That's good because it will make me miss my mommy too and I don't like missing her even at my age. My mommy liked to dance and make my daddy really red too. And I'm positive it had something to do with her 'hellos' too."

"Your mommy is gone too?"

I nodded.

"When did she go away?"

"She and my daddy went away when I was six."

Her eyes widened. "I'm six. My mommy died in a car accident. How did your mommy die?"

I tried to think of a nice way to explain it to her. Somehow, telling her that vampire and shifters attacked us in the middle of the night and slaughtered them while I watched wasn't going to work. "Well, that's a little hard for me to talk about. One, it hurts in here still." I touched my chest. "And two, it's not something that people talk about. Not because they're worried about hurting my feelings but because it was very, very, very bad."

Hilary touched my hand and I felt her power wrap around me. The second she surged it through me, searching for the answer, I pushed her power back into her and held it there. She gasped and ripped her hand away. She stood quickly and stared at me. "They were very bad men and it wasn't your fault. You were too little to stop them."

"I still should have tried," I whispered, more to myself than to her.

"Sweets?" Amber asked, sounding confused but managing to draw me out of what could have been a sorrowful moment.

I looked at Hilary and tipped my head. "Did mommy give you rules about certain things?"

"Like what?"

"I think you know what I'm talking about, Hilary."

She bent her head down, clearly ashamed. "Yes. I'm sorry. But I wanted to know what happened to them."

"I gave you an answer."

Amber gasped. "Don't scold her. She doesn't normally..."

I put my hand up, cutting Amber off. "No. They," I pointed at Riston and Eric, "can try to tell me not to scold her as well and they'll get the same answer. This little girl is more than just a little girl. She's very special. And..."

Hilary sighed. "Being special doesn't mean I can do anything I want. I have to think about other people. They have feelings and I could hurt them if I'm not careful."

Snickering, I leaned forward and tapped her nose. "You got that speech too, huh?"

"Yes," she pushed her hand around it the grass. "My Uncle tells me that all the time. I get sick of hearing it."

I nodded. "Well, that is almost the same speech I got when I was little. My daddy was the one who gave it to me. And do you know that I would give anything to hear him say it again."

"You were a daddy's girl too?"

I snickered and nodded my head. "I thought my daddy could hang the moon, sweetheart." I decided it was time to lighten the conversation. "I most likely got that idea because of the whole lycan moon thing. What do you think?"

"I think that you don't get hugged enough," she said, tossing her arms around me. I held her tight and she kissed my cheek. "You're wrong."

"About what?" I asked.

She smiled. "Not everyone who loves you goes away."

I couldn't have responded to that if I tried. It took everything I had to keep my emotions under wraps. Hilary reached out and lifted a stray strand of my hair and began to twirl it around her finger.

"You have pretty hair. Is it long?"

I nodded. She beamed. "Your daddy told you that he liked your hair long and you kept it that way."

Not wanting to break down, I simply smiled. She was right. My father did like my hair long when he was alive. "You have very long hair too. Did mommy like it that way?"

"Oh, yes because she had lots and lots of hair. It hit her fanny even."

I laughed. "Well, mine only goes to my mid-back. Because..." I stopped short of spilling the truth.

Hilary didn't. "Because the bad men use it to grab you at times and the longer it is the easier they can get it."

"Yep. Hardly seems fair, does it?"

"*Men.*"

I snorted.

She giggled. "You have dirt on your face."

I nodded. "Amber already told me. Since it's only dirt I don't mind. I can think of worse things to have on me."

Tears came to her eyes and I had to fight to keep from hugging her. "The day mommy went away we were supposed to go to a birthday party. She told me not to get all dirty because I was in a nice dress. I didn't listen and got mud all over my pretty dress. Daddy stayed home with me while I took a bath and mommy went to the store without us to get a present. She said she'd be right back. She lied. She never came back."

"Is that what you really believe? Do you really think mommy lied?" I asked, leaning in close to her.

She was quiet for a moment. "No. I don't think so. But why did she say she'd be back if she wasn't going to come home?"

I twirled my finger in her pigtail and gave her a soft, warm look. "Because mommy didn't know she wouldn't be able to come home, Hilary." The urge to kiss her was great. I gave in and kissed the tip of her nose. "Have you ever fallen and hurt yourself?"

"Yes," she answered so low I almost didn't hear it.

"Did you know you were going to get hurt before it happened?"

"No."

"Mommy didn't know either."

She looked up with tears in her green eyes. "Why would someone make mommy go away? She wasn't bad."

"My mom and dad weren't bad either, Hilary. In fact, my daddy's job involved protecting people from very bad things. He worked very hard with other men like him to make sure that innocents didn't have to worry about what else lives among us. But he and mommy still had to go."

Talking about my parents made my entire body tight and I desperately wanted to cry but the little girl before me needed someone to be strong for her. "Do you know what I think?"

"What?" she asked staring at my charm necklace. She tipped her head a bit and her eyes lit up. For a moment it looked like she wanted to touch it. She didn't.

"I think that the powers and the angels above needed your mommy and my parents to help them there. And when they help there, they help everyone, not just us. What do you think?"

She continued to stare at my necklace with awe. "I want Mommy here to help me."

"And I want mine but if we all took them back who would be left up there to help everyone?"

"Angels."

"They need help too." I touched the tip of her nose. "In fact, some of the mommies and daddies that go to them to help were already angels to begin with."

"Really?"

I nodded. "Yes, angels exist here too. Some were born among us, to live, work, even learn to love what they were born to protect."

"Are you telling the truth?"

"What if I told you that my mommy was a full angel and my daddy was part?"

Amber made a choked sound and I knew she was disapproving of my topic of conversation but Hilary wanted to talk about it and I was telling her the truth.

Hilary gasped. "Your daddy was part angel, part lycan?"

"He sure was. I think that made him very special. I bet your mommy was extra special too. Wasn't she?"

"Yes."

"Some people that the angels and the powers need to help them are able to do *other* things, they're different but powerful and can help fight the war on a big," I put my arms out wide, "huge scale."

"Like they can do special things?" she asked, still staring at my charm.

"Yes. And the ones who can do special things are ready to lend a hand because they have spent their lives helping and are very good at it."

"My mommy is very helpful to them then."

"I am positive that she is one of their best helpers, Hilary."

She bit her lower lip. "I think he is too."

"Who? My daddy?"

"Yes, but the other one who had to go play with the angels. The one with the green eyes. The one you didn't kick in the head when he asked to have a wedding."

I heard the words coming from her tiny mouth and my chest tightened to the point it was painful. I knew who she was talking about and I missed him greatly. I tried to smile but failed.

Hilary touched my chin. "He watches you a lot." She looked up towards the sky and smiled wide. "He says that you know he does, that you even talk to him when he's around because you know he's there and that," she closed her eyes tight, "he heard you singing. He came to watch you play with me."

She lowered her voice as tears filled her eyes. "He says that he was very worried that you might never play again. He says that he loves you and always will. He is a bit upset that you don't want to see him. What does that mean?"

"It means that," I swallowed hard, "I have the ability, when I sense him near, to actually see him there but I don't use it."

"Why? If I could see my mommy I would." She touched my cheek and pushed her power through me again, this time only enough to find the answer to a bit not the story of my life.

I pulled her hand away fast and gave her a stern look. Yelling at her wasn't an option. Huge tears ran down her tiny face as she shook her head. "It wasn't your fault. You always blame yourself. If you would let him by you, see him and hear him he would have told you that already. But you're stubborn." She laughed through her tears.

I wiped them from her face. "Don't cry for me, Hilary."

"You don't cry for you. Someone has to." She cupped my cheeks firmly. "I cry for me, late at night when I know daddy is sleeping, I cry because I miss mommy. But I don't tell him because I don't want him to be sad anymore. He just started smiling and laughing again. Amber makes sure of that."

"She's good at that, huh?"

"Yep. She helps take care of me. If it wasn't for her, my daddy and my uncle would still have a hair brush stuck in my hair."

I laughed hard and Hilary gave into it as well. She reached and touched my triple knot charm, I smiled. "How did you get one of those too?"

"Did mommy wear one too?"

"Yes."

I felt it then, the loving, warm energy that moved in around Hilary and held her close. It was so familiar, so loving, so warm--it was a mother's love. Her eyelids fluttered closed for just a second and she swayed back and forth.

"Would you like me to give you a charm like mommy's?"

She nodded. "Yes, she didn't give me one."

The energy moved over me, seeming to concentrate its power point directly at me. I listened to the silence and understood it. "Hilary, what if I told you she did?"

She shook her head and then stopped fast, staring up at me with wide eyes. "Ooo, my doll, Morgan has one. Mommy and daddy got her for me for my birthday last year."

"I'll tell you what. I have lots of these. If you want, the second I find the box they're in, I'll give you one. You can take Morgan's and give her the one from me. How does that sound?"

"Good."

"Hilary," I lifted her chin and gave her a warm smile, "do you think you could get the dress I gave you all dirty? You can get this one that I have on all dirty too. You can even roll in the mud in it."

"Really? Why?"

"I get the feeling that you think you're making mommy happy by doing what she asked. That's why you worried so much about the two dresses you have on after you showed me your rockin' somersault, isn't it?"

She nodded and looked away.

"Honey, that's nothing to be embarrassed about. It shows how much you still love her."

"It does?"

"Yep."

Hilary stood and tossed her arms around my neck. "Will you come back and visit again?"

"I'll do one better." I tried to get up but Hilary wouldn't let go of my neck. "Sweetheart, if you let me stand, I'll tell you where I live so you can visit as often as you like."

She let go instantly. Getting to my feet, I smiled down at her. "Close your eyes."

She did.

I turned her around several times and then stopped, leaving her facing my house. Bending down, I pressed my mouth to her ear. "Open them."

The second she did, I watched as the realization of what I was telling her sunk in. She squealed and leapt into my arms. I stood and held her up high. As I turned, I found Amber crying and holding Eric's hand as tears streaked his cheeks as well. I carried Hilary over to him. "You need to go to daddy now, Hilary. I think he needs a hug."

He held his arms arm out and practically tore Hilary from my arms. He squeezed her tight and closed his eyes. "Thank you, Miss."

Chapter Two

I glanced at everyone and nodded before turning and walking away. I didn't stop to look back. Instead, I headed into the house and went straight to the kitchen. For some reason, I felt comfortable in that room. The dining room also had a strange pull on me. It was as though my body recognized it as a safe haven. I only hoped that were true. For the first time in a long time, I felt like I was home.

Putting my hands on the counter, I let out the tears I'd been holding back. I let them all go. For so many years I'd kept it in me, not wanting to show my weakness to anyone. Seeing Hilary going through what I went through had been the final straw.

I pulled the red rag from my head and ripped the tie out, allowing my hair to spill down to my back. Leaning down, I turned the icy cold water on and began to scrub my face to get the dirt off it.

I struggled to get out of the wedding dress as I cried. Not quite able to reach the zipper, I dropped my head and let out a shaky laugh. "It figures I'd get stuck in asshole's dress at a time like this. Is someone trying to tell me something?"

I wiped my tears away and did my best to stop crying. Suddenly, I felt something tugging at the zipper and undoing it for me. The dress dropped to the floor on its own. I stepped out fast. I kicked it far from me before turning to face the person who helped me. Riston stood there looking like he wanted to help but wasn't sure how. Why hadn't I sensed him in the room with me?

He rubbed the back of his neck, giving me a great view of his bulging biceps. "Eric wanted me to thank you again for what you did."

"It was nothing."

"Paula died eleven months ago and Hilary hasn't brought her up once the entire time. It's a huge thing you did for her." He locked gazes with me. "I'd like to thank you too. Hilary is my niece."

"Niece?"

He nodded and cast me a pained look. "Paula was my sister."

"I'm sorry for your loss." As I stood there looking at him, the feeling of knowing him crept over me again. I pushed it down. It flared back to the surface. Sometimes, my powers were as stubborn as I was.

He shrugged. "I'm sorry that talking to her opened old wounds for you."

"Yeah, well, if someone would have sat me down like that after *it* happened, I might not be in the ridiculous crying fit I'm in at the moment. You know what? I feel like letting out some aggression. Want to burn a dress with me?"

"Umm?"

I smiled. "Sorry, Amber must have forgot to tell you I'm crazy, creepy and don't seem to have an off switch."

"Crazy and creepy?" He arched a dark brow. "I think you'll find some stiff competition in this town if you're hoping for top spot there."

"Stiff? Top spot?" My gaze went his groin as a slow grin spread over my face. As I traced my way up his torso I found him staring at me with shock etched on his face. "What? Was it something I said?"

Leaning against the peeling white doorframe, he nodded. "I'm Riston Wallace."

"Nice to meet you, Riston. I'm Karri-Lynn O'Higgins. Most just call me Karri."

"O'Higgins?" he asked, staring at me as though he expected me to pull a demonic bunny out of my pocket. I could. I didn't.

"Yes."

"Karri-Lynn?" The wide-eyed expression he gave me made me think that pulling the bunny out might just draw enough attention to get him to stop staring at me.

"Yes." I would have offered more but he was beginning to creep me out and that was damn hard to do.

He reached out and made a move as though he were going to touch me, but stopped. "No. It can't be. Kars?"

Kars? I hadn't heard that nickname in a long time. A bit taken aback by Riston's sudden weirdness, I just nodded. "Yes, people, or rather someone used to call me that. Why?"

Riston's jaw dropped as his blue gaze raked over me slowly, lingering in places it shouldn't. He shook his head and he drew in a sharp breath. "Jack's daughter?"

That got me. Backing up, I narrowed my eyes suspiciously on him. "You're not much older than I am. How do you know my dad?"

"You don't know who I am?"

"I said you looked familiar. Do you know me?"

Riston was quiet for a moment. Something moved over his face

Mandy M. Roth

that I couldn't read. If I had to guess, I'd say he was digging for an answer that would make me happy. "I was, umm, I mean my father was friends with your father. I crossed paths with your father several times and knew that my dad thought very highly of Jack. In fact, I'd venture as far as to say, they were *very* good friends." He drew in a deep ragged breath.

I arched a brow. "So, did we play together or something? You really do seem familiar to me. I can't place you though. I have to say that I don't remember playing with any little boys. I led a rather sheltered life when my parents were alive. In fact, I only remember playing with my dad and his best friend, RJ. I think they took pity on me because I was different from other children."

A slow, lazy smile spread over Riston's face. "Yes, you were."

"Huh?" I waited for him to enlighten me. He didn't. "I take it that we did play together or at least met when I was little. Sorry about not remembering. Some of the time I try hard to block out that part of my life. Especially the day I lost my parents."

"You were there..."

I put my hand up, already knowing where he was going. "Yeah, I watched it happen. I do my best not to think about that anymore."

"I'm sorry, I didn't mean to..."

"No. You're fine." As I stood there it hit me who he reminded me of. My brow furrowed as I lifted my hands towards his crisp blue eyes. I'd seen eyes just like that almost daily when my parents were alive. But it was the day they were killed that I began to believe they belonged to my guardian angel. The man, my father's best friend, RJ, who'd come in and took hold of me, saving my life, had eyes just like Riston's--as blue as the sky, with black thick eyelashes lining them.

I moved Riston's face from side to side before lifting his wire-framed glasses off his face. It was him. No. That couldn't be right. "What the...No. It's not possible."

Moving into him, I stared at him with questioning eyes as an array of emotions tore through me. Closing my eyes, I remembered being there the night my parents died, outside of the car on the ground at my father's side. Trying desperately to save him somehow, to keep him with me anyway I could even though I was just a child. Things, monsters like I'd never seen before were all around me, trying to break through the magikal barrier that was up. RJ had swept onto the scene then. He went at the monsters, taking them down one by one before staring down at my father, then me. He picked me up fast and cradled me to his chest as he stared down in horror at my father.

As I opened my eyes, I found myself cupping Riston's face. Heat flared through me, stealing my breath and making my body cramp with need. Riston's arms wrapped around me and he held me close to him, staring at me with nothing short of lust in his eyes. The heat, the power that ran through me demanded I get even closer to him. Since we were already pressed together, I did the only other thing I could think of, I kissed his jawline lightly. It was a bold move, even for me.

The music playing from the front porch changed to a slow, orchestra-accompanied darker song. It thumped in my chest and my breasts heaved forward as my breath hitched. His hands seemed to be everywhere yet they never moved. Somehow, it felt as though he was caressing my back, arms, my face all while simply standing still.

Riston's breathing was choppy at best as he stood there with his arms around me. If it wasn't for the rise and fall of his chest and tightening of his arms, I would have thought him a statue. I couldn't help but kiss his jawline again, closing my eyes at the contrasting feeling of his skin to my lips. I sighed and he tightened his hold on me. The second he gently swayed our bodies to the music, I lost myself in his arms.

A flood of emotions continued to rage within me, leaving me clinging to him as we continued our torturously slow dance. It was beyond insane to think Riston was the same man who had saved me over twenty years ago. He was too young and too close to me, making my body do its own series of internal summersaults. The odds of him being the one that I'd come to think of as my guardian angel were a billion to one but it didn't matter. Something about Riston called to my body on a carnal level, demanding my attention.

He held the lead, moving our bodies perfectly to the music as he held me equally as tight. What was happening? Why was I so drawn to him and why in the hell did I never want to let go?

The orchestra took a very dark, haunting twist and I instantly ran my hand up the side of his neck and clung to him. I couldn't have let go, even if I tried. He felt so safe. It was something I hadn't felt in a long time.

Riston dipped me back a bit. Our eyes locked, leaving our lips dangerously close to touching. Every ounce of me wanted to kiss him, yet I stayed there, staring up at him with nothing short of rapture. He made a move and I thought for sure that he was going to kiss me. He didn't. I bit back a plea for him to take me and let him pull me back towards him as we made another circle.

The minute his warm lips brushed over my neck before kissing my earlobe, I realized what it was I was doing--clinging to a man I didn't know. I pulled back quickly and let my natural instincts for dealing with people kick in.

"If you're not a member of the town's welcoming committee, you should be."

Riston moved towards me and stopped before pulling back to his spot. His blue gaze seemed to swallow me whole and I loved it. I had to fight to push thoughts of him above me, looking down at me while he slid in and out of my body from my head. He ran a hand over the back of his neck again and let out a soft laugh. "Yeah, I'll have to check into joining that."

"Let me know how it works out for you. If you get in, I'll think about moving away and returning a week or so later in hopes of getting another greeting like that one."

"Sounds good to me." He licked his lower lip and bit it softly, doing nothing to help my state of need. "I'll be sure to keep room in my schedule for you."

Laughing, I glanced around the kitchen. The old, worn cabinets had paint peeling everywhere and the ceiling looked as though there had been water damage at some point. I sighed. "Do you think it's safe to stand out here? I'm a bit concerned that the ceiling will fall in on us."

"Nah, this place just needs a face-lift that's all. You're not planning on trying to do it yourself are you?" he asked, not looking very sure of my handyman abilities. Not that I could even blame him.

"What? I've only hot-glued my fingers together twice and nailed my shirt to the wall once."

A sly smile spread over his face. "Only twice?"

Rolling my eyes, I laughed. "Okay, three times but that has to stay between us. If it gets out, I'll lose my fix-it girl status."

"We wouldn't want that to happen, Kars."

Tipping my head, I stared at him. "Why do you keep calling me that?"

"Sorry," he said, putting his hands in his front pockets. The action gave me a tiny glimpse of the perfect V etched in his hips. The man had the body of a god and I wanted to explore every single inch of it with my hands before using my mouth. "I didn't know that you didn't like it."

"It's not that I don't like it, because I do. It's just that I can only remember one person in my life calling me Kars and it sort of was his thing. No one else's. It's hard to explain." That was RJ's nickname for me.

His lips twitched and it looked like he was doing his best not to smile. "I'll stop."

Suddenly, the idea of Riston calling me Kars sounded appealing. "You can call me whatever you want. It was just different to hear it again after so many years. It just reminded me of someone I once knew."

"Is that good or bad?"

"I honestly don't know anymore. At one point I thought him a god. I was six so that tends to happen." I winked. "I'm not sure how I feel about him now. I promise to stop associating you with him."

"Ohmygod, don't you dare step too close to her, Riston. She bites and won't sit still for her shots," Amber called out from the front entrance.

"I resent that statement. I *so* sat still for the last round of them. Besides, I'm harmless."

"Really? Then would you like to explain the chest full of weapons in your attic?" Amber mused.

I shook my head and covered my eyes with my hand. "No, but I'm sure you will."

"Riston, you have got to see the chest of weapons that used to be her dad's. They look like some of the ones you collect."

That piqued my interest. "You collect weapons?"

"Sort of."

Amber grabbed hold of his arm and tugged hard. "Come on. You'll love them. I promise." She glanced at me. "Karri doesn't mind, do you?"

Like I can really say no now.

I smiled. "Nope. I just got them out of storage so it would be neat to see all of what's in there. I never got to look through it when I was little. What I did see looked kind of cool."

And damn deadly.

Amber paused. "Wait, you mean you just finally got your parents' things out of storage? Karri, you've had the keys since you were eighteen. You had to have at least gone and got photos or something. You didn't have one to show me of your family."

"I still don't." I forced a smile to my face. "I only grabbed a bit from the storage units. I might have some pictures in the boxes that are here. I honestly don't know, though. I wasn't there when things were originally packed and put into storage. And I just sort of grabbed some things at random when I stopped in to pick stuff up."

"But weren't you the least bit curious all these years, at least for the sake of nostalgia to go through your parents' things--your things even?"

Wanting to be close to family and friends was a very Amber thing to do. I'd grown numb to it over the years. Riston watched me close as though he were personally awaiting my answer. I said the first thing that popped into my head. "I wasn't really ready to deal with that part of my life, Amber. To be honest, I'm not sure I'll ever be ready to."

"But, Karri, don't you want to remember all the good times you had with them before they passed? Don't you want to..."

"Be reminded that I'm alone in this world? That they were the only people who understood who and what I am and that they're gone?" I asked, not showing any signs of the tears that wanted to run free. "No, not really."

"You're not alone, Karri." Amber winked. "You're sort of stuck with me."

"And *you*," I put a lot of emphasis on the word, "are the only reason I'm standing here. I'd still be in New York if I hadn't missed you so much. Not that I have anything against the Midwest but it wouldn't have been my first choice. Though," I glanced at the wall and shook my head. "this place seems familiar to me. Like I'm supposed to be here. It's weird."

Riston coughed.

"So, have you found someone to put your other house up for sale yet?" Amber asked.

Taking a deep breath, I prepared to tell her the truth even if it wasn't what she wanted to hear. "Amber, I'm not selling my other house. In fact, I'm not selling my apartment in New York City either." My job demanded I keep various safe points and I considered my homes just that. There was no way I was giving them up.

She wrinkled her nose. "But why? It seems silly if you're going to be living...Karri, you told me that you were moving here."

I glanced around and wiggled my feet. "Uhh, just in case you missed it, I did move here. I just can't always be here. I'll do my best, hon, but in all honesty, it's hard for me to find down time. This will be a place I come to relax and get away from the hectic thing I call life."

"Quit your job. You don't need the money."

Riston continued to watch me closely. I shifted a bit and focused on Amber. "I can't. Not yet just anyway." No. I had a group of men to save. Hell, to be honest, I had a world to save but one who fought evil always did so it seemed to lack luster.

"Karri, are you in trouble?" she asked, suddenly looking a bit pale.

I'm always in trouble.

"No. It's complicated, Amber, and to be honest, I'm good at what I do and wouldn't have a clue as to what to with myself if I wasn't busy all the time. It won't matter much soon."

"Why is that?"

Shit. I hadn't meant to say that. "Weren't you going to show Riston my father's chest of weapons. Maybe he'll be able to show me how to use them all." I laughed on the inside. I already knew how to use them all.

Riston didn't look too happy about my request. I wasn't really sure why. Maybe he thought I'd put my eye out or something.

Not waiting a second more than need be, Amber headed toward the staircase with Riston in tow. As I followed them up, I realized what a great view of his ass I had. It was apple-shaped, I was sure of it.

Amber let out a soft laugh. "Karri, stop staring at Riston's ass."

It didn't surprise me that Amber knew what I was doing. She'd lived with me long enough to know how I was. "I can't help it. It's right there. Mmm, close enough to touch."

Riston glanced back at me with a shocked expression on his face and missed a step. Somehow, he managed to avoid falling flat on his face. Amber and I snickered. "I really need to have warning cards drafted up for everyone I introduce you too, Kari. They should have to sign off on the hazard better known as you."

"Want a picture of me naked to use? We could ghost it down and have the warning printed over it?"

Riston shook his head. "It seems like just yesterday that you were coloring and..."

Amber gasped. "Tell me that you don't already know her."

"Why?" I asked. "Am I really that bad?"

"Just crazy, sweetheart." She snickered as she headed into the attic and went straight for the chest. "Case in point."

"Hey, don't blame me for what my father owned. I have my own set of weapons."

"You do?" they both asked.

Riston slowed his pace and I accidentally ran right into him. Running head on into a cement wall would have hurt less. I lost my balance and went backwards fast. In a flash, Riston was turned around and seizing hold of me. He pulled me to him and the burning deep inside me returned. I gasped and he smiled.

I sensed someone coming and stilled. Unsure who it was and picking up on even more than one, I placed my palm on Riston's chest. "I forgot something. Feel free to look around with Amber. Oh, and thanks for the catch. You have amazing reflexes for a human...errr...hunk. Yep, hunk. Where is my head at?" I cringed at my slip of the tongue.

For a moment, I wasn't sure he even heard me. He was staring at the doorway looking as though he sensed someone too. "What?"

"Riston, are you okay?"

"Stay here with Amber. I'll be right back," he said, as he went to go around me.

I caught hold of him and tugged gently. He glanced back at me and winked. I couldn't help but step closer to him. Before I knew it, I was pressed tight to his chest and staring up into his crisp blue eyes. I went to my tiptoes, putting my lips dangerously close to his. He didn't pull away. Instead, he dropped his head down just a bit. Our lips brushed slightly and my power slammed to the surface.

Amber cried out and I jerked away from Riston, ready and willing to kill whatever had caused her fear. When I looked down to find her clutching her hand to her chest with tears in her eyes, I ran to her. I dropped down and took hold of her injured hand quickly. The minute I spotted the African-throwing knife lying half in and half out of the chest I knew that she'd cut herself on it. With its multitude of killing points, it was not a toy.

"Honey, we're home!"

Amber's eyes widened at the sound of Branson, one of my men's voice. "Your hunky movers are back. Think you can get them to shift into something cool? I want one of them to turn into a monkey."

"Well, one's a Fay so no on him. One's shy about getting naked in front of people he doesn't know but I'll ask. He's a lycan so you'll have to settle for a wolf. The third will dance naked in a rainstorm so I'm guessing he'll do it if you promise not scream or faint. He's a different situation. He can shift into several different large cat breeds. Oh, Branson, the Fay, is an ass so he still might work for something close to a monkey."

"I," she hissed as blood began to pour from her hand, "promise not to scream."

"Branson!" I called out, needing the use of one of his many gifts.

As a Fay, he possessed a limitless supply of magik and raw power. As a man he seemed to have limitless pick up lines.

A tall, toned, sandy, blond-haired guy with a recently acquired full beard came rushing into the room. His gaze went instantly to Riston and hardened. "Who the hell is this, Karri?"

"Questions later. Freeze them both now!"

I didn't have to say it twice. Branson put his hand out and pushed his magik out and over the room. Amber stilled and I knew it had worked. As I pulled her hand towards me to see the damage, I drew in a sharp breath. She'd split it wide open. "Amber, I can't believe that you would grab that thing."

"Damn, what the hell happened to the sexy redhead?"

I shot Branson a nasty look and he winked. "Hey, inquiring minds and all. Plus, she is sexy, Karri. We all noticed. Do beautiful people flock to you or what?"

"I used to think so," I said, grinning. "That was right up until I met you and ended up with your sorry ass as a friend."

"Karri, you're killing me here."

"Where are the other two fools?" I covered Amber's hand with my own and let my magik out. It rushed through her, healing her from the inside out.

Branson chuckled. "Well, here's the thing, darling, Matty's team called and needed him right away. He took off to rendezvous with them. He said it sounded big and that he'd be getting in touch with us as soon as possible so be prepared to head out. They wanted you with them but Matty told them that you needed a break. I agree."

I rolled my eyes. It was just like Matty, the guy who could shift into several different types of large cats to be pulled away. "Yeah, well break ended less than an hour ago when some half-demon came looking for Hilary."

"Hilary?"

I nodded. "A little girl who lives across the street. She's amazing, Branson. She's so full of life and laughter. It's infectious."

He stared at me without blinking. "Yeah, I know the type. So, what the hell would the other side want with a..." He stopped and clenched his fists. "You didn't let them find her, did you?"

"Give me some credit. Though, I was sure to deliver what he was looking for--a magikal female."

"What did you do?" he asked, not bothering to hide the fact that he sounded almost scared to know.

"Remember that girl you dated, the one who wanted me to be her best friend in the whole wide world because it meant she could be close to you all the time?"

Branson shivered. "You mean Stephanie? The one who had it in her head that we were going to get married ten minutes before she even knew my name? The one who stalked me until you finally did what I couldn't." He grinned. "Oh, thanks for that. The minute you kicked her ass off my front porch, I swore my undying allegiance to you."

Laughing, I thought about that night. It was kind of fun getting to hit her.

Branson made a choking sound. "Shit, you pulled a Stephanie on him, didn't you?"

"Yep. Worked like a charm. I never knew men were so phobic of commitment. I'll have to use that one again."

"Aww, man, I almost forgot to tell you that Jason missed check-in. Before you panic and go off taking on a third-world country all on your lonesome, our informant on the inside says he's still alive and will contact us as soon as he can. I think that about sums up my morning."

I continued to push magik through Amber's hand while I stared at Branson. "What are you leaving out?"

"Now why would you think I'm leaving something out?"

"Because you haven't made a pass at me yet and normally you'd have tried at least twice to get into my pants."

He raised his brows and bit his lower lip. "Shit, I knew I should have told you how hot your ass looked when I walked in. You know that those shorts leave a tiny bit of cheek showing on each side?" He wagged his brows. "Seger told me you'd know something was up."

"I sure did," Seger, an equally tall man with brown roots and bleached out tips said, as he entered the oversized attic. The spiky hair look he had worked well for him. He entered the room and stared at Riston. He put his hand out and claws erected from it. The look he gave Riston scared me. He was a powerful lycan. One that not many dared to cross.

I thrust magik up and held him in place. "No! What the hell is going on? I just got done telling Amber you were shy about shifting in front of others. Care to explain the big bad wolf routine?"

Seger kept his eyes locked on Riston like Riston was about to leap free of Branson's magikal hold him and go nuts. "Who is the new guy and what do we know about him?"

"Seger?" This was strange behavior for a man I'd known for years. Something was wrong.

He pointed at me with his clawed hand. "Karri, you have pissed way too many people off with this project. You've got the powers and the normal scum on your heels. The price sitting on your head is the biggest I've ever heard of and I for one am sick with worry every time you're out of our line of sight. I'm convinced that we're going to walk in to find you dead. I will question everyone's intent when it comes to you, doll."

Shocked by his outburst, I couldn't help but laugh. He didn't seem as amused. "Oh, yeah, it's real fucking funny that they want you dead, Karri. We've been friends a long time now and I am not about to stand by and let you put yourself at risk."

"Hold up, Seger." I glared at him but kept a level head. "I gave in. I moved back to the house by campus and stayed out of the forefront in New York for the last month. You were the one who told me that here would be best. That if I missed Amber that much to come to her. I said, no. I said that I would only lead evil right to her. You swore to me that all of that price on my head bullshit had blown over, that I wouldn't risk anyone's lives here."

"Yeah, well I thought it had, Karri. Someone shed some new light on the matter this morning. But I'm sticking with my gut. Here is where you need to be. I can't explain it but I know I'm right."

"Time out!" I stood fast, not caring who knew I was pissed. "Who is in charge here, Seger?"

His jaw tightened as his breathing grew heavy. "You."

"That's right. Yet you continue to make decisions without consulting me. And these aren't split-second life and death ones-- these are ones regarding my life. What the hell crawled up your ass? Huh? You weren't always like this." The Seger I knew was caring, funny and full of life not paranoia and anger.

"Sometimes, I wish you were a man," he said between clenched teeth.

"For the record, I'm extremely happy you aren't. We are the only team with something to stare at while on missions that makes us horny as all..."

I pointed at Branson. "One more word, I dare you." Turning to Seger, I put my hands out. "Well, you tossed that out for a reason. Why is it you wish I was a man?"

He snorted. "So I could knock some fucking sense into you. You bitch at me about not consulting you but do you ever stop and consult me when you run off and put your life on the line? Do you, Karri? Do you ever open up and tell me everything so I can make sure the rest of us are there to back you up? You used to. You used to tell Tripp everything. When he was your first hand man, you went to him and filled him in on the details. Do you respect me less? Is that it? If you think I'm less of a man, just say it."

I rolled my eyes.

"What?" he asked, his temper clearly rising. "Do you think I'm less of a warrior, Karri? Do you think that I can't protect you? That I can't lead the men in your absence?"

I stared at the ceiling as I shook my head. "That's not it and you know it."

He snorted, giving me a hard stare as he did. "Could have fucking fooled me, Karri. You've become a lone gun who is now dangerously close to ending up dead. I can and I will continue to tell you exactly what I think. And I will do what I see fit when it comes to your safety. You can think what you want about me."

"Seger, I am not questioning your manhood." I glared at him. "I'm scared to death that I'll get you killed. Tripp is dead because of me. He's dead because I shared everything with him. I will not do that to another of my men. I can't and I won't risk any of your lives. You're like family to me and I can't…Seger, I can't bury another one of you. I can't." It took all I had not to cry.

He stilled. "Karri, shit. I'm sorry. This isn't what I wanted to do. I just worry about you constantly. And then I walk in to find you with your back to--" he stared at Riston, "him."

"Seger, you really need kids of your own. Parenting me must get tiresome." I winked. He growled. "Oh, you are just precious."

I went to him and wrapped my arms around him. He hugged me tight and lifted me off the ground with ease, careful not to scratch me. "Aren't you happy I'm not a man? This would be weird for you then."

He chuckled.

"What if I promise to tell you everything? Will that help you calm down a bit? I feel like I'm walking next to a rabid wolf with the way you've been acting lately."

Exhaling, he hugged me tight. "Yeah, it will help. Not letting men you don't know into your house will help me too. And putting Branson on a fucking leash would be a plus," he said, grumpily.

"What happened? Did Branson do something stupid while you were at lunch?"

"Hey, I do not do stupid things." Branson grinned. I'd seen the expression countless times and knew exactly what it meant. Branson really did do something stupid.

Seger growled, no longer seeming concerned with Branson's

antics. His gaze was on Riston. "Karri, who is the new guy? I want an answer now. I tried to calm down but it's not working."

"A friend of Amber's." I watched Branson and Seger closely and noticed Branson favoring his weapon. "If either of you shoot him or attack in any form, you will have me to deal with. Are we clear? He's not a threat to me."

Why did I add the 'to me' part?

"But, Karri, don't you sense that he's a..."

I stood quickly and glared at Branson. "That he's a nice guy? Yeah, I got that much out of him. I also know that the two of you will stay away from him. I think I already addressed the issue. Did I not? He is not to be touched. In fact, he's to be protected."

Seger nodded, still watching Riston closely. I would have commented but the price of healing Amber decided to pick then to surface. Instantly, my hand split wide open. I held it out and gasped. "Ouch, damn. I friggin' hate it when this happens."

Branson moved towards me quickly. "When is the last time you ate, Karri?"

I thought about it and drew a blank. I shrugged. He growled. "Damnit, woman. It's not a hard thing to remember. When you feel hungry, stop and eat something. Christ, without us around you would go days and days without eating. I'm starting think we need to remind you to breathe."

"Not true," I said, doing my best to try to control the bleeding.

Seger came to me, put his un-shifted hand over mine and the wound closed instantly. His healing power was different than mine. He didn't suffer by having to take on the injury. He just healed and was done with it. He offered a small smile. "Branson may be a dick but he's right, Karri. If you're serious about staying here you need to remember to eat and sleep. We can't get to you as fast as we normally can. If you'd let us relocate here to be with you, we could."

"Guys, come on. I'm not that bad. You have your own lives to live. You don't need to follow me wherever I go. Besides, I'll be back in a bit anyway and then just take time off here."

"You," Seger growled, "are our life, Karri. It's what being a team means. I know you have it in that pretty little head of yours that we're all just here to pass the time and can't wait to hand you off to someone else but that's not the case. In our own weird way, we're family now. Like it or not, Karri, you have people who won't walk out of your life now. Learn to deal with it before I take you over my knee and let Branson spank you."

Putting his hands up, Branson took a step back. "Hell no, she'll rip my arms off. You're on your own, Seger. Matty might help but I'm guessing he'd do something to distract you just to see you get pissed off. He and Karri get a kick out of that."

"You guys do realize that you have to adopt Amber too, right?"

Seger laughed. "Branson, I get the feeling that two women, under the age of thirty are going to make a bunch of us old timers stay on our toes, what do you think?"

I went to laugh and staggered a bit. "Whoa, anyone else feel that?"

"Feel what?"

"Like something up to no good was close?" Evil tended to affect me in weird ways. The buzz I was suddenly getting had made me lose my balance a bit.

Branson snorted. "When is the last time you got some sleep?"

When I thought about it, I realized that I hadn't slept in two days. Not wanting to alarm them, I just smiled. "I'll catch a nap or something later today. Now, I want to know what Branson is hiding."

Seger grinned. "You are good. The guy can get away with lying to the rest of us but can't be in a room two seconds with you before you pick up on something being off."

"She's always been that way."

The minute I heard the voice from the hallway I froze. Staring at Branson and Seger, I did my best to make sense of it. "No. Tell me that you didn't bring him here. Tell me that you did not drag that no good, son of a..."

Seger put his hands up. "Karri, wait. You don't understand. He's not..."

I threw power out, grabbed hold of Riston and Amber and let it coat them. For a second, I was positive that Riston moved. That was ridiculous. There was no way he could. Branson, while an ass, was still powerful. I moved in front of Riston because he was closest to the doorway and prepared to do what needed to be done to protect him.

As I watched the tall, raven-haired man with piercing green eyes enter the room, my chest tightened. He tipped his head. "Karri, do you really think you needed to protect your friends from me?"

"Yes. And I would strongly advise you to turn around and go back to the hell you came from, Hansen."

I watched as Hansen grinned. "I have to hand it to you, Karri-Lynn. You certainly take every precaution to keep the ones you care about safe. Well, almost every precaution. You will remember to mention that the crystals you put around any of their houses need to stay in their spot and not be moved to keep evil things out, right, Karri?" He put his hands out and smiled. "Funny, I didn't sense a barrier here. Are you taking to tempting fate now?"

Seger glanced at Branson and then me. "I swear that Branson read him. He cleared the test, Karri."

Hansen grinned and walked in a slow circle. "Tests are so easy to cheat on."

"Hansen, I'd advise against the attitude. She'll kill you in a heartbeat. Don't encourage her," Branson said. "I'm shocked you're still standing if that tells you a thing, man."

I glared at Branson. "What the hell were you thinking? He crossed the line and I for one can't trust him."

Hansen laughed and I wanted to punch him just because it sounded fun. "Now that hardly seems fair. You cross the line all the time. Why is it okay for you to do it but not for me?"

"Have I ever put any of you in danger or allowed you to be hurt during my crossing of the line?" I took a step towards him and he backed up.

Seger stepped forward. "No, Karri. You have never done that. I can't say that of all present." He leveled his dark gaze on Hansen.

"Hey, you can stop the backhanded remarks, Seger. Branson gave me a clean bill of trustworthiness. Isn't that enough?"

"No," I said, not bothering to even put on the pretenses of liking him. "You yourself admitted to pulling one over on him, dickhead." It was hard to fool Branson's magikal senses. To do so meant one had to either be born evil or have the help of some powerful backers.

"Aww, are you still upset about what happened? I thought you'd be happy to see me. You seemed to more than enjoy yourself on our last meeting, Karri. Or don't you..."

I went to go at him and found Seger and Branson next to me in a flash holding me back. I kicked out hard and they held me up and off the ground. "Put me down!"

Hansen winked, taunting me. "Come to daddy, sugar. I can teach you things you've only dreamed about."

"And I can rip your head off and shove it up your ass. Want to see?" I thrashed out, almost freeing myself from Seger and Branson's hold.

"Shit, Karri, you're a girl. You aren't supposed to make me work this hard to hold you in place," Branson said, sounding strained.

Hansen let out a soft laugh. "See, even your own men believe you should be elsewhere, not wrapped up in this mess we call the war. You should be lying in a bed, spread out and eagerly awaiting me to..."

I thrust a hefty dose of magik at him, striking his groin. He cried out and grabbed himself.

I grinned from ear to ear. "You were saying?"

Seger dropped his head down onto mine, pulled his claws into his body, letting his hand return to normal and hugged me tight. "Calm down, Karri. He's doing it on purpose. He wants you to come at him. He needs you on the edge, doll. Don't give it to him."

"What are you talking about?" Branson asked. "I scanned him for evil and found none."

Hansen smiled wickedly. "Care to explain why that is, Karri? Careful, you might have to confess what you tried so desperately to keep hidden from all of them."

"Karri?" Branson asked, letting go of me and putting his body between Hansen and I. "What the hell is going on here? I thought that you'd be ecstatic to know that he managed to break the hold they had on him."

I couldn't help but laugh. "They never had a hold on him, Branson. He came out of the womb on their side. He was born to the darkness--to evil."

"What?"

Hansen licked his lower lip. "Always the perceptive one, aren't you, Karri? Oh, but wait." He made a move towards me and found Seger pushing him backwards. He just laughed. "Tell your guard dogs to back away, Karri. They aren't like us. They don't share the common thread. I think you and I both know what will happen to them if I'm feeling provoked. Now, come and give me what it is that makes men flock to your side, give their life for you and swear allegiance to you and not the powers."

"Kiss my Fay ass, you punk bitch," Branson said, reaching for his weapon. "She isn't handing you shit."

I knew that Hansen was right. They wouldn't survive an attack by him. Drawing on my powers, I thrust Branson across the room and pinned him there. Before Hansen could react, I did the same to Seger, leaving nothing standing between us.

Hansen walked in a small circle. "Tell me how it is you know so much about how things work when you're as young as you are? I've lived for over a hundred years and am still learning. But you, Karri, seem to know it all. That's funny because I heard that just ten short years ago you didn't even know what you are. That you found yourself under a beast that even the strongest of evil's warriors would admire. And that you were within inches of death, feeling your power trying to surface but terrified of what it was and what it meant you were."

"Karri, lift the hold, now!" Branson shouted from his corner of the attic.

While I didn't let go of him, I did give him some company. I used my power and moved Amber to him quickly, encasing them in protection as I went. "Guard her with your life. She's like a sister to me."

I went to do the same and send Riston to Seger but stopped when Seger shook his head. "Save your energy, Karri. He'll be fine where he is. You seem to be missing out on something huge when it comes to him. Let me go and I'll help. You can't take Hansen on alone. He's a first level warrior for them, isn't he?"

I nodded.

Seger glared at Branson. "Way to go, asshole. Drop the devil at her doorstep again some time. I'm sure she'll love it about as much as she loves this one. Now, Karri, let me go. Amber is safe with Branson and your new friend is fine on his own. Let me..."

Hansen shot power out, hitting the barrier I'd put around Seger. While I could protect him from death, I couldn't stop the impact. It hit Seger and sent him hurdling backwards. Hansen laughed. "I take it that you didn't bother to tell them what we are, Karri. Did you not want to brag, even a little? I know I always do."

"Seger?" I asked, afraid he might be hurt. "You breathing, buddy?"

He groaned. "Still alive. Pissed. But still breathing."

"Want me to enlighten them, Karri-Lynn? Want to tell them the extremes that the war has come to? Want to share exactly what each side is now being forced to use to fight the other? There was a time when our race was created to be the mediators, but no, no now we're the pivotal players in it all. Tell them, Karri. Tell them what the powers kept hidden from all. Tell them what we are." Hansen said, glancing at Riston. "And who is your new friend? Don't tell me that you went and found yourself another fill in. A powerful..."

"You will not touch him," I said, taking a firm stance in front of Riston and preparing to battle the purest form of evil, a fallen angel.

Branson struggled against my hold, demanding more of my attention than I was willing to put out. "Damnit, let go of me!"

"Stop fighting it, Branson. It makes Karri use her powers on you and not conserve them." Seger got to his feet, using the wall to support himself. "She's too friggin' stubborn to let us go until she feels like it."

Even though Seger, who I trusted with my life, told me that Riston would be safe, I wasn't willing to take that chance. I wrapped my power around Riston and thrust him across the room for Seger to protect. It took way more of my energy than it should have to move him.

Seger's eyes widened as he stared at Riston. "I tried to tell her. You tell her to drop it, maybe she'll listen to you. I doubt it but it might be worth a try."

"Huh?" I asked, unsure why the hell he was bothering to explain anything to Riston who had no clue that anything was going on.

Hansen didn't give Seger time to answer. He closed the distance between us fast, grabbed the back of my neck and tried to kiss me. I put my hand over his mouth, preventing him from making contact. He tipped his head back and laughed. "Now, sweetheart, is that anyway to treat your dear loving husband?"

I shoved hard on his face. "Oh, would you please shut up. We are not, nor were we ever married you delusional, psychotic, pathetic, excuse for a man. I would rather shackle myself to a rabid hellhound than to you, so stop dreaming and get a hold of yourself."

Hansen laughed and licked my palm. "That could be arranged."

I cringed. "Oh gawd, I'm not going to break out in anything am I?"

"Did you break out when I dropped in to help you and you assumed I was someone else we know?"

I froze.

He grinned as I lowered my hand from his face. "No, you didn't break out. Did you, Karri? Hmm, I never did find out what tipped you off that I wasn't who you thought I was."

It was my turn to smile. "You can't kiss worth a shit and you kept pawing me like a schoolboy out for a quickie in the back of his car. Sort of a dead giveaway."

Branson snorted and I had to bite back a laugh too.

Hansen's mouth captured mine before I could blink. He thrust his tongue in and I bit down on it. He stopped and put his hands in the air. He mumbled something, his eyes wide.

I laughed.

"Holy shit, she's going to bite his tongue off," Branson said, sounding impressed. "Damn happy I never tried that one on her. I like my tongue in my head."

Hansen moved quickly, attempting to insert his hand down the front of my pants. I beat him to it and had mine down his and a death grip on his cock before he could blink. I knew exactly what to expect when I reached down, he was after all an identical match to someone I had been more than intimate with--Tripp.

He shook his head slightly as I held tight to his tongue and I twisted his most prized passion to the point where I knew he was in pain.

He mumbled something else. I gave in and released my hold on his tongue, but increased my hold on his cock. "I'm sorry, did you say something?" I asked, gagging slightly at the idea of him having had his tongue in my mouth. "Mouthwash, anyone? I think I'm going to puke."

Hansen grimaced. "Kar-ri, let go."

"No."

I met his gaze, refusing to look away. "Did you or did you not have something to do with the enemy knowing where and when they could find Tripp? Before you answer you should know that I can and will rip what you hold so dear from you." I laughed. "See, you took from me, I think it would only be fair."

"You wouldn't?" Hansen looked hopeful.

Seger laughed. "The last guy who tried to call her bluff is probably still singing soprano as we speak."

Hansen tried to strike out at me and I caught his hand with mine and tightened my hold on his dick, twisting him almost all the way around. "Ahh, enough. Enough. You win."

"Did you have something to do with Tripp's death?" I fought hard to keep my voice from cracking and failed. The very thought of Tripp made me ache for him.

"Not purposely," he said. "I swear, Karri."

"Is he lying?" Branson asked.

I shook my head. "No." I released my hand from his cock and wrapped magik around it instead. I gripped it hard, the threat of removing it still there. His eyes widened more. I smiled. "No hands required. Quite a perk if I'm fucking you. Not so fun when I'm ready and willing to rip your dick off."

Hansen's gaze went to Riston and his eyes widened more. "Unfortunately, you aren't the only one who is willing to do that at the moment. To be honest, I would rather take my chances with you, Karri. Your new friend is most disconcerting."

I ignored his comment and wiped my hand on my jean shorts. "I need to be dunked in bleach now. Thanks."

"Karri," he closed his eyes a bit, "I miss him too."

"You miss him? That's all you have to say?" My anger seized hold of me and I fought hard to keep any darkness from filling it. "Tell me what happened, Hansen. Why turn Tripp over and not me? Why?" I slammed my fists into his chest. As he caught my wrists I dropped my magik, unable to keep both it and my feelings in check.

"You really don't know?" Hansen asked, sounding surprised.

I shook my head as a tear ran down my check. Something passed over Hansen's face that I couldn't read. I didn't care how he felt. I only knew that I hurt because of him. "You let him die. You knew the enemy read you enough to know what Tripp's part in it all was and yet you didn't warn him. You made up all that shit about needing a break from it, that the evil was getting to you so he stepped up to the plate because he was scared of losing you to them, Hansen." I punched out hard and caught the side of his face. "He took your fucking place!"

The fury within me needed to shout, needed to let it all out. "You used his love for you against him! Why?" I hit him again. It did little to calm my rage. "I can't believe that you hated him, Hansen. I saw the two of you together. You were different with him. You cared about him. What in the hell changed that?"

"You."

"What?"

He shook his head and laughed. "You still don't understand why. How is that, Karri? How can you be so smart and so oblivious all at the same time?"

Taking a calming breath, I regained control of my emotions, at least temporarily that is. "I don't know, probably the same way you were able to deliver your own brother into the hands of the enemy. Takes some skill and practice but at the end of the day you realize you pulled it off without a hitch. Though, that could just be the bitch in me talking."

"He had something I wanted, Karri. Something that wasn't supposed to be his but they," he glanced up, "still gave him."

I glared at him. "Cryptic talk will gain you a one-way ticket to getting the shit beat out of you. The only reason you are still alive is because I can't physically bring myself to kill you. Don't think I won't find someone who can, Hansen. Someone who won't see Tripp when they look at you. Someone who doesn't care, who won't be at the mercy of a fallen angel." I smiled as the perfect person came to mind. "Someone like Jean-Paul."

Hansen stiffened. "Would you really have your pet vampire come after me, Karri? I don't think you would."

I kicked out hard and fast, catching him in the gut. He fell to the ground and I seized hold of the knife I knew he carried in his boot. I pressed it to his throat and winked. "You don't know me as well as you think, Hansen. No one does."

"That's it, Karri. Open up to the hate. You're so close to being one of us, aren't you?" Hansen touched my cheek and I fought down the urge to slit his throat. "Tell me, do you still wake in cold sweats with the urge to kill everything around you? Do you still hear the demons whispering to you when you're on the verge of sleep, when you're not strong enough to keep them at bay? Is that why you look tired, Karri? Do you find ways to stay awake?"

That caught me off guard. "What? How do you know that?"

Hansen smiled, running his hands up and over my thighs. "Until you came along my brother and I were close. He came to me for advice when he needed it. He told me all about how you'd shoot up from a fitful sleep, your eyes filled with black, clutching your chest as your heart slowed, preparing itself to stop altogether--allowing you to be a member of the living dead. A powerful force of darkness. A force like me. He told me how he'd struggle to get you to understand where you were mentally and to bring you back to yourself. He wasn't your anchor, but he tried all the same, terrified that one night you would never come back, never recognize who he was and forever be one of us."

I shook my head, not wanting to believe that Tripp would tell something that personal to Hansen.

He smiled. "He was scared to death that you'd turn and he knew he didn't have it in him to kill you, Karri. Tripp knew that he'd stand by, helpless while you slaughtered millions if you ever gave in to the darkness. That's why he came to me. He knew that I did have it in me to kill you. It was the hardest thing he'd ever done, at least that is what he told me, but he had to ask, had to know that someone would be able to stop you if or should I say when the time comes."

I pressed the knife to him more and shook my head. "You lie. Tripp said he could do it. He said he would keep me from hurting anyone. He swore that he could." My hands trembled. "He promised me that he'd be the one to kill me if it came to it. He said..."

"He lied," Hansen whispered.

I shook my head, not wanting to believe him. "No. You're twisting things. He knew I couldn't ask Seger or the rest of them. He knew that in the end they won't be powerful enough to stop me.

He said that no matter what happened that he'd transcend time and space to make sure I don't hurt innocents. Tripp wouldn't lie to me."

Hansen nodded slightly. "Listen to the way you talk, you know that you're on borrowed time, that you've done what it takes other angels hundreds of years, if ever to do. You've seen too much, been through too much and have found yourself on the wrong side too many times. They did it to you. The powers knew that you were too young to handle what they wanted from you but they didn't care. They needed a woman, someone the men would let their guard down around, someone who could appeal to both sides--someone like you, Karri."

Hansen locked gazes with me, reminding me so much of Tripp that I almost forgot he wasn't. "It hurt him to lie to you, Karri. But he knew you needed to hear that he could do what you asked. As much as I'd like to be the one to tell you that there was a point when Tripp could have carried out what he, as your second in command, should have been able to, I'd only be lying. He couldn't hurt you. From the moment he met you he set his job aside, not caring who he put in danger in the process."

"Shut up," I whispered, not sounding the least bit threatening. "He was one of the best soldiers I've ever seen in action. I tried to tell them that. I told them to make him be team leader--Captain. Not me. They didn't listen."

"Karri, you let us all think we're good at what we do but we know that you carry something we don't. It's something I can't even put my finger on but if I have to guess it's that you genuinely have no fear of death. You almost seem to welcome the idea."

Dropping my head down, I bit back my emotions. "Did he tell you that too?"

"He didn't have to, Karri. I heard the two of you talking." Hansen's gaze ran over my face. "I felt his pain, his fear, it hit me out of nowhere. I rushed to him. That's when I knew. I watched from the shadows as he lay in your bed, holding you, rocking you while he tried desperately to wake you up from whatever self-induced hell you'd put yourself in, Karri."

Seger cleared his throat. "Umm, Karri, why was Tripp with you in your bed to start with?"

Hansen's face lit with amusement. He was getting way too much pleasure out of airing my secrets. "Tell them how you broke one of your own golden rules. Tell them, Karri."

"What are you doing here?" I asked, ignoring his request. "You didn't come to play catch up, so why are you here. And," I pressed the knife to his throat more, drawing blood as I went, "don't think I haven't noticed your hands on my ass. Get them off me now or I will keep them as souvenirs."

He winked and put his hands out far from my body. "I'm here to collect you, of course."

"Like hell you are," Branson shot out. "Karri, go. Get the hell out of here! We'll handle him."

"You couldn't possibly handle me. You are an inferior race. You couldn't even sense what I carry in me. The darkness, the hate, the rage. Your little mind can't possibly grasp what we are. The idea of a being sent forth from the gods themselves is too much for you."

"I know you're an asshole."

I glanced back at Branson and snickered. "I think that summed it up nicely."

Hansen seized hold of me and flipped me onto my back fast. He took the knife and pressed it to the side of my face. Another power thrust hard against my magik and it wasn't Hansen's. No. It was one of the people I was holding in place. They were powerful and wearing me down fast. It was clear they wanted out but I wouldn't let them.

As I went to push Hansen off me, he let his eyes swirl to black. Before I could prepare myself, Hansen pushed his dark power through me, calling to my own dark side. The side I'd inherited from my father.

"What the hell is he doing to her?" Branson asked.

"He's trying to force Karri's dark angel powers to the surface."

Hansen stopped and stared at Seger. "She told you what she is? What she carries in her?"

He shrugged. "She's not ashamed of who her father was. He may have carried all the genetic traits of someone who should have been evil through and through but from what I've heard about him, he was anything but."

Hansen smiled. "That may be so but he had what Karri has never had, an anchor, a true mate to keep her grounded to the side she was destined to serve. She is fair game. May the strongest side win."

I knew better than to fight it at this stage. I'd need my energy to hang on to the shred of goodness I had left in me. I gave in, slipping into character as I called it when I went the way of darker part of myself for the sake of a mission. My eyes burned and I knew they'd filled in black. I stared up at Hansen before turning my head and licking the knife blade. A rather smug look moved over his face.

"There you are." He kissed my forehead and I let him. "Since you didn't fight as hard as I anticipated I'm willing to let your friends live."

"What's the fun in that?" I asked, knowing he was testing me.

He ran his hand over my cheek taking the knife away from my face in the process. "It really is you. For a moment I was worried you were simply playing me for a fool. If you're willing to sacrifice your friends then you've given in fully. The council was right. You were past the point of being able to stop."

"Karri?" Branson asked, sounding concerned.

"Hansen," I ran my hand over his chest seductively. "Let me kill that one before we leave. The man has been on my last nerve for years."

Hansen couldn't look happier if he tried. "Very well." He rolled off me and helped me to my feet, kissing my hand as I came up. I resisted the urge to smash my fist through his face.

Putting my back to Hansen, I locked eyes with Branson. It was easy to read the confusion on his face. I winked. He stopped looking confused and played the part. "Karri, you don't want to do this."

"No, I really do."

Chapter Three

Something flashed before us. I looked down to find the CD player from the front porch sitting on the floor. It clicked on and what sounded like a choir of angels signing sounded from it right before it morphed into *Tubthumping*.

I paused and stared down at it. I wasn't the only one who found that odd. Everyone seemed to forget what had been going on.

Branson laughed. "Turn it off. I'm going to throw up just hearing it again. Seger remember when you, me, Matty and Tripp got super shit-faced and decided to sing karaoke? We must have stood up there doing shots and singing this for hours."

Seger laughed. "Yeah, we made fun of Tripp for weeks because he kept saying that he was in love with Karri and that she said yes to marrying him." He gasped and then whistled. "Aww, looks like big brother is watching. I'm guessing he is pissed. I'd like to take a moment to apologize for telling him that he was crazy when he was drunk and saying that."

Hansen snorted. "He can't interfere. Not when it involves her. It doesn't matter how big of a player he is for them now, he gave up his right to interfere where Karri is concerned."

"What the hell are you talking about?" Branson asked.

I locked gazes with Branson and waited for Hansen to spill it all. I didn't have to wait long. "You see, Fay, for us, if you tamper with another man's mate and attempt to make her your own, you have to make certain sacrifices. You are required to give up a power."

Branson laughed so hard that he snorted. "Tripp and Karri were never an item. They were friends. His confession was caused by booze. None of us touched Karri. She has a strict not-dating-any-of-us policy."

"Well, she did right up until Tripp."

I didn't stop or let on that I was beyond pissed. Instead, I bent down and picked up the African throwing knife that Amber had cut herself on. Her blood had now dried to it. Since she was technically an innocent, someone who was permitted into the gates of heaven without question as were almost all humans, it would burn like hell when it cut Hansen. I smiled.

"What are you planning to do with that, Karri?"

I froze at the sound of Tripp's voice. Branson's jaw dropped. "Holy fucking shit!"

"Karri?" Tripp asked, his voice every bit as soothing sounding as I remembered it being.

"Oh would you take your celestial ass back to the plane it belongs on?" Hansen asked, not sounding a bit shocked that Tripp was there. "Don't you have a harp or something to play?"

"Fuck off," Tripp said making me smile. I knew then that Hilary had been trying to prepare me to see him when she'd talked about the green eyed one who watched over me. She knew Tripp wanted me to see him soon and she'd given me the time I needed to adjust to that. I made a mental note to hug her the next chance I got.

"Wow, didn't know they were letting their top guns talk like that, brother." Hansen laughed from the gut, sounding as evil as he was capable of being. "You can't help her or bring her back. She's mine now. If you would kindly move, I will take her and be out of your hair."

"Tripp," I said, softly, wanting to say so very much more to the man who stole my heart only to take part of it with him to the grave. "Patrick Swayze it."

I didn't wait, I spun fast and sent the knife spinning through the air. It passed right through Tripp and slammed into Hansen's chest. He fell back, clutched himself before smiling up at me.

"You missed my heart."

"I wasn't aiming for it. I just wanted it to hurt really fucking bad. I'm guessing Amber's blood will burn like hell later, buddy. I told you already that I can't kill you. You look too much like Tripp for me to take your life."

Laughing, Hansen pulled the knife out and threw it at me. Tripp put his hand out to stop it and it went right through it. "Karri!"

I slammed my palms together quickly, catching it in mid-air and stopping it just before it would have gone through my skull. Branson let out huge sigh and I think Seger did too.

It was Riston who I felt compelled to look at. I found him staring at me with what looked like worried eyes. That was silly, he was under Branson's control, right? There was no way he could understand what was going on. I tore my gaze from his and glanced at Hansen. "At least mine struck its target." I dropped the knife.

When Tripp turned and faced me, my hands began to shake. I tried to look away but he held my gaze. A slow smile spread over his face. "You figured it out, didn't you?"

"Well, I didn't think they'd send a boy to do a man's job if that's what you're asking." I shifted a bit wanting desperately to run to him and hold him in my arms but knew better than to try it. "You look good, you know, for being dead and all.'

"So do you, for umm, being alive and all."

I smiled, thinking back to Hilary and sitting in the front yard, discussing the spirits of our loved ones still surrounding us. "I'd appreciate if you didn't use six-year-olds to send messages to me, though. I almost lost it in front of her and she didn't need to see that. I needed time to adjust to you being gone, Tripp."

Tripp smiled wide, melting my heart. "Well, she's stubborn but not near as bad as you. She insisted on being allowed to tell you how I felt. Plus, she told me I was handsome so I used that to my advantage. I'll apologize later. I didn't know how else to get you to really listen to me, Karri."

"Oh, I hear you fine but you're always bitching about me not taking enough safety precautions or forgetting to eat. You never say anything helpful."

"My brother is an ass," he said, with a lop-sided smile.

I couldn't help but laugh. "Gee, thanks for that. Though, I knew that Hansen was an ass a long time ago. You forgot gullible. That seems to play to everyone's advantage lately." It was awkward, trying to talk to him with everyone else standing and watching us.

Tripp's warm smile softened the hate that I felt over his death a bit. It was better than I ever hoped for, seeing him there, unharmed, and radiating power, love and energy. "Hey, didn't I get you that shirt?" I asked, as my gaze ran over the cream-colored ribbed shirt that he was wearing. "It's kind of kewl that they let angels wear jeans there too."

"Karri, I explained this to you long before I had to leave. We don't die. We move to another plane of existence and continue the fight there."

"I know," I said softly, wanting to ask him if he'd met my mother and father but keeping the question inside.

Tripp nodded. "We'll talk later about it. Okay?"

Smiling, I nodded.

"I'm impressed. I thought you'd give into the urge to slit Hansen's throat, Karri."

Evil radiated off Hansen, drawing my attention to him. He narrowed his gaze. "What's going on?"

Tripp didn't bother to face his brother, he kept his eyes on me. "You forget how strong she is, brother. You had centuries of practice pretending to be on our side but still fail to get past her guard. Karri, on the other hand, mastered the art of playing both sides less than seven years ago."

"She wasn't playing, Tripp. I felt the evil in her let loose. I felt it. And the council knows she's close. They sent me to draw it out and bring her to them."

It was my turn to laugh. "No. They sent you in hope I'd kill you."

He looked shocked. I couldn't blame him. "Don't take it personally, Hansen. They needed someone they were positive I would jump at the chance to kill. And they needed that person to be powerful enough to call out my bitchy side before I did strike. That way..."

Tripp nodded. "Karri would turn completely. She's too close to the edge to kill a fallen angel now and they know it. So does she. They also knew their chances of her being blinded by hate could push her far enough to allow herself to switch over. They underestimated her, as usual."

"I'd go away if I were you, Hansen, before I let one of the 'inferior' races here slit you open."

He snickered. "You know as well as I do that they can't hurt me, Karri."

Glancing down at the CD player, I arched my brow. "Okay, the grand entrance thing is getting on my nerves, Tripp. Please do something with it. It makes me think of vomit too and I wasn't the one drinking or throwing up." I cast an angry look at Seger, Tripp and Branson. They all laughed.

"I thought it was funny," Tripp said, winking.

"You would."

Branson exhaled loud enough for me hear it. "See, I told you they were just friends."

Tripp and I locked gazes. He shook his head no and I understood. He didn't want me to tell them the truth. Why, I wasn't sure. The music stopped and I heard it then, the call of the demons that the evil ones had obviously sent in the event Hansen should fail in his set mission--converting me to the darkness. They shrieked as they entered the room, swooshing in as dark shadows.

I sprung into action. I let my power cover me.

Tripp reached out for me, his hand went through me. "Karri, no!"

It was too late. As I felt my hair pulling upwards and my clothing changing over, I knew that I'd crossed that thin line between good and evil once again, each time putting myself closer to never returning. Glancing down, I found myself wearing a black leather cat suit that left my breasts almost hanging out and nothing to the imagination. It formed to every spot of my body. The now four-inch spiked heeled boots I wore made me the giant Hilary had claimed I was.

The shadow demons would go for the purest forms of good they could find. It didn't surprise me when they went at Amber. Branson threw his magik up, protecting her from their onslaught. The ones that went at Tripp found themselves passing through him with no luck. When they turned their attention to Riston, the evil and the good side of me shared a moment of perfect understanding--Riston was not to be harmed.

I put my hand out fast. "Come," I commanded. They didn't hesitate. No. They switched directions fast and came directly to me.

Hansen gasped. "Karri, no. They'll kill you. I didn't know they would send them. I didn't..."

Tripp came at me fast. "Don't you dare do it, Karri-Lynn. Don't you dare merge with them. You won't walk away from..."

I began the merging process, allowing all the evil they held into me before Tripp could get it out of his mouth. It was the only way I could be sure that they couldn't report back to their superiors or harm anyone I cared about. If they ate away at me, they'd die. So would I but it was all I had.

The force of them entering me and the evil that they brought sent me flying backwards. I slammed into the wall. Plaster cracked and fell to the floor as I bit back a cry of pain.

"What the hell is happening to her?" Seger asked, breaking my hold on him and charging towards me.

He couldn't have been more on time if he tried. As I felt my body lift high off the ground again it lunged backwards. Pain followed by the sound of breaking glass told me exactly where I was headed. Out the window.

Seger grabbed hold of my hand, yanking me to him. My power brought the breaking glass back with me, making the window whole once more. The momentum I'd been carrying left me crashing into Seger. We tumbled, me falling over him and him fighting to keep hold of me.

"Switch back," he said, sounding labored.

I heard him talking but it seemed far away. I knew then that bad Karri was holding the reigns. I smiled and scratched my fingernails over the top of one breast. Blood swelled to the surface. Seger stiffened as he tipped his head back, fighting the blood call I'd just put out unwillingly.

"Karri," he bit out as his teeth began to lengthen. The beast within him fought for control and the evil in me wanted it to win the battle.

"What the fuck is going on?" Branson asked, sounding as panicked as I felt on the inside.

Hansen moved towards me and pulled Seger away from me just as Seger's eyes began to swirl with shades of amber. "Get a hold of yourself, wolf."

Tripp put his hand out. "Karri-Lynn, release them. They're feeding on your darkness."

A wicked laugh tore free from me. "Do you wish for us to be free, to share with you what we have learned, angel?"

That wasn't my voice I heard talking. I knew then that the shadow demons were in league with the evil I already carried and that gave them the power to control a good deal of me. They seemed drawn to Tripp.

Branson got a pained look on his face and rubbed his beard vigorously. "Why is my cock as hard as a rock? Don't get me wrong, our Karri's always been able to keep it on its toes," he pointed at me, "but that Karri is making me want to fuck a hole through the wall."

Tripp kept his eyes locked on me as he answered Branson. "It's because Karri isn't in control of herself. She has a natural ability to regulate how much sexual energy she gives off when it's just her. The shadow demons have blocked her ability to do that. Watch her, she's not herself. She can and will use sex as a weapon right now. And she can and will kill you if given the chance."

"So, you're saying that our Karri is some sort of sexual seductress?"

Tripp nodded, slowly as he began to circle me. "She was created for a powerful mate," he glanced behind me, towards Riston, "one who is a natural born alpha, so much so that his appetite for sex would be hard to fill with a normal mate. Before he shut himself off from the urge to procreate, he was insatiable. So much so, that even his friends would worry about him."

Hansen stood next to his brother, watching me closely. "Why would someone like that shut off their natural sexual urges?"

The shadow demons within me began try to toy with my powers, making things in the room shake and move slightly. I opened my mouth and spoke but had no clue what the hell it was I was talking about. It wasn't even my voice that came out. "It's simple, Dark Angel. Males of the supernatural kind outnumber females greatly. Often, they live for hundreds of years before their mate is even born. Should they meet their mate before she is of age to perform the mating ritual, their bodies automatically shut down the urge to find comfort, to seek pleasures and do not respond again until their mates have been put through the ritual needed to awaken their sexual side."

"Anyone else think her head might spin?" Branson asked. "That does not sound like Karri's voice."

"It's not," Tripp said. "It's one of the demons she's holding in to keep you all safe."

The demons within me held tight to their grip on me. "She can hear you, green-eyed one. She can hear all of you. She fights hard, hoping we will die within her. We will but that matters not to us. We answered the call of our master and his wish was that if she could not be brought over, then she was to die. We will have served him well. It will be a great loss to our side for she is remarkably close to being one of us and would have been unstoppable. It is her concern for all of you that holds her to the light. With no anchor, she would have lost the fight soon anyway."

Tripp locked gazes with me and for a moment, it felt as if he was able to see the real me, trapped within the demons grasp. "Karri, set them free. There's someone here who can destroy them. He's not banned from interfering but if he tries now, baby, he'll kill you too. He knows this and that's the only reason he's not acting out right now."

"Baby?" Branson asked.

Seger growled out and charged at me. I could smell his arousal dripping in the air. He wanted to fuck me and the demons I carried wanted to let that happen. They forced my hands up and over my body, making me sway to an unearthly beat that played out around me. "Have you thought of her before, wolf?"

Seger's nostrils flared.

The demons surged within me, sending my power out in a massive wave. It made the entire room vibrate. I twirled in a circle, even though I didn't want to. Laughing, I tipped my head back. "So much power left unchecked in one so young. Do you realize that she is only allowing us a tiny portion of the magik she carries? It is most remarkable. Our master would be most pleased. And the horrors this child," I tipped my head and laughed, "for that is what she is in comparison to the rest of you, has seen are remarkable, horrors you can only try to imagine."

The demons were attracted to Tripp. So was I so I gave in to the urge to go to him. They tugged at my magik, using it to caress Tripp. He gasped. I smiled. "Green-eyed one, she knows your body well. Tell us," I ripped opened the front of the leather outfit, leaving my nipples just barely covered, "how well do you know hers?"

"Karri," Tripp said, softly. "Let them loose, baby. I give you my word that someone here can destroy them."

The demons laughed through me as they felt my struggle with hearing Tripp promise anything. They moved aside, mentally, long enough for me to comment. "Like when you gave me your word that you'd be the one to kill me?"

A pained look passed over Tripp's face. "Karri-Lynn, I'm sorry. I didn't mean to lie to you. I swear. But I couldn't--I can't be the one to hurt you. I don't have it in me. "

"Is she back in control?" Branson asked.

The demons seized the reigns before I could respond. Staring at him, I licked my lower lip seductively. They used my magik against me, changing what I was wearing once again. Cool air brushed over my body and I realized just how little I had on. Glancing down, I found myself wearing only thin strips of black leather. Nothing more. The strips just barely covered my shaved mound and my nipples.

Branson drew in a sharp breath. "Guess not."

Something heavy appeared around my neck. Reaching up, I found myself wearing a collar and a silver chain. The demons laughed again, holding the chain out towards Seger. "Come, wolf. Seek your prize. Smell her blood. Her sex. Her power. Take her and claim her as your own. Better yet," I turned in a small circle, thumping thin air as I went, "just fuck her until she bleeds."

Seger growled. It was plain to see that in his current state, he'd more than fuck me. He'd tear me to pieces. I sensed it then, the power I'd felt earlier. It moved around me. The demons drew back a bit, frightened at first before laughing wickedly through me. "Ah, she receives the help of a powerful warrior of good. A," they forced my arms high into the air, "man who has a personal stake in what happens to her."

I fought back, pushing against their control. Staring at the chest full of my father's weapons, I concentrated on them, drawing on every bit of strength I had. The weapons shook and then lifted into the air.

Tripp's gaze went to them. "No! Karri! Don't do it! We can beat them. Set them free. Killing yourself isn't the answer."

I kept fighting, using my power to try to fully control the weapons. Tripp shook his head. "Karri, if they get control of those weapons, they'll use them to hurt Amber."

I stilled but didn't release my hold.

Tripp stared at me. "They'll use them to hurt Riston. Do you want that? Do you want them to kill Riston?"

Instantly, I sent the weapons and slamming back into the trunk and withdrew my power, holding what I could to me tight, terrified they'd hurt someone I cared about. The demons seized the opportunity to act out through me. "Green-eyed one, you may have found a way to appeal to her sensible side but we control her sexual side. And," they forced my nails over my bare stomach, cutting deep into the taut flesh there, causing blood to flow freely, "we say that she will fuck the wolf in front of you all. He cannot help but answer to us."

Seger lunged towards me, howling out. Tripp, Hansen and Branson charged him, tackling him and taking him to the ground. I bent down and ran my hand through the blood on my stomach, sending Seger into an even bigger struggle to break free. As I brought my fingers to my lips and licked my blood from them I turned and focused on Riston.

It was then that I felt the demons within searching for answers. "Interesting," they said through me. "We are unable to find information on you within her. Yet we sensed her fear of harming you. It is there but she has hidden it from us. How is that?"

Tripp was the one who answered. "She's locked it away from herself too. Stop digging for it or you'll kill her and yourselves."

"We care not."

Leveling his gaze, Tripp nodded. "Branson, take Amber and get her out of here. Hansen, see to it that Seger is controlled and as far from here as possible."

"What are you planning on doing?"

"I'm planning on getting those things out of Karri," Tripp said, his voice calm.

Instantly, the demons within collected their power with the need to destroy Tripp on their mind. I fought back hard and clung to them. There was no way I'd let them harm him. "Two can play at this game. I'm not about to play wrap me in nothing more than fucking ribbons anymore, assholes."

"Karri? That was her voice. I heard it!" Branson shouted. "What's going on?"

I turned and found all of them staring at me with shocked looks on their faces. "Tell me how to kill them, Tripp. I know you know. I can't remember. They're..." I held my head tight as pain shot through it. "They're blocking the answer from me."

"Karri?" he asked. "How the hell are you talking to us?"

"It's not easy. Could you hold the questions until after the demon-athon is complete please? I think I've raised enough demons now to meet our quota. What do you think?" They clawed at my sides. Everyone gasped as I cried out.

"Fucking tell her how to stop it, Tripp," Branson said fast. "They're tearing her body from the inside out. Look at the claw marks on her!"

"How do I kill them? I know that I can. I just can't remember..." They fought back, sending evil power ramming through me. I felt my nose begin to bleed and I grabbed my head as the pressure increased.

Before Tripp could answer the demons within thrust me upwards, sending me right at the ceiling. Someone grabbed hold of me and I could almost hear the demons within shrieking. They shot out of me so fast that I fell backwards all the same, knocking whoever had a hold of me over, as well.

I turned and found myself laying on Riston who was still under the influence of magik, at least I hoped he was. My eyes widened. "Shit, I knocked over an innocent and," I glanced down at myself and drew in a sharp breath, "I think I lost the 'Morticia Does Dallas'--look on top of him too. He got a nanosecond of a naked me on him."

Branson let out a nervous laugh.

I swayed a bit, doing my best not to pass out. "Who hit me with a two-by-four in the head?"

"No one," Tripp said, softly. "Are you hurt?"

"Nah, another day in the life. Nothing to get worked up about. Same old same old. And whatever the hell else works as a response here."

"Karri, your body can't take much more of your 'just another days.' You don't take care of yourself like you should."

Rolling my eyes, I dropped my head down on Riston's chest, enjoying the feel of him. "And he wonders why I don't listen when he talks."

"I heard that," Tripp said.

I groaned. "I wasn't trying to hide it from you. I was simply talking to my friend's friend." As I went to roll off Riston, he put his arms around me and held me close. That wasn't supposed to be possible. Was it?

You probably did it yourself, needing comfort. You probably thrust your power out and forced him to respond. Pathetic.

Deciding my explanation worked, I couldn't help but hug Riston as I sighed. "It would be my luck to have this crap happen the same day I finally meet a nice, normal guy I'm interested in. The day I meet you."

"Hey, technically dead but still standing here," Tripp called out with a laugh.

Tripp had a point. He was a great guy when he'd been alive. He'd also been a great lover and so much more than I even wanted to admit to myself. I didn't want to let the pain of losing him back in so I did my best to block it out. Humor was my weapon of choice to help with that. "I said normal. Did you miss that part? I never thought I'd say this but I don't want a supernatural who is prone to having things chasing him too. Gawd, I just got done telling Amber how I wanted someone dark and dangerous. Can I change my vote to shy and innocent?"

I lifted my arm to push up and pain shot through it. I hissed. "I did not sign up to be a punching bag for things that go bump in the night. Yet, here I am, sore as hell. Why is it that I have never been on a date that didn't involve stakes, guns, death and evil things?"

"Just lucky I guess," Hansen said, actually making me laugh.

"When I watch a movie with Amber she's always amazed that I'm all swept away when the hero and heroine are doing something simple like going for dinner. It's when things start exploding and people start dying that it gets boring. Is it too much to ask for a normal life?" I went to roll off Riston and stopped when his lips curved into a tiny smile. "Guys?"

Something crashed and I heard a loud thump. "Ouch. Yeah?" Tripp asked.

"I didn't think angels could get hurt."

"Then you didn't read the manual very thoroughly," Tripp said, laughing.

I didn't move. I stayed on Riston, staring down at him, searching for a sign that he was understanding what was going on. I tipped my head and gave him a questioning look. "Branson, are you sure your holding spell worked?"

"Amber hasn't budged. Are you questioning my skills?" He hissed. "Damn, they burn."

"They?"

Seger chuckled and it was music to my ears. "Yeah, boss, the demons that came out of you are slowly kicking our asses. There's nothing like trying to hit something that doesn't seem to really be there. Though, they're managing to get good licks in on us. Hardly seems fair if you ask me."

Part of me wanted to peek and see exactly what Seger was referring to but since they were fighting shadow demons, I already had a pretty good idea. It was like fighting thin air.

"He's right," Hansen said, surprising me. "They're winning."

"Tell them to go home. Tell them we forfeit the game and they can play in the attic. We'll all go play in the kitchen or somewhere else." I sighed, not wanting to play the game that was anything but fulfilling anymore. "Oh, and I'm happy that you're done trying to fuck me like an animal, Seger."

He laughed. "Me too. Sorry about that."

"No problem. Happens all the time. And to be honest, normally it's evil shit trying to hump my leg. Even though I'm sure you'd have ripped me to pieces I can smile knowing that you aren't a man-whore or evil."

"Uhh, thanks. Wait, are you saying you're happy I almost did that?" he asked.

I chuckled. "Think about my life. Who would you rather have kill you? Them or one of us?"

"Point taken."

"Karri, if I let them leave this room they'll report every detail of what happened here. If the council thinks they can't convert you they'll kill you," Hansen said, sounding strained.

"You hate Karri. What the fuck do you care?" Branson asked, stealing the question I had.

He laughed. "None of you get it."

"I do," Tripp said. "Hate is the furthest thing Hansen feels for Karri. And before anyone argues please keep in mind that he is my twin. Our bond didn't go when I did. It's how I knew he was here."

"Why can't you help with these things, Tripp? Isn't this the same thing you fight on a global level now?" Seger asked, falling down next to me. He turned and blushed. "Sorry again about the whole..."

"Attempt at mounting me?" I asked, winking. "Don't worry about it. I should have warned you about the oversexed problem. Though, I didn't find out exactly what happens when it's let out until recently."

"That would have been good to know. I'd have brought my own collar or something."

"Seger."

He arched a brow. "Yeah."

"That's fun too."

His eyes widened and I giggled. "I was kidding. At least to a point. I think you're safe from my evil clutches now. But for future reference, whatever happens to me when that starts, seems to affect lycans and other angels the most. I don't know why."

"So," he said. "You're warning me that if I ever find you trying to kick the shit out of someone when you're in stiletto boots, I should get my ass to a cold shower fast?"

"Hmm, I think so. It's trial and error. I learn something new about myself on a weekly basis. For instance, did you know that I can't cook?"

He laughed hard. "Yeah, but I'm happy to hear you finally figured it out. I don't think I could have stomached another one of your meals."

"Ass."

He winked. "And you, my dear Karri, are one of the bravest women I know. We've had hundreds of years to get used to all of this yet you're the one who makes us laugh and joke during it all." He sat up. "Speaking of which, do you think you could stop laying on your new boyfriend and help your old one?"

"I guess so." I nodded and froze.

Seger chuckled. "I think they pulled the wool over our eyes, Branson. Care to share how long you and Tripp were a couple?"

"Karri," Tripp said in a warning tone. "Know that I'm here only because someone more powerful than my superiors is allowing it."

"So that means she can't answer the question?" Seger got to his feet and put his hand out to me. I took it. "What? Was it longer than a month? Karri never dates a guy longer than a week, two at the most so that would be like a record for her."

Tripp's jaw tightened. "Seger, enough. There are things greater than you can imagine at work here."

Rolling my eyes, I sighed. It seemed pointless to keep up the charade. "Four years, Seger. Tripp and I were a couple, a very serious item for just over four years."

His breath caught. "Well, that explains the rampage you went on when you found him, uh, when he passed away. You should have told us. We'd have tried to help you through it better than we did."

I smiled. "Killing things helped a lot. Knowing that in the fucked up world of angels, Tripp wasn't really dead helped the most though."

"Karri?" Seger touched my cheek softly. It was a kind gesture, one I appreciated more than he'd ever know.

"Yeah?"

"It's okay to say that you miss him. We all do."

A lone tear ran down my cheek as I locked gazes with Tripp. "I do miss him. So much that it hurts to talk about."

Tripp averted his gaze. "Karri, don't."

Seger gave me a tight hug. "It'll be okay, kiddo. We'll get ya through it. See, he's not really gone."

I stood and watched as demons flew right through Tripp. "Ohmygods, you really can't interfere."

Hansen moved fast and stood before his brother, stopping the demons in their tracks as they tried to take another swipe at him. "I bet it still hurts though."

Tripp ran his hand over his chest and nodded. "Thanks. Though, I'd like to point out that I would be able to help if you hadn't gotten me killed, jackass. Way to keep your thoughts to yourself. Did you have to race back there half-cocked because you found Karri and me in bed together?"

Hansen glanced over in my direction and then to Seger who had somehow managed to get Riston to his feet. "We wouldn't be here now if you were still alive, Tripp. She would have never come-- never moved on to the path she was born to follow. You know that. Hey, you knew going into the thing that you couldn't stay forever."

A shadow demon moved past me fast, slashing out as it went. It caught my upper arm and tore it wide open. I cried out and slapped my hand over the wound. My other marks had healed. This one only seemed to grow worse. "Okay, that hurt. Tell me how to kill them."

Before anyone could answer the room around us seemed to spin. I tipped to the side and landed in sand. Confused, I sat up fast and found that we were all standing on a beach. "What the..."

"Who is the hot chick?" Branson asked.

I followed his gaze to find a young woman and a little girl spread out on sheets with an umbrella over them. The woman's long white-blonde hair matched the little girls, and hung to the ground as she sat with her back facing us. The little girl began to sing. The song she'd picked, *Wishin' and Hopin'* sounded so cute coming from her that I couldn't help but smile. It made me think of Hilary and our dance earlier.

"I don't know. I think the better question is, what the hell just happened?" I touched my arm lightly, wincing as the wound began to grow more. "Anyone want to tell me why this thing is getting bigger?"

"It's feeding off your darkness," Tripp said. "Seger can't heal it either, Karri. You'll need holy water and something to bite on. It's going to hurt like hell. We need to get out of here fast or it will keep growing."

"Okay, the arm is the least of my worries." I did a head count and realized that both Amber and Riston were with us. Amber's eyes were wide. "Umm, Karri? What's going on?"

Branson cursed under his breath and pushed his magik through her once more. "You could have told me that she has supernatural blood in her."

"Sorry, forgot. Can you make them forget this?"

Branson cast a nervous glance at Riston before looking at me. "Yeah, Amber won't remember a thing."

I pointed at Riston. "What about Drop Dead Sexy? Will he remember?"

At that moment, I could have sworn that something passed between Branson and Riston. Branson shook his head.

"Good. Now, anyone want to take a guess where we are and why we're here?"

"Karri-Lynn, what are you doing?" the woman asked, loud enough for all of us to hear.

I knew that voice. Turning slowly, my breath caught. Unable to make sense of what was before me, I just stood there with my mouth open. It couldn't be her? No. There was no way my mother could be before me. This had to be a trick, something the bad guys had figured out they could use against me.

As I stared harder at the little girl, I knew who she was too--me when I was a child. My pulse sped. This wasn't happening.

"Why did the hot chick just say your name?" Branson asked.

Seger cleared his throat. "And why does she look like she could be your sister?"

The little girl shook her tiny hips, sending the ruffles on the bottom of her pink swimsuit bobbing around. She stopped singing and giggled. "I'm singing, Mommy. Try not to be so silly."

"Mommy?" Branson asked. "Is that you, Karri?"

"Tripp, what's going on?" I moved towards him fast and reached for his hand. When mine went through his, I shook my head. "Make it stop."

"I can't, sweetie."

"Sweetie?" Seger asked, with a grin on his face. "Old habits die hard? Oh, pun intended on that one."

Branson coughed. "For the record, Karri would have beat the living shit out of me for calling her that."

"Shut-up, Branson." Tripp brushed his hand through mine as I stared out at the scene unfolding before us.

"Mommy, why does the song talk about making yourself pretty for a boy to marry you? How come you have to do that?"

I watched as my mother laughed. "Why do you ask? Don't you want to get married someday, Karri-Lynn?"

"Not if I have to kiss him."

She laughed harder. "Why is that?"

"Because RJ said I have to punch any boy who tries to kiss me and I don't want to have to beat up my own husband. Would you want to hit daddy every time he kissed you? Geesh, you'd be hitting him all the time. Poor daddy."

She held her arms out to the little version of me. "Oh, RJ said that, huh? He should have clarified that you can kiss your husband without having to punch him, darling."

"Why?"

"Because, he's going to be your…umm…better yet, I hope he doesn't correct that. That will teach him to try to keep you away from boys until you're of an age and I can perform the ritual."

"Ritual?" Branson asked, appearing next to me. "What's your mom talking about?"

"I don't know."

"Karri," he touched my cheek, "you're crying."

Seger moved to my other side. "Leave her alone, Branson. She's allowed to break down when need be and I think seeing her mother for the first time since she was a little girl warrants that."

"How come you do that?" the little girl, or rather me, asked my mother.

"Do what, honey?"

"How come you get the same smile on your face that Daddy does when you talk about RJ and me? You look all weird, like you know a funny secret. RJ does it kind of too, 'cept he doesn't make me feel silly, like I'm a joke or something."

My mother stood and put her hand out to the younger version of me. I couldn't help but walk forward and whisper, "She seemed so tall to me when I was little."

"She is tall, just not as tall as you," Branson said. "Don't get pissed but your mom is hot. I see where you get it from…ouch! That hurt."

"Then shut up and I won't do it again," Seger said, ready to punch the Fay again.

I watched as my mother led the little girl, for ease of explanation, to the edge of the water. "Karri-Lynn, what would you say if I told you that one day you'll grow up and marry a very nice man?"

The little girl seemed to think about it. She squinted. "I'd say that I think you're wrong."

"Why?"

"Because I don't think RJ or Daddy will ever let me date a boy, nice or not. I asked about it once. I wanted to know about where I could find a prince like Cinderella and they both started telling me that boys were bad and that I wasn't allowed to ever talk about them again. Is that true, Mommy? Are boys bad?"

"No, sweetheart but your daddy doesn't want to think about his little girl growing up at all and RJ doesn't want to think about you growing up dating other boys. It's all very hard to explain to you right now but when you're older I'll tell you everything."

"Mommy?"

"Yes, darling."

I pointed at her breasts. "When am I going to get ones that look like that?"

I laughed and took another step forward. "Oh gods, I really was just like Hilary when I was little. How did they not tape my mouth shut?"

As my mother tossed her head back and laughed, I moved closer to her, needing to touch her. Something powerful surged around me, causing a disturbance in the illusion. It faltered but didn't go away.

"Karri-Lynn."

Turning, I found my mother standing next to me in a long provocative white gown. I looked back at the version of her with the young version of me and arched a brow. "What the hell is going on here?"

"Watch your mouth, young lady. That is not talk for a woman," the mother in the white dress said. I leaned back a bit.

"Mom?"

She smiled as a breeze seemed to come out of nowhere. It blew her long hair all around her, causing it to whip around and mine to do the same. "It's me, honey. This," she pointed at the scene of her and me before her, "is taken from your memories. It's an illusion. It's the demons way of trying to tear you down from the inside out. Do you understand?"

She put her hand out to me. "They want you to think that everything that's happened was your fault, Karri. It wasn't. Don't let them win with that. You carry so much love for everyone around you that it's easy for you assume responsibility for things you had no control over."

I felt evil beginning to press in all around us. My mother lifted her arms and it stopped instantly. "I can't stay long. I wanted to see you again." Tears came to her eyes. "You have grown into a beautiful young woman. Though," she touched my shoulder and turned me around slowly, "you're too thin. You should eat more."

"We keep telling her that!" Branson yelled out.

My mother laughed. "I can see why you keep him around, he's rather amusing. In fact, you have made wise choices about those you keep close to you. Tripp has told us so much about you and the others. Your father hangs on his every word, still shocked his baby girl followed in his footsteps."

I glanced at Tripp and he nodded. "Mom, it's really you?"

She laughed. "You certainly got your father's need to be leery of everything."

I grabbed hold of her and hugged. Standing a good three inches above her I kissed the top of her head. She laughed and squeezed me tight. "I think I'm shrinking."

Evil did its best to push in on the illusion but failed. My mother drew back a bit and lifted my arms out. She didn't look a day older than I did. Seger was right, we looked like sisters. "Karri-Lynn, please tell me that you haven't been playing in the mud again."

"Who me? Never."

She laughed and I felt her power moving all over me. When I glanced down, I found myself completely clean, my hair silky and flowing free around me. I now wore a long white gown similar to hers. Straps of two-inch thick material covered my nipples and crisscrossed over my toned abs before moving into a larger bit of material that covered my crotch. A matching band of it covered my ass, hanging down to the sand. The sides were open all the way up. As the breeze continued, I realized what I was missing. "Mom, why am I not in underwear?"

"Well, darling, I would think you'd have figured that out by now. After all, Tripp is very attractive and was in perfect health."

I jerked slightly. "Tripp, this is not my mother! This woman is talking about you and I having sex!"

"Yes it is. Trust me, Karri, I was as shocked as you to find out just how very much like you she is when it comes to a lack of modesty. Oh, and you get the sex thing from her. No question about it."

My mother beamed. "Isn't it great? Being in complete control of men that in theory could tear you apart is a high that you'll never come off of."

I covered my eyes. "Ah, I just got a mental image of you and Dad.

I think I'm going to be sick."

"Karri-Lynn, there is nothing wrong with your father and I having sex. It's natural," she laughed, "well, maybe not natural when it comes to your father, he is quite a handful, but..."

I covered my ears and fought to keep from being sick. "Are you trying to get me to join a convent? Is that what you want? Just say it and I'll do it. No more of this. Good gods, hordes of evil things have tortured me to the point I thought I wanted to die and they had nothing on this. Dad never had sex. You never had sex. End of story. They just beamed me down or something. It was an immaculate conception. No sex. None."

She laughed hard. "Honey, we're similar to Tripp. We didn't die, we moved on to another plane where we are together and still very much in love."

I paled considerably. "You're saying you're still doing Dad, aren't you?"

She wagged her brows.

"That's it. I'm done. I can't ever have sex again. It's your fault."

"While knowing that would normally make your father a very happy man, I'm afraid that he'll not agree with your decision. He wants grandchildren." She glanced over at the group of men I'd brought with me and nodded her head. "You found him. I knew you would. I'm sorry it took so long, Karri."

"Found who and would you please put me in some underwear or something?"

"Okay, if you insist." She snapped her fingers and I glanced down. I moved the thin bit of material out of the way to find a teeny, tiny white thong on me. I snapped around fast, checking my backside. There was a simple, thin, string of white there. "Mother, this is dental floss not underwear."

"You own undies smaller than that," Branson yelled out.

"And how do you know that?" Seger asked, crossing his arms over his expansive chest.

Branson shifted awkwardly. "I sort of went through her box of undergarments when we were moving her in this morning."

My mother touched my upper arm and shook her head as she put healing energy over it. "Karri-Lynn, get out before you can't. You will die long before you've had a chance to live."

I cupped my hand over hers and smiled. "I have one last thing to do, Mom. Then I'll stop."

She shook her head. "You can't hide your intentions from me, Karri. It may work with everyone else in your life but I know you better than you know yourself. He won't let you do it."

"Who?"

"RJ, of course."

That made me laugh. "Mom, I don't know if you know this but I haven't seen him since I was six. I wouldn't know him if he walked right up to me. Well, I might if he proclaimed the day to be green bean day but that's a whole other story. Besides, he doesn't care what happens to me. He's got his own life. I've got mine."

My mother's look hardened and I felt her energy scanning me. She hit horrific memories of my childhood after she died, memories that I'd kept hidden from everyone. Her eyes widened and she moved towards me fast, wrapping her arms around me and holding me tight. "Oh gods, baby, he didn't know. None of us knew. We, your father and I, can't get to your level of existence without the aid of one of our kind among you so we couldn't have known, Karri."

Ashamed of myself for not learning to be stronger sooner, I pulled back from her and refused to let her hug me again. "It's no big deal. I'm fine."

"Fine? That existence was not fit for an animal, let alone my baby girl."

"Mom, I'm good now. Really. But trust me when I say that RJ couldn't give a shit."

When she didn't correct me for my choice of words, I looked up to find her staring towards the group of men with tears in her eyes. I touched her arm lightly. "I didn't meet any of them until after the fact. They don't know what happened and I don't want them to. Please don't say anything about it."

Nodding, she took my hand and turned to watch the illusion of the two of us playing in the surf. I could feel the love radiating off her. It wrapped around me and held me tight.

Suddenly, another person joined us on the beach. When I saw my father running full force at us, I covered my mouth. "Daddy!"

My mother clutched my hand tight. "That's your memories honey, not really him. Do you remember what happened on this day?"

"Yes, Dad and his men were attacked in broad daylight without warning. They were over that ridge going over some plans for something and it happened. Dad said that one of the demons they killed had a picture of me on him. So I assumed..."

"That the attack was your fault. RJ got hurt and you blamed yourself for it, even though he was healed within a week and it was not your fault. I couldn't get you to understand that." She looked behind me at the men. "He couldn't get you to understand that either."

Evil pressed in hard, this time breaking free. Two large *sparterous* demons fell from the sky and dropped on both sides of my mother and myself. She gasped and I rolled my eyes as I struck out hard and fast, ripping the red jewel from one of their foreheads with one hand and smashing my other hand through the hole. It caught fire and I kicked it away from me--silently cursing the outfit she put me in.

"Karri?"

Pulling her backwards I went to snatch the other *sparterous'* red jewel. It caught my arm and bent it back fast, taking me to the ground. I spotted the guys running towards me out of the corner of my eye and grabbed a handful of sand.

"Hey," I said, catching the demon's attention. It looked at me and I threw sand in its eyes. It jerked back fast and I spun, kicking its feet out from under it and sending it to the ground. I crawled over it fast, yanked the jewel out and punched its empty hole. Rolling quickly, I narrowly avoided going up in flames with it.

Riston was next to me in an instant, shocking the hell out of me. Reaching down, he pulled me to my feet fast. "Are you hurt?"

Why wasn't he frozen? Worse yet, why did he glance at my mother? He could see her? This was not good. Confused, I glanced past him. "Branson, I thought you tossed a magikal whammy on him. Why the hell is he walking around fine?"

Branson swallowed so hard that I could see his neck muscles working overtime. That was never a good sign. "Uhh, just go along with him. I swear that I'll, uhh, wipe him clean when we're done. Yeah. That's it. I'll clear his memory then."

My mom laughed as she grabbed my arm. "Karri-Lynn, where did you learn to fight like that? I am certain that you did not learn it from me."

"A vampire taught me most of it but these guys have done more than their share of teaching me how to handle different types of demons. Are you planning on yelling now because I feel like I should go to my room or something?" I glanced down at the outfit she put me in and sighed. "I also feel like I'm going to pop a nipple. Can you please fix this?"

Riston stared down at me with a look, which had me worried that he was about to tackle me to the ground and have his way with me.

"And being under him would be a bad thing, how?" my mother asked.

My eyes widened. "Tell me you weren't just reading my thoughts."

"I could, but that would be a lie."

Tripp stood behind Riston with a huge smile on his face. "I can't believe you remembered to kill them that way. I didn't think you were paying attention that day, Karri."

My mother snorted and wagged her brows. "I can't see how she learned anything with you teaching her like that."

"Like what?" Branson asked.

Tripp shook his head. "No, don't...."

My mother grinned. "Well, he was a very good personal tutor. His reward system would have made me study hard too. I especially like how he'd ask Karri to recite the various demons and how to kill them while he was," she glanced downwards, "doing a little research of his own." She winked. "Withholding when she stopped saying them was genius, Tripp. What do they call that way of teaching? Orgasm incentives?"

"Victoria, are you trying to get me killed a second time around?" he asked. "I thought we were friends."

She laughed. "Oh, don't worry about *him*. After what I just learned being in my baby girl's head, he deserves to be reminded of what he never made an attempt to claim. It serves him right that another man won her heart before *he* did."

Something crashed into Riston, sending him flying backwards and hitting the ground fast. I ran to him, worried that he was injured. He winced as he got to his feet but seemed fine. Tentatively, I ran my hand over his arm. "Are you okay?"

"Yeah," he glanced at my mother, "I'm fine."

"Mom, did you just knock Riston on his ass with your power?"

She didn't answer. Instead, she put her hand out to Tripp. "Tell them how you were finally able to do what no others could."

Tripp shook his head. "Victoria, I don't think that's really something that needs to be advertised."

She put her hand up. "Tripp."

He shrugged. "Fine. Karri really did agree to marry me."

"Don't sound too happy about it," I said, hurt that he had to be forced to even admit it.

"Karri, it's not like that. I'm just trying to give someone the same respect I'd want if I was in their shoes. I wouldn't want it thrown in my face that you were happy with someone else. Would you?"

My mother smiled. "I was right to pick you, Tripp. When word came to me that my daughter still hadn't been claimed I knew that she needed someone special in her life to fill that gap. You," she ruffled his black hair, "more than stepped up to the plate."

"What are you talking about? You didn't send Tripp to me and I didn't need anyone."

I looked at Tripp, expecting him to back me up. What I got instead was something I wasn't expecting. "I'd do it again in a heartbeat, Victoria. She's as amazing as you said she'd be, even more so."

Backing up, I shook my head. "You were with me because my mother asked you to be? Wow, umm, I don't even know what to say to that." It felt as though I'd been hit in the stomach. I snorted as my emotions raged. "And the academy award goes to, you my faithful second."

He made a move to come to me and I put my hand up. "No. Don't."

"Karri-Lynn, please, you're not understanding how things work."

"I understand that you didn't think twice about playing with my emotions, Tripp. Am I wrong?"

The illusion began to crumble. My mother reached out and hugged me tight. "I love you."

"Mom, what's..."

She hugged me tight and then looked at Riston. "Take care of my baby."

Riston wrapped his arms around me tight as the illusion began to swirl. I tried to go to my mother but he held me to him. When the swirling stopped, I found myself standing knee deep in the snow in what appeared to be a blizzard. Riston held tight to me, his fingers skating over my exposed skin and dancing close to the edge of the strips of white cloth. My skin burned with pleasure everywhere that he caressed it.

Tipping my head back, I sighed and rocked my body against his. "Why did my mother say that to you? Why would she tell you to take care of me?"

He ignored my questions and held tight to me. "Are you cold?"

"No, and I should be. There's snow everywhere. Why am I not freezing?"

"Because it's an illusion, Kars." Riston growled slightly as I shifted a bit.

I turned into his arms quickly, placing the palms of my hand against his steely chest. I bunched the black material of his tee shirt in my hands and gave into the comfort of his arms. "I'm so sorry that you got pulled into this. I never intended to involve anyone else in it. Branson will make you forget. He has the power, and I do mean that literally, to wipe your memories of this, Riston."

"What if I don't want to forget?"

"I'm sorry but you don't get a choice. This is my life and I don't want to share it with strangers, Riston." I couldn't help but to slide my arms around his waist. "I don't understand what's going on and that's scaring me. I don't scare easy anymore."

"You don't have to be afraid anymore, Kars. I'm here now." He ran his hands through the back of my hair and kissed the top of my head. "I've got you now."

Energy seemed to move through us. I held tight to him and couldn't help the tears that came to my eyes. "I didn't get to tell her that I love her. I..."

"Shh," he tilted my chin up, "she knows." Riston pressed a tiny kiss to the tip of my nose and I could have sworn that I felt love radiating from him.

Stop dreaming. A man like him isn't for you.

"Where's everyone else?" I asked, noticing we were alone and needing something other than him to focus on.

"They're coming. Don't worry, Amber's safe."

"How do you know?" I thought about what he'd said before, in the kitchen. His father and my father were friends. Hilary had special gifts and wasn't human, neither was her mother. It hit me then. "You're not human either. Are you?"

I glanced down and spotted the blood in the snow. My breath hitched as I pulled out of Riston's grasp.

"Karri?"

"Make it stop, Riston. Please make it stop. I don't want to be here. Please."

He tried to pull me back to him but I didn't give in. "Kars, talk to me. What's wrong?"

"It's that night--the night my parents died. It's..."

"There they are," Seger called out from somewhere behind me.

Something pushed past me. It was evil at its finest. It ran around me fast and then dissipated.

"Why am I stuck in one spot?" Branson asked.

"We all are," Tripp said. "They know that one of us here can stop this but they don't know which one so they're temporarily binding the rest of us. They don't want us to interfere and help Karri."

Instantly, a very life-like illusion of my father appeared before me, laying in the snow, covered in blood. I covered my mouth and shook my head. "It's not real. It's not real. Not again."

"Karri. Karri, look at Daddy," he whispered, his breathing

labored. "Karri, baby."

I looked at him. His big brown eyes locked on mine. "I need you to listen to me." He coughed. "I need you to ask RJ to take you to his sister, sweetie. No one else. She's right. I can feel it. Do you understand?"

Suddenly, it felt as though I were six years old again. My clothing changed back to what I'd had on to start with and I could feel the tug inside, the power trying to take me back more.

"Baby, focus on daddy, not what's around us. They can't hurt you if you keep up the bubble I taught you."

I looked down at my father. "Daddy?"

He nodded. "Did you hear me? You need to make sure RJ knows to take you to his sister, no one else."

I caught movement out of the corner of my eye. Turning, I saw something, half-man, half-beast running straight at us. I screamed and shook my head madly. It kept coming. It hit what seemed to be an invisible force field all around my father and me and lurched backwards, shrieking out as it went.

Another one of the beasts came at us. I screamed out as it hit the shield I'd somehow put up. It reared its hideous teeth mere inches from my face. Crying, I flung more power out, and barely pushed it a foot away. Somewhere deep inside me I knew I was more powerful than this and that I wasn't a child anymore but it didn't come out in my actions. The beast launched at us again. I threw my body over my father's head. "No more. He's hurt enough already."

"Shh, Karri, baby. Look at me."

I sat up and stared down at my father as he lay, bloody and dying in the white snow. Evil things slammed into the invisible barrier that I knew I'd put around him when he'd fallen. I also knew why he'd fallen. "I should have listened. I should have stayed hidden like you said but I saw them hurt Mommy and I had to..."

"Shh, Karri-Lynn, look at Daddy."

I looked at everything evil around us not him. This wasn't right. He died when I was six yet here I was, an adult sitting next him. I fought hard with my inner emotions but failed.

"Karri, I know this is too much," he clawed at the snow clearly in pain, "for you. But please try. He's coming for you. I knew the minute that you screamed for me to wait," blood splattered onto the snow as he coughed, "for RJ before we left the house that he heard you. Tell him, Karri, tell him...his sister...he'll know then. That's all Daddy needs you to remember. Can you be a big girl and remember that?"

"Daddy, there's more of them now. Get up. Get up and we'll go home."

"Karri, you have to listen to me. Tell RJ. He knows that you're the one. He's known for a while now. I told him that I asked the goddesses to help him find happiness like I found with your mother and then you came into our lives, Karri. They sent you to us to care for and love before giving you over to him to love for the rest of your life. I know this is a lot. You're just a baby yet but you have to listen."

I only half heard what he was saying, too fixated on what was happening around us. As I stared at the beasts trying to break through the barrier it was like I really was a child, mentally at least. They terrified me as they snarled and snapped their jaws at me.

"Karri. Please."

"Daddy, I want to go home now. I don't like it here. I want pink pancakes. Tell mommy to get up and make you pink pancakes." I tugged on him. "Please get up."

"Pink pancakes?" he asked. I watched as he registered what I was telling him. He closed his eyes tight and tears streamed down his face. "Karri, baby doll, I have to go soon but I can't leave until I know you're safe. Call for RJ. He'll hear and be able to find you. They're blocking me from contacting him. But they don't know, honey, they," he hissed in pain, "don't know that you're his mate-- that you can reach him with your mind, with your words even."

Another large demon thrashed out, catching my attention and holding it. I screamed out as it thumped madly against the protective barrier.

"Karri-Lynn O'Higgins," he said sternly. I stopped and stared at him. "Call for RJ..." His eyes closed.

I shook him gently. "Daddy don't go to sleep now. Please get up. I can feel you. You're just playing sleep. I don't want to play. I want to go home. I want pink pancakes." I hugged him tight. "Daddy, get up. I'm scared."

He coughed again. "Karri, call RJ to you. He can sense you. You just have to call out to him and he'll be able to find you and protect you. Trust me, baby, he will give his life for you. You are his world, his future."

"Daddy..."

"Karri-Lynn, this is an order. Call RJ, now!"

I sniffled and called out to my father's best friend and right hand man, "RJ!"

My father gasped, seeming to choke on nothing. A small smile spread over his face. "I love you, honey. Ne-ver…forget that."

The second he went limp, I screamed. Something moved over me fast, going right through the barrier but not harming me. I knew then that RJ had made it.

"Enough!" I shouted. I jerked back fast and the illusion broke and another one replaced it. I stood, holding a bag of groceries as I stared at an open green door. My mind fogged and it felt like I was there, living the day over.

"Tripp, is there a reason the door is open or are you psychic now to boot. Even you, wonder of all wonders, couldn't have predicted I'd stop at a, dare I say it aloud, grocery store."

I shifted the groceries and closed the door behind me. The sound of jazz music surrounded me, soothing me with the soulful sounds of Billie Holiday as I dug into my shirt and pulled my silver chain with the triple knot charm on it out. I glanced down at the engagement ring laced through the chain, hanging next to the charm and shook my head. "No offense, but I'm still shocked I said yes. Not that I'm second-guessing you. It's just…something is nagging at me…something inside. Tell me it's not cold feet. I believe anything you tell me so make something up. I'll go with it."

"Oh, I got the junk food you like and fruit for me. If you throw any of it away again because it's taking up cold pizza space we are going to tangle and I don't mean that in a good way."

As I started past the oversized foyer I glanced into the formal living room. It was in shambles. "Uhh, Tripp, I know you mentioned getting a dog but I thought I vetoed that. But I did give some more thought to your idea of adopting a baby."

I walked into the living room and looked around. "Seger made mention that his sister and her husband have adopted a little boy who is like us, not human. I asked him more about it and after lying to his face," I shook my head, "which I hate, I managed to find out that older children need a home too. I think I'd be lost with anything little. I don't think I come with maternal, tiny baby instincts. Maybe we could adopt one in the double-digits. How about Branson? Shit, he's triple digits. That won't work."

I set the groceries down and went to work straightening up the room. "Tell me that you and Branson didn't get into another who is stronger fights again." I picked a table up and found a picture of the two of us. Its glass was shattered as was the lamp that had been sitting next to it. "Tripp?"

He didn't answer. I grabbed the bag of groceries and sighed. "Gee, no worries, I'll just put the cold stuff away and clean up your mess," I said, laughing slightly.

I heard something moving around upstairs and shook my head. "He showers more than any man I know."

"Karri," someone whispered near me.

I turned, expecting to find Tripp but found nothing. "Tripp?"

"Run, baby! Run!"

My chest tightened. "Tripp, what are you doing? I can't see you."

Something thumped on the level above me again and I headed towards the stairs. I made it all the way up only to find that the hallway was littered with broken pictures, clothes, torn sheets. "Okay, Tripp, answer me. You're anal about your house and it looks like a tornado went through it."

Something dark whipped past my head, its evil brushed past me and I knew instantly what it was--a vampire. "Tripp!"

He didn't answer and panic seized hold of me. Something crashed through the wall next to me and slammed me into the other one quickly. It seized hold of my neck and lifted me high. Looking down, I found an oversized, partially shifted were-hyena holding me up. He snarled, showing off his bloody mouth and teeth. I clutched onto his clawed hand, fighting to breathe.

A vampire came rushing out from another room. "Who do we have here?"

Someone else appeared, another man, this one shorter than the other two. "It's the chick from the pictures."

"We're here to find out who else he was working with, not some dumb fucking blonde. Kill her and keep looking," the vampire said, staring at me with hard eyes. "We need to report back that the angel is dead."

Dead?

I shook my head as much as I could.

The vampire smiled. "Oh, yes, blonde one, your lover, the spy sent to infiltrate us, the one who honestly thought we wouldn't discover who he really was, is dead. Don't fear. You're going to follow him soon enough. Kill her."

The idea of Tripp being dead was unimaginable to me. I kicked my legs out fast and caught the short man around the neck. Raising my power up, I used it to burn the were-hyena's hand on my neck. He let go as I twisted my body around, snapping the short one's neck.

I dropped to the floor and punched out hard and fast, catching the were-hyena in the groin. He went to slice out at me and I flipped backwards. His clawed hand raked past me, missing me. I threw magik up and around Tripp's house, determined that these men would not leave.

I rushed into the master bedroom and slammed the door shut. I let my power coat it, knowing it was only a temporary hold but a hold all the same. I turned and it took a moment for my mind to register what my eyes were seeing. It was Tripp, spread out wide against the wall. He'd been pinned to the wall, crucified.

My breath came in shallow pants as I covered my mouth and shook my head not wanting to believe what was before me. Shaking, I moved towards him slowly, sure that he'd look up and smile at any moment, that he couldn't be dead. He didn't move.

I lifted his head and found that his face had been mutilated. Screaming, I stepped back fast, too fast, tripping over my own two feet and falling into a puddle of his blood. I began to hyperventilate as I fought back the vomit that wanted desperately to rise.

"No, no…no."

I pushed to my feet and forgot logic, forgot reason. I went to him fast and began trying to figure out what was holding him to the wall. When I realized it was magik, I threw my own around it and sent it spiraling off into the abyss. Tripp's body fell fast, too fast. It hit me, taking me to the floor and leaving me under him.

I pushed up but couldn't budge him. The reality of it all set in and I found myself fighting to keep my own darkness from rising. It was then I realized that this had all already happened once. It wasn't happening again. It was an illusion. An illusion that I was allowing the shadow demons to use to get me to tap into my darkness, my hate, my rage.

"It's not real," I whispered to myself.

The illusion around me began to shake. Tripp's body vanished, as did the blood that I'd had all over me. I closed my eyes and concentrated hard. I found the answers I need. "I call on the archangels…before me, Raphael."

Wind whipped around me madly and the illusion dropped completely. I found myself laying on the attic floor. I struggled to get to my feet, the wind was strong. Shadow demons shot up and began to buzz past me, slicing out as they went. "To my side, Michael."

I kept going, calling upon all of powerful angels. One of the shadow demons came surging forward, headed straight for me. I prepared for impact but someone moved before me quickly, blocking it from hitting me.

The demon shrieked out as it evaporated. The other shadow

demons began to evaporate as well and the wind died down slowly. When I realized it was Riston standing in front of me I couldn't stop myself. I wrapped my arms around his waist and squeezed him tight, resting my head against his back. "Thank you."

He touched my arm lightly. "You're welcome."

I stood there, not wanting to let go but knowing I had to. "Branson?"

He approached slowly. "Yes?"

"Make him forget," I whispered, still holding tight to Riston.

"But..."

"Do it."

Branson cleared his throat. "But, Karri..."

"Please do it before I lose the will to make you. I want to keep Riston and that scares me. Make him forget. This isn't any life for him, Branson. It's not fair for me to do this to him."

"You're not understanding. I can't..."

Riston nodded. "Do it, Branson."

"But it won't..."

"I know," Riston said running his hand over my arm lightly. "She needs this right now. Give it to her the peace of mind. I'll take care of the rest."

Branson sent his magik out and over Riston. It sprinkled around me and made me sneeze. A tiny giggle erupted from me and I glanced at Branson. "Trust you to be the one to make me laugh after all of that."

"Hey, at least I'm good for something." He looked behind me and nodded. "I think Tripp has to go now."

I turned fast to find Tripp beginning to fade away. I tried to go to him but something mystical held me in my place. When I realized it was his power I shook my head. "Tripp, let go of me?"

He smiled. "Thank you."

"For what?" I asked, unable to believe I'd done anything to deserve a thank you.

"For teaching me that I wasn't too old to have fun and for teaching me how to love again while I was here with you. And Karri, none of what we had was staged. I was sent to protect you, to guard you until you and your mate found one another, not to fall in love with you. That just sort of happened. I wasn't supposed to let it and they told me that you could never love me, that it was impossible. We beat the odds, Karri."

"Tripp." I bit back tears. I wanted to tell him that I loved him but the words wouldn't come to me.

"I don't need to hear you say it, Karri. I lived it. I know that you do."

"But..."

"You're in good hands now, sweetie, and that's how it's supposed to be. I picked up where another angel left off. She handed the reigns to me and now, I've seen you to the one you were created for. Take care of yourself, sweetie."

"Tripp?"

I felt his magik, his power moving over me. "What are you doing?"

He smiled. "Taking the pain away. You've grieved enough for me already, Karri. It's time to let go. I didn't get to give you that dog or Branson as our kid but I can give you this--the ability to move on. To love again."

"He faded before I had a chance to ask him what he meant about delivering me to the one I was created for. "Damn, he's a fast one now isn't he?" I asked, laughing. That caught me off guard. "Uhh, why am I not killing something or bawling my eyes out?"

"Because whatever he did worked," Branson said. He smiled as he approached me. "Thanks for picking me as your adopted kid possibility."

"You saw that?"

He nodded. "Yeah, we were trying to reach you, trying to get you to hear us but they kept you from sensing or seeing us. Not even your new buddy could get you to hear him." He pulled me into his arms and hugged me tight. "You're all right, for a girl."

"Gee, thanks." I looked around to find that Hansen was gone too. "Did Hansen take off on his own or did someone kill him?"

Seger grinned. "As tempting as that was, he fought hard, controlling those demons and refusing to let them leave with the knowledge they'd gathered, Karri. He made his mistake. He sacrificed his brother in the hopes he'd win what Tripp had, but found out that he couldn't take what belongs to another."

I gave him a questioning look.

"You, Karri. He couldn't take you." Seger motioned to Branson. "We're leaving too. Amber won't remember us even being here."

"In her time, only seconds have passed," Branson said, ushering Seger towards the door.

"Wait." I drew back a bit. "You mean in *their* time it's only been seconds, right?"

"Uhh, yeah." Branson grinned as he practically shoved Seger out the door.

I glanced down to find Amber bent over the chest of weapons where she'd been before it all started and I let out a shaky laugh. "Another day in the life of Karri." I rotated my head around, doing my best to work the kinks out in my neck. "No tears. No anything. It's just another day. Nothing more. Nothing less. Gawd my life sucks major ass. Maybe I'll luck out and not wake up tomorrow."

Snapping my fingers, I pushed Branson's magik off the room and dropped down by Amber fast. I took her hand in mine and smiled. She came to and hissed. "Ouch. I think I..."

She looked at her hand. It was healed.

"You think what?" I asked, doing my best to look innocent. It wouldn't do her a bit of good to remember what really happened. No. She'd never sleep at night if she fully understood the terrors around her. "You screamed and scared the hell out of me, Amber."

"Really, so does this mean you no longer believe in demons since I scared the hell right out of you?"

I simply laughed. It was shaky but I could do little to stop it. "Oh, I don't know about that. What do you say we stay out of the weapons trunk?"

"I think that's a very good idea." She looked over my shoulder and smiled wide. "So, Riston, see what I mean? Her collection is full of stuff you'd love. If I could get her to act semi-normal for more than hour I think you'd really like her. In fact, I'd venture to say that the two of you would be perfect for one another."

A new song kicked on and I realized that the CD player was still sitting on the floor not on the porch where it should have been. The woman sang about being a bitch yet having so many other levels that she was not only complete but comfortable in her skin. Amber arched a dark red brow. "I don't remember you bringing that up here."

My mind raced as I keep a cool look on my face. "Because you were too worried about me staring at Riston's ass to notice me grab it."

Amber snickered. "Gawd, I can't hear this song and not think about you, Karri. Remember when the hot guy with the black hair and green eyes told you that you should really carry this on you at all times and demand it be played when you enter a room?"

I let out a soft laugh. "Yeah."

"What was his name? He was super hot and never picked on you about your vampires and werewolves thing. In fact, he seemed to share your obsession. He also seemed a little iffy on Jean-Paul."

"Lycans, not werewolves," I winked at her, "and his name is

Tripp." The very fact that I didn't talk about him in past tense was a testament to Tripp's power and his helping me overcome my hidden grief.

"That's right. He was really nice. I can't believe you didn't know he was into you."

The last thing I wanted to talk about was Tripp but that wasn't Amber's fault. "I figured it out eventually. Hey, why don't you go ahead and dig through some of this stuff? Not the weapons though," I smiled, "It might bring back good memories. I'm sure the penis pictures are up here somewhere. I have to confess that I threw away the ones that were so pathetic that I was mad we wasted film but I kept the really good ones."

"I still can't believe you did that."

"Hey, you said that you'd never seen one. I gave you a thousand because I love you."

Her eyes lit as she wrapped her arms around me. "I have missed you so much."

Taking her hands in mine, I lifted them high and spun her in a circle. She giggled and I followed suit. We continued on, dancing around the room and laughing as we went. As we approached Riston, Amber came to a grinding halt.

"Oh, I forgot you were here."

Laughing, I put my hand out to him, to my surprise, he took it. "I would say you can be an honorary girl for the next five minutes but you are *way* to alpha to accept that as a compliment."

Amber snorted. "You just called him alpha."

I bit my lower lip, a bit embarrassed by my slip of tongue. "So I did."

Riston shrugged, not looking the least bit offended. In fact, he looked rather pleased. "Hey, I'll take it."

"I'll be right back," Amber walked towards the door, "I want to go check on Hilary and Eric."

"Are you taking *your* Riston with you?" I asked, not really sure what the hell I'd do with him once she was gone.

"No. I think *my* Riston would rather stay here with you but I could be wrong."

"Wait, how did I end up being handed off to Amber?" Riston's blue eyes seemed to sparkle as they stared at me. "How about I hang out here? I'm guessing you could use a hand with things and I have no desire to watch my brother-in-law cry every time he looks at Hilary today."

"Eric will not cry every…oh…you were joking, weren't you?"

Amber asked.

Riston nodded and took a deep breath in. "It's good to know that you guard him like a hawk, Amber."

She waved, blew him a kiss and headed out of the room. "Karri, try not to scare him away!"

"No promises." I glanced down at the trunk on the floor and sighed. "Why in the hell did they decide the middle of the attic was a great place for this stuff? Amber's lucky she didn't cut her hand off. Err, I mean…yeah, lucky."

Way to go, moron. You force Branson to take his memories only to tell him what happened.

I went to try to budge it and groaned as pain moved throughout my body. "I guess it's staying right there."

"Here," Riston said, pushing past me, sending tiny sparks of pleasure throughout me as he went. I let him go, even though I knew it took two supernatural men to carry the thing earlier. When he picked it up I gasped. He put it down fast. "Gee, that's heavier than I thought."

He didn't look strained in the least. Something was going on. It wasn't heavy for him but he wanted me to think it was. Odd. I didn't comment. I just put my hands on the chest and helped push it towards the back corner of the attic. As we pushed it almost all the way to the wall I lost my balance, something I did a lot when I was on the verge of exhaustion, and ended up falling to my left.

Riston grabbed me just in time for me to accidentally bring him with me. We tumbled to the hardwood floor. I hit first and Riston landed on top of me. He was a hell of a lot heavier than he looked.

I pushed up hard on him. "Gods, you're solid muscle."

He propped his upper body up with his hands and stared down at me. The look on his face was neutral but from the feel of the erection pressing against my upper thigh, it was safe to say he wasn't unaffected by the predicament we'd ended up in. As my inner thighs tightened and my chest heaved, I knew that I wasn't immune to it either.

Riston dipped his head down and I took in his manly scent. It was so familiar and so exciting that I was left no choice but to inhale deeply. He chuckled. "What are you doing?"

"Mmm, trying to figure out why you smell so familiar." The second I said it, I wanted it back. The song changed again and the minute I heard The Beatles my eyes widened.

Riston chuckled. "Something wrong?"

As *Here Comes the Sun* pumped out I couldn't help but laugh.

"No. Nothing's wrong. I just have memories of annoying the hell out someone with this song."

"Really? Who?"

Shifting beneath him slightly, I felt his bulging erection dig in more. I drew in a sharp breath and locked gazes with him. I would have made a smart-ass comment but he leaned down more and touched the tip of his nose to mine. I smiled. "You look so different with glasses on. And I like your hair short now. Never thought I would. Did you cut it because I said it was pretty? I didn't mean it as a bad thing. I just meant..."

I swallowed hard when I realized what it was I was doing. "Umm, wow, I think the heat is getting to me. I don't suppose you'll just ignore my last comment? Or better yet, all of what I just said? You remind me of someone."

Riston licked his lower lip and grinned slightly. "So you've said."

I closed my eyes as an overwhelming feeling of exhaustion hit me. I blinked and tried to focus on Riston but failed. "Why am I so tired?"

"Because you haven't slept in days and I can sense the toll it's taken on you." He kissed my forehead lightly.

Fearing I'd slipped into that state between reality and dreams, I didn't question Riston's comment. Too many times the demons picked then to mentally wage a war on me. I couldn't risk it. I had to stay awake. As I felt his weight moving off me, I reached or at least hoped I reached for him.

"I'm going to move you to the sofa downstairs," he whispered.

"No." I tried to open my eyelids but they were too heavy. I shook my head. "I have to get up. They'll come. They'll come and I'm not strong enough to fight them alone anymore. Please, Don't go."

"Kars, I'm not going anywhere ever again. I promise you that."

"I don't want to be alone anymore, RJ...err...Riston," I mumbled, correcting myself. Riston wasn't RJ. So, why did my mind keep slipping up?

"You're not alone, honey. I won't let them come, Kars. I'm strong enough to keep them away from you. Keep you safe and I will."

Why didn't he seem the least bit offended to be called by another name? I drifted off before I could think too much harder on it all.

Chapter Four

I jerked awake and tried to get my wits about me. I blinked and
found Amber staring down at me. "Hey, sleeping beauty, I would
normally let you rest because it's so rare but you are going to have
one hell of a sore back and neck if I leave you here."

"Huh? Sleeping Beauty?"

She put a finger to her lips and hushed me. "Yeah, it's pushing
three o'clock. You've been out for close to four hours, sweets. And
before you ask, I did write it on the calendar. No fear. We'll never
forget the day you actually slept longer than twenty minutes without
waking up screaming." Amber nodded towards something behind
me. "I was going to make fun of you for passing out with one of my
closest friends wrapped around you, but if he had something to do
with you finally getting some sleep I'm not about to comment.
Though, he's going to be sore too if we leave him like that."

"Him?" Turning slightly, I came face to face with a sleeping
Riston. My heart hammered in my chest as my entire body began to
tingle. Amber went to touch him and I caught her wrist gently. "No,
let him sleep a little bit longer."

"Karri, he'll end up stiff and sore."

"I don't think he will. I get the feeling that the man can sleep
anywhere. I also have an uncontrollable urge to crawl onto his back
and tickle him. Care to shed some light on that one?"

"You're freaking me out, Karri. You've known Riston for six
hours and you've got him not only holding you but sleeping. He
doesn't just pass out in mid-day. In fact, Eric complains that he
doesn't sleep enough--ever. You waltz in and the man seems
instantly drawn to you and so relaxed that he finally lets his guard
down. You have one of those personalities. It's kind of off-putting
but works for Riston."

"I'll go," I said fast, not wanting to upset Amber.

Her brow furrowed. "What do you mean, go?"

"If this is too weird for you, I'll go, Amber. I didn't show up with
the intention of having any of the things that happened today,
happen." I couldn't tell her all the details but I knew them. I also
knew that she wasn't as safe as I'd been led to believe.

She gave me a puzzled look and shook her head. "Oh no you

don't, Karri. You like Riston so you want to run in the other direction. Nice try, sister."

"Aren't you lil' Miss Adamant?" I snickered. "Go ahead. I'll be down in a minute. I'm going to grab him some blankets and a pillow."

She beamed and I could almost hear the wheels spinning in her head. "Take as long as you need."

"I am not about to seduce your friend."

She bit her lower lip. "Could have fooled me. But, Karri."

"What?"

"Don't hurt him. He's a good guy."

I stiffened. "Thanks for the vote of confidence, Amber. I said I wouldn't do anything and I meant it. But hey, let's just toss that out there in case I was lying. Care to add anything..." I stopped just as I began to raise my voice. "Never mind."

"What in the hell is your problem?"

I snorted. "My problem? Right. I'm sorry but from the moment I picked you up this morning you've been taking nasty, uncalled-for jabs at me, Amber. Tell me what I did to deserve this."

"I have not been taking nasty jabs at you, Karri. You just need thicker skin."

Easing Riston's arm off me, I sat up and smiled. "Excuse me, but if my skin was any thicker a bunch of beefy guys would show up with stakes and semi-automatics to protect the world from me, Amber. I have spent the greater part of my life being made fun of, called crazy, a bitch, a man-eater, which is my personal favorite plus loads of other things." I wasn't even going to get into the parts of my childhood that my mother had found my memories from. No. Those were best left hidden. "Whatever. That's fine but to have you, my best friend, doing it isn't fine. If this is how it's going to be between us now I want to know."

"Why, so you can disappear for another seven years without a word before you pop-up like nothing happened?" She narrowed her blue eyes to the point they were hard. "How could you cut off all contact with me, Karri? I thought you were dead. I called the local police department near you, begging them to check in on you."

"You can't honestly think I'd cut ties with you for the fun of it, can you, Amber?"

She put her hands in the air and shrugged. "I don't know what to believe. I never thought you'd do that to me. If you were in trouble you should have come to me. I would have helped. You know that."

I snorted at the idea of Amber fighting evil. "Yeah, the next time I'm standing in the pits of Hell fighting things you can't even imagine I'll be sure to call you to lend a hand. I should probably warn you that they have mongo huge spiders down there. I know how much you hate those."

"You can be such a bitch, Karri."

I smiled, knowing that it was one I used often when I was playing on the side of evil. Amber took a step back. Tipping my head back, I let out a throaty laugh. "You have no idea how much of a bitch I can be. Pray you never find out."

"See," she pointed at me, "there you go being a bitch again."

"In my defense, I came this way. What the hell is your excuse? Does bitchiness grow on trees around here or you just planning on holding things I couldn't control over my head forever?"

"Bitch."

"Thanks," I said, smiling sweetly at her.

She snickered. "Wench."

I laughed too. "Thanks."

"I hate it when you do that."

I shrugged pretending to be innocent. "When I do what?"

"When you take being called a bitch as a compliment." She giggled and put her hand in the air. "I will never forget the party you threw to celebrate your PMS that month."

"Ah, Menstrual Madness. I almost forgot about that one." It felt like a lifetime ago when I'd hosted that campus party. "I was shocked at how many men showed up."

"Karri, please, they follow you like homesick puppies. I knew the night of that party that you were some sort of female pied piper."

"Pfft, right."

"I think Hilary nailed it when she asked if a guy showed up with a wedding. That about sums it up, Karri. Not many women can claim that. Jean-Paul did it twice."

I laughed.

Amber sighed. "I'll be back in a bit. Hilary is calling me."

I didn't hear anything, but that didn't mean much. Amber had a way of bonding with people, giving her an extra level of perception when it came to them. She clearly loved Hilary. I couldn't blame her. Hilary was a doll. "Okay, I'll meet you downstairs in a bit."

She glanced at the still sleeping Riston. "If I asked you to give him a serious chance, would you?"

"Five minutes ago you were sure I'd take him and rip him to emotional shreds. Now you want me to let him in?" Giving up, I waved my hand in the air. "I surrender. I told you that I won't try to..."

Amber smiled. "Why do I get the feeling that if it's meant to be you won't have a say in it?"

"Probably because you have Fay blood in you."

She shook her head and laughed as she headed out of the attic. I waited until I was sure she was gone and snapped my fingers. Two pillows and a blanket appeared in my arms. I bent down and lifted Riston's head gently.

There was something so familiar and so safe feeling about him. I undid the blanket and laid it over his large frame. I felt compelled to talk to him, so I whispered, "What is it about you that has me in a knot, Riston Wallace? What makes me want to keep touching you?" I ran my hand through his hair and cupped the side of his face, careful not wake him. "Are you hiding something from me?"

"Psst."

I turned fast to find a set of dark brown pigtails attached to a very happy little face as Hilary stood in the doorway. "Can you come out and play?"

I snickered and bit my lip. "I think I can do that."

She grinned from ear to ear. "Karri?"

"Yes?"

"You felt her too, didn't you? You felt her come and hug me when we were sitting in the grass, didn't you?"

I watched her closely, doing my best to judge the situation. "I felt something move through you, the energy was so warm and so loving that I think I know whose energy it was."

"My mommy."

I nodded.

"I was right, my mommy likes you a lot. She says you're the one he's been waiting for." She pointed at her uncle who was still sleeping on the floor.

That made me laugh. "Hilary, that is...umm, sweet to say but I think you may have misunderstood what she said. No one waits for me."

"He did."

"Okay, I'll leave this alone if you promise not to start talking about it when he's awake."

She seemed to think hard about it, going as far as to touch her cheek and tip her head as she hummed. "I can promise that. But you should probably know that most adults don't tell kids to keep a secret from someone they love."

I groaned. "Listen, kiddo, I've got absolutely no parenting skills. We're lucky I managed to parent myself let alone come away with any type of morals. If you're looking for that, go find Amber. She tends to be the one who explains right and wrong to me too."

Hilary giggled. "No one else would ever dream of talking to me like that. They think I'll cry or something."

"Are you planning on crying now?"

"No."

"Good. I don't think I could take anymore sadness today."

She gave me a puzzled look. "Mommy's right, you don't ever see the effect you have on people, Karri-Lynn. She says even when storm clouds sit over your head, you shine light."

That caught me off guard. "Oh, Mommy sounds like she knows me well."

"I think she does."

I smiled. "I wish that were true, Hilary. I think I would have really liked her."

"Can you play for a little bit?"

"Hilary, I need to say something else. Something else that you don't need to tell everyone about. Okay?"

She nodded and came towards me fast. I put my arms out to her and she moved into my lap. "If something should happen, something different than you're used to around me, and I tell you to run," I took her hands in mine and held them tight, "put your hands up like this and think extra hard of Mommy as you run to Daddy or Uncle Riston. Can you promise me that?"

"But I wouldn't leave you alone with bad things, Karri."

"This is non-negotiable, Hilary."

She glanced back looking extremely confused. "Huh?"

"It means that I'm not budging on it. If you don't agree and promise me to do it you are not allowed to come over without your uncle or daddy with you. Am I clear?"

Hilary whistled. "Whoa, you sounded just like a mommy there."

"Give me a bit while I try to figure out if that's a good or bad thing."

"It's a good thing." A slow, sneaky smile spread over her face as she turned all the way around in my lap and cupped my face. "Listen close, it's about those cousins. I want a girl one for sure and a boy won't be too bad either. I don't think so anyway but I want lots of them."

For a second, I thought Riston had moved. I put my hands over Hilary's and swallowed back the laugh I had. "I think you should talk to your uncle about that."

"Why? You're the one who has to get a big belly. What does it matter what he thinks of it?"

I choked on nothing and shook my head. "Oh no, don't you dare get it in your pretty lil' head that I'm going to be..."

"My aunt?" She smiled. "You will be."

"Hilary."

"Aunt Karri?"

I growled. "You are quite the little diva."

"I bet they said the same thing about you when you were little," she said, giggling.

"Well, I may have had the ability to drive a select few, one in particular, batty. So maybe."

Hilary stilled and her face took on a serious look. "Aunt Karri, if something happened to my daddy you won't let Uncle Riston give me away will you?"

"What?" I asked, the topic hitting closer to home than I liked.

She chewed on her lower lip and averted her gaze. "You wouldn't let him leave me with strangers would you?"

"Why are you asking me this? Your daddy is fine."

"Don't let him, please. I don't think Daddy is going anywhere but it scared me. When I saw inside you, I saw you being given away when you were my age and it scared me bad."

I fought to control my emotions. Every ounce of me wanted to whisk her up and hold her tight. I chose to hug her close to me instead. "How much did you see when you were in there, Hilary?"

"Enough to be scared."

I stroked the top of her head and rocked her gently. "I promise you that I would never let someone be that *heartless* with you. I would take you myself before I let that happen, Hilary. And I don't think your uncle would ever do that. I think he loves you with all his heart and would never hand you over to strangers. People who love you don't do that."

"But he..."

"Hilary!" The sound of Amber calling filtered up the staircase.

Hilary's eyes widened. "Oops, I think Amber just figured out I wasn't napping."

I gave her a stern look and she giggled. "Okay, off with you. Go apologize to Amber."

"I will." She stood and looked me in the eyes. "Don't go away. Don't leave like you're still thinking of doing. Stay with us. Please."

I pointed towards the door. "March."

"Yes, Aunt Karri."

I growled playfully. "Don't make me turn you into a pink elephant."

Her eyes widened as she ran for the door, giggling all the way.

Riston groaned, reached out fast and caught me around my waist. Before I could blink, he had me on my back and his body over mine. My breath caught as I stared up at him.

Riston smiled. "This is even better than I hoped."

I gave him a questioning look and he laughed. "I'm talking about waking up to find you under me."

"You weren't really sleeping, were you?"

"Maybe, maybe not," he said, not bothering to move off me.

There was no way that I was going to let Riston get away with eavesdropping. Even though technically he didn't. "I guess you heard your niece's request for cousins. You should hurry up and get on that. I could drag you around and find you someone to have them with. I'll do anything to get her off my case. She's like a pit-bull."

He laughed. "She's stubborn. Kind of like someone else I know."

"Really?" I asked, doing my best to not get aroused and failing.

"Mmmhmm."

"You should get off me now, Amber's afraid of me eating you alive one minute and wanting me to drop a ball and chain around your leg the next. The people here are crazier than me. I think something is in the water. To make a long, drawn out explanation short, get as far away from me as you can. I'm insane and will no doubt leave you, at best, alive but emotionally damaged."

He chuckled. "Kars, I'm capable of making my own decisions and if I..."

I grabbed the back of Riston's neck and pulled his head down towards me. I didn't wait or give him any type of a warning. Instead, I pressed my lips to his and eased my tongue into his mouth. Not one to shy away from taking the lead, I found his warm tongue and began to trace tiny circles around it as I sucked gently.

Riston moaned and I took that as a good sign. Pressing onward, I tipped my head to the side and laughed softly as Riston began to kiss me back. We searched each other, tracing a path through the other's mouth. As it went on, I found my breathing growing shallow and Riston's mirroring mine.

His rigid cock pressed against me and I fought to keep from begging him to give it to me. It didn't help that I seemed to need to have him in me to the point it was almost painful. My nipples ached to be touched by him, caressed with both his tongue and hands. Sensing I was the one who was about to lose myself, I drew back from the kiss and pressed on Riston's chest.

Reluctantly, he pulled back but not before stealing one more, tiny kiss from me. He let out a small sigh and shook his head. "Karri, where in the hell did you learn to do that?"

"What? Kiss?"

"That was no kiss. That was...it was...a kiss."

I snickered. "Yeah, I think I said that already." I patted his back gently, savoring the feel of his muscles as I did. "So, you were starting to lecture me on how you were more than capable of making your own decisions. I missed the rest of it. What were you going to say?"

"That I might have been mistaken. Ignore everything I said. I can't think for myself when it comes to you." He bent down to kiss me again and I put my hand over his mouth.

"Hey, Romeo, up. I smell like I've been rolling in the mud. Oh, wait. I was rolling in the mud." I let out a small laugh as he tried to talk into my hand. "What was that? You want me to shower so you can stand to even be in the same room as me? I understand. No need to be that way about it. I can take a hint." I let go of his face and he nipped playfully at my hand.

"I think you smell wonderful."

I snorted. "Something's wrong with your sniffer. Now, up, big boy."

"Big boy?" He arched a brow and smiled.

"Please, as if you don't already know that you're sporting one hell of an impressive cock. It's been hard and digging into my leg for the last five minutes. I have to say that I'm a little concerned that it might rip me in two so don't be coy and pretend you don't already know that."

"Kars?" Riston blinked several times. "Kars?"

"Echo, echo." I winked. "Let me guess, you haven't had a woman announce that before? I find that hard to believe. In fact, I find it hard to believe that you aren't with someone. I'm guessing every woman who has taken a ride on Riston has wanted to make the vacationland permanent. Care to share how it is you manage to chase them off?"

"I found out that I had a very special ticket holder and closed entrance to the park some time ago," he said, taking me by surprise by playing along.

"Hmm, I'll have to ask Uncle Joe if I've got a golden ticket." I batted my lashes and licked my lips before doing something I'd warned myself not to--I kissed him again.

He ground his hips, pressing his erection into me more. The layers of clothing between us suddenly seemed like they were miles thick. Riston must have felt the same way because he slid his hand up and under my tied red shirt and stopped just shy of touching my breasts.

"Say, yes," he whispered, as he kissed his way down my neck.

I fought with all my inner might to be strong and say no. That wasn't what fell out. "Yes."

He slid his hand up and over my breast, closing his eyes, seeming to savor what he found. He sucked gently on my neck, nibbling just enough to make my entire body responsive. I lifted one leg slightly, sliding my foot up his jean-clad leg.

Sliding my hands down, I cupped his ass and pulled on it with each thrusting motion he made. I squeezed trying to find any indication that he wasn't pure muscle. I got none. He moved his hand up more and as his fingers glided over my nipple, my breathing became even more erratic.

Riston kissed my neck causing tiny noises to escape me as I began to undo his zipper. He held his breath as though he were unsure if I really would keep going. As I began to actually pull his zipper down he exhaled. I slid my fingertips in, encountering a thatch of well-maintained hair and felt my pussy flood with cream in anticipation of what was to come.

"Karri! I'm in the house. If you two are doing anything freaky please tell me now. I do not want to walk in on anything," Amber called out from the lower level.

Riston groaned and planted a kiss on my collarbone. "She has impeccable timing."

"Saved by the Amber." I winked as he rolled off me, adjusting himself and zipping quickly.

He got to his feet and extended his hand to me. I took it and laughed. Riston offered a fake frown. "You think this is funny, don't you?"

"Yes, and I have the strongest urge to punch you in the face." I grinned. "Something made me think of my mother today and a conversation we once had. It just seems like it would be fitting to just sock you one. Almost like you deserve it. I must be mad that you got me all worked up without a finish."

Riston pulled me to him and gave me a tight squeeze. "I've missed you."

"Huh?"

"Guys," Amber called out, being sure to make a ton of noise as she stomped up the stairs. "Are you decent?"

"I'm dressed. Riston, on the other hand, is butt-ass naked and all I can say is damn. You should see the size of his penis. We need a picture of this. Quick, get the camera. I think we finally found the winner."

He chuckled as he winked at me. "Can I get a rain check on that golden ticket admission?"

"Most certainly."

Amber entered the room with her eyes covered. "Please tell me that she's joking, Riston."

"I'm dressed."

"Whew." She uncovered her eyes and looked a bit upset. "You didn't do it, did you, Karri?"

"Didn't do what?" I went to step away from Riston but he took hold of my hand, not letting me go anywhere.

"You didn't seduce my friend," she said, in an almost pout-like voice.

Much to my shock, Riston lifted our joined hands and planted a tiny kiss on mine. He stepped into me, leaned down and captured my lips with his. I was too stunned to do anything beyond give in, so that's what I did.

He traced the inner edge of my lips with his tongue, paying special attention to my lower one before seeking my tongue out. I took a tiny step back, overwhelmed by the passion he'd put into it and he followed me. My free hand fell to my side as I stood there limp, completely caught up in his kiss.

Cupping my face with one hand, Riston began moving his head back and forth, sliding his tongue in and out of my mouth artfully, teasing mine in the process. I was powerless to him and from his stance, he knew it. He drew back and I was left standing there with my mouth partially open.

I touched my swollen lips and stared up at him in wonderment. "Amber?"

"Uhh, yeah?" she asked, sounding as floored as I was and I'd been the one to get the kiss.

"I think your friend is seducing me."

"Is it working?"

I glanced at her, ran my fingers over my lips and nodded. "Yeah, I'm fairly positive it's going well for him."

Amber gasped. "Riston, you're smiling."

"He smiles a lot. Why is now different?" I glanced up to find him staring at me with a goofy look on his handsome face. "Okay, this one is different but he really does smile a lot."

"Not around us. At least not for close to a year, Karri." Amber shook her head. "Oh, your phone rang when I came in. I left it downstairs, sorry. I wouldn't have interrupted but I know how you are about your phone. You're all dramatic, life and death with it."

"Thanks."

"Karri, ignore it and go back to letting him seduce you." She smiled wide. "I heard through the grapevine that somebody put in a request for lots of cousins."

* * * *

I searched around the kitchen for my phone and found Amber holding it with a huge smile on her face. "Still leading the life of a spy I see?"

"A spy?" Riston asked, eyeing me up.

Amber laughed. "Yeah, Karri, I've known you for years and you still won't tell me the truth about what it is you do. I've done a lot of thinking about this over the years and I think I have it figured out."

I bit my lower lip and snickered. "And, what did you come up with?"

"That you're either some CIA agent, the highest-priced call girl ever or a member of an organized crime operation." She winked. "That or an actress."

Riston coughed and choked on air. "She's a what? How the hell can you not know what she does, Amber? She's your best friend."

"And she's insane. You should see her when she's in the thick of the *part* she's playing. In normal, everyday Karri land she's eccentric enough. Add in her creepy business acquaintances and you try to figure it out. She can go from dumbass blonde to I'll-eat-you-and-your-little-dog-too in about a second. Plus, it doesn't hurt that Karri's degree is in physics."

"Physics?" he asked, looking more than surprised.

I smiled. "Shock of all shocks, I have a brain. Though, I have to take the time to throw props to someone from my childhood. He was a science geek, in the cutest way possible."

Amber snickered. "You would grow up with sexy, smart men around you."

"Yeah, lucky me." I wagged my brows.

Amber sighed. "You think it was just another day at the office. Those movers of yours are hot as hell. The one with a beard is funny." She pushed Riston slightly. "Ask her something. She's really friggin' smart."

"I've got nothing," Riston said, giving me a soft smile and a slight nod.

Amber gave him another push. "What do you mean you have nothing? You teach physics at the University during the school year when your normal job doesn't keep you busy enough to satisfy your need to always be doing something."

I glanced at him. "Physics? This is all a little too coincidental for my taste."

"What is?" Amber asked.

"If you tell me that he got put on academic probation for building a weapon that generates varying pulses too then I'm going to think you're making this all up. And for the record, I had no intention of wiping the campus grade computers out. It just sort of happened."

"No, I don't think he did that but then again I was young when Riston first started working at the University."

I laughed. "You couldn't have been that young. He doesn't look any older than thirty-five and I'm being generous there, folks."

Amber hummed softly as she thought about my question. She pushed Riston lightly. "Hmm, you know, it's weird but I think I'm messing up dates because I keep thinking you were around on occasions when you couldn't have been. That or you're like eighty but have managed to find the perfect skin cream."

"That would be a *no* on skin cream," he said, laughing. "I can't imagine rubbing something all over my face."

Arching a brow, I gave him a seductive smile. "Really? I could think of a few things I'd like to rub all over my face and I'm sure I could come up with something you wouldn't mind rubbing all over yours."

"Time out," Amber shook her head, "if you're going to seduce him while I'm in the room then I'm going to need a sign or something. I can't deal with it."

"Now, we're back to me seducing him, huh?" I shook my head. "What sort of call out do you need?"

She shrugged. "How about a long look or a triple wink or..."

"I could say, hey, Amber I'd like to fuck your friend until I can't walk straight and have to stay in bed for three days to heal. Would that do?"

"That'll work," she said, clearing her throat as she rubbed her neck. She blushed instantly and I couldn't help but laugh. "Don't laugh. We didn't all come out of the womb being able to say anything in regards to sex."

"Oh, it's not something I came out doing, Amber. In fact, I've already told you that I was a rather late bloomer in regards to sex. I think I'm just playing catch up."

"Somehow, I don't believe you were a late anything."

"Had you kissed a boy by the time you got to college?" I asked, staring down at my phone.

"Yes, of course. Didn't you?"

"Nope."

Amber's eyes looked as though they'd pop from her head. "No way, Karri. I see the way men are around you, present company included."

I looked her dead in the eyes. "I swear to you, Amber. Until I got to college I'd only held hands with one man that wasn't my father and I was six at the time so it doesn't count. I wasn't allowed to date growing up. Hell, I wasn't even allowed to look in the direction of a boy but it didn't matter. I didn't want to anyway."

"Excuse me, Karri but when I met you, you were wearing a see through pink genie costume to go to your first period class. You tripped over me while staring at Dom."

"At who?" I asked.

"Dom Bates, the big football hero there."

I shook my head. "Not ringing a bell."

"Tall, dark hair, brown eyes, about six-three and over two hundred pounds of muscle?"

I sighed. "Amber, I said I don't remember him and I don't."

"Okay, do you remember this about him," she stuck her face out a bit, "you went to homecoming with him and dated him on and off for about a year and half. Granted, I use the term date loosely on your end but in his mind you were his girlfriend."

I stood and thought about it.

"Karri!"

"What? I'm thinking. Give me a minute."

She groaned. "He had a tattoo across his back of an eagle and one on his ass cheek that you showed me when he was passed out."

"A devil," I said smiling. "I remember that."

"Finally, for a minute I really thought you couldn't remember a guy who you were with for so long. Or kind of with."

"Amber, I remember the tattoo, not the guy. It was cute. The ass it was on wasn't bad either."

Riston made a choked noise, not sounding very happy about the topic of conversation. Too bad.

"Ohmygod you're making me crazy only because I'm positive that you don't remember him, Karri. How about Josh?"

"Who?"

She sighed. "Please tell me that you remember a guy that wasn't one of 'your men,' Karri. Any guy will work. Please throw me a bone here. I'm worried about you."

I nodded. "I remember a guy who was chained to a bed with a blindfold on that I met when I was eighteen. He was super pissed and scared the hell out me. Hot as hell though. Mmm."

Riston tipped his head. "You met a man in chains?"

I nodded. "Yep, he was in his jeans and nothing else. His buddies had decided that he needed to loosen up and a friend of mine decided to send me in to," I glanced at the wall a moment, "umm, dance for him."

Something moved over his face that I couldn't read. I took a step towards him almost instinctively and put my hand out to him, feeling the need to comfort him but unsure why. "Hey, I didn't do anything with him, Riston. At first, he terrified me the way he sniffed the air and then tried to break his chains. I thought they were overkill, that his buddies were being asses but when I saw him almost bust free I couldn't even move. I was paralyzed with fear. I wasn't like I am now."

Amber snorted. "Yeah, now you'd be the one chaining him to the bed."

I did my best not to laugh but lost the battle. "No. I'd never do that to someone like him. It may have been funny in the eyes of his buddies but it went against his very nature. He was an alpha for sure and being chained isn't acceptable to that type of man. It doesn't matter if it's in the spirit of fun and sex or not. Being put in a room to act as a submissive for a woman he didn't want was even worse. I'd have let him loose but each time I tried to get close enough to do it, he'd ask me to back up."

Amber put her hand up. "Hold up, the guy's supposedly this badass but he asks you to back up?"

It didn't make sense to me but it was what happened. "Yes. Right before I opened the door I sensed that something was wrong. I sensed his anger and when I saw him there like that I didn't feel sorry for him. No. I felt sorry for anyone who had to deal with him later." I put my head down and noticed that Riston had taken hold of my hand at some point. "The man told me that he wouldn't hurt me and I knew he wasn't going to break free and tear my head off or anything but I knew he could hurt me in other ways. So did he."

"Meaning?" Amber asked.

"It means that Karri sensed that he wouldn't be able to stop himself from taking her if he broke free, Amber. And if Karri wasn't ready for him, it would have been rape. He didn't want that. Neither did she."

I stared up at Riston wondering how he knew that. He gave me a small nod, seeming to take the talk of other men well, not that he had any reason not to. It wasn't like he owned me or had any sort of ring on my finger. Hell, he'd only really just met me. He continued on, "And Karri knew that he didn't want to hurt her and that powers beyond him were in control."

"How the hell did you get talked into being in that type of situation?" Amber asked, looking like she might actually believe the truth for once.

I stretched my back and rolled my shoulders, doing my best to work out the kinks. "Someone thought it was high time I lost my virginity and had picked him to be the one to take it."

Amber shuddered. "Someone wanted you to lose your virginity to a dude who was chained to a bed and damn near breaking free of them? Uhh, I'd have run like hell from that situation for fear he'd rip me in two and I don't mean with his hands."

"Yeah, that's pretty much what happened. Although, I had a hard time running away and leaving him like that so," a tiny smile crept over my face, "I made sure he was free after I was far enough from him that he couldn't track me."

"Track you?" Amber asked. "You make him sound like an animal."

I stiffened. "No! Not an animal, Amber. A man who was fighting part of who he is--what he carries within him. Never an animal."

She put her hands up. "Whoa, take it easy. A little over protective of some guy you didn't even get a good look at or find out his name, aren't you?"

"Leave her alone, Amber." Riston pulled me close and kissed my forehead. "She was doing what came naturally to her."

"You two are so perfect for one another. I knew that before Karri came but didn't tell her, because she'd have made a point to do the exact opposite of what I wanted her to when it comes to men." Amber looked altogether too pleased with herself. "Hey, Riston, why are you fine with talking about men from her past? You don't strike me as a sharing kind of guy when it comes to women in your life."

A knowing look passed over Riston's face. If I didn't know better, I'd have guessed that he seemed happy that I had an encounter with another man. Weird. My luck, he was the guy who had been chained to the bed. As I thought it, my stomach tightened.

No.

Dismissing my own foolish thoughts, I snorted. "Probably because I'm not his woman and we just met. And way to go on the Karri reverse psychology thing. You know me well."

She glanced down at our joined hands and huffed. "That's funny, from the way he holds your hand to the way he pulls you into him in this odd protective manner, I'd beg to differ, Karri. You look like a very kept woman." She grinned. "And before you go running in the other direction, there are worse things to have happen the first day you move into a new house."

"Don't I know it," I said, partially under my breath. "Shadow demon welcome committee sucks major monkey balls."

Riston laughed and gave me a tiny squeeze before I let go of his hand and took a big step backwards, needing air. Amber must have sensed that she'd pressed too hard because she went to work on changing the subject.

"My favorite thing to do is dig through Karri's voice mails on her cell phone and then make her return the calls just so I can hear first hand how wacky she can be. I have no doubt that she has one of her endless male worshipers call just to leave creepy messages so I get all excited and curious."

"Creepy messages?" Riston asked, staring at Amber. "Endless male worshipers?"

"Yeah, vampires, werewolves, witches, demons, death, destruction, so on and so forth."

Riston directed his attention to me but didn't saw a word.

Amber snorted. "You know how you zipped her wedding dress up because she didn't think to do it?"

"Yes."

Riston zipped the wedding dress? That means he heard everything about my breasts shrinking. My cheeks instantly flushed. I glanced at him and he offered me a small, shy grin. I blushed more.

Amber pointed at me. "Holy shit, you never get embarrassed. We're keeping Riston around if you're going to actually start acting semi-normal." She threw my cell phone hard and several feet from me. She liked to test my unnatural reflexes.

I tossed my hand out and plucked it from the air. "You throw like a girl."

"Bitch."

"Thanks," I said, pretending to tear up. "Who called?"

"A guy who called himself D and wanted to talk to Lynn. I

explained that you were indisposed. He asked me what I was wearing and then wanted me to tell you that he can only get half of what you need."

"Half?" I asked, knowing that I didn't sound pleased.

Amber tossed her hands in the air. "Half. What are you trying to get your hands on? An atomic bomb?"

"Don't be silly. Given enough time, I could build one all on my own." I opened my phone and glanced at her. "I need enough equipment to supply a unit of operatives in the area in preparation for second and first level demon attacks. They're the last mission I absolutely have to complete before I can take some time off."

I grinned. "The attacks are unconfirmed, but I'm the one who gathered the intelligence and I trust my gut. It says there's something big headed their way and that they have no clue it's coming." Going into a detailed Armageddon discussion seemed like it was called for but I held back. It was enough that Amber knew what she did, cluing her in on just how fragile the balance between good and evil was seemed like overkill. I still wanted the girl to be able to sleep at night.

She tossed her hands in the air and growled. "Just tell me the truth for once. Come on, Karri. Riston is standing here. Don't let him think you really are crazy. He's a nice, decent guy. Don't scare him off."

"I always do tell you the truth. It's your choice if you believe it. And I really don't care what Riston thinks of me." That wasn't entirely true but I wasn't about to tell her that.

"Karri, you are crazy and I love you for it. Now, call D back so Riston can hear what I'm talking about."

"Okay, but if he guesses what I do for a living the first time out after you've spent how many years trying, I will never let you live it down." I'd already told her the truth, I fight evil and get paid to do it, but she never believed me. "If he gets that I'm a team leader for a special ops group of supernaturals then I'm going to laugh at you for like eternity."

Amber giggled like a little girl and stood next to Riston. "Up," she said, motioning to the countertop. He lifted her quickly. She nudged him. "You're going to love this. Even knowing she's just being silly it's still a hell of a good performance. Oh, Karri, be sure to add the bits where I'm supposed to believe you're using magik."

Biting back a laugh, I nodded. "I'll give it an academy award winning performance just because you haven't seen me do it in seven years. You'll enjoy it even more now."

"Why? What happened? Did one of them threaten to shoot Jean-Paul? Wait, that sounded like I wanted that to happen. Hmm, maybe I did." She sat of the edge of the counter completely hooked. To Amber it was all a make-believe soapish drama. To me, it was very real.

"I," I spun in a slow circle, "am no longer a member of anything. I'm an independent. Think of it as still working for the powers but with no rules restricting me. The way it was supposed to be."

She gasped. "Oh, I like this addition to the story. I can only imagine you working with these types of people without any restrictions. So, what's the scoop. Give me a legit reason to believe this addition. "

I offered her a warm smile. "I spent four years undercover for the powers." I glanced up. "Think of them as the good side's committee of guys with too much time and power on their hands. One year was spent with first level of demons in the New York area. I pretended to be one of them without breaking cover once the entire time and came out alive. That earns you anything your heart desires where these assholes are concerned because their other men can only spend about twenty-four to forty-eight hours in that type of environment without giving into their darkness and becoming the evil they fight everyday. They're still a bit shocked that a chick under the age of two billion was able to pull that off."

Riston's face hardened. "First level demons? You spent a year with them? Undercover?"

"So, you've heard of them. Makes sense. Hilary is different as well." I nodded. "Yeah, one full year and still do freelance as needed. But if I had to put a title on what I do, I'd say that I kill bad things. You know," I put my fingers out and began to make list-like gestures with them, "ghouls, demons, vampires, lycan, weres, shifters of different natures, anything that thinks it can kill innocents, human or not. Granted, just because you're one of these things doesn't make you bad. Killing innocents does." I grinned. "All the things that want to see mankind be fodder. They want to rule the world. It's my job to help in the fight to prevent that from happening. There are others like me. Not as many as we once had."

His jaw tightened.

"In fact," I sighed, "our numbers have dwindled."

"Why in the hell would you willingly go undercover at all let alone for those extended periods?" he asked looking like he wanted to toss me over his knee. While that sounded good, I didn't think now was the time for it.

Amber's eyes widened. "You aren't buying her story are you?"

Riston just stared at me. That told me he more than believed me.

"My dad was a great man, Riston. The organization he worked for, the one that I was contracted to, the powers, those supernaturals that think they're gods but they're not, have a lot of flaws. So many that people in high places were, and are, more corrupt than the evil they fought on a daily basis. Not all of them are, but I'm a hundred percent sure that my father died because of that and I refuse to stand by and watch it happen to any other men.

"At least, not if I can help it. I wanted access to classified documents, to the men who work for them--men like my father and his team. I also wanted the right to act as liaison as I see fit--not as the powers deem. These men deserve more. They fight for mankind. Who fights for them?"

There was another reason I did what I did. It involved Amber and my need to see her well. She'd been so sick and had literally died from it that I'd been left little choice. It wasn't something I wanted to think about let alone tell her. She'd blame herself and that wasn't acceptable. I'd willingly traded my freedom and signed on to fight for good in order to save her life. Now that, according to her, she was free from the cancer-like illness that had eaten away at her, it seemed even more worth it.

I sighed. "I served my time, did their dirty work to gain that. The first year was the hardest. The rest went by without me really noticing it."

"What? Did you stand around in a bad mood for the first year with them?" Amber asked, doing her best to mock an ugly situation.

I scrolled down in my cell phone to find D's number and let out a soft laugh. The man was the older brother of my main weapons supplier, Owen, and was also a certified dumbass. Lucky for him he was sexy or I'd have deemed him too stupid to live. "Uhh, no. It means I had to make them believe I was every bit as ruthless as they are and more so. Since they have even fewer women on the frontlines than we do, that was interesting."

"Ooo, let's hear what you supposedly did."

"No." I pushed the send button and waited as the phone rang. "It still keeps me up at night, Amber."

"Hey?"

Taking a deep breath, I looked at the floor and let my voice be light, airy, breathy. "D, how ya doin', baby?"

D moaned. "Getting hard listening to you."

"Mmm, you say the sweetest things. A girl could get used to that."

"Fuck, girl. You can kill a guy with just your voice."

I turned and faced the doorway instead of Amber. She still got to see my profile but I didn't have to do an acting job to her face. "D, I think we both know that I can kill a guy with even less than my voice." I purred. He sounded like he was in pain. "Baby, I need you to get your brother on the phone."

"Ah, Lynn, he's, umm, not in right now."

Grinning, I reached over and started pulling wallpaper from the wall completely bored with talking to the man. It was rather sad that the entire time I'm doing a half-hearted attempt at phone seduction I felt the need to redecorate but in truth, it was very telling as to how uninterested in D I was. The man was a box of rocks with a penis. If it had two legs and a pulse, even that was optional when taking vampires into consideration, D wanted to fuck it. He'd spent the greater part of six years trying to work his way into my pants. I spent the same time frame thinking of ways not to lose my temper and kill him.

"I understand. It's hard on you with him being dominant and all." I picked hard to get a piece of wallpaper off that was stuck. "That's like so weird that the second born would wear the pants in the family. I mean don't get me wrong, you're...umm, you're you."

"Lynn, Owen doesn't rule me," he said, tension filling his voice.

I glanced at Riston, who was staring at me with a not-so-friendly look on his face. I pointed at the scrapper on the counter behind him. I covered the phone and whispered, "I need something to do so I don't fall asleep talking to this ass. I've heard his pick-up lines so many times that they're almost background noise now." His eyes widened and for a minute I thought I saw him smile. Picking it up, he handed it to me.

"D, I wasn't sayin' he rules you. I'm just sayin' that you listen really well. I have this puppy that's giving me a hard time and if you could teach it to listen like you do I'd be forever in your debt."

Riston snorted. I bit back a laugh.

"Hold on, I'll get him."

"Thanks, D. See, I know who is really in charge." I bit my lips to keep from laughing and ended up having to hold the phone up, run to the sink, blast the water to hide the giggles that came from me. Amber leaned down and ruffled her hand through my hair laughing as well. It was something she did when she was convinced I was toying with her.

I glanced at Riston, impressed he was taking all of this as well as he was. My guess was that he thought it was a joke too. If he started ruffling my hair I'd have issues.

"Lynn?"

At the sound of the deep voice on the other end of the phone, I held up my hand to silence Amber. She stopped. Running my hand over my mouth, I laughed once more before standing tall. I dumped the dumb blonde routine. "Owen, how are you this fine day?"

"Owen?" Riston asked. I ignored him.

"Lynn, come on, don't be mad. I tried to get everything you needed. I did. But..."

"Owen, Owen, Owen, making your brother screen your calls is low. Even for you. Now, stop kowtowing and tell me exactly what's going on. I used you for this because you guaranteed it could be done in the time frame I needed it done and because you're always talking about wanting to keep what happened to my father and his men from happening to anyone else."

I walked to the kitchen window and stared out at the large backyard. "You came to me, Owen. When you heard I was working for the powers it was you who made first contact. You couldn't wait to see Jack's little girl in action. You saw it, want to fuck with it?" I let out a throaty, scary laugh. "I think your work is exceptional and your attention to detail unrivaled. That's why I'm talking to you on the phone and not standing before you, handling the matter in person."

"But, Lynn," he pleaded. "I'm having trouble moving your supplies through all the channels. That's all. It takes a lot to bribe them. I've got to get the stuff moved around under the human government's noses while I'm also trying to avoid detection from our own kind. You ever try moving a shipment the size of yours past the DEA and the powers? Yeah, it ain't easy or cheap."

My temper flared. My power rose fast. "Owen, I get that you think because this project is so important to me you could exploit it, take it for all its worth. But did you stop and think that I'm going against the powers and the council to the underworld on this. If I'm willing to take on them, men who wouldn't think twice about killing me, what makes you think I'll hesitate to take on you?"

"Come on. I was friends with your dad. Lynn, you need me. You can't move this..."

Lifting my hand in the air, I let out another wicked laugh, seeing the image of Owen in my head, pinned to the wall high off the ground. I knew it was really happening. That my magik had reached out and taken hold of the man. Amber would no doubt assume it was part of the act. "I'm sorry, Owen. What were you saying? You were friends with my father? Hmm, you like to tell me how very much like him I am so I'm guessing he'd have beat the shit out you by this point too."

"Damn straight," Riston said, catching me off guard.

I shook my head, a bit confused and kept talking to Owen. "So, you think I need you because I can't move what? Ooo, scared of heights?" I laughed again, enjoying toying with him a little too much.

"Put me down, Lynn. Put me down!"

I lifted my hand higher knowing that it in turn lifted him as well. "No. I like having your attention. Now, are we understanding each other's position on the matter? I want these men equipped with what they need and I can and will kill to assure that happens."

"Yeah, Lynn, just tell me what you need."

I growled. "I sent you a very detailed list. If you lost it, I'll kill D now just because he annoys me. While it's a shame since he's only guilty of thinking with his dick, its par for the course in our line of work."

Owen gasped. "Lynn, I know you aren't one to fuck with but even you wouldn't kill D just for that."

"Normally, I would just fax you a friendly reminder that you assured me it would be done. This isn't normal. I can't explain, even if I tried. I know that these men have been abandoned by the powers, who are too concerned with everything else. They think it's one team. A few men, no great loss should something go wrong. They're wrong. It would be a great loss to me. Even setting my feelings aside, they guard one of the largest portals to hell known to us. Yes, for the most part it's remained quiet or at least we think it has. They could be kicking the shit out of things on a daily basis for all we know. And after the day I had here I'd believe it. Hell, the ice cream man is a fucking demon."

"Really?" Owen asked. "That's weird, what kind of demon?"

"Something that isn't lactose intolerant," I bit out. "Owen, I don't know what kind of demon he was. The point I was trying to make is what better place for the enemy to send armies through than the section that is not only one of the biggest but one that's team of protectors is fractured, forgotten and vulnerable because they have no backup?"

Taking a deep breath in, I let out a tiny laugh. "They do now. They have more back-up than they'll want or need. At present count I've got over a hundred other teams ready and willing to come in and help them if what I suspect is coming actually shows up."

"Over a hundred teams?" Owen and Riston asked in unison.

I lifted my eyebrows but didn't question that. "Yes, and I'm pretty sure I can get another hundred within a day or two if needed. People bitch about team leaders all the time but I've found them to be very easy to deal with."

"It's the legs," Amber whispered.

Laughing, I shook my head. "No, I don't think so, hon. I think it's because they are all a little skeptical that the powers are up to no good." I thought about it a minute. "Okay, the legs probably don't hurt my chances of getting them to say yes. So far every team I've asked has set up and went on call so I'm not complaining."

I could feel Owen's fear as I lowered him to the floor. "Get a pen, Owen."

"Ooo, I want to talk to Owen when you're done." Amber laughed kicking her foot out to catch my attention.

I shook my head and laughed. "Are you ready?"

"Yeah, I've got it in my email somewhere. Just refresh my memory and I'll hunt that email down. "

I pulled my power back into myself and covered my eyes as I thought of things they'd need. "Get M16's, oldies but goodies. FAMAS, for sure. Not a ton but I know one, possible two of the men in the unit are left-handed and I'd like to keep everybody happy. Send some AK's too. They tend to be boys' favorite toys. I want some M60's. I've got a few of my guys with me on this and Branson likes his lawn mower if you know what I mean. I told him to learn to aim."

"How did he take that?" Owen asked, chuckling.

"He told me that I was still bitter about our break-up."

Owen snorted. "You never went out with him."

"Yeah, I reminded him of that too. On second thought, if the ass wants to keep claiming we were an item when we weren't, send PKM's instead. He hates those."

"You are an evil woman," he said, laughing.

"Aww, thanks. Damnit, that will bug me. I was going for the evilest woman on earth. Send what you can get me for sustained firepower. I want some M85's as well. At last check, they had three members able to snipe. I can't find any information on their fourth. The one record I was able to find indicated that he was deceased so, I have no clue who replaced him. I'll snipe if I have to but that is my weakest area and that's why I need the accuracy the M85's provide. I'm beginning to think that if it has a membership with us and a penis, it has a thing for .50 cals, so send me some of those as well."

"What do you need in the way of camouflage for the snipers?" Owen asked.

I shook my head. "Here's the weird thing, Owen. I went through every shipment roster from these guys and I mean every. They never once bothered with sniper camouflage."

"What, do they think they're invincible?"

I laughed. "No I don't think invincible is it at all. I think invisible covers it."

"Invisible? No one can do that."

Going to the fridge, I opened it and pulled out a bag of cut veggies, lunchmeat and condiments. It had been all I'd had time to grab on my way into town. "It is possible to do that, Owen. You need to have the right genetic make up for it. My dad and a few of his friends could pull it off. I've been told that I can but someone I trusted emphatically told me not to try it until he could show me. He told me I'd get stuck like that and my stupid ass still believes him after all these years so I just hope for the best."

Riston snickered and I joined him. I wasn't exactly sure what part of my conversation was funny to Riston but the very thought of the memory of RJ making me swear I'd never try to make myself invisible without him there to guide me had me smiling. The man had known me well when I was little. Well enough to know that if he scared me then, it'd stick with me later in life.

"So, do they walk around looking like a floating rifle?" Owen asked.

I snorted. "No, when my dad would vanish, he and everything he had on him and with him would go too. I do know that he couldn't do it wounded but that's a story I don't want to see anymore of today." I shuddered at the memory of my father bleeding in the snow.

"Shit, that's deadly. I never knew Jack and the guys could do that. Now I know why they scared the hell out of me. Watch your back, Karri."

I thought about them all. "Yeah, I guess they were deadly but I felt safe with them. Though, as I learn more about them I start to wonder why and how they managed to come across as gentle giants to me. And I appreciate your concern but I don't think these men will hurt me, Owen. I'm here to warn them and see to it they're safe. If, in the end, they decide to kill me for it so be it. I'll die with that nagging feeling finally gone."

"Do you have a handgun wish list, Karri?"

"Mmm, baby, stop talking dirty to me. Of course I have a handgun list." I pulled bread out of the drawers and searched for paper plates. Amber opened the cabinet behind her head and handed them to me, grinning from ear to ear. "I'd like to get this out in the open, if a 9-mm comes in here with anything other than Sig Sauer marks on it we will have issues. I get these guys are like two thousand if you combine their ages but they can come the way of the Sig or lick my left ass cheek. They, in my opinion, are the finest manufacturers of handguns in the world."

Owen snorted. "Watch what you offer up there. They are males."

"Hey, if they're hot I'll lick theirs too." I laughed as I washed my hands. "Okay, kidding on the last comment. Toss Dessert Eagles in there. Again, big and boy toys. Eagles make me feel like I'm lugging a bowling ball. That's just me, I guess. Oh, don't forget RPG's. They make me all warm and fuzzy inside when I see them blow shit up. No one understands why I'm horny as hell after leveling groups of the bad guys. Pfft, like it's not obvious."

I laid the plate out on the counter and went to work on fixing lunch. Amber hopped down to help. As she went to cut the bread I grabbed her arm. "Amber, cut Riston's thin like mine, he has to watch his carb intake if he wants to stay awake."

"Huh?" she asked.

I began picking through the bag of veggies. "Okay, sorry about that, now I want fatigues across the board. For all I know they each have a thousand pairs. I don't care if that's all they wear. They could use them as pajamas for all I care. Until I see what they have here, I'm operating with the assumption that they have nothing."

Amber went to put bologna on Riston's. I grabbed her hand. "For goddess sake, don't put that on the man's sandwich. He'll bitch for a week about the smell. Eat a piece and try to kiss him. He'll love that."

"Karri?" she looked at me with wide eyes.

"Hmm?"

"Nothing," she said smiling.

Shrugging, I focused on Owen. "Get me full sets of fatigues for all members. My list has their measurements according the database."

Owen made an odd noise. "But, what if they're different now? Will you still be pissed even though I can't help they changed?"

As Amber pulled the ketchup out and went to dump it on Riston's sandwich I grabbed the bottle and held it in the air. She jumped up and down trying to reach it. "Okay, give me that. Everyone likes ketchup, Karri."

I pulled the phone away from my mouth. "Unless you want a lecture on how a salami, ham and cheese sandwich is sacred all unto itself, do not put anything on it. Just leave it plain."

She rolled her eyes. "Do you want to do this?"

"Move," I said, bumping past her. I opened the veggies and went to work, picking out only the celery, green peppers and cauliflower. I dropped them onto his plate and shoved it at him without bothering to look at him.

I rubbed my brow harder. "Owen, we'll use the team leader as an example only because his measurements are the only ones I can remember off the top of my head. Unless he lost so much weight that he's now emaciated and incapable of supporting his lycan frame and has had his legs chopped off at the knee then he's still six-five, two-hundred and thirty-two pounds give or take a bit. Shoe size, thirteen, his inseam and other measurements are on the original list. If you fuck that up and leave him digging to get his pants to stop cutting circulation off to his cock I'll shoot you and then let him do it too. Don't forget what I said about the sizable pant waists and gun belts."

"Come on, Lynn," Owen said, sounding desperate. "Cut me some slack on that and I can push this through faster."

"No, I want at the very minimum a fifteen percent stretch factor for them. If you can get me twenty-five percent I will personally hand you the heads of your enemies as thanks. And I mean that literally. If they need to do a partial shift they can do it without worrying about walking around naked."

"They're shifters." Owen snorted. "None of us care. It happens."

"Owen, if I was with you when you needed to shift, at least partially, would you be slightly uncomfortable with the idea that I'd be able to see everything you have or may not have to offer the rest of the night?"

"Hell yes."

"Right, I don't want any one of them to hesitate to do what they need to do to stay safe. If I can provide them a tiny bit of maneuverability with the ability to maintain their modesty then I will. I have the luxury of knowing the men on my team who are shifters sizes by heart." I smiled as I thought about Seger and Matty. "I also keep extra clothing for them. Trust me when I say that the first time Seger ended up with nothing to wear and he realized that his new team leader was female, he shifted back into a wolf and stayed that way the rest of the night."

"What the hell did Matty do?"

I laughed. "Matty doesn't have a modest bone in his body. He stood tall, smiled and said that he was fairly sure I'd seen a naked man in my life but if I had any questions then he'd be happy to answer them."

For a second, it sounded as though Riston growled. I glanced at him, only to find his face a mask. Shaking my head, I continued talking to Owen, "Yeah, Matty also laughed because it was a cold night when he first got stuck being naked in front of me." I snickered. "It certainly wasn't very flattering for him to be that cold if you know what I mean."

Riston stiffened and I gave him a questioning look. He smiled. It looked a bit forced. I ignored him. "I still have to practically dress Matty myself because he thinks it's funny that I'm not comfortable with just how carefree he feels in his birthday suit. And I'm sure Branson is still holding out hope that I'm the one woman in all the history of lycan half-breeds that got the shifting gene just so I'll be stuck walking around naked all night in front of him." I snorted. "As if the costumes I have to wear to be a walking diversion for them cover anything. Please, dental floss covers more than they do."

I thought of my mother and the outfit she put me in. I couldn't help but chuckle. "Guess I should be bummed that I didn't get my mother's affinity for the dental floss look. Don't get me wrong. I'm not ashamed of myself but it's kind of scary to think there was someone with an even more open outlook on life than me."

Owen laughed. "Your mother was something else, Karri. She was amazing."

"Yeah, she was. My dad was a lucky guy."

Owen laughed hard. "Now, what about shirts?"

"Don't worry about the shirts. They go so far already, beyond that if they rip they rip. I'm guessing any man other than D would rather walk around with no shirt instead of missing his pants."

Owen cleared his throat. "What about the belts. Can we please skip them?"

"Hey, dipshit, if we're going out of our way to make sure they can do partial shifts and stay dressed why not make sure they can stay armed? Right--do it. If their weapons are thrust from them when they do a partial what's to say the enemy won't be there to pick them up? We're also in the middle of a populated town. There are children here. It's easy to lose count of how many you've picked up at the end of the day. I personally wouldn't be able to live with myself if an accident happened, Owen."

Amber pulled three beers out and went to hand one to Riston. He lifted his hand to signal no but I'd already snatched the beer out of her hand and put it back. Going to the cabinet, I pulled out one of the sixteen-ounce plastic cups I seemed to buy tons of and went to the freezer. I pulled the tray out and Riston took it from me. He twisted it hard and ice went flying everywhere. I moved the cup fast, catching the cubes in mid-air. Not one hit the floor.

"Karri?" Amber asked, sounding shocked.

"Yeah? Hey, can you dump half of these in the ice cube bin? He drinks like a gallon every time he takes a sip and complains if the cup is full of nothing but ice. Oh, there's lemonade in the fridge. It's the only thing diet I have besides soda until I can beg you to go grocery shopping for me. Those places scare me. If it's not frozen, I don't know what to do with it. Plus, old men have heart attacks there so I avoid them now."

"Karri, Riston doesn't drink lemonade." She gave me an odd look. "He told me he didn't like it once."

"Amber, I've had your lemonade. You put enough sugar in it to rot someone's teeth. Remember how I had a sip and slept for the afternoon?"

She nodded. "Sure do, Sweets."

"He'll do the same thing. He was being polite. He likes lemonade."

"I think I've got everything," Owen said, sounding pleased. "What about you? I heard you took twelve to the chest last week."

I tipped my head to the side. "Aww, Owen, you've been keeping tabs on my health. No, sorry to disappoint you but I did not take twelve to the chest. I took eight to the torso, one to my left hip and one only grazed my inner thigh. That reminds me, send a couple of those vests you make me that hide under those tank tops. I love the corset ones too. Also toss a full one in."

"Karri, your men have picked more bullets out of you in the last month than all of them combined. I'm sending more than that."

I snickered. "Owen, it's not that bad. I've been a little bit worried about these guys stationed here so my head hasn't been in the game. That's all. And on a good, normal month I go through eight vests so I don't think fourteen is too bad."

"Fourteen?" Riston asked.

I nodded but didn't look back at him. "Owen, send what you want but I can't wear them if I'm standing there pretending to play on the bad guys team. See, they think they're *uber* cool and invincible. While that plays to our favor, it sucks shit when I have to stand on that side and hope I'm not caught in the crossfire again. Branson is still having issues about that."

"Branson shot you?" Riston asked, his voice low, scarily so.

I put my hand up in a dismissive manner and listened to Owen.

"I don't know how you do it, Karri. Most of us can't hold onto that rage for more than a few seconds without our dark side overrunning us." Owen sighed.

I smiled. "I'm used to it. But the lines are starting to blur a bit. Thankfully, I've pissed enough of you off to know you'll put one between my eyes when the time comes." I laughed. "Anyway, please listen to me this time. My breasts are not a C and not D. I'm a C and three-quarters, Owen. I'm either swimming or trying to breathe with the other jackets you send. I'd appreciate being able to move normally."

"Karri-Lynn."

"Oh, I got a Karri-Lynn. We back to being friends?" I asked, chuckling. "I do so love it when you call me by what the bad guys think my name is--Lynn. Always let's me know when I'm being a bitch."

Owen groaned. "You're the scariest friend I have. But, you should know that you aren't the monster you think you're becoming. Far from it."

"Thanks for trying to cheer me up on that front but I've heard what they call me now. The sad thing is, they're right. Sorry I threatened D." I put my head down and rubbed my neck. "Speaking of D. Send him away this afternoon. When I first called you for all of this, a few weeks back, I knew what a big order it was so I put in a few calls to show you that I do appreciate the risks you take for me."

I lifted the beer on the counter and put it back. I grabbed a bottle of water instead. "Owen, let the group of people that will show up on your doorstep today in. They're human, don't eat them. They'll give you a selection of engagement and wedding rings to choose from, locations for the ceremony and reception options. Look them over. Narrow the list to make easier on Maxine. I picked the honeymoon location already. You'll be taking your bride to Scotland to finally meet the rest of your family. D will be following on a separate flight several days later and will not be staying at the castle I rented for you and Maxine."

"Huh?"

"I bumped into Maxine a couple of weeks ago. She's expecting but doesn't know it yet. I sensed it immediately. Do the right thing and make it look like you asked her to marry you without knowing about the baby. Trust me. She'll be swept off her feet. I didn't put a spending limit on it to show trust. Handling what I need for these men and keeping them safe is that important to me, Owen. I can't thank you enough for helping with that."

He was quiet. For a moment I thought he hung up.

"Owen?"

"I'm going to be a daddy?"

Laughing, I tipped my head back and sighed. "Yep. That means you're going to be a father. I should point this out. I don't make idle threats. I think we understand each other now. So, if you hang on the line for a bit, you can share your good news with my friend Amber who doesn't believe in anything paranormal. And I'm not sure if her friend Riston will want to talk to you as well. Somehow, I think he might already be a believer."

Owen gasped. "Riston?"

"Is there an echo? Yes, Riston? Why?"

He snickered. "Umm, uhh, Karri-Lynn, what's he look like? Riston just sounds like an interesting name."

I glanced at Riston who was now leaning against the countertop holding his plate with his legs crossed, looking at me with a sexy smile on his face. "I don't know. He's about six-five, has a rather large…aww, hell, he's got the body of a god. Dark hair, cut close, super blue eyes and lush, full lips. If I had to guess his weight I'd say about two-thirty?"

Riston tipped his head slightly, licked his lower lip seductively and nodded. He lifted his leg slightly and wiggled his foot. "I'm a thirteen in case you're wondering."

"Owen, did ya get a visual?"

He laughed hard. "Oh, I got a visual all right. Good luck, Karri. I think you're going to get so much more than you bargained for out of this."

"Thanks, I think," I said, handing the phone to Amber who actually squealed.

I grabbed my plate and water. "I have no kitchen table yet. Any suggestions?"

He stared at me for a moment, seeming to be soaking me in. A slow, lazy smile came over his face. "I'm fine wherever. We can sit out back if you want."

"I'd like that." I glanced down at his plate and froze. My mouth dropped as I set my lunch down and tried to take his plate from him. "Ohmygods, I just realized what I did. I'm so sorry. Tell me what you like and I'll make it for you. I wasn't thinking. I just..."

"Kars, its okay. This is *exactly* what I would have made myself." The warm look he gave me made me relax.

I narrowed my gaze on him. "Your father's name isn't RJ is it?"

Slowly, he shook his head no. "Why do ask?"

"No reason." I didn't tell him that he reminded me so much of RJ that it was getting harder and harder to keep them separated in my mind.

Chapter Five

I stared down at the contents of the box and shook my head. When I'd seen the bed frame in a magazine I thought it would be like any other one, four little pieces. No. This one was anything but that. I'd been thinking of putting the thing together since I arrived but had yet to do it.

"Want some help?"

I jumped and spun around fast. Riston leaned on the doorframe and smiled. "I thought you were still downstairs with Amber."

"I was," he said, shrugging. "I think she's going to be on the phone a while. It's been several hours and counting. D got on to talk with her."

I moaned. "Great, she will have heard every lame pick-up line out there when she's done talking to him."

"She's actually lecturing him on treating women like queens, not objects."

Laughing, I shook my head and glanced at the bed again. "What happened to simple bed frames?"

"Can't you zap it together or something?" he asked, amusement running through his voice.

"If you want me to, I can. But I'll offer you this piece of information. You'll most likely think it's a cop-out but I don't have an anchor so the more I use or rely on magik the more I open myself to the darkness I carry. Trust me when I say that after a year in hell I have a hell of a lot of dark side in me. This wouldn't cost me much but I still would rather try to do it by hand. I used a lot of power today. More than I should. But I'm talking out of my ass because you have not idea what I'm talking about. Right, forgot about having Branson erase your memory…umm, okay." I counted slowly in my head, ready for his skepticism. It didn't come. "Aren't you going to say 'likely excuse' or something like that?"

He shifted slightly, watching me closely as he shook his head. "No. I do want to know about the anchor thing. Why don't you have one?"

"You mean, why don't I have him?"

He crossed his arms. "Okay, it's a him. So, why isn't the guy with you?"

"I don't know. I'm not sure he's even still alive. I mean, the last time I saw him I was six so a lot can happen between then and now." I glanced downwards not wanting to show any emotion. "He has to be dead, right? They tell me that a true mate would have come for me by now. I highly doubt he's my true anything. I mean, it's ludicrous to think I was made for only one person. I'm me. Not some man's possession." I knew that I sounded like I was trying to convince myself because I was. The idea that my mate, the man my father told me would protect me with his life, never came for me. He didn't care.

"Wait, your mate is your anchor?" he asked, standing straight.

I nodded as I drew in a deep breath. "I should have guessed that you'd at least have a little bit exposure to supernaturals."

"Why's that?"

"Because Paula had the gift of magik and so does Hilary." I put my hand up blocking the protest I saw coming. "I know she did. Hilary used her power on me to try to figure out what happened to my parents and found more than she bargained for. You can scream at me now, hit me and call me crazy. I'm fine with that."

"Do men hit you a lot?" he asked, moving towards me as a dark shadow moved over his face.

I nodded and dropped down to start putting the bed frame together. Picking up the instructions, I once again tried to decipher them. "Right now, you'd never guess the physics thing was true. I can't concentrate much anymore. It's a side effect of things I'd rather not discuss. Anyhow, I think I need some sort of middle piece."

"I think," Riston said, sitting down next to me. If he moved, even a little, he'd be touching me. "You should tell me more about the anchor deal."

I reached for the screwdriver. "I can't. I don't know anymore. I just know that I need one. I guess it's someone who doesn't have to work at keeping my darkness in line or controlling my magik when I can't. But yes, in my case, my anchor would also be my mate or as the rest of the world calls them, my spouse. I highly doubt I even have one of those. Why everyone keeps telling me I do and that he's who they say he is, is a mystery to me."

Riston took the screwdriver from me, pushed the directions away and began fiddling with the bed. "Why don't you think you have one?"

I held two portions of iron together for him as he fastened them. "Because my parents used to tell me that it was someone close to them, their best friend."

"And?"

I sighed. "Mom would tell me stories about how mates are drawn to be together and although they may care for someone else, be with someone else, they don't ever have a perfect thing until it's their mate that fills the roll. She then apologized to me because she didn't think I'd be able to love anyone but the one I was made for. Something about my case being special. She also said she was afraid that went for him as well. So, I'm thinking if a guy knew he couldn't love anyone else, he wouldn't have handed me to strangers no matter how much he blamed me for my father's death."

"Karri." He ran his hand over mine.

"Don't worry, I'm not holding out any hope that this man will ever be in my life. I'm ten years past when he should have shown up so he's either dead or hates me. Either way, I'm not on his to do list." Laughing, I moved close to Riston to help with the next portion. "I always got so mad when my mother would say that I was made for my mate. It was insulting to think I wasn't just me-- someone special just because. One day, I took her a list. She asked what it was for. When I told her it was my list to give the gods so they could make a mate that was just mine, exactly how I wanted him, she laughed so hard she cried. My dad stopped home while he was working and thought something was wrong."

My arm brushed Riston's as I helped hold the bed frame. I did my best to ignore the heat that flared through it. It was difficult, especially when I already knew how good it felt to kiss him. "Dad went nuts, rushing to her, pulling me into him. He checked me for injuries and kept trying to get mom to tell him why she was crying. That only made her laugh harder. Dad's friend, RJ, came in and thought something was wrong too. Mom gave him the list. He read it. Looked at her. Read it again. Looked at dad and then laughed too. He was a jerk."

Riston coughed and kept going on the bed. "A jerk, huh? Because he laughed at your list?"

"Yes, at the time I was five. I put a lot of time into that thing. I decided that I wanted someone as tall as my daddy, with big muscles so he could pick heavy things up that I couldn't, dark hair, blue eyes and he had to be smart because I wanted him to teach me lots of things. It's silly, I know but it's what I decided I wanted. I know it had to be horrible looking. I was little, had just learned to read and write and couldn't spell worth a damn but still. It was me being honest and I really wanted mom to give it to the gods or God if that's what you believe. Instead, she let that ass put it in his pocket and keep it. He had the nerve to pat my head and thank me. What was that about? I bit his hand. I should have bit hard enough to draw even more blood. Maybe that would have taught him."

"I take it you didn't care for this guy very much."

I leaned forward more, my breast rested on his upper thigh as I reached and held the frame. My breath caught and I had to let out a slow breath to stop the raging need that filled me. Riston stiffened and I knew he was doing his best to ignore that as well. "You know, you remind me of him."

He let out a soft laugh. "Gee, after the 'ass' comment I feel so honored."

I laughed. "For as much as he got on my nerves, I still liked it when he was around. Dad laughed and carried on like a big kid with my mom whenever RJ was close. They were happy and not so worried about me. When he wasn't there, I had to stay close to one of them all the time. Something about a threat and it involved me. I don't know. They didn't tell me about it, RJ did. He didn't go into detail. He only said that bad men had bad things that made my mom and dad want to keep me extra safe." I snorted. "I can't believe I let that fly as all the answer I needed. My only defense was that I'd just turned six and used to trust the man completely."

"Used to?" Riston asked, stiffening a bit. "What changed that?"

"An evangelist and a woman who was so far removed from my mother's family that there was no way she should have counted as a relative."

"What happened?"

Leaning back, I stared at the frame. "Okay, want me to help with the other side? If you say yes, I may not let you leave here anytime soon."

Riston crawled over the put together portion and moved to the other side. "So, if you're thinking of keeping me could you let me know for sure if me reminding you of someone from your past is helping me out?"

"Helping you out with what?" I asked. The second I glanced up and saw the sexy, hungry look on his face I laughed. "Ahh, with that."

Riston let his gaze run over me as his lips curved upwards. "Yeah, that."

I smiled wide and crawled to the next spot. I could feel Riston's hot stare on my ass and loved every minute of it. Glancing over my shoulder, I looked down the length of my body and met Riston's blue gaze. "So, do you want to screw or not?"

A wolfish grin spread over his face as he moved onto all fours and crawled over me. The feel of his hard body slinking over mine left me tingling, and tightening. The second he was completely settled above me, he pressed his mouth to my ear and whispered, "I would be more than happy to screw, Kars."

His rapidly growing erection pushed at my ass. I knew if we didn't have clothes on that I'd have him in me and from the obvious thrusting motion he made, he knew it too. I tipped my face up and concentrated on his lips.

Riston brushed his over mine, sending my body into a state of need. My inner thighs tightened and I found myself pushing back against him, causing his bulge to dig deeper.

Running my tongue out and over his lower lip I left him breathing heavy and simulating sex even more, adding mini-thrusts combined with tiny, breathy moans. Riston nipped playfully and growled when I began to rub rhythmically against his clothed cock.

"Mmm, enjoying yourself?"

He held his erection to me, thumping against my ass twice. "What do you think?"

"I think that something about you makes me think about sex almost non-stop and that's never happened to me before. I'm hoping I can fuck it away. Want to help me try? I don't want to wear you out or anything."

Riston's breath hitched. "You can't fuck me out of your mind, Kars. In fact, I highly doubt that you will ever wear me out. I have what could be considered a downside by some women."

"What's that, a monster of a cock?"

He kissed my earlobe and chuckled. "My, you certainly are all grown up now." Reaching down, Riston skimmed his fingers over my bare torso, coming to a stop at the top of my cut-off shorts. "Once I get started, or rather, now that I am back in the game, I'm dangerously close to falling back into old habits."

"Which are?"

He licked a lazy line down my neck. "Mmm, needing to have sex multiple times a day."

I let out a sultry laugh. "And women think that's a problem? You've been sleeping with the wrong women, Riston."

"You're right, when I used to date, I always seemed to pick the wrong ones," he whispered in my ear, his hot breath skating over my neck, making me shiver and my pussy spasm. "But I think I finally might have picked the right one. What do you think?"

"I think that I'll need to take you for a test drive before I confirm that. I'd hate to say yes only to find that you aren't all I think you'll be."

"Mmm, honey, the urge to take you here and now, to mount you is so great that I'm having a hard time refraining from ripping your clothes off."

Instantly, my pussy began to moisten more, leaving my thong damp. Riston took a deep breath in and for a split second I was positive he could smell the changes in my body. Every ounce of me wanted that to be true. I wanted him to just know when I was hot for him, when I needed the large piece of flesh between his legs in me, when I needed him.

I'd known him less than a day and he seemed to consume me. That in itself should have sent me running from him. It didn't. It made me want him even more. There was something about him, something I couldn't put my finger on but I knew I would soon enough.

"You want me, don't you?" he asked, pressing against my jean shorts in just the right spot, causing them to pull a bit and rub my clit in the process. "You want me deep in you. I can smell it."

Still looking back at him, almost touching his lips, I ran my tongue out and over the corner of his mouth. He nipped playfully at me, causing even more moisture to settle between my legs.

"Answer me, Karri. Do you want me in you?"

"Yes."

"How bad?"

I kissed him, no longer able to hold back. "Mmm, I'm soaked because of you and I want you to be in me more than I've wanted anything in a very long time, Riston."

"What if I can't promise to be gentle our first time, Karri? Would you still want me in you or would you still be scared of me."

Still be scared? I thought about it and kissed him slowly before drawing back to answer him, "I trust you."

That was an odd thing to say.

"That's all I needed to know, baby." The second he went for my zipper, I sensed Amber's presence.

"Amber's coming."

He growled and nodded, moving down. "Impeccable timing." We settled in so we were both seated. Riston sat behind me and went to work on the bed frame again. A head of red appeared in the doorway.

"Hey, Owen is nice. His brother D is a total jackass."

"I know."

She grinned as she glanced at the two of us. I'd say she looked hopeful but I knew Amber well enough to know that there was no way she'd really want me making a move on Riston--not if she liked or valued the man's friendship in any way, shape or form. "They even played along, trying to convince me that they're cat shifters."

Smiling, I nodded at her. "Yep, cougars. I've heard they're good in bed--not D and Owen but that breed in general."

Amber tossed her hands into the air. "You would have thought of that angle too. How do you get all of these men to play along? Ever since I've known you, men have done anything you said."

"That is so not true, Amber. You just got to see a tiny portion. They didn't want to scare you, hon and I'm only telling you what I heard. I've never been with one. In fact, I've never been with any sort of a shifter in the area of sex."

"I'd prefer to know that you haven't ever been with anyone," Riston said so quietly that I almost missed it. I gave him a questioning look but he ignored it.

Amber giggled. "What's your story for no shifters in the bedroom? I've got to hear it."

A bit embarrassed by what I was about to say, I found my shoulders slumping and my cheeks flushing. "Umm, don't laugh but whenever I've been around men like that I just get this odd feeling."

"What kind of odd feeling?" Amber asked, grinning as she did what she assumed to be play along.

I wrinkled my nose a bit. "Well, I always get the feeling that I'd be crossing some imaginary line, some thing laid forth ever since I can remember. It leaves me with this overwhelming, almost suffocating feeling that if I dare cross it I'd be putting their lives in jeopardy and would be doing something that someone close to me would have a hell of a time forgiving. It's a lame excuse, I know but it's true."

Riston ran his hand over my thigh slowly and I was sure with the angle he was at that Amber couldn't see it. "Doesn't sound the least bit lame to me."

The 'oh brother' look that came over Amber made me laugh. She shook her head. "So, your excuse is that you think you'll kill them if you screw them. Gotcha."

"No, I don't think that I'll personally be the one killing them, I think it would be someone else--someone who would show no mercy regardless of who he was dealing with. That being said, when it comes to other men, men who aren't shifters of any form, I have the strangest urge to teach that same someone a lesson, Amber. It's almost like I feel as though this person who'd hurt other shifters deserves it. Deserves to know that what he didn't want had to go somewhere so it chose entirely different types of lovers, ones he'd have no idea how he measured up against. Ones that he wasn't born to lead."

Riston let out a slow, deep breath.

"Shit, say I bought into it all," Amber said. "Then what you're saying is that you're screwing men to get back at one you don't even know."

"Yeah." I put my head down, disgusted with myself.

"Karri?"

I looked up at her. She crossed her arms. "Tell me why you look sick to your stomach about what I just said. I would have thought you'd be ecstatic. You can be *hella* ruthless in the area of males."

"Because *almost* every time it happens--you know, the urge to take a man, toy with him, fuck him and then leave him, I try to stop it but it feels like I'm standing in front of a tornado and asking it to please stop, to please go around me, anything but touch me. It doesn't work. The harder I fight it the worse it gets. That's why I tend to..."

"Keep the men you date at arms length."

"Yep."

Amber leaned her head against the doorframe. "You said almost all. Why?"

"Because two," I thought about Riston and raked my gaze over him, "okay, three men haven't made that sick feeling in my gut appear."

"Who?"

"I'm not answering that."

She snorted as she came in. I watched as she seemed to trip on nothing. She didn't fall but shook her head, looking confused. "Damn, did you see that? I tripped and nothing was there."

Glancing towards the ceiling, I closed my eyes and could almost feel Tripp's energy. "Ha, ha, very funny, Tripp. Yes, I was counting you as one."

"What?" Amber asked.

"I was talking to Tripp...err...about you tripping. Yep. Funny. Glad you weren't hurt though."

She snickered. "You are so strange but I love you all the same." She went to a box and opened it. Bending down, she began to unpack it slowly. "Well, Jean-Paul seemed to hang around a lot. Did he give you that weird feeling? The blood-sucking piece of shit is sexy but not right for you. I can't believe he's still in your life. Stop hanging around eccentric people. They're bad for your health."

I arched a brow. "Then does the same go for you because I'd miss you as my best friend? Especially since you're one of only two girlfriends I've ever had. The rest of my friends are male. They suck when it comes to just talking. Well, most of them do. Matty, he was here early this morning. The one with the chin-length auburn hair. He's really good but it's because he's also an empath in addition to being a cat shifter so he flat out senses my mood before I do.

"Seger's not too bad when it comes to heart-to-hearts but he's also taken a very odd protective stance that's always there. I asked him about it once and he told me that it was instinctive--like he felt compelled to assure himself that I was delivered safely somewhere. We never did figure out where that somewhere is." I laughed. The bad Karri damn near got the man to break that private promise earlier.

"What about that Branson guy? You know the one with the beard?" Amber asked.

"Uhh, hell no. He'd do anything for you but heart-to-hearts aren't his thing. It's weird. I got caught in his crossfire about a week ago and that first night I wasn't worth a shit in the 'know what's going on around me' category but I'm positive that Branson sat there talking to me the entire time."

"What was he saying?" she asked, not looking the least bit skeptical.

"I think he was telling me the story of who he is, where he comes from and all of that because when I felt better I just knew everything about him. I can't even tell you how amazing that feels to me. Men hide things from me all the time. Most because they assume I can't handle it or some have ulterior motives. Not Branson, no, he told me everything and I've never had a man trust me like that before. I thought that one other had but I found out I was wrong."

I couldn't help but look up. Finding out that Tripp had been sent by my mother, even if in the end we fell in love with one another hurt. He should have told me the truth. "The guy held things back, important things and that hurts. If you ask me something I'll be open and honest about everything in my life. All I ask is that it is offered in return."

"I told you everything about me," Amber said, winking.

"And you are the only family I have. Does that tell you anything?"

"Now, I feel like it's you who is getting the short end of the stick, Karri."

I rolled my eyes and held the frame for Riston who was making rather painful sounding noises. My guess was the hard on he had wasn't enjoying being denied, yet again. "Knock it off. You are the best thing that could have come into my life, Amber. I think they sent you to replace the sister I would have had. Well, that's my theory anyway. Though you're older than she'd have been now. She would have been six years younger than me."

Riston dropped a screw and banged his head on the rail. "Umm, a sister? You were an only child, Kars."

"That all depends on how you look at it."

He touched my arm lightly. "Explain."

"Before I went to sleep the night my parents passed away, my mom kissed me goodnight and said that dad would stop in as soon as he could. I knew that, he always did. But I felt something different about her. I know now what the feeling is. But then it took me a minute to understand it. The second I figured out what it was, I blurted it out. She laughed and confirmed my suspicions. She'd just found out that she was pregnant but hadn't told dad yet. She made me swear not to let him know until breakfast when she'd make him pink pancakes again." I laughed. "Apparently, she did some sort of pink everything meal when she found out she was having me. She was like that--very out of touch with reality but wonderfully so. I've also come to find out she is, umm, was quite the sex kitten."

"Yeah, gee, I wonder where you get it all from," Amber mused and I knew she was trying to keep the mood light.

I waited, holding the frame for Riston. "Amber, you know that you don't have to walk on eggshells when it comes to them or their passing. I, uhh, recently had a chance to see how I would deal with it. I'm okay."

"Right, that's why you cover it in a veil of dark fantasy and paranormal instead of just saying they died in an accident. But I can understand why you do that, Karri. Seeing them pass away had to be the hardest thing in your life."

"Do you remember all of it? I mean what lead up to it?" Riston asked, softly.

I nodded. "Sort of. Mom left the room after kissing me goodnight. I fell asleep. The next thing I knew my dad was yanking me from my bed and running full force towards the car. I remember seeing men, I think the men on his team, fighting big things that my father was somehow keeping hidden from me. They were fuzzy when they shouldn't have been."

I let myself reflect on things I swore I never world. "He told me that it was okay. That they weren't really there and that when we were safe he would make sure I didn't think about them again. I know now that he would have wiped my memory of it, had he lived. I was dazed, confused and scared. Something inside told me that I'd never be back. It told me that I needed to look hard and try to always remember because it'd be important later but I believed my dad was a god and if he said it would be fine then it would be fine."

"Jack had a way about him. Didn't he?"

It was such a warm feeling to hear Riston talk about my father and actually know him, even if it was through his own father. I couldn't help but smile. "He sure did. Though, I was sometimes guilty of questioning his authority, which seemed to make the men on his team laugh so hard that some of them had to leave the room to keep him from blowing up. One didn't. No, one was brave enough to stand there and snicker when I'd start my endless line of 'but whys' that I loved so much."

"Oh, the 'but whys'. Please don't remind me." Riston didn't wait for me to question him about that comment, he kept on going, "If it's not too much, what else can you remember leading up to what happened, Kars?"

I shrugged wondering why it was so important to him but not questioning him. "That night, when we were running toward the car, I knew that one of the men wasn't there. That he wasn't in the protection of the group."

I took a deep breath and tried to keep my emotions under wraps. "I knew that he'd somehow been separated from the others who were trying to hold off the things attacking because…umm, I think because of me."

"Maybe they were trying to protect you, Karri. The demons who came might have been after you for a reason so horrible that the idea of allowing them to be near a child was sickening and infuriating," Riston said, taking me by surprise. He shrugged fast. "Just a guess."

I didn't comment on that.

"What about the guy who was separated from the group? Did he die?" Amber asked.

"No. Not then, anyway. I'm not sure if he's still alive or not. But I do know that I was terrified of leaving him that night. Not that I thought he couldn't handle himself but something inside me felt like it was tearing, Amber. Like my father was pulling me in one direction and the guy who was separated from us was pulling me in the other direction. I kept yelling for my dad to stop and, in all the confusion, he forgot RJ. He told me that he was coming and that we couldn't wait. It physically hurt, Amber. My mom kept touching me, trying to heal whatever was happening but she couldn't. She kept yelling at my father."

I put my head down and sighed. "She told him that if he wasn't careful he'd sever the bond and that I wasn't made to survive without it in place. That's the only thing that gives me any sort of hope that RJ is still alive. If my mother was right then I'd have died if or when he does."

"RJ?" Amber asked. "The same RJ you spent years trying to find? The one that kept your parents' estate out of your evil friggin' guardians, Madge and William's clutches? That one?"

"Yeah, he and my dad were good friends. I can't speak for him but I think they may have been best friends. And I think he was my dad's right-hand, his second in command. Why?"

"How the fuck could you have some bond with that asshole?"

Riston cleared his throat. "Hmm, that must be a common assumption."

"Assumption my ass," Amber bit out. "How could he hand you over to those people if he had some bond with you, Karri? Hell, even if he didn't. How could he give you to monsters?"

She came in and sat down on the floor with us and put her hand out to me. I took it and she held mine tight. "Seriously, I get that a guy doesn't want anything to do with someone else's kid but to hand you to *them*…gawd…he could have kicked you, beat you and put you through hell himself and saved William the time or better yet, dumped you on the street. You would have been treated better there, Karri."

I dropped my head down, not wanting to discuss this anymore. "How's the bed coming? Do you think it will be sleep-worthy soon? I still need to try to lay down for another hour or so before I go out on patrol again."

Amber huffed. "You still call it patrolling when you are partying all night? I love it. And for the record. I'm right, you would have had a better life living on the streets than with them. No child should grow up like that. You were loved by your parents and you went from that straight to Hell. He literally took a scared little girl who had just lost her parents and handed her over to the devil himself then never looked back. He should be shot in the head. Or better yet, put through what you went through. How can you even say his name, Karri?"

I shrugged. "I don't know. I get that he didn't want to deal with me. Hell, I don't even like dealing with me at times. I should have fought back. I might have been able to keep my dad alive long enough for RJ to help him. I didn't mean to be so scared. I couldn't help it and if I really could have changed it I'd have never let my father die. You know, I don't want to talk about this anymore, Amber. It wasn't that bad," I said, lying through my teeth.

"Right," Amber glared at me, "so me waking up to hear you screaming in your room on an almost daily basis was no big deal, huh? I guess that means that it was nothing when I ran in to find you in the middle of the mother of all nightmares. Karri, you were cradled in a ball trying to protect your head from something crying, shaking, mumbling about RJ."

Riston touched my shoulder gently. "Was it a nightmare about your parents?"

Amber snorted. "Not unless her parents made a habit of using a horse whip on Karri and fucking trying to brand her for being some demon thing. And not unless her father tried to...I can't even say it."

"What?" Riston asked, grabbing hold of my waist and pulling me back against him.

My temper flared. "*Someone* here opened those letters Madge used to send and it wasn't me." I gave Amber a knowing stare completely forgetting that Riston was with us. "Did you enjoy getting detailed accounts? I know she liked writing them out. I'm so happy she found a receptive audience, Amber. Did you like the details? Huh? Did you like hearing what a man will do to a six-year-old he hates? Oh, I bet you loved hearing what he'd do to a teenager that woke up one day when she was sixteen to find herself with the body of a woman--no longer a child, and terrified."

Amber shifted, not backing down a bit. "I read the letters from Madge because I couldn't fathom the idea of someone who had no other family and no friends when I met her not answering or even opening mail from her aunt."

I went to stand but Riston held me in place. "Madge was *not* my aunt. I didn't know her and had never heard of her. How *he* even found her is beyond me." I snickered. "Maybe RJ looked up psycho in the phone book? I'm sure they were there."

"No doubt."

"I was placed with them and I didn't get a say. So, can we move on now? I'll tell you all about lycans or prove that I can do magik. At this point in time I'd summon a demon and kill him in front of you if you want. Anything but this topic. Please. You pick."

"No," Riston said, sternly. "What did this woman do to you?"

Amber shook her head. "No, not just the woman. The lady was shacked up with some evangelist preacher named William. Together they were going to rid the world of evil. I only know this because the crazy bitch repeated it about a hundred times in the letters she'd send, Karri. I want to know how a man who is friends with your family, best friends with your dad even, can hand an innocent little girl over to monsters and never look back."

"Leave him alone, Amber."

She balked. "Karri, how can you defend him? The man handed you to a woman who beat you with a bible, who handed you over to a man that tried to 'exorcise' the demons in you in ways that are *more than* against the law, Karri--they were hideous and sick! He was a sick man who should have been locked up, not left with a little girl in his care. You're a dreamer. A sweet wonderful person with an imagination that knows no end, Karri. Not a devil bent on seducing the world. And for that man to beat you, telling you that you needed to stop whoring around with RJ, the devil himself, was beyond uncalled for."

"A whore? What? You..." Riston sounded a mortified as I felt.

I shook my head. "No, of course I never...RJ never...gods no. RJ saved my life. He came out of nowhere, swept me up and kept me safe from the evil that would have killed me too. Not only that, he didn't make me leave my dad's side until he was gone. He let me say goodbye."

Amber snorted. "Only to drop you at evil's doorstep." Her nostrils flared as she clenched her fists. "I hate him for you, Karri. I hate them all for you. Do you even know why they treated you the way they did when it came to RJ?"

I shook my head no. "I told them he was just dad's friend. Then William...umm...he begged to differ. At that age, I didn't argue with a knife stuck in my hand." I looked away, sickened by it all. "I don't want to talk about this anymore."

"Knife in your hand? Karri-Lynn?" Riston's breathing was shallow as he held me to him. I could have sworn that he was shaking.

"Yes, a knife in her hand, Riston, pinning it to the dining room table," Amber said, her gaze heated. "You should have read those letters, Riston. That bitch had the nerve to say that no man would go out of his way to assure a child that wasn't his was set for her life. She was pissed that they couldn't dip into the funds RJ had ensured Karri had, that only so much was allotted monthly for them to raise Karri. Let me just say that teachers make less in a year than what RJ made sure was there financially each *month* for her care. But it wasn't enough for them. She was a greedy, psycho bitch. She had the nerve to say that Karri was born a demon whore and that RJ…Gawd…I can't even say it."

Taking a deep breath, I laughed hysterically. "Sorry, got a mental image of RJ pimping me out to the underworld and it was so ridiculous that it was funny. I sliced my foot open on glass once at the beach when I like five and he almost passed out. No joke. I remember telling him to sit down because I was very afraid that if he did pass out he'd crush me. I told him I'd fix it and to stop making that face he was making."

"Face?" Riston asked.

"Yeah, it was sort of a cross between, I want to sweep you up and make this better and I'm going throw up because you're hurt. See, he'd have left a hell of a trail of dead demons before letting one lay a hand on me. He told me that if a boy ever tried to kiss me that I should punch him on the nose and run get him so he could hit him again. I'm telling you, he could get on my last nerve but he was all right. Plus, he was the only person ever to understand green bean day. In a way, he helped invent it. He knew how much I hated them and how my mother seemed to think I'd pass out dead without eating them. He made it a game and had the cutest green bean costume made for me."

Amber snorted. "Ohmygod, Karri. I found myself celebrating green bean day a few years' back and damn near died of embarrassment. I was trying to help Paula get Hilary to eat them. It worked. Somehow, it got her to try them."

Working my way out of Riston's arms, I pushed to my feet quickly and walked to the window nearest me. As I stared out the darkening sky I wondered what RJ was doing, how his life was or even if he was alive at all.

"I still want to slap that RJ upside his head. Leaving you with Madge and William was just wrong." Amber appeared next to me.

Staring down at her, I smoothed a stray piece of red hair from her pale face. "Please don't blame him."

"He dumped you off, handled your parents' affairs and got the hell out of there. He sounds like a *real* friend. A champ. Karri, you have a romantic view on life. Everything is some fairy tale. Some bigger than life event. I love that about you but you don't deal with things. You lock them away and enter make-believe land. You even defend..."

"Amber, I don't want to talk about this anymore. I'm past all of that. You may not understand where I go," I touched my head lightly, "but I do. And most of the time I find a way to bring it out and share it with you. I've seen and done things that I wouldn't wish upon my worst enemy. I do not view life as a fairy tale. I view it as what it is--a struggle between black and white, good and evil. A struggle that I have all but lost. I love you but you can't change who I am. William and Madge couldn't. The people in my life now, my men as I call them, can't and neither can you. Everything happens for a reason. I would appreciate not discussing this in front of strangers. It's *beyond* personal."

Covering her mouth, Amber nodded. "Shit, Karri, I'm sorry. I didn't mean to bring it up with Riston here. I don't know why I was comfortable talking about it in front of him. Part of me wanted to shout what you went through while he was sitting there. Like it was high time he heard it all. What the hell is that about?"

"I don't know." Looking out I stared at the white house with green shutters and laughed.

"Karri?"

Glancing down at Amber, I touched her cheek and smiled. "Let's call it a day. I can drive or walk you home. You pick."

She looked away and nodded slowly. I could feel her pain. "Karri, you're right, since the moment you got here this morning I've taken nasty jabs at you. I've waited for the day you'd come and then I do this to you. Don't leave. I know you. You find a way to distance yourself when it all becomes too much. Don't do that." She wrapped her petite frame around me and hugged me tight.

I held her close and kissed the top of her head. "Come on, we're burning daylight. I need to thank Riston for helping, get you home and get some sleep." I turned, expecting to find Riston by the bed frame but found nothing. "Amber, I don't remember seeing Riston leave?"

"He's quick like that and he's a great guy. I'm guessing he decided we could use some privacy and that I'd stuck my foot in my mouth." She pulled back and wiped her eyes. "You don't have to walk me home. I'm going across the street to Eric's for the night."

My eyes widened. "Oh."

She chuckled. "It's not like that, Karri. After Paula passed away, Eric drew into himself, so did Hilary. Eric had always stopped for coffee and he'd always talked to me. Riston asked that I open the lines of communication more--be an ear for him to let things out on. I did. We're good friends now."

"Who sleep at the other's house," I said, winking and nudging her. She blushed and gave me a shy smile. "I'm glad you're here."

"Me too." I took a deep breath in and stretched. "I think I'm going to have to break down and get curtains in here. Blinds too maybe."

"Ohmygod, are you really Karri-Lynn?" She mused, doing a rather bad acting job of being shocked. "The Karri-Lynn I know and love had to be yelled at for almost a year about putting blinds in her bedroom windows. You used to tell me that you couldn't sleep without being able to see the sun or stars--whichever was out while you were down."

"I'm still like that. When I lived with the people who we aren't going to talk about, my room didn't have windows and I despised it. I hated not knowing if it was day or night." I pointed at the windows directly across from mine on the white house next door. "I've never had a neighbor who had windows that lined up with mine. And I have a tendency to..."

"Walk around naked or almost naked when you're alone. I know. Though, I have to wonder if that neighbor will mind. I think he might actually be okay with that. I think you should keep the blinds off the window. He's a nice guy and has earned an exciting view."

I snorted as I ran my hand over the window frame. "Since when did you become an advocate for men?"

"Since I got to know some of them better. That one there may be on the quiet side but he's a great man, Karri. He cares so much about everyone in his life but he doesn't admit to it. He's there at the drop of a hat and never asks a thing for himself." She touched my arm as I stared at the white house. "And until today, I hadn't seen him smile in almost a year. No joke."

"Oh, assure me that the guy with the sports car and the 'if it has legs, I'll bang it' attitude isn't my neighbor. I'm telling you, Amber. That guy had you mentally undressed in less than a second. That takes skill and a whole lot of practice."

Amber chuckled and patted my arm. "No, Seaton is not your neighbor. I wouldn't have let you buy the place if he was. Not that you'd have given me a say. You took one look at the email I sent and said this was the one. It's weird, Karri. You even seemed to know the layout before you set foot in it." She shook her head.

"Don't get me wrong. Seaton's harmless. But you pegged him right. He likes the ladies and life in the fast lane. Still, Eric, Thatch and Riston hang out with him."

"Thank the gods it's not Seaton then. Branson is enough of a life in the fast lane guy for me to deal with as it is."

"You know. I came back from New York saying 'thank the gods' and all of these people just snickered and went on about their day. I feel like I'm sitting on the outside of a secret society. You people need handbooks for visitors."

I stared at her a moment, taking in just how wonderful she truly was. "Keep hanging around Eric and I think we might give you one and make you an honorary member. Come on. I'll walk you over. Then I'm hitting the shower."

"You don't have hot water yet."

I grinned. "I know. So, odds are, I'll really *hit* the shower. Hope I don't put a hole in the wall. I know that I swore I was going to renovate this place myself but I'm fast losing interest in it. I might just hire some people to do it for me. Mmm, we could make them take their shirts off while they work, sip my lemonade and get out score cards. I love men who can fix things. The idea of them getting sweaty and using their hands is a complete turn on. Yep. That settles it. You and I will start screening sexy handymen tomorrow."

"Hey, what do you think of Riston? He's handy, you know?" she asked, suspicion all over her beautiful face. "He's hot, like Jean-Paul kind of hot."

"Wait, are you trying to get me to like him or run like hell from him?" I winked at her.

"What? Jean-Paul may be the French's version of a mob lord but he is sexy as all can be. Plus, he's the only guy I can think of that's been consistent in your life."

"French's version of a what?" I smacked my forehead. "Oh, right, it's called a vampire. Or, asshole, depending upon the mood I'm in when you ask."

"Right, vampire."

I walked in a circle shaking my head as I went. "I go out of my way explaining that all he wants is a new flashy toy with all the latest bells and whistles on it. I am perfectly honest and tell you that he is a creature of the night. I say, don't look him in the eyes, Amber. What do you do?"

I walked more, growling slightly. "You ignore me and walk right up to him demanding to see his fangs. So much for not looking him in the eyes. I then say, do not let him in our house--no matter what. I come back after a class to find him naked on my bed with roses. He can't just waltz in. It's against the rules he's forced to live by. When he told me that you let him in before heading out on your date I wanted to smack you in the back of the head."

"Sure, Karri, he's an ass but you have to admit that his attempts at wooing you were pretty damn funny. Please make a note that I am in no way suggesting you have a relationship with that man. I merely needed a drop dead sexy benchmark to compare Riston to." Amber moved quickly away from me winking as she went.

Covering my face, I groaned. "Dead being the key word there."

"Okay, say I buy into the vampire thing. Mmm, immortal hot guy who is rich with a hot accent and huge ego, not bad at all. That's do-able in my book, Karri. You should be able to marry him off easily. Want me to take out an ad for him?"

"Money means nothing to immortals, Amber. It means nothing to me."

She snorted. "Yeah, I know. When you started 'patrolling,' you were suddenly so busy that I had to ask you to pencil me in, you asked me to handle your checkbook and the expenses. I thought you were selling drugs for a bit there. Come on, the amount of money you had flooding in every month was obscene. That didn't even include your trust or any of the estate assets that RJ kept secure for you."

She laughed and pointed at my six drawer dresser, sitting sideways towards the back of the room. "Okay, you have more money than a rock star and you buy things at auctions, second hand shops, you never buy anything new."

"Not true. I bought a bed frame and new mattresses last week."

Amber made a twirling motion with her finger. "Let me guess, you needed to wipe the memories having to do with your old bed. You're always touching things, judging if you can live with its aura or not. I love your strangeness but when we crawled through the bin of door knobs at that antique shop so you could touch every one, I did want to have you committed."

"But it was fun. Admit it." I winked at her. "You even put a lampshade on your head and told the owner that a piece of your ship had broken down and that your home planet told you that you could find the replacement part there."

Amber laughed so hard and she stopped breathing. I held her to me and smiled. "Oh Amber, remember the *squeezie-gezzie* door knob we found. You picked it up and made an odd face. When you handed it to me I knew instantly that its previous owner could have made masturbation an Olympic sport. That's when we dove out head first, bought what we wanted and ran home to shower."

She tipped over and we both crashed to the floor. "Ohmygod, you bought that and told Jean-Paul that you were thinking of him. I wonder if he ever put that in his house."

I nodded. "He did."

We broke down in laughing fit and stared at the ceiling as we calmed down. Taking hold of her hand, I gave her a warm smile. "I am so thankful that they heard me."

Amber made an alarm bell sound. "Alert, alert, Karri spooky moment fast approaching."

"Ha, ha. It's true. I was scared. William kicked me out the night after all that. I was terrified of the dark and there I was. I'd just turned eighteen and graduated from high school. I had nowhere to go. No friends. Between the way I am and the way they were, people ran when they saw me coming. That was the first time it hit me how alone I was. I'd never asked the powers for anything. Not when Mom and Dad died. Not even when RJ handed me over to strangers and all I wanted to do was cling to his leg. Wait, I did cling to his leg. I also asked him to stay. He said no." I laughed. "I wrote him a letter once when I was like eight or nine. All it said was 'sorry for biting you.' I was a dork. I thought he left me there with them because he was mad that I bit him."

"You bit him?" Amber asked.

Something brushed over my arm and I stared around, trying to figure out what it was. When I found nothing, I relaxed. "Long story. Anyway, I didn't ask the powers for help then either." I took a deep ragged breath. "My mom told me that if you were really good you could ask the powers or the goddess of your choice for help. I broke down that night and asked for help. My clothes were in shreds. I was bleeding from just about everywhere, tired, cold and in so much pain."

I cleared my throat. "I was scared of myself and positive that they'd been right, that I was a demon. I could feel the evil pressing in on me. It was moving so fast that I was sure I wouldn't make it through the night. But I asked and closed my eyes tight, trying so hard to go away to one of the many places I have in my head but I couldn't."

I moved our laced hands around in Celtic patterns while I continued to talk. "That's the night PJ came to me. She told me that someone special, someone who would need me as much as I needed them would come when she left. It was you."

"Oh, the lady who said she knew me but I'm positive she didn't? I'd remember meeting a PJ. Not a common thing to go by. Though, you seem to have a lot of nicknames around you--PJ, RJ, it's kind of cute. I love the way you always make her seem so magikal too. Did she get you some sort of medical attention?"

I let Amber continue thinking in human terms. "Kind of. I hurt so bad. Especially my cheek. William split it wide open and I'd been too weak after what I'd done to heal a thing. Plus, I knew I was being hunted. I'd had my first brush with what evil feels like when it's hungry and coming for you when my parents died. I felt that everywhere the night he threw me out. I know now that by finally recognizing my powers and having them overthrow me for a bit, I'd sent up a huge flare for the bad guys telling them to come and get it. I didn't mean to but it happened. I was terrified, Amber. And I do mean terrified."

My hands shook just talking about it. "When my parents died I had my father there, doing his best to calm me down. RJ showed up then too, like some giant knight in black." I let out a soft laugh. "But I was completely alone the night William finally snapped. When this huge flash of white surrounded me I was pretty sure I'd died. I was actually really happy about that."

"Karri."

"What? When would it have been okay to surrender? I had nothing left in me. You seem to think I'm some sort of superwoman. I'm not. I hurt too. William spent years screwing with my head, so much so that I really believed what he said about me. I believed I was bad, some abomination that the devil made. Amber, I was scared to eat the food there. He'd..."

She gave me a knowing look. "Begun experimenting in how much poison your system could handle without actually killing you," she said, with a long sigh. "It was in one of the letters. But the crazy bitch kept saying that William really did manage to kill you several times that way and that you rose from the dead, your eyes black and the look of evil etched on your face. She was delusional and he was sick. She mentioned that he tried that with you the first time when you were ten. Feeding a ten-year-old rat poison is...it's...it's something they don't even have words for, Karri."

No part of me could argue. It was horrific. Thinking about it, about him, still left me shaking. "I know," I whispered. "When I'd get used to the smell of what he was trying to put in my food or drinks, he'd switch to something new, convinced that it was one more sign that I was a demon. It all started after he shoved me down the staircase and broke my leg. I healed it without knowing how I did and he stood there and watched it happen."

Amber covered her mouth. "Ohmygod, he tried different ways to kill you. That's what she meant by the demon child resists the blade, the poison, the snakes, the powder and the rod of justice. Whatever that was."

I cringed and took a deep breath. "Amber, she meant William--the rod of justice was a euphuism for his…I'm going to throw up if we keep talking about this. Each time he tried to…umm, I'd emit some sort of protective energy that I still to this day don't know how I did it." I choked up and Amber wrapped her arms around me.

Her eyes widened. "You mean that he tried to rape you, Karri? Oh fuck, that's what she meant by the rod of justice, William thought..."

I nodded. "He could exorcise the evil in me by screwing it out of me. He thought that he was someone touched by the hand of one who is right--his own personal savior."

"What exactly did he manage to do to you, Karri? Did he rape you?"

Something banged hard on my bedroom wall, leaving the perfect indent of a fist. It magikally eased away, smoothing over until it was perfect but I'd seen it. I just couldn't figure out what had caused it. I knew that Amber hadn't done it. Hell, she was clinging to me, not ever paying attention to it.

My hands shook harder as I held tight to her. "He punished me for something I couldn't help, for something I couldn't change. And I was too young, too naïve when it came to who and what I am to stop him."

Huge unshed tears filled my eyes. "Amber. I didn't understand that I had the power to stop him. I should have known. I should have figured it out. No child survives what he'd do to 'test' my demonicness. No child can take an ax to the gut and live to tell about it. They don't ingest enough poison to drop an elephant and survive. They don't wake to find themselves covered in poisonous snakes, scream, try to get away only to find the snakes biting them everywhere and somehow manage to live to see another sunrise, another day for William to test his theories, prove the evil in me was real."

"Why don't you hate RJ?"

I laughed, it was choked but there. "To be honest, a little part of me does. It just didn't feel right to admit that in front of Riston. A little part of me, which hides in the darkness I carry wants RJ to have to be the one that puts me down. It wants him to have to kill what he had such a hand in creating. I try to stop it. I, the me that's normally in control, doesn't want that. I just want RJ to be happy wherever he is."

"I can understand that," she whispered. "At least you had PJ come to you when you needed her most."

"If you'd have seen her when she appeared out of thin air you'd have thought she was a goddess or an angel too. She was so tiny. Shorter than you, even. Her hair was as long as mine but instead of stick straight and blonde, it was dark, dark brown and hung in huge ringlets." I laughed. "If it wasn't for her big blue eyes, I think someone might have actually thought she was all hair. Gods, Amber, she was stunning."

"Hilary's mom was like that." Amber smiled at me. "She had so much hair that I'm not sure how she didn't tip over. She was petite, almost child-like but held herself in a way that you knew she was all woman."

"Yeah, so did PJ. Sexy, compact and damn dangerous when provoked."

"Was?" Amber asked.

I nodded. "Yeah. Just under a year ago, I was running on the treadmill, doing my normal thing and instantly felt like someone had hit me with a bat in the chest. I couldn't breathe. The second the nothing that hit me tossed my ass into the garage door I knew it was bad."

Her eyes widened. "Tell me you moved the treadmill because I'm sort of believing this story and that's a *helluva* far way to go."

"No. It was in the same spot. But that didn't matter. All I felt was her pain. I lay there, wrapped her in a blanket of my power and took it all from her. I tried over and over again to bring her back, Amber. I tried to heal her from a distance. Her wounds were mortal but she was still alive. She fought me tooth and nail. She said that I wouldn't walk away from that. I don't know, something about being similar but not the same and that in the end we'd both end up dead. I kept trying and that little spitfire," a tear fell down my cheek, "she started to bind my power so I stopped. It was then that she told me to come this way--that the people *we* loved would be threatened in the near future."

"The people *you* loved?" Amber asked, arching a brow. "Karri, this is weird but I believe you. So, no laughing on the inside for me asking this but why did she say we?"

"I won't laugh at you. But I can't answer that question. PJ was adamant that she knew you. When she left and moved back home she had told me that she'd send my new roommate to me very soon. She also said that I didn't need to know her name. When the time came I'd fall into her lap. And I literally did. In fact, she was adamant that she also knew RJ. When she showed up out of the blue, kissed my forehead and healed me instantly, she cried and cried. I had to hold her to get her to stop saying that he didn't know."

"How'd she know him? And who didn't know what?"

I shook my head. "I don't know. PJ was cryptic but funny. She was this little ball of energy. She talked a mile a minute. I did catch that she was related to him somehow. She refused to be specific. Though, once, when she was at the bank, showing me all that RJ had done for me, she told the bank manager that she was my sister-in-law and that my husband had left papers there regarding the matter. Then she pinched me hard when I opened my mouth to object. She had bony lil' fingers."

"Husband?" Amber asked, her eyes wide and face pale.

"Yeah, that was about my reaction."

Amber pinched my arm and laughed. "Sorry, couldn't resist."

"Laugh now, but at the time, I hyperventilated in the ladies room. She couldn't stop instigating the rest of the time. I almost lost my lunch on the bank manager twice. It's kind of strange though that when William accused me of horrible things, I hated him. But when PJ used RJ to have fun at my expense, calling him my husband, mate and even asking when the baby was due while we were standing in front of the bank employees," I covered my mouth again, "I didn't hate her. I did get sick to my stomach though."

"What? Was RJ that bad looking?" she asked, nudging me.

I shook my head. "I honestly don't really remember a lot about what he looked like so much as his presence. I remember that I thought his eyes were windows to the sky. See, mom told me once that he was some mix of a good angel from the light and a lycan. I got it in my head that the gods used his eyes to check and see if I was behaving. Looking back on it, I'm sure they were just very blue. My imagination has always been rather big."

"So, all you got of this guy is eyes?"

I groaned. "I was like five. I remember he was a giant at least compared to me. So was my dad. I put my foot next to his once and was convinced that if he stepped on me, I'd die." Looking at Amber, I drew my lips in. "This goes nowhere but when I met your friend, Riston, he reminded me of RJ. I can't explain why. Could be the blue eyes. I have never done that to a guy--thought of someone else when I'm staring at them."

"Holy shit, Karri. The sandwich. You fixed that because..."

I nodded. "I got him confused with RJ again. It just felt right. I could almost hear all of them like they were still alive, still joking. My dad and RJ would argue about the stupidest things. They weren't fighting so much as goading each other."

Amber snicker. "Kind of like us?"

"Yep."

"They had a "deep discussion" about the perfect sandwich once." I giggled and it must have been infectious because Amber did, too. "I got so sick of hearing it when I was trying to be a secret agent that I hopped up and told them they were both wrong. Peanut butter and butter was the best. When PJ came into my life and gave me a lecture about the perfect salad I couldn't stop laughing at her. She got mad, tossed her hands up and stormed out of the room. I called out and told her that she forgot her 'perfect' salad and I ended up wearing lettuce."

"Don't get mad, Karri, but whenever you bring her up, it seems like you viewed her in a slightly maternal manner."

I let a tiny bit of power up and coated our joined hands. Amber didn't seem to notice. "Why would I get mad at that? PJ did fill in where I clearly had needed a woman's guidance. Before you ask, she tried to teach me to cook and gave up. She had the patience of a saint and I did her in. But for the most part it seemed like we filled gaps in the other's life. Did I ever tell you that she was the one who had the sex talk with me?"

Amber nodded, a huge smile broke over her face. "Yes, but I refuse to believe that you needed one. You ooze sex. Like you came out of the womb knowing it all," Amber said, pinching me one more time. "You bat your lashes and guys run into walls. I still remember losing count of how many guys walked up to you, opened their mouths to say something and then walked away shaking their heads. And I'm not believing you were a virgin for as long as you say you were."

"Amber?"

"Hmm?"

"If you survived a place where a sick man mentally and physically abused you, before moving to trying to rape you--but not succeeding, would you want to be with a man? Would you trust them?"

She sucked in a deep breath. "Karri, I'm sorry. I never thought about it."

"And I haven't always oozed sex. It didn't happen until after I was out of William's home. It didn't happen until after PJ came into my life."

"So, how did PJ handle the sex talk with you? She knew what you had gone through."

I raised my voice and did my best to impersonated PJ. "Karri, honey, think of your body as a temple. A whole lot of men will worship it. Only a select few will be allowed to enter. Now, ideally, only one man would get to bathe in the shrine within but he's a bit slow on the uptake so by the time he figures things out your temple doors will have rusted shut. I'd stick a billboard out front for you but the boy has tunnel vision and would drive right past it. Please don't share our little heart-to-hearts with him. He might not like me encouraging you to let others play in your healing pools."

Taking a deep breath, I continued on, "To make a long, rather bad explanation short--if your made to order mate doesn't show up soon and the urge for sex strikes, screw the guy but don't bother getting his phone number. And for the love of the goddesses, do not tell the guy who you marry I said that. Should he ever ask about your past, give him that big smile of yours right before you give him some of you. If he forgets what he asked you, you're golden. If he doesn't just say three. He can handle that. I think. Better make it two. Yeah. Go with two."

Amber laughed so hard that she snorted. "Ohmygod, if mystery man ever shows up and catches you in the fib, just tell him you misunderstood the question. Tell him you thought he wanted to know how many men you've had at one time."

I wanted to laugh at her joke but something in my gut told me not to. It felt like someone was in the room with us even though I knew no one was. Amber nudged me and laughed more.

"Come on. That was funny and you know it."

"I know nothing of the sort," I said, grinning at her. The feel of being watched was great. If I didn't know better, I'd have said that Riston was still in the room, invisible, but there. That couldn't be. Could it? "I'm feeling like this is one of those moments PJ would have urged me to smile pretty."

Amber rolled onto her side and stared at me. "I would have liked her. She sounds like you. Plus, if nothing else, she designs kick ass tattoos. The one she designed for you is gorgeous."

I sighed. "Amber, it was hard to let her go, to let her pass away, when the time came. I mean, the whole time I'm keeping her pain in me instead of her, she's thinking about the people she loved. She tried to push images of them at me so I would know them when I saw them but I couldn't stop thinking about the day she'd come to me, while you were home for the holidays. She flashed into the room and accidentally knocked me over. The second I got up, she tackled me to the floor anyway, laughing and talking a mile a minute again. When I caught the word pregnant, I couldn't believe it. She was so excited. She couldn't stay long, something about needing to sit the two-hundred-year-old pain in her ass down and tell him before he found out from someone else. She was worried he'd try to kill his best friend, the father of the baby."

"Oh, she was a mom?" Amber asked, pain her voice. "After seeing Eric and Hilary go through losing a wife and mother I would never wish it on my worst enemy."

I nodded. "Yep, PJ was mom. She told me, didn't even bother to ask, she just told me that I was the baby's godmother. Yeah, I asked if she'd fallen and hit her head. I'd break a kid. She looked me dead in the eyes and told me that I was perfect for the job."

Amber snickered. "She must have been crazy to let you anywhere near a child. Who's the godfather?"

"I think it's the two-hundred-year-old pain in her ass but I'm not sure. I said yes, like she even gave me a choice and then fell into some deep shit with work. I'd never endanger anyone I care about so I cut off communication with her and with..."

"Me." Amber glanced away from me.

"Yeah. I didn't have a choice, honey. I had a debt to pay. Going and playing with the biggest baddies on the block completely absolved that plus some. I lost myself in it all, Amber. The lines blurred for me."

"What do you mean you were in debt? You had and no doubt still have money falling out of your ears." Amber squeezed my hand.

I couldn't tell her the truth. She'd blame herself. I had to sign on the dotted line with the powers in return for Jean-Paul's assistance with watching my body as I healed a death that was brought on from taking Amber's sickness into me. "I needed a favor, a huge one. It had nothing to do with money. It had to do with something far more important to me. Jean-Paul could help but the people he's with knew an opportunity when they saw one. I didn't have much choice."

"Gawd, Karri, you should have told me. I could have..."

I let out a soft laugh. "You couldn't have done a thing, Amber. I wasn't even qualified to be there at the time. I was young, powerful, female and someone the bad guys didn't know." I took a deep breath. "I could feel PJ's magik when she checked in on me from time to time. She was so disappointed in the situation and hurt that I hadn't come to her either. But she had a family to worry about and I'd never jeopardize that." I sat up and stared at my dresser.

"Amber, I'm a terrible person. I know that PJ had a baby girl but nothing else. I wouldn't let her tell me. It was safer that way."

"Safer that way?"

I nodded. "Do you remember when you had that headache that you were convinced had split your skull open?"

"The one I got while I was on that blind date with the king of creep?"

"Yeah, remember how I showed up and crashed your date?"

She narrowed her gaze on me. "Yes. I was never more thankful to see you in my life. Why the hell did you make me go with Tripp while you stayed behind?"

"Your blind date wasn't what you thought he was, honey. Some vampires can do what's called a psychic attack. He was attracted to you because you're special too--you just don't acknowledge it. It's a way for them to see inside, see your dreams, your nightmares. I think some may actually feed off it. I'm not sure. Anyway, the attacks hurt like hell at that low level. Imagine someone doing that to you while you're getting the shit beat out of you."

"I'm not special and no way would I want that headache back. I threw up for days and my nose even bled all night," she said, her eyes locked on me. "Oh, shit, that's why you didn't learn anything new about any of us for all those years. You didn't want to accidentally spill it."

"Yeah."

Sitting up next to me, Amber shook her head. "Karri, you didn't want them…umm, us to get hurt."

I shrugged. "Yes. But I did something else to PJ. I betrayed her trust in me and I think I'd do it again if put in the same situation." My breath grew ragged and sweat beaded on my brow. "Once PJ was calm and almost gone I went against her wishes and opened her link with her daughter, with her family. I kept every bit of her pain locked in me so her little one wouldn't know how much pain her mommy would have been in. All I let her have was the feeling of her mommy's magik, her essence around her. I wanted her to know that PJ was thinking about her. PJ had been adamant I not do that. But I just felt like they had a right to say goodbye, even when she didn't want to hurt them more."

I got to my feet and rolled my shoulders, trying to let the pain out.

"The woman helped me through a horrible time in my life, sent me you, trusted me enough to give me an important position in her child's life and I repay her by going against her final wishes. I just couldn't let them miss their chance to say goodbye, Amber. I couldn't."

Chapter Six

Amber gave me a soft smile. "I think her family appreciated that."

Untying my red shirt, I took it off and held it up. "Remind me to burn that. It stinks. Ugg. I stink. I need to take a shower and get my ass out on patrol."

"Karri, give it a break. You don't need to keep it up. Sleep tonight. Pretend again tomorrow. I know you were in town before you came and got me this morning. You only got a few hours of sleep with Riston today. I didn't mean to get you talking but I just wanted to catch up."

"Stop worrying. I'm fine. Though I'm thinking the neighbors might toss me out soon. I spent the day blaring polyester flashback music, I have the local eyesore and I'm next to someone who measures his grass. I'm sure of it."

Amber snorted. "Wait, you still don't know who your neighbor is?"

"Mr. and Mrs. Meticulous?" I undid my jean shorts and let them fall to the floor, leaving me standing in my bikini. Amber drew back fast and covered her mouth. Glancing down, I noticed the ragged puffy pink scar from the bullet wound on my left hip. Right under it was a nice claw mark for effect."

She looked in me eyes and gasped. "What in the hell happened to your hip?"

"Gunshot," I pointed at it, "and were-panther." As I pointed at the claw marks, Amber moved towards me slowly. "Relax. It will all be gone soon. I, umm, sort of forgot to eat yesterday so it takes a little longer to heal. But I ate today. You were there. No yelling at me again."

"What?"

Shaking my head, I lifted my hair. "Untie me."

"Owen told me that you really did get shot last week. I thought he was as crazy as you. How are you walking?"

"Well, I put one foot in front of the other and hope for the best. How about you?"

Amber moved up behind me and went to untie my suit. She gasped and ran her finger over my tattoo. "Ohmygod. Karri, you know how I've always liked this tattoo? How I thought PJ did a kick ass job with it? And how it seemed so familiar?"

"Could you hop to that point you're trying to make? I plan on making you gather up my gear again for me."

"Umm, Riston has this same one on his upper back too."

I laughed. "Right. Okay. I'm going to shower in the ice cold water that the no-show plumber left me with. You should have added that Riston has a brand mark near his too. I could get even more sick to my stomach."

"Hey, setting the obvious weirdness of this aside, what's wrong with Riston?"

I held my bikini top up with my arm. "Changing topic now. Could you gather my stuff up? It's all in that sideways dresser."

"I'll get it all but let the record state that I'm not lying. You've got almost the same tattoo as him. And all this crap is beginning to make a believer out of a die-hard skeptic." She walked over to the dresser, giving me a dirty look the entire time.

As I turned to go into the master bedroom's bathroom Amber screamed out. Instantly, I threw magik up and over her. She jumped back fast and stared at the nothing around her. With wide eyes she poked out into the air and her finger hit an invisible barrier. "Karri, what's going on? What is it? Did you really do magik?"

"Promise you won't freak out?"

She nodded.

"Yes," I said, sheepishly.

Amber screamed out again this time jumping up and down. At first I thought she was scared of me. When I saw her smiling, I knew better. "Holy shit! Holy shit! Holy..."

Waving my hand the barrier dropped. "Yeah, shit…I get it. Did you officially snap? It's not like I haven't been preparing you for this for like ever."

"Yes, I mean no. I haven't snapped." She stood there smiling wide at me. "First off, can you do that magik thing again? It was cool?"

"Will you take a rain check? It's not very wise for me to use that much while running on empty. And trust me, honey, what I tossed around you was a hell of a protection spell."

The hurt look on her face broke my heart. Lifting my hand, I drew on my power and made a white orb appear. "Here," I tossed it to her, "play with that. It's Amber-friendly so you can't hurt yourself."

She beamed. "You are the coolest."

"Yeah, it's just great to be me." I went to head into the bathroom and Amber screamed again.

"Oh, I almost forgot the most important part."

"Part of what?" I asked, positive I didn't want to hear her answer.

She played with the ball of light as she spoke, "Well, when I asked you why you were positive you'd never have kids you told me that story about a mate. And you explained that you were made different from other women of your kind. That you'd been created for only one man and that he was the only male who could ever create a child with you. That the idea of birth control was absurd because you couldn't catch human diseases and could never have a child without your mate. Remember?"

Yawning, I nodded. "Yeah."

"Did you ever find him? Did you ever find your mate?"

"Nope, but I stopped looking after we graduated from college. I got a job and didn't look back. I don't want children. They'd hate me and I'd no doubt break them or something." I made a move and Amber shook her head as she held up a handful of photos.

"Karri, who is the woman in the pictures with you?" she asked, smiling wide.

"Damn, I almost forgot about those. I finally found them. I swear they grew legs and walked away when we lived together. Every time I wanted to show you them they weren't where I left them." I yawned again. "That's PJ."

Amber made a choked scream sound and nodded. "Okay, how many years ago did she come to you tell you she was expecting a baby?"

"Amber," I covered my eyes and thought about it. "I don't know, you'd just moved back home so shortly after graduation."

"That's seven years ago."

I gave her a droll look before heading towards the bathroom again. "You don't say. Thanks for clearing that up."

"Hey, Karri," Amber called out. "Did PJ ever tell you if her daughter liked the dollhouse you send her for her fourth birthday? What was that again? A big grey shopping mall thing right?"

"I didn't send a big grey shopping mall dollhouse. How fun would that be? No. She was PJ's little girl, so she's a princess in my mind. I gave her a dollhouse that looked like a castle. I had it made for her."

"Yeah, she loved the dress up set you sent with it. She walked around in that frilly pink skirt all the time."

That made me smile. "Did she like the wings? I couldn't find a pair that small so I had Owen make them for her."

"Oh, yes. So much so that her uncle had to pull her off the front porch banister because she was sure she could fly."

I cringed. "I didn't think of that when I sent them. I hope he wasn't too mad."

"Yeah, well she also made her uncle be the prince. He didn't look too happy about that either."

Laughing, I started the water to the shower. "You know, every little girl needs a prince. It should be a law or something."

"I agree."

"Shit, I forgot to grab a towel." I turned to head back out and stopped instantly. "Amber?"

"Yeah?"

"Sorry to put you through the whole PJ story since I clearly already had."

"You really must need some sleep. You're not thinking very clearly." She laughed, sounding so enthused about something that I almost went back out to check on her. "So, you never did answer me when I asked what was wrong with Riston?"

I climbed in the shower, screaming, I jumped back out of the line of water. "Ohmygods, that's fucking cold. That's it. I'm going over to the Meticulous' next door and using theirs. I need a towel and heater."

"Are you going to answer me about Riston? You know, any guy out there could be that one guy, Karri. Riston could be him. You said he reminded you of RJ." She growled. "I want permission to hit him in the head with a frying pan if he is."

I snorted and poked my head around the corner. "Pfft, honey, no. He's not *him*."

"But how do you know. You can just remember RJ's eyes. He could be Riston."

Shaking my head, I smiled wide as a thought came to me. "It took you five minutes to go from not believing me to being an expert on the supernatural. Care to tell me why you seem stuck on Riston, a man I just met, on accident, while flipping around my yard covered in mud and wearing a wedding dress is RJ?"

"Karri, do you get the feeling that someone's in here, watching us?"

"Yes." I looked around and raised my brows. The place had an old, spooky, yet oddly familiar quality to it. One that made me love it instantly. The feeling of being watched was still there but the presence didn't feel evil. No. It radiated concern, love and protection. Those were all things I was lacking so I was just fine with that.

I grinned. "How cool would it be if the house was haunted? I want a ghost I can name Gilchrist. It's not like the opportunity to use that odd of a name will pop up again in my life."

She gasped. "You would think that was cool. I changed my mind. Walk me to Eric's."

Laughing, I nodded and turned the cold water off. "Fine. Can you put those pictures back so nothing happens to them?" I asked, walking out of the bathroom still wearing my suit and motioning towards the pictures.

"Oh, I will treat these like rare gems." Amber winked. "But tell me one thing."

"What?"

"Why is your hair short and black in one of these pictures?"

I laughed as I thought about the one she was talking about. "Because PJ slapped her magik on me and I found myself standing there in skimpy black leather lingerie, with short black hair blue eyes and a man in the next room."

"A man?" she asked, eyes wide and smile bright. "Wait, you mean the guy chained to the bed?"

"Yep."

"Karri, what if Riston really is RJ? What if he was the one chained to the bed?"

I sighed, not wanting to acknowledge the very thing that had been eating at me. "Then something that my heart tells me would be beautiful will never be."

"Why?"

"Because I don't want anything to do with RJ or with all that he represents--a family, a future. It's too late for me now. I just want to live the remainder of my life as drama free as possible, Amber."

"Okay, I'm ignoring that." She waved her hand in the air dismissing it. "Tell me this, if Riston is your mate and you have sex with him, can you get pregnant?"

Groaning, I rubbed my hands over my eyes before letting a laugh slip out. "Why do I have visions of you rummaging through my things and his to make sure that no condoms can be found?"

She laughed. "I'm just asking, Karri. Suppose he was your mate and the two of you have sex. Could he get you pregnant?"

"Gee, since I've never had sex with my mate I'd have to say I don't know. Probably. It would depend on how damaged my reproductive system is."

"Damaged?"

I sighed. "I put my body through a lot, Amber. The word immortal is just another way of saying that I'm harder to kill than most. It doesn't mean I can't die."

She grabbed my hand. "Karri, is there something you're not telling me? Something about your health?"

Oh, shit. Think of anything but the truth.

"Umm, no. What gave you that idea?" The idea of telling her how worn and torn my body now was wasn't an option.

"You call me a month ago, after having not talked to me in seven years to inform that you're moving here to be close to me. You're not normally one who makes a lot of long term plans but you haven't once talked about what will happen now that you're here. You haven't said, oh, hey, Amber this Christmas let's go do this or that. In fact, you've made a lot of comments about being on borrowed time."

Shit. She was right. I had. It wasn't like I realized I was doing it. "Hmm, well, I don't know why. Guess I've changed in seven years."

Amber put her hand on her hip. "If there was something wrong with you, you'd tell me right? I mean, you sat by my side when everyone, the doctors included, said I wasn't going to make it. You gave me hope and refused to take no for an answer. You'd let me do the same, right?"

The doctors had been right. By human standards, Amber had no hope. That's why I'd stepped in and healed her, even with the knowledge that I'd take on her injury, her death--her illness. I took on the negative effects of not using her powers. They were mine to carry.

"Amber, I'm fine."

"Then tell me that if Riston is your mate and you ended up pregnant, what would you do?"

"Come and find you so I could knock you over the noggin for jinxing me." I smiled. "I don't know. I honestly have never thought about it, Amber."

Chapter Seven

I adjusted my headset and kept pretending that I'd gotten a cramp running and needed to stretch. I bent low, extended my leg and glanced at my upper thigh. I loved knowing that I was armed to the teeth but looked like a young woman out jogging in the middle of the night. Owen had helped me perfect the outfits. The white tank top was reinforced to stop most bullets and not shred at the first touch of a claw. My navy running pants unbuttoned down each side in a flash, allowing me to get to my thigh holsters. They held my P226's and extra clips of silver bullets. The navy boy-cut shorts I wore beneath the pants gave me something to keep my ass covered should I need to rip the pants off.

The matching navy jacket hid my arm sheaths. Both contained six-inch hunting knives. I wore my hair in a high ponytail. The supernaturals seemed to take that as an even bigger sign of innocence. The entire ensemble was so great at night that I had it in almost every color combination imaginable.

I hadn't been able to shake the feeling that I was being watched since I woke up. As I was getting dressed, after a rather ice cold shower, I could have sworn that I'd felt warm air near my ear as if someone was breathing on me. My entire body had lit with desire. If it was a ghost and could make my body jump like that, it was welcome to stay. Though, I'd have to seriously consider changing the name I'd selected for it. Somehow, Gilchrist didn't seem as sexy as the ghost had.

I felt it then. Evil. It was stalking me. I knew how enticing I looked to it. In the eye of the demons that stalked humans, I was prime pickings, female and alone. I went to start to jog again. Evil was apparently impatient.

A tall man with sandy blond hair that hung to his mid-back stepped out from the side of the building nearest me. I gasped, pretending like I hadn't sensed him. His pale grey eyes locked on me. His body was toned, not extremely muscular but that meant little in the world of supernaturals. This vampire was as deadly as any other thing out there. Maybe more so. He wore the obligatory monochromatic outfit all the bad guys seem to have. Basically, they went with black from head to toe. He smiled. I cringed.

"It is not wise to be out on your own at such an hour," he said, evil lacing his voice. He took a step towards me. "It is most unfortunate for you that you took this path."

I stood still.

He moved next to me quickly. Had I been human I wouldn't have seen him move. Since I wasn't, I watched the entire thing. I gasped and played the role of victim perfectly. "How?"

Smiling wickedly, he raked a fingernail down the back of my jacket, splitting it open. "It matters not, human. All you want is for me to touch you, to be near you, to have you." The compulsion he was laying on with his voice was thick enough to choke on. I laughed so hard on the inside that I almost shook with it.

He pulled my jacket open, exposing my upper left back. Instantly, his hand went to my tattoo and branding spot. He laughed and the sound made me sick to my stomach. "Someone has placed the mark of the devil on you. Oh," he laughed, "are you the devil's whore, Karri? That's what he thought, wasn't it? William told you that you were evil, spit forth from hell and delivered to them so that you could have the demons within you exorcised."

I stood, sensing more of his buddies close to us. Watching us. I couldn't make my move too soon or they'd run. I had no choice but to stand there listening to a soulless demon bring up horrific memories.

The vampire ran his fingers over the outside of the brand. He traced each symbol on the tattoo and laughed again. "So, you are more than just human, yet not so much so that you resist my hold on you. Your mind has been exposed to shadow demons most recently, making it so easy to read. It is an open book, young one. It is a shame for this mate your back speaks of that you shall not live to see him."

He took a deep breath in. "I am right, you are not mated. I wonder, would you have told him of the man who burned your flesh knowing he would see it? Would you have revealed the number of lashes you took defending his honor? How William tore your arms open, ripped your face open wide, thought of taking you in ways only your mate should?"

The vampire ran his hands over my arms lightly. I shivered. He laughed. "Ahh, Karri, so young, standing up to such an evil man. Was defending a man who cared nothing for you, your mate, worth what William put you through." He touched the brand on my upper back again. "What became of the rest of these? The ones you received while screaming and crawling on the floor? What of the rest of the scars from the whip? And the bite marks, Karri? What of those? Did you make them go away or did the angel that came to you and held you trying to make you believe that her brother did not know that it would happen--did not know that you would spend your life being treated like an animal, not able to look your foster parents in the eyes or be seen with them in public, do it? Did she heal them?"

Brother?

"Yes, the one who abandoned you and let you be William's demonic play toy is the brother to the one you held so dear. Ah, yes, PJ? Yes, let your mind race, little one. Show me it all."

That couldn't be right. Evil ones loved to lie. I pushed him from my mind and stood still.

He laughed as I let off a signal of fear. I had no fear of *him* so it was completely invented. "That is it. You are still afraid of William today. You can still remember screaming out for a man who never came as William bent your lush body over the table and offered to show you what it was the hero in your head would do to you. What all men did to sluts, to demon whores."

Tall shadowy figures walked out into the street and joined us.

"Did you like it when William made the woman--Madge bind your wrists and begin to undress you? You must have liked the bites, Karri. For he bit you when you struggled and you struggled non-stop. What was the horrible rage burning in you? Did you wonder if it was the evil they accused you of being surfacing? Was it?"

A slow smile crept over my face as I waited for him to get to my favorite part.

"You knew what William was going to do. You knew he was going to take you and ram himself in your body until you renounced all that was evil. You knew that the way he'd watched you for years was wrong. You lay there bound, staring at the floor, screaming for a man who would not come. A man that had put you there. A man who could leave a child in the hands of that sort of evil is a man I can learn to admire. Did you like growing up with William? Never knowing if he'd done something to your food again because he liked watching you be so sick you could barely move. He got great joy out of his psychological torment. I can only imagining the joy he had when he had you laid out before him, a dark angel offering."

As he said dark angel I broke into a full smile. Waiting for him to put it all together.

"Tell me why you are not as terrified as you should be, Karri?"

The other vampires moved in on us slowly. Once I was sure they were all in an area I could contain them, I laughed.

"This is funny? It is funny that a man raped you while you screamed, begging him to stop. While you screamed out for someone named RJ to come but he never did."

I snorted. "Just like a vampire to get some of the story only to invent the rest."

He stepped back fast, clearly realizing he didn't have quite the hold on me that he thought he did. "You will remain silent."

I shot power up and around the area, locking them in with me along with any sounds of a fight. "And you will remain here with me."

I felt him draw on the last of my memory of William. He hissed and backed away quickly. Pulling the ripped jacket off, I turned a bit and wagged my brows. "Oh, did you get to the part where I figured out what that rage inside was and what it was trying to do?"

"It cannot be. You are too young to be her."

"Yeah, I get that a lot." I pulled my knives from my arms sheaths and smiled. "Oh and about the rape thing. It was a little hard for William to rape me, being pinned to the ceiling by pitchforks and all." I laughed at the thought. It was sick but called for. Besides, I didn't regret it.

The vampire looked at his friends with wide, horrified eyes. "Go, go now!"

All of them scattered. I leaned against the building and waited for them to figure out what I already knew. They weren't going anywhere. One of them shrieked and shot a wave of power at me. Putting my hand up, I batted the invisible wave of it back at the vampire, sending him hurdling into the air. Another tried to use his power on me too and I did the same thing. "Well, boys, we can continue our game of volley power or we can jump to the part where I kill you. You decide. Keep in mind that I'm meeting a friend for coffee in a few hours and I'll need time to pretty up."

They all rushed at me, doing partial shifts as they came. I giggled slightly and nodded my head. "Morons. It must be a male thing."

I sheathed my knives and ran at the charging group. That seemed to shock them. I thought it was funny. A second before we where to collide, I sprung high into the air, twisted as I went over their heads, yanked the button legs of my pants open, grabbed my P226's from my thigh holsters and fired at the line of them as they ran in the other direction. Each shot was a direct back of the head hit. A ball of dust erupted in place of where each vampire used to be.

As I landed, I sensed one behind me. Turning fast, I brought the gun up and pressed it to his forehead. He snarled. I pulled the trigger. I shook my head as dust went fell all over me. "Mmm, breathing in dead guys is the highlight of my job," I said, sarcastically.

"Combine powers, quickly, the Dark Angel cannot fight us all at one time. She works to separate us," the blond vamp yelled.

Why the idiots believed the rumors they'd heard about me was beyond me. Knowing that in a minute they would hit me with a huge shared wave of power and that I'd be knocked backwards, I holstered my handguns.

I felt it coming, the huge rush of evil energy. Bracing myself, I waited. It slammed into me, throwing me into the air. Every inch of my body burned from the pressure. The second I struck the side of the building, pain shot through every limb. I hit the ground hard and fast.

Something moved over me. It didn't seem evil nor did seem to really be there. Opening my eyes, I blinked but saw nothing. I still felt it though. As a hand touched my cheek, my eyes widened as I stared at nothing but air. "Tripp?"

The nothingness caressed my cheek before lifting my arm as if it were checking me for signs of injury. It didn't feel like Tripp. "Who and what are you?"

It didn't answer.

"See she cannot fight us all," the vampire yelled.

"Men." I raised my hand and let my magik out. I tried to stand but the nothingness pinned me down. I pushed up hard, the nothingness that held me eased but didn't stop touching me. I got to my feet quickly. "Thanks. Though, I should say that the bad guys do that all the time." I smiled at thin air. "Neat, are you the ghost from my house? How cool would that be? I'm working on a new name for you. I'll admit the other doesn't suit you. Oh, and if you interfere again, odds are, I'll be joining you on the whole ghost side."

I looked at the row of vampires suspended in various positions by my magik and glared at them. "That does not kill me, idiots. Who the hell started that rumor? All that does is piss me off. And when I'm pissed," I drew my handguns, fired into all but the blond one's hearts, "I am not a nice woman to deal with."

The blond one stood frozen in place, glaring at me. Something smoothed over my tattoo and pressed lightly on my brand mark. My entire body warmed instantly. My breath hitched as I looked over my shoulder but found nothing. Stunned, I dropped my magik on accident.

Instantly, my body was ripped backwards. Evil power had hold of my hair and neck, yanking me straight towards the vampire. I fought hard to turn with no luck. The second the vamp actually got his hands on me, he laughed, pressing his mouth to my ear. "The dark angel so many fear is nothing but a child. A gifted, foolish, traumatized child. One who I will enjoy showing exactly how William should have ended things."

His dagger-like fingers nails raked over the side of my neck. Warm blood ran down. He took a deep breath in. "She is nothing but a shell of bad memories that haunt her every waking moment. She is..."

"Sick of hearing your voice." Throwing my head back, I struck his face hard. He released his hold on my neck, giving me the edge I needed. Dropping down fast, I spun and swept his legs out from under him. He flipped into the air and defied gravity.

"You are nothing. In our world you are a legend, a myth to be feared. A monster even bigger than we are." He laughed. "You are nothing but a devil's whore. A zealot's whipping post. Without your weapons you are but a gifted Fay."

"Hey, asshole. I'm missing the equipment to play mine's bigger so stop trying to get me to toss my weapons. Pissing matches aren't really my thing. Oh, and I'm no Fay."

"I can smell your fear, your terror each time I merely say William's name, Karri." The vampire licked his fangs. "Karri-Lynn."

I froze as he mimicked William's voice perfectly.

The vampire seized the opportunity to keep going, using William's voice as he went. "Get up! Stop cryin', girl! Madge, stay out of this. It's between the demon and I. You're the one who let the devil bring this...this...monster into our lives." The vampire stared at me. "You didn't need a baby that bad that you had to open us up to evil. Just look at her. Years and years of tryin' to rid her of her demons ain't done a damn thing. Oh, Lucifer knew what he was doin' with this one--makin' her so she would tempt any man. Take a good God fairin' man and give him thoughts he need not be havin'. Thoughts of lewd, sinful acts. Things only the devil and his whore would dare do."

I tried to move but couldn't. It had been over ten years since I'd heard that voice and the vampire was right--it still terrified me.

"Shut your mouth, Madge. She don't need no doctor. She needs to beg for forgiveness from the Lord." The vampire dropped and stood before me. He slashed out. Pain radiated throughout my cheek. I knew it was an illusion but that didn't stop me from touching it. "Ain't you the lucky little demon? I was aimin' for those eyes. They're always watchin' me, lookin' at me like I'm the evil one. I know what goes on in your head. You think of ways to kill me. You still hope someone will come. Someone will take you back to hell."

The vampire ran his magik over me. Instantly, I was covered in lacerations, burn marks and bite marks. Barely any skin was left untouched. I knew it was an illusion to make me remember exactly what William did. It didn't stop the pain of the actual ordeal from sneaking up on me.

The vampire continued on, goading me. "You're thinkin' of him now ain't you, temptress? Hoping he'll show up and fix it all, take you back among the other demon waste that seem to huddle together. You have ideas that he might forgive you for what you did--lettin' your father die while you just sat there cryin' your lil' eyes out. He hates you. He won't come. He won't listen to your cries anymore. No, not unless you promise to give him what he wants. Tell me the truth, you thinkin' about him?"

Another laceration appeared on my upper arm, this one showed bone.

"What do you mean who? Don't pretend you don't know who I'm talkin' about. No man does all that for a child that ain't his. What have you been doin' for him all these years? Huh? Are you throwin' those legs around him, lettin' him drive himself in until you're full of his evil seed? Are you?"

I felt something pressing in close around me. It helped to shield me from the awful memories. "It's not real, honey. It's just an illusion. A vampire's trick. He's feeding off the memories that the dark shadows found. Fight him. You're stronger than this. I'm here with you, honey. I'm not going anywhere."

My breath caught as I tried to figure out if the wind had just carried what sounded like Riston's voice to me or if I was officially crazy.

"What's this, Karri-Lynn? Do you have the help of someone close by? Maybe you'll get lucky and your protector, your mate will show and finally do his job." The vampire leaned into me, his voice instantly going to William's again as he held an iron brander with the mark looking like a devil's head with horns burning and sizzling. "Now, girl, he'll know his whore when he sees her and he'll know she was taught a lesson she'll never forget. Hold still, this will only take a minute. Then we can get to what you know you want, me in you."

The darkness I carried within me surged forward. My eyes burned for a second as they always did when they filled to black. Reaching out fast, I seized hold of the vampire's throat and lifted him off the ground. I'm not sure who was more shocked me or him.

Shaking my head, I thrust his illusion off my body, once again back to myself. "You want to pretend to be William? Then I will pretend you are. Trust me when I say even after all he put me through, in the end justice was served."

I let my power loose and watched as the vampire was ripped from my grasp by it. It pulled him into the air and locked him in spot. He screamed out as the first bit of flesh was ripped from his body. I smiled and waved.

"This is so much more fun now that I'm not eighteen and scared to death. I kept begging myself to stop. But I didn't know how. I didn't understand what was happening. I terrified myself. I really believed the bullshit he fed me, that I was an evil demon. Now, I not only know that he hit the nail on the head, I don't care. See, I'm not begging for anything or anyone now and I am well aware of how to stop it. Now," I waved my hand through the air dramatically, "let the fun begin."

The vampire's skin continued to peel, piece after agonizing piece. He screamed, begging for mercy. I showed him none. Smiling, I winked at him. "We here at Karri-Lynn Memory Land would like to remind you to keep your hands and arms inside the magik zone at all times. We cannot be held responsible for any lost or damaged vampires." I thrust power out, whipping him madly around in the air, peeling faster, digging into muscle, bone all of him. "Oh, and be sure to come again. But wait, you won't be able to because you'll be dead."

Ashes fell from the air and I knew the vampire was long gone but I couldn't seem to get my power to return to me. It wanted more. It wanted justice. It wanted blood, death, destruction. Tears flowed down my cheeks as I closed my eyes, caught in the struggle between light and dark that waged within me. The harder I tried to pull it back the less it listened to my command.

"No," I bit out. "Not today. I won't give in..."

My power whipped around me, lifting my hair and bringing thoughts of evil to my head. I covered my ears, hoping to ignore the voices that now whispered to me, encouraging me to go on a killing rampage.

"Kill him. Your mate is so close. Find him," they chanted, filling the air around me. "Show him what you have become. Rip his still beating heart from his chest."

"No," I pushed out as I fought to keep my inner demons inner.

They pushed back just as hard. "Hunt him. Kill him. Force him to choose between killing you or dying. Force him."

The voices were nothing like mine, and it hit me then. It was evil's attempt at trying to get me to give in. They wanted me to the point that I was theirs or no one's. I stood tall, letting the wind whip past me and the demons press in on my mind. I laughed and shook my head. "Come on, show yourselves! Stop hiding and pretending to be my inner thoughts, because I do not want RJ to have to make that choice. That would mean I'd have to face him and let him see what I've become. I'm too ashamed of myself to do that so try another fucking one, assholes."

Black shadows rushed at me from every angle whispering, "He knew. He knew all about William and wanted the human to kill you after he was done teaching you a lesson. He never looked back. Give in. Kill him."

"No."

The evil ripped me up into the air and slammed me into the brick wall. Still, I remained strong. "I won't let myself hurt him. I won't let you take me to that point." Reaching out, I gathered what power I was still in control of and shouted out, "Knife!"

One of my knives began to move all on its own, shaking on the cement. It lifted high into the air and came barreling at me full force. Pushing to my feet, I shook slightly, my body riddled with pain and waited for the end to come. I took a deep breath in and tipped my head back. Something slammed into me and it wasn't the knife.

Suddenly, if felt as though strong arms were wrapping around me. My breath grew short as an intense heat washed over me, drawing my energy back to me. It ran through me hard, leaving me crying out in agony. The arm-like feeling brought me up and off the ground a second before darkness washed over me.

Chapter Eight

After adjusting the baseball cap on my head, I pulled on the ponytail that hung from the back of it. I glanced down at my cut-off, orange T-shirt and loose thin cotton grey exercise pants. I walked towards the kitchen and smiled wide as I found Amber there.

"Mmm, I knew I smelled coffee."

She gave me a nervous look. "You okay this morning?"

"I actually feel amazing." It was the truth. I hadn't felt this good since I was a child. "I haven't a clue how I got home or how my bed got put together and I don't care. I can't believe I slept in this late. I never sleep in."

"Pfft, correction. You never sleep," Amber said, wryly. "Also, you slept for two days, sweets. It scared the hell out of me but Riston assured me you were fine."

"Two days?" I asked, positive I'd heard her wrong.

She nodded. "Two days, sleeping beauty. I checked on you all the time and you were dead to the world. I have to say, it was hard to get past Riston. He watched over you like a hawk, Karri. He even helped me get you cleaned up. He brought you to my house and I gave you a bath." She smiled wide. "Though, I'll tell you now that he had to lift you but I tossed a towel over the front of you even though I know you and know that you wouldn't have cared if he saw you naked or not"

Dead to the world? Riston watched over me? Tossed a towel over me? For me to sleep for two straight days I had to have expelled a hell of a lot of power and energy. If that was the case, I was damn lucky I wasn't dead. "How did I get home?"

She shrugged. "All I know is that Riston showed up with you in his arms and from there, he's done nothing but watch over you. I think the boy has it bad for you, Karri. Correct me if I'm wrong but I think you have it equally as bad as him."

"If you give me some of your famous coffee you can say whatever you want about me."

Amber gave me a cautious look at she poured me a cup of coffee. "You need to eat."

"Yeah. I need to go grocery shopping first. If I beg will you come with me? You get everything I need. When I go alone I get half, forget the rest and end up mad and throwing things away."

She winked and opened the refrigerator. "I already handled that. Now," she tossed me a banana and winked, "eat."

I was starving so I didn't argue. Instead, I began to peel the banana.

Amber seemed pleased with herself. "Karri, I worried about how you would survive without me cooking for you. I can't believe that I had to show you how to make a peanut butter and jelly sandwich."

I took the cup of coffee from her and smiled, my mouth full of banana. "Hey, my 'guardians' taught me to dance with live snakes. Not cook."

Her green eyes widened.

"Lighten up, Amber." I put the banana in my mouth and wagged my brows, holding it there with my lips.

As I went to take a sip, the door to my left opened fast. I hadn't sensed anyone else in the house. I drew in a sharp breath and dropped my coffee. A large hand shot out in front of me and caught it, never once spilling a drop. I visually traced my way up the arm, following every curve, bulge and tawny inch of glory. The second I found myself staring into a pair of crisp blue eyes I backed up so fast I cracked the back of my head on the kitchen doorframe. "Ouch, okay, hitting the one has already begun," I mumbled with the banana still in my mouth. I pulled it out fast.

Riston stared at me intently, seeming to soak me in with his hot gaze. He arched a brow. "Glad to see you're up and about." He glanced at the coffee in his hand. "Drop something?"

I couldn't seem to get my mouth to do anything other than hang open as I stared at him. I actually considered putting the banana back in it just to act as a filler. If Amber's theory was true then Riston was the man I'd waited all my life for. He couldn't be. Could he?

No. He can't possibly be RJ. He'd have said something. Right?

After giving it some thought, I realized how ridiculous I was being. PJ was not Riston's sister.

"Karri?" he asked, giving me a smug smile.

I nodded. "Umm, why were you in the basement?"

"I fixed your hot water tank."

"You did?"

He laughed softly and took a step towards me with my coffee in hand. "I also hooked up your washer and dryer. I hope that's okay."

"Wait, are you telling me that I'll now have the ability to have a hot shower and clean clothes?"

"Yep."

I arched my brows and smiled. "You're making me wet here, buddy."

"Karri!" Amber shouted.

"What?" I thought about what I'd said and laughed harder. "Opps, fell out. Sorry, RJ…err…umm, Riston." I stared at him, waiting for him to yell at me or show some sign of being upset that I'd slipped up on his name.

He just smiled. "Dare I tell you that I hooked your stereo system up?"

My eyes widened as I tossed my arms out and around his neck, still holding the banana in one hand. I kissed his cheek and squeezed him tight. "I think I love you." The second I said it, Amber dropped a dish. I released my hold on Riston and I backed up fast hitting her. "Shit, sorry. Are you okay?"

She looked at me with wide eyes. "Oh, great and you?"

"Great."

Riston chuckled and we both looked at him. "I'll stop laughing if someone gets me some coffee too."

Amber actually raised her hand. "I'll do it. Umm," she leaned in close to me and whispered, "your cell phone rang while he was in the basement. The guy said his name was Jason and that he's your husband. When in the hell did you get married?"

I walked cautiously past Riston, as though he'd bite and unplugged my cell phone from the wall. "Amber, where did you put my PDA?"

"It's in the drawer," she said, sharply.

I rolled my eyes. "You can stop now. I'd have called to let you know I'd gotten married. Geesh. I'm a lot of things. But come on."

She turned around and glared at me. "I took the message right, Karri. He asked for Hope and when I said you were indisposed, my standard response, he asked that I tell you that your husband Jason called."

"Amber, he's one of my men."

Her eyes grew even larger. "One? How the hell many husbands do you have?"

"At present count forty-two. I also have thirty-one fiancés, twelve brothers, countless lovers and about six cousins."

"What?" she asked looking as though she was going to strangle me.

Unable to help myself, I laughed as I reached over and took my coffee from Riston's hand. As my fingers skimmed over his, heat flared through them. I kept my gaze on Amber enjoying the look on her face too much to stop teasing her.

"I lost count of kids. That's why I needed my PDA." I wiggled it as I searched for Jason's name.

Amber charged at me. I moved to the side and hit a solid warm wall. Leaning into it, I laughed more. She looked like she was about to spit fire. "Karri, what in the hell happened to you?"

"Well, you left and there was no one to invent new theme parties with. Jean-Paul sucks, pun intended, at being social with anyone so I went into that call girl business you always accused me of belonging to." I backed up more into the mass of muscle. "Thankfully, only half my men are into role playing."

She smacked me in the arm. "You…you…oh, you."

I took a sip of my coffee and was vaguely aware of an arm around my waist as I smiled at Amber. "Amber, say that you're married. Your husband has been out of the country for months on business, leaving you with," I peaked at the PDA, "three children. What's the one thing you'd want him to do?"

Tipping her head, she gave me a dirty look. "I don't know. Come home I guess."

I took another bite of banana as I laughed. "So, say you're an operative. You're up a creek without a paddle, knowing the enemy is watching and listening to everything you say and do. You also know you need to get out fast. You call someone you trust. Someone the enemy would never suspect would one, know you're into that life style and two ever know enough about it to help you. Who do you call and what do you say?"

She shook her head. "I don't know."

"I'd call a female operative. If she answered, I'd tell her that I missed her and couldn't wait to see her again. If someone else answered her phone, I'd leave my name and the fact that I'm her husband. Because she'd then know…" Riston stopped short of completing his statement.

I handed my banana to Amber who gave me a stern look. "You took three bites. Eat more." She shoved it at me fast, practically cramming it down my throat. I let my throat relax and took it all the way in. Her eyes widened. "Only you would deep-throat a banana."

I laughed, pulled it out and threw it at the trashcan. It hit the lid and fell straight in. I snorted. "And Branson had the nerve to say I throw like a girl. Mmm, now back to Jason. Riston is right."

Reaching up behind me, I cupped the side of Riston's neck, caressed it gently and nodded at Amber. "Leaving that message would let her know that he needed to come home and soon."

"Oh," Amber said.

"I need to get him out of there. Phone."

Amber tossed it at me. I caught it and handed her my coffee.

I pushed twenty-four on it. It rang twice before a man picked up. "It's Karri-Lynn. I need to get an extraction unit to Jason within the day."

"Will do," the man on the other end said. "I can have it there by eight."

"Thanks." I ended the call and scrolled down to the number Jason had called from. I hit send. It rang four times.

"Hello?"

"Jason, honey is that you, I think my connection is bad. I hate our cell phone service. You should have gone with the one I told you to."

Jason sighed, clearly happy to hear it was me. "Yes, Hope, it's me, hon. I'll change the service the minute I get home. I miss you."

"I miss you too." I held the PDA up and read the names of our supposed children. "Little Jason is so excited he made the soccer team. Oh, and Christopher finally slept through the night."

"Mmm, good you got some sleep then?"

I rocked against the warmness that held me close. "I did get some sleep. Couldn't you tell? I only yelled a little about the phone service." I pulled the phone away, covered it and stared at Amber before pinching her arm fast.

"Oww!"

Smiling, I brought the phone back to my ear. "Hon, Fern just scrapped her knee."

Jason let out a soft cough. "I'm sure she's fine."

"I know she's fine but she has a dance recital at eight tonight and I can hardly take her looking like she got hit by a bus."

"It'll be fine," he answered.

"Well, I'm so happy that you don't see a problem with this. You're how many miles away while I'm here. The idea of taking her up there, you know what…forget it. I need to go. I'll call you back when I drop everyone off at school."

"I love you," he said, softly.

"Ditto, hon. Ditto."

I shut the phone and handed it to Amber. She looked extremely confused. "What did that mean? You never once told him that you found a way out for him."

Riston chuckled. "Amber, she picked an argument about the

phone service because I'm guessing she's not one hundred percent sure Jason would be the one to pick up."

"Yep." I traced circles on the large arm holding me.

"He answers back that it's him and seals it with a promise to change the service as soon as he gets home. See, he wants to come home. Following?"

Amber nodded.

"Great, the by referring to a little Jason making the soccer team, Karri was telling him that she had gotten the ball rolling on his extraction. When she mentioned the sleeping through the night, he knew that it would take place tonight. The part about the recital and the knee told him when and where."

"How did it tell him where?" Amber asked, her brows drawn in.

He snickered. "Did you catch the mention of Fern looking like she'd been hit by a bus?"

"Yes. Oh, he needs to get to the nearest bus station at eight."

"Right," Riston answered softly.

Amber put her hand up and motioned with the phone to me. "So, why did you say ditto? See I wasn't close enough to hear Jason's side too."

"I said ditto because he said I love you--or translated is thank you."

She grinned. "What? Is ditto, you're welcome?"

"No. Ditto is my way of avoiding saying I love you back without saying it."

She shrugged. "What's the big deal with just saying it? It's all an act."

I let out a soft laugh. "Yeah, it is one big, dangerous production. I have so many supposed relationships that I need a PDA to keep them straight. It's impersonal even when I'm standing with them playing the role in real life. It's removed. A lot of these men have wives and children at home waiting for me to return them in one piece. And I'm not looking to fuck anyone. Most of them don't register on my radar as anything other than as a co-worker."

"Most?" Riston asked.

I ignored him. Talking about Tripp wasn't something I wanted to do.

Amber snorted. "It's three words, Karri."

"I know. If I love you, I tell you. If it's business you get any other form. I have given this cause, these men so much of me. I'm allowed to hold a little bit back. It's also hard not to remember my dad doing all this. My mom was his world and he was hers. Should he ever have had to call for help similar to what I offer, I'd have wanted to know he kept it all business and saved himself and his heart for mom."

"He did," Riston whispered in my ear.

Confused, I glanced back him. Realizing how close he was to me, I went to pull away. He held me in place. "Karri, I'm not working today unless something dire comes up. Would you like to spend the day together? I know you have a lot do here so we can work on that if you want?"

I looked at Amber, my eyes wide and my heart thumping a mile a minute. Normally, I was Jenny on the spot when it came to polite turn downs. Nothing came to me. It hit me then that I actually wanted to spend the day with him.

A shit-ass grin spread over Amber's face. "I should probably go down to the coffee shop and check on things. I'm sure Wendy has everything covered but it's good to stay on top of things." She locked eyes with me. "I'll be sure to take Hilary with me. I'd hate for the two of you to have any interruptions."

Groaning, I patted Riston's arm. "I smell a fix up."

"Me too," he said, his warm breath skating over my neck, making my entire body stiffen. "I don't know if I could stand to see Amber upset. She does so much to help my niece and brother-in-law out that I feel like I owe her."

I tossed my hands up and made a T. "Time out. I get a day out of you because you feel obligated?"

"No," he laughed, "you get it because I asked and you don't want to turn me down."

"Oh, I don't, huh?" I shook my head and smiled. "Mmm, I'll tell you what. I have to get a bit of real work done today and I think its going to take up a huge chunk of the day."

Riston rocked our bodies slightly. "I'll help. That'll still count as time together. I think you'll find that I can stay out of the way, almost like I was *invisible*, but be there the instant you need me."

There were so many ways I could read into his statement that I didn't even bother trying. "Here's the deal. I am one hundred percent sure that vampires, lycans and demons are not only real but everywhere. I sensed power in Hilary so I get that you aren't an average guy, but I don't need another guy hanging around me telling me I'm crazy." I pointed at Amber. "I have her for that. I don't want to spend time pretending that anything I am willing to offer extends beyond a bedroom, backseat, shower, broom closest, confessional booth..."

"Karri! You're going straight to hell," Amber said, laughing.

"Thanks." I glanced back at Riston. "If you'd like to meet up around six or so I'd be more than willing to fuck you but I have to leave by ten. I have a previous engagement and cannot cancel it. It's work related. As for my day, unless you can help me out with the paranormal para-military team I'm looking for then I'll have to put you in for six."

"Did you just tell him that you'd fuck him at six?" Amber asked, sounding excited. Since she was never pleased with me when it came to men, I looked at her.

"See, I did the spiel that makes all men run and you go ape-shit. Why is he still here and why are you smiling?"

"My guess is that he's happy he's getting some at six." Amber winked. "I'm smiling because I couldn't agree more with your decision. Doing Riston at six is just what you need."

Riston cleared his throat. "Can I say something?"

"No."

"Of course," Amber interjected. "Ignore her."

"I don't want to be penciled in at six, Karri. I'm not going to lie and tell you that I haven't thought about it *a lot* but I want to spend time with you." He lifted my chin to face him. His blue eyes locked on me. "Can you understand that I'd like to get to know you just as much as I'd like to get to know *you*."

Amber sighed. "Oh, he's good. If you don't want him. I'll…uhh…I tried to say take him, but sorry Riston, that just creeps me out."

"But blondes with green eyes, boyishly handsome faces and daughters do it for you."

"Right," Amber said fast. "Oh, I mean no. No. I'm a fan of bald men. Yeah. Who look old, very old. No kids."

"Yeah, right." I looked at Riston and touched his face gently. "Spending a day with me is like joining the circus. Go play with nice, safe girls, who don't attract chaos."

Thinking of men in peril, my mind went to the operatives. "Hey, Amber. Can you think of a group of beefy men that pal around together more than most do? They'll live close to one another. No more than a couple of blocks. Should one be outside of that immediate area, he'll have a fast sports car of some sorts, possibly a liking for the ladies and be your quintessential bad boy. He'll be the one who butts heads most with the guy in charge."

She looked as though she were thinking about it. She grinned. "All I can think of is Riston and his buddies."

I shook my head. "Uhh, okay. I can see this isn't working. The alpha or team leader will not only be big but naturally ooze something that makes others want to seriously consider taking his advice. He'll have someone he trusts beyond a shadow of a doubt as his right-hand man. Doesn't have to be family but most often is. The rest of the mix will vary. One thing will be clear. Everyone who knows them will understand that one doesn't come without the others. They'll also be all about protecting each other's friends and family. If one suffers they all suffer." I tipped my head. "I'd kill for an apple right now. The banana didn't do it for me. Anyone else hungry?"

"Does she change topics like this all the time?" Riston asked.

Amber nodded. "You have no idea."

"I'm out of ideas. If I find them then my big day of work is chopped in half, allowing me to move Riston up to around three." I laughed and poked his abs gently. They didn't move. "Geesh, is all of you that hard? Wait, I already know the answer to that. It's a great *big* yes."

His eyes widened as a huge smile splayed over his face. "Amber's right, you have no stopping point. It's great."

"Really?"

"Mmmhmm."

I grinned and ran my hand over his. "Whew, glad you passed all that. I really wanted you to spend the day with you and would have hated to kick you out."

His jaw dropped. "That was a test?"

"Yeah. Karri doesn't bother dealing with assholes if she can help it. Had you seized the six o'clock offer, you too could have ended up kicked in the head," Amber said, snickering. "I've seen it happen many a times. It's never pretty."

Riston exhaled deeply. "Damn, I am a happy man right now."

"Why is that?"

Running his hand through the ponytail coming out of the back of my cap, he stared down at me with an expression I didn't recognize. "For a minute I thought you offered every guy a time to be with you every time you..." He looked away.

Cupping his face, I brought his attention back to me. "No, Riston. Contrary to popular belief I'm picky and not so fun and fancy-free when it comes to certain things. And if you dare ask me how many men I've given the test to and that have passed I'm going to say two. I agree. I think that's all you can handle."

Amber snorted and I buried my head in Riston's chest laughing.

As I peeked out at her, I found her smiling so wide that I thought her face might break. "Tell him what PJ told you about the temple. The bathing in the shrine's pools thing was the best part. Oh, umm, anyway." Amber stood straight and glanced at Riston nervously. "So, Karri, why can't you find these guys? You seem to know everything about other ones."

"Because the cord between the powers and the unit here was severed. I don't know which side did it. But somehow, they started to fall off the radar slowly about thirty-five years ago. I can only find bits and pieces about them. And when I try to concentrate on them I get a migraine. I can't explain it. I think my head would rather not lend a hand in this one."

Waving my hand out, the counter tops filled with boxes of files, several laptops and all of the necessary equipment that would have me up and running."

The second I did it, I froze. "Oh shit, Riston I told you that I could..."

"Shh," he took the cap off my head, letting my hair flow free and smiled softly, "It's fine."

My heart beat wildly in my chest as I stared up at him. I couldn't help but touch his temples, lift his glasses and smooth the line on the bridge of his nose. I knew then that he had the power to hurt me. He was a man I could fall for and that was bad considering I had only one mate. Closing my eyes, I took in his manly scent and sighed.

Amber gasped, drawing me out of my Riston induced stupor. "Cool. Did you only have to click your fingers to get the information too?"

I whipped my head around and stared at her with wide eyes. "No!"

She took a step back.

"I have hunted in the worst areas to find leads on them. The powers seemed to have conveniently lost what they had. I'm beginning to think they put it into the wrong hands on purpose. I have tracked operatives that were strays so to speak to figure out if they were this team. I thought I'd found two of them. One, I'm still unsure about. But the other was not a member of the unit here."

Amber began leafing through files. "Christ, you have all of their specs. Hey, the powers keep notes on likes and dislikes?"

I laughed. "No. That's just something I used to see dad and RJ do."

Riston tightened his hold on me. I twisted in his arms and faced Amber.

"Your dad and RJ let you learn how to do this stuff? My God." She cast a nasty look towards Riston. "Don't you agree Riston James Wallace?"

I smiled. "Your middle name is James?"

Riston nodded as he kept his eyes on Amber. A knowing smile passed between them and Amber squealed, startling me. As she began to jump up and down I reached out, worried that she'd over do it. It was childish but for Amber, it seemed appropriate at the moment. Besides, who was I to question her maturity when I played dress up on a regular basis, in my front yard no less. Sanity wasn't my strong suit. No news flash there.

"Amber?"

"I knew it!" she cried out, shaking her hips and doing an odd little dance combo. "I knew it." She stopped and gave a warning look. "Oh, you've got a date with an ass kickin' from me. But for now, I'm going to keep having Karri moments."

"Huh?"

She grabbed me and began to dance around to no music. "It's a themed party moment if I ever felt one, Karri. Quick, snap your fingers. It's time to celebrate."

"Celebrate what? Have you finally lost it?"

Riston laughed. I looked at him for guidance. He provided none. "No clue."

Amber snorted. "Yeah, right." She looked at me and seemed to get hold of herself. "So, where were we? Oh, right. Your dad and RJ teaching you military stuff."

"No," I said fast. "Dad and RJ never taught me any of this. At least not one on one. I would work my way slowly to the edge of the door while playing with some toy or another. I just liked to listen to them and pretend I could help. Keep in mind, I was most likely dressed like a bumble bee or something. But, hey, I was going to help my daddy, damnit."

"They never noticed?" Amber asked, staring at Riston.

I snorted. "Oh, they noticed. At least RJ did. Half the time I'd fall asleep because they'd be up until the wee hours of the night. My mom never once interfered. She stayed far away from their discussions. It made her sick to her stomach to know that dad put his life on the line everyday with the world's most deadly creatures. Owen tells me that I got the eccentric behavior from her but the rest of me is my dad through and through. He said that my mother wasn't capable of killing anything--that she came from a long line of straight light angels and that she physically couldn't harm anything, not unless it was dire. He also said that was a good thing, that dad's darkness, his lycan and dark angel blood was so powerful that if they hadn't found each other he'd have been on the end of RJ's gun."

I laughed. "He was right. My mom wouldn't even kill spiders. She'd put a jar over them and leave them for my dad to dispose of. In fact, I know first hand that she won't, umm, wouldn't defend herself even demons drop out of the sky right in front of her."

"Kars," Riston whispered, holding me tight to him. "Don't blame her for something she couldn't control."

"Don't lecture me like a child, Riston. Those years are done. Remember that." Surprised that I snapped at him like that, I ran my hand over the top of his and snuggled back against his warmth. "Sorry."

He put his chin on my shoulder and rocked our bodies lightly. Amber smiled wide as I just gave into the safe feeling he gave me.

"Karri, you can do all of this, yet you can't find RJ?" Amber glanced over my shoulder at Riston.

"No. And I don't do this to him," I said, motioning to all the research. "RJ's life isn't on the line. At least I don't think it is. He could be dead. I really don't know. Hell, he's probably playing golf in his checker pants with the rest of his country club buddies. I know a few men who opted to grow old. He might be one of them. If he did then I'm betting on the ugly pants thing. He had this horrible brown shirt that he wore a lot. He'd defiantly have ugly pants as an old man. What do men that age do anyway?"

Amber laughed hard as she stared at Riston. "I don't know. Any guess, Riston?"

"Checkered pants?" he asked, sounding shocked. "Ugly brown shirt?"

Covering her mouth for a moment, Amber calmed her giggles down and took a deep breath in. "Hey, what if he didn't opt to grow old?"

I didn't respond. Instead, I waved my hand and a file appeared in it. I opened it and rubbed my eyes, knowing that I was fighting a losing battle with tears.

Amber touched my arm as her forehead creased. "What's wrong, Karri?"

"Nothing." I lied.

She stood there a moment before her blue eyes widened. "Oh gawd, it's because I asked what you would do if RJ didn't age."

I bit my lower lip, doing my best to keep it from trembling. "I don't want to talk about that."

"Why?" she asked, running her hand down my arm until she bumped into Riston's. "What if he was still young, still the way you remember him and..."

"And what, Amber?"

"Karri?"

I shook my head. "No, don't Karri me. Think about it, Amber. If he is then do you know what that means?"

She shook her head.

"It means that he didn't go off and grow old. It means that he dumped me with William and never looked back. That he had all the time in the world to check in on me but never did. It means that my father was right, RJ could sense when I needed him but ignored it. When I called out to him, when I need him most, when I was so scared of William that I couldn't control what was happening to me, he chose not to come."

"Kars, that's not..." Riston pulled me tight to him and I pushed his arms off me.

I needed air. I twisted away from him and took a deep breath. "I screamed his name but he didn't come. Even years later, he still didn't show. It's easy to think of some guy pushing sixty getting the shaft of having a twenty something year old mate and wanting nothing to do with her to the point he was willing to give up his gifts. It's a whole other story when you're talking about a man who will forever be locked in his thirties turning his back on me."

"Karri, stop. You don't mean that," Amber said.

"You were the one who said I should hate him. You said I live in a fairy tale with a romantic view on life. The veil can't withstand finding out he just didn't give a shit, Amber. Even my skin isn't that thick." I laughed. "I will understand if I find out that he really does blame me for what happened. Trust me, I, of all people, can understand hate. It makes people do funny things."

Amber shook her head slightly as a tear fell down her face. "Karri, this doesn't sound like you. You have the biggest heart and have never blamed any one for anything. Why now? Why Riston...umm, I mean RJ?"

"Because I sensed him hesitate, Amber." The minute I said it out loud it felt as though a huge weight had been lifted from me.

"Huh?"

I let out a soft laugh as I ran my hand through my hair, letting it spill over my shoulder in waves. "The day he took me to my guardians, I sensed him hesitate when he handed me over. I thought

I was talking to him. I thought I was telling him that Dad wanted his sister to take me but when I realized that my lips weren't moving and that his weren't either I couldn't think straight. I didn't understand then that it was possible for me to communicate with him by using my mind."

Amber sighed. "You were six and scared. You'd just seen your parents be slaughtered so I would think the *guy*," she put a lot of emphasis on that, "would take some time to explain things to you."

"Picture Jean-Paul trying to explain something to Hilary."

The sneer that Amber tossed in my direction told me that was a bad example. "Okay, picture Riston trying to deal with losing his best friends, having to take over a team of immortals that may or may not have been set up by the people they fight for and having an insta-kid. One that he knows or suspects is supposed to be his wife someday. What do you think he'd do?" I nudged him. "Sorry, you get to be the example since you're in the room."

Amber's jaw tightened as she leveled her blue gaze on him. "My guess is dump the kid off as far from him as he could get her and then be damned surprised when she showed up, a grown woman. One that he would no doubt think of as his idea of the perfect woman. Tall, long blonde hair, brown eyes, a body to die for and a sparkling personality."

Laughter erupted from me as I stood there. "Well, when you find her, send her my way. I'd like to kick her ass and bring her down with the rest of us."

"I'm also betting that he'd be sweating what would happen next. Would she accept him into her life, only to use him and discard him like she's done to so many others, would she blame him for everything that happened or would he be lucky enough to have her love him?"

"Done with the hypothetical, Dr. Amber? You're starting to freak me out."

"Maybe, so what would you do if you had RJ standing before you right this minute?" she asked, touching my chin lightly.

"Honestly, I'd just ask him where Jack and Victoria O'Higgins are buried and walk away."

"You wouldn't tell him who you are?"

Riston rubbed my arms lightly and I couldn't help but shiver. "No. I wouldn't."

"But you'd be giving up your chance at having a family."

I tapped Riston's hands and he let go of me. I glanced nervously over at Riston and then Amber. "Let's go out back and talk about this. I'd rather not have this discussion in front of..."

"Oh, he can just stand there and hear it all, damnit. I don't care what he thinks or how he feels," she snapped, taking me by surprise. "Don't you dare come to his rescue either. Riston is a big boy and I am positive that he will not think you're crazy, Karri."

"Still, its personal, Amber. He's seen and heard more about me in a few short days than anyone else I know. I'm not normally like this and I don't like the idea that I'm sharing so much with someone I know so little about."

Amber glanced at Riston. "Karri, tell me something about those lycans you're always talking about. Do they really have excellent hearing like you said?"

"Yes."

She took my arm and headed for the back porch. "Great, let's talk about it out back. Riston can just keep his ass right there."

"Umm, Riston? I didn't realize she would become scary, sorry about..."

"Don't you dare apologize to him, Karri O'Higgins." Amber ushered me out and onto the back porch. "Hear me out, Karri. PJ came. She answered your call for him."

"Are you doing drugs?"

"No, shut up and focus." She motioned in the air with her hand like it would clear every thing up for me. "I can only imagine what kind of shape you were in when you called out for help and I don't even want to think about what the scene must have looked like when William was trying to…yeah. What if PJ came to keep RJ from seeing all of it."

I stilled, thinking about what Amber was suggesting. "What? You think she thought he wouldn't know how to help?"

"No, I think the woman was smart enough to know that her brother would go crazy the minute he saw what he'd left you with and that there might be no bringing him back, Karri."

"Her brother?" The vampire had suggested that but I'd ignored him. What in the hell made Amber suggest it too? "Amber?"

"It makes sense, Karri. You told me that you were able to hide her pain from her family when she passed away. Wouldn't it hold true that she could feel your call and block your pain from him?"

"I guess." I thought more about what she was suggesting. As off the wall as it sounded, it was a very real possibility.

"You said it yourself, Karri. You said that RJ would have killed an endless line of demons if any of them tried to touch you. Do you think he'd have left you with something as hideous as William and not looked back?"

"Umm, do I point out the obvious that he did or do I shut-up and smile pretty here?"

"Did you call out for him before the night William finally lost what little hold on reality he had?"

I shook my head no. "I didn't want to be a burden."

"If PJ wouldn't have blocked you from getting in touch with him, saying she did, then he would have shown up and most likely done what, Karri? Killed everyone in sight? What do you think he'd have done if he had to stand there and see you like that?"

"I don't know, Amber."

"My work here is done. Go spend the day with Riston. We'll talk more later. I have a few things I need to take care of."

"Amber?"

She pointed at the door. "Go, spend time with Riston. Don't worry about work. The team you're looking for isn't going to get any more lost in a day. Take this one to yourself, Karri. Be yourself and have fun."

I watched her walk away before turning to head back into the kitchen. The minute I got in the door, Riston was on me, picking me up and pressing his mouth to mine. My breathing was choppy to say the least. He'd caught me so off guard that I was powerless to stop him, not that I would have. His tongue searched the crevasses of my mouth, leaving no place unexplored.

My entire body tightened in respond to his kiss. As my nipples hardened against his powerful chest I moaned, unable to resist him. He lifted me higher and I wrapped my long legs around his waist, leaving my heated core pressed to his erect cock. Something moved around us, some sort of power, a magik that wasn't mine but was extremely powerful. Since it didn't seem threatening, I ignored it.

Riston began walking towards the dining room, still holding me with our lips locked together. I pulled back a bit. "You're going to hurt yourself. Put me down."

"I can't. Not yet," he said, drawing my lower lip into his mouth just a bit.

"Why?"

He smiled as he kissed me quickly. "Because where I lay you down is where I'm taking you, Kars. I think it would be more comfortable for you if we used a bed and not the dining room floor."

"Mmm, that sounds very promising. What if I told you to put me down now?"

"I'm not kidding. I can't wait another minute to be in you. I know I said I wanted to spend time with you and I still do but I..."

"Have the overwhelming urge to fuck me until I can't walk?" I asked, smiling.

"Yes. How did you know?"

I kissed his jaw line and let out a soft laugh near his ear. "Because I've had the urge to do the same thing to you since the moment I came up from a flip in my front yard to find you standing there." Reaching down between us, I unbuttoned the top of his jeans and then went to work on getting his tee shirt off him. I was just about to pull it over his head but stopped. I grabbed his glasses and eased them off his face, then went back to pulling his shirt off.

I tossed it aside and focused on Riston. His broad, muscular shoulders drew my gaze in and forced it down his well-defined pecs. Continuing on my visual trace of him, I couldn't help but lick my lips as my gaze trickled over six-pack and fell upon a thick line of black curls that disappeared under his jeans. "Yep. You are most certainly not human. They don't come built like this."

"And how is it you know how human men are and are not built?" he asked, giving me a stern look.

Ignoring his question, I took his glasses and put them back onto his face. He went to open his mouth, no doubt to repeat his question and I pressed my finger to his lips. "Hold that thought." I took hold of my orange, ripped tee shirt and pulled it over my head.

Since I wasn't wearing a bra, Riston now had a full view of my bare breasts. His gaze went instantly to them. As his jaw dropped, I snickered. "I'm sorry, honey, what were you asking me?"

He didn't respond. Instead, he lifted me higher and captured one of my nipples in his moist mouth. He circled the erect pebble with his tongue and moaned as he walked quickly towards the staircase. Tipping my head back, I savored every second of the sensations that tore through me as he continued to climb the stairs while sucking gently on my nipple.

We made it almost all the way up before he switched breasts, taking that nipple into his mouth as well and moaning yet again. My hands went to his hair and I held tight as he brought me close to my zenith by only touching my breasts. He headed straight for my room, never bumping into anything even though I was blocking his view.

As he began to lay me down, I knew we'd finally made it to my bed. Riston set me down gently but didn't stay with me. Instead, he kissed his way down my torso, licked my belly button making me giggle and stopped when he reached the top of my light grey, loose-fitting exercise pants. He tugged on them and began to pull them down, exposing my shaved mound. The outfits I wore were too revealing to leave anything there and by the looks of it, Riston didn't mind in the least.

He kissed my *mons* and slid my pants off the rest of the way, quickly returning to the apex of my thighs. He parted my slit and licked my swollen bud, sending a shockwave of pleasure through me. I arched my back letting out a soft moan.

Riston moved down just a bit and inserted his tongue into my pussy while he began to tweak my clit with his fingers. I clawed at the sheets, needing anything I could find to ground myself with. My magik was pushing hard, trying to surface and I didn't want it to.

"Riston, please..."

He shook his head no with his tongue still in me. The movement made my inner thighs quiver and my magik beat wildly against my hold on it. I had never felt anything like it. "Gods, please. I can't hold in it. It hurts."

"Let it go then, Karri," he said, inserting his finger into my pussy and licking my clit. "Let it go."

"But, please, uh."

"Mmm, you taste so good. I'll never get tired of sampling you, Karri. Never." He added another finger and I squirmed. "So tight, honey. So sweet."

"Riston?" I fought to stay in control and knew I was losing the battle. The second Riston began to finger fuck me my pending orgasm hit. My legs acted of their own accord as they moved together, cupping the sides of his face. He chuckled into my pussy and lapped up my cream. When he didn't stop licking me, rubbing me, fingering me I pushed up hard, sliding my entire body up the bed and away from him.

"No more," I panted.

Riston moved up and over me faster than a human could and gave me a sexy smile. "Oh, Karri, we are only just beginning. That was just one small taste."

He stopped and unzipped his jeans. I tried to sit up and help him but he picked that moment to cover my mouth with his, letting me taste myself on his lips. It was his turn to moan as he kissed me wildly, moving around a bit as he worked his jeans off.

Riston settled his body between my legs and the second I felt the rounded head of his cock pressing against my pussy my eyes widened. There was no way he was going to fit in me. I tried to move out from under him but he picked that moment to insert into me, ever-so-slightly.

Crying out, I clutched onto the back of his arms and held on for dear life as he spread the lips of my channel wide. I was convinced that if I hadn't been wet from him going down on me and bringing me to peak, he'd have torn me open wide. He pushed in more and a tiny scream tore free from me.

He stopped. "Kari? Am I hurting you?"

I nodded as I fought for breath.

Suddenly, the magik I'd sensed downstairs was back, running through my body and settling in my groin. Riston's eyes widened. "Kars, you feel so fucking good to me that I didn't know I was causing you pain." He went to pull out and I seized hold of his arms.

"No, don't go. I just need a minute to adjust to you, big guy."

"Big guy?" he arched a brow and smiled. "Mmm, I could get used to hearing that."

Reaching up, I took hold of the back of his neck and pulled his mouth down to meet mine. His cock entered me even more and he tried to back away. I bit at his lower lip, hard enough to catch his attention. He made an animalistic sound before pushing his tongue into my mouth. The very act of kissing me left my pussy relaxing just enough to help him ease in and he did. As he continued to enter me, I wondered if he'd ever end. He hit my cervix, causing me to jump a bit. He moaned. "Karri."

Wrapping my legs around his waist, I helped him slide in the rest of the way. "I hope you're all the way in because you have run out of space in there, Riston."

He chuckled as he began to ease out of me slowly. "I'm a very happy man, let's leave it at that."

I held tight to him as he began to work himself in and out, slow at first, allowing my body time to adjust. As he covered my mouth with his again, he began to thrust, taking me faster in a more aggressive manner. I knew it was the alpha in him and if it didn't feel so good, I'd have thought to challenge him just to say I did.

"There, right there," I whispered, clinging to him.

"Karri." He bit his lower lip and looked away from me. "Maybe you shouldn't talk."

Smiling, I cupped his face, directing his attention and his gaze back to me. "You feel so good in me, Riston. Mmm, filling me completely." As his jaw went slack I tipped my head up bit, knowing the effect I had on him and loving it. "There, Riston, mmm, more."

Riston shifted a bit as he drilled me into the bed, leaving his lower abdomen caressing my swollen, ripe clit as he fucked me. I bucked beneath him, savoring the feel of having him filling me. Tiny bursts of pleasure radiated throughout me with each pass he made. I kissed at his jaw line, his neck, his ears, anything I could get to, panting softly as I went.

As I felt a pending orgasm fast approaching, I began countering Riston's moves with more aggression, speeding it along. My power picked that moment to tear free of my grasp. It hit the foreign power around us and instantly merged with it. Suddenly, everything seemed even more intense, more pleasurable than it already was--as if that were even possible. I knew then that the power was Riston's that I felt and I knew that it was familiar to me.

Riston arched his back at the same moment that my pussy clenched his cock tight and my orgasm hit me. He didn't move. I shook my head, not understanding the strange sensation in my pussy. It felt as though his cock was swelling deep within me, filling me with its expanding girth. "Riston?"

"I'm part lycan," he whispered, sounding incredibly strained.

Shocked but somehow not freaked out by his admission, I pressed my lips to his. "In that case, roll over."

I felt a hot wave of his cum fill me just as Riston's jaw dropped. "Karri, I can't pull out right now. I'll hurt you."

"RJ, I didn't ask you to pull out, I asked you to roll onto your back."

Something moved over his face as he stared down at me. Another jet of cum filled me as Riston rolled onto his back, taking me with him and leaving me straddling his waist as I lay on top of him. He suddenly felt even bigger in the new position. I gathered my wits about me and relaxed as another wave of his cum filled me. I began to sway my hips slightly, mixing tiny thumps in as I went. He growled and arched his back.

"Kars," he bit out. "What are you doing?"

"Does it hurt?" I asked, knowing it didn't by the rate at which his cock began spitting more and more seed into me.

He shook his head and clenched his teeth. "No. It feels so fucking good that I don't think the swelling will ever go down. You're so tight. I can't make it relax, baby."

I swiveled just a bit, making tiny half circles on his cock. It left my clit rubbing against his hard abdomen and me stimulating his cock. Another orgasm took hold of me, leaving me throwing my head back and doing, fast, short, jerky movements that made my pussy toy with his expanded shaft.

Small animalistic noises sounded from me as I rode him. Riston growled out and held tight to my hips, holding my body to him as if I'd even dream of going anywhere. "Kars, stop. Please."

More cum filled my womb as he remained locked in me, jetting again and again. I rode him with the tiny movements even more, savoring the feel of him and tweaking my clit as I went. Something big began to build in me. Gasping, I put my hands on Riston's chest to steady myself as I continued to ride him.

"Karri."

His cock picked then to fill me full of his hot, jetting cum. As a lycan, he could come again and again and I wanted all that he had. Dropping down, I began to rub my body against his, allowing my nipples to run over his hard chest while I continued to take his insanely thick cock deep into my pussy. I nipped playfully at his lips. When he closed his tight I drew back. "Riston?"

He shook his head and refused to meet my gaze. It hit me then. "You have the urge to bite me, don't you?"

When he closed his eyes slowly, I knew the answer to that was yes. I pulled my hair to one side and leaned down towards him, offering him my neck. "Open your eyes."

He did.

"Do it," I said, feeling the swelling in his cock easing a bit. I took the opportunity to begin moving up and down on him, fucking him with full motions while I offered him my neck. "Take it, Riston."

"No," he bit out without moving his lips. "I have to tell you something first. You have a right to know..."

My power surged, sending a jolting amount of magik through us both. It whipped us around, keeping our bodies locked together but putting Riston back on top. It was then that I understood--he was dominant and needed this, needed to be in control of it all.

Another power moved around us, this one came from him and moved through me as Riston brought his head down. I waited for him to bite me but felt only pleasure as he began thrusting into me again. Slowly, I started to notice the feel of tiny thread like pieces of power weaving back and forth between us.

"Riston, what's happening?"

He didn't answer. He kept his head buried in the crook of my neck as he slid in and out of me, pushing me closer and closer to culmination. I held tight to him, scared of what was happening but gaining too much pleasure from him to want to end it. The invisible cords seemed to wrap tighter around me, mystically attaching the two of us together. My head said fight it but my body wanted it more than life itself.

I began to feel light headed and tried hard to stay focused but the feel of him in me and the orgasm that was working its way over me left me a splendid stupor.

"Mine," Riston said hoarsely as he pulled back a bit. The moment I spotted blood on his lower lip, I knew that he'd used his power to take the pain away while he bit me. "Mine."

My stomach clenched tight. I fought to keep from crying out but gave in, letting what felt natural come to me. I yanked hard on him. "Riston."

Nodding, he lifted his hand, let one claw eject from the end of his fingertip and cut a line into his pec, leaving blood welling to the surface fast. Something primitive took over, making my breathing shoot off the charts and my body tingle everywhere.

Riston cupped the back of my head as he lowered his upper body down to me. I didn't hesitate. I did what felt natural--I ran my tongue over his wound and moaned as the copper taste of his blood filled my mouth. I swallowed, taking him into me, feeling the threads that were between us mystically pulling up together so tight that I thought we might never separate.

Swiping my tongue over his wound again, I stopped and sucked just a bit. Riston went into a frenzy, pushing and slamming into me, driving his cock so far into me that I couldn't even cry out. I drank him down while I accepted every inch of him into my body. Slamming down, he held firm, filling me with his seed yet again.

"Riston," I panted as I hit my zenith yet again. A sudden veil of fatigue seemed to drift over me and I fought to keep my eyes open but failed. "Riston…what's…?"

He continued to make love to me, leaving my orgasm lasting longer than it should. I felt his cock swelling once more and did my best to stay awake. He apparently had other ideas. "Sleep, Kars."

"RJ? What's…happening?"

He chucked lightly as his seed filled me. "It's okay. I promise. You're tired because I had to take a good deal of blood to complete the bonding, honey. You're a hell of a lot more powerful than I thought and it wouldn't have worked any other way." He kissed my lips gently. "I'm happy that you know it's me, Kars."

"Happy I know what? Bonding? Riston?"

He sighed. "It's me, Karri-Lynn. It's RJ."

"Riston?" I slipped further into a state of relaxation and felt my hand slide off his arm.

"I'm sorry, Kars. I am. I couldn't stop the natural urge to claim you because you're my mate. If I'd have known it was going to be that intense I would have told you everything. I wouldn't have taken you until you knew the truth, baby. I thought that the ritual of acceptance needed to be performed on you for mating to take place. I didn't..."

I couldn't help but giggle. "Now you sound like PJ."

Riston took a sharp breath in. "Karri, did my sister perform the ritual on you?"

"She painted me with symbols and chanted like a crazy tribal woman. Is that what you mean?"

It was Riston's turn to laugh. "Trust her to think of everything."

"She also said she performed the blessing twice." I thought about PJ grinning when she did it. "She told me that it would teach that two hundred-year-old pain in her ass a lesson." Giving in, I began to slip into a state of total abandonment. A tiny giggle erupted from me.

Riston held his position, continuing to fill me with his seed. "Ha, ha, but you won't be laughing if her blessing worked."

I gave off a very tired laugh.

"Kars, I can't pull out of you yet and have already filled you with more cum than your body could ever accept. If PJ's blessing worked, we'll be having twins, wife. You're mine, Karri, my mate, my wife now. And I will never let you go again."

* * * *

I blinked several times as I seriously considered waking up. Snuggling closer to Riston's warmth, I purred lightly as a shiver ran over me. He chuckled and the sound warmed my heart.

"Cold?" he asked, pulling the covers over me more.

"I wasn't until I realized how hot you are."

"Mmm, thanks." The cocky tone in his voice made me laugh.

I peeked out and found him staring at me. I groaned and shut my eyes again. "Okay, that's weird."

"What's weird?"

"Waking up with someone next to me." I ran my hand over his chiseled chest and traced small, lazy circles on it. He felt so good, so right and I couldn't get enough of him. "Do you think we should get up? We seem to be prone to late day naps."

"Wait, are you telling me that you've never woke up with someone else in the bed?"

"Once I had some sort of magikal mishap." I cleared my throat. "I, umm, sneezed and gave myself the chicken pox but they weren't like normal children get them. They were unique to say the least. Anyway, I fell asleep listening to someone reading a book to me and woke up with them still reading. Does that count?"

"Magikal mishap?" He laughed. "I like the soft spin on that. And no, that doesn't count."

"Then no, I haven't ever woken up with someone else in the bed with me." I snuggled closer to him, desperately seeking his warmth. "Not that you haven't already picked up from hearing every little detail of my life but I have issues with abandonment." I laughed and ran my finger down the center of his chest.

Riston hugged me tight and kissed my forehead. "I am so sorry, Kars. I swear to you that I will never leave you..."

"Whoa!" I put my hand up fast, covering his lips so he couldn't say anything else ridiculous. "I have equally as many issue with commitment. I have issues that have issues, buddy. No more of that talk or I won't bother to ask for your phone number. And why are you apologizing? It wasn't you who..." I stopped as I thought about what was said before I'd fallen asleep. It was foggy but there.

I'm RJ.

His words hit me hard, sucking the air from my lungs. There was no way that Riston was RJ. My imagination must have been on overdrive before I'd fallen asleep. I let out a small laugh as I shook my head. "I think Amber and everyone else might be right. I really might be crazy."

"Why is that?"

My gaze moved over Riston's tawny flesh and I couldn't fight the need to taste him. I planted a tiny kiss on his chest and propped myself up on my elbow so I could see him better. "How is it that you're tan all over?"

He chuckled. "What kind of question is that and how is it that you can bounce from one topic to another on the spur of the moment?"

"I don't know. It's a gift. Why?" I glanced down the length of him and stopped when I hit the portion where the white sheet had him covered.

Riston reached out and caressed my exposed nipple, causing it to harden instantly. "That's some gift. I'm almost afraid to ask what it is you're thinking about half the time."

"Right now," I looked up at him through hooded lashes, "I'm thinking about sliding down the length of you and sucking you off. I think it would be interesting to see how much of you I can fit in my mouth. Don't you?"

Riston lay there staring at me. If he hadn't blinked I'd have thought I'd given him a heart attack. Waving my hand in front of his face, I tried to gauge if he was alive or not. He blinked again. I took that as a good sign.

"Riston?"

He didn't respond.

The opportunity to completely knock his socks off seemed perfect so I went with it. I moved over him and my hair fell forward, cascading around the two of us, leaving me staring into his crisp blue eyes. I kissed his full lips chastely before sliding down and planting tiny kisses on his torso. I neared the thin line of dark curls that originated under is navel and ran my tongue through it.

He jerked. "Karri."

"Mmm, yes?"

Riston grabbed a fistful of sheets as I continued lower, licking, kissing and nibbling on his taunt abdomen. I moved down more, taking hold of his semi-hard cock and running my tongue up the side of it. For a split-second, I thought Riston might actually leap off the bed. I chuckled. "I take it that you like that."

A rather pained expression covered his face as he gave a slight nod. "A little, yeah."

"Just a little, huh?" I asked, easing my mouth over the head of his penis. With him not quite fully erect, I was able to not only get him in my mouth but slide almost all the way over him.

The feel of his pulsating shaft, twitching, growing in my mouth left me feeling wanton and free. I raked my nails lightly over his thighs causing him to jerk once more. I sucked on him then, drawing out his erection and fighting my own gag reflex as he hardened to full length. He hit the back of my throat and I stared up at him through hooded lashes to find his mouth open and his upper body straining.

The angle was familiar. Too familiar. Images of the man PJ had sent me to, the one who had been chained to the bed flooded my mind as I began to work my head up and down.

Riston slid one hand down and eased it in my hair, cupping the side of my head as he went. "That's it, baby. Yeah."

I wrapped my hands around the base of his cock and began to alternate twists with them. Pulling off just a bit, I allowed saliva to build in my mouth and pushed it over the tip of his dick. He moaned and stared down at me as though it were the most erotic image he'd ever seen. I only hoped that were true.

Taking him deep into my mouth once more, I moved my hands through the moisture running from my mouth and began to stroke him as I sucked. I added my teeth then, scraping them gently up the length of him, holding back my excitement as Riston moved his hand out of my hair fast just before claws broke free from it.

"Kars," he panted.

Humming softly, I arched a brow in question and found him flipping me fast. Before I even knew what was happening Riston had me on my hands and knees and was pressing his distended flesh into my wet core. He didn't wait for me to be ready. No. Riston drove himself to the hilt and hooked an arm around my waist as I tried to scurry away from him.

Gasping, I clung to the sheets as the balance between pleasure and pain was balanced perfectly when Riston reached down and began to rub my swollen clit. He pumped feverishly into me, each time filling me past the point of acceptance, reminding me of just how much of a man he truly was.

"That's it, Kars. Come for me. Come all over my fingers, baby. Soak 'em."

My body obeyed, instantly tightening as an orgasm seized hold of me. My hot channel fisted his dick, holding him to me, causing him to moan. I clenched my muscles as even more pleasure washed over me.

Riston howled out and began drilling his cock into me with such a force that I found myself fighting to support our combined weight. He pushed in hard and stilled, his balls drawing up tight as he filled me full of his semen. Exhausted, I went to collapse onto the bed face first but found Riston holding me to him.

"Riston, I can't believe I'm going to say this but I..."

"I love you."

I stilled, positive that my ears were playing tricks on me. Not wanting to make a big deal out of what I had to have imagined, I didn't comment. There was no way in hell that Riston could have fallen in love with me in a matter of days. That was ludicrous. Wasn't it?

Brushing my hair to the side, Riston bent over me and planted a kiss on my brand mark. It heated for a moment. I hissed and glanced over my shoulder. "What the..."

It was gone. Infuriated, I glared at him. "How dare you?"

A confused look came over him. "I healed it, honey."

"I never asked you to heal it."

"But, Kars..."

It hit me just how irrational I was being. Taking a deep breath, I collected myself and dropped my head down. "I'm sorry. Thank you."

Riston withdrew from me slowly, a wet sucking sound accompanied him. He growled slightly. "Damn, I was just in there and I already want to go back. Karri, you're killing me."

"I'm killing you? Pfft. You won't be walking funny for the next day. I will."

He eased us to the bed and instantly drew my body to his, spooning me so perfectly that it felt as though we were made to fit together. As I stared forward I found myself looking out the window staring at the house with the green shutters. "I really need to get some blinds."

Riston chuckled, the manly sound reverberated through me. "That or you just call me when you're about to undress."

"Why?"

"So, I know to watch from my bedroom window to be sure not to miss the show."

I turned a bit. "You're Mr. Meticulous?"

"I'm not that bad," he said, as his lips curved upwards a tiny bit. "Okay, maybe I am that bad."

"So, we're neighbors?" The realization of what that implied hit me.

"Mmmhmm."

I took a deep breath, not wanting to have the discussion I knew we had to have. "Riston."

"Hmm?"

"It won't be weird between us now will it?"

He ran his hand over my arm. "Weird doesn't come to mind when I think of watching you undress, Karri."

I laughed. "No, I mean what just happened won't make being neighbors weird will it?"

"I'd say it makes things more convenient but I'm getting the sense that you're not too sure about that." Letting out a deep breath, he pulled me into his arms tight. "Say it."

"Say what?" I asked, doing my best not to ruin what we'd just shared.

"You're trying to find out what I'll do when you bring other men home with you, aren't you?"

"Riston, I'm just trying to be practical. Things like this don't last."

"Things like what, Karri?" He laughed but it sounded anything but jovial. "So tell me, honey. Did you start thinking about someone else during sex or right after we finished up?"

I rolled out of his hold and tried to get up only to find him pulling me back to him. "Riston, please."

"Please what? Please don't be upset that you've already got someone lined up for your bed and are a little concerned about it being *weird* between us?"

"Riston, don't."

He let go of me and sat up fast. I could feel his anger, his confusion but most of all his pain as he turned his back to me. Sitting up, I went to touch him, to comfort him and stopped when I spotted the tattoo on his upper left shoulder. It was almost identical to mine. I stared at it, unable to believe what I was seeing. That was PJ's artwork if I'd ever seen it. Everything seemed to hit me at once. Amber's comments, Riston's knowledge of my father, his being a lycan and something that could work magik, the comments my mother had made on the beach--all of it swarmed over me, filling my head completely.

It clicked. Riston James Wallace was RJ.

"You didn't answer me, Kars. Did you start thinking about someone else during or after we were together?"

"I'll answer your question," I did my best to hold my tears in, "if you answer mine first."

He shrugged. "What's your question? Do you want to know if you can take a picture of my penis for your collection or to remember me by?" he asked, biting each word out.

"No. I just want to know where Jack and Victoria O'Higgins are buried, RJ."

He sat up straight and stared ahead for a moment before turning to face me. The moment his crisp blue eyes locked on me I lost my battle to keep from crying. He made a move to touch me and I scattered off the bed fast, pulling the sheet with me.

"Kars." He stood and faced me. "I didn't know how to tell you."

I gasped when I heard his confirmation. Taking a deep breath, I held myself together as best I could. "Where are they buried?"

"I'll take you there."

I shook my head. "No. You won't."

"Karri-Lynn, please..."

Looking around the room, I began to see flashes from when I was younger. "Ohmygods." I put my hand up, let my magik go and fought back a scream as it coated the walls and repaired the run-down state of what had once been my parents' room. "I used to live here." That's why it had seemed so familiar, in a dark, yet comforting kind of way.

"Kars." Riston came towards me fast and I thrust magik at him, keeping him away. "Let me hold you, honey. I know this is a lot for you."

"This was my house, our house and you lived," turning slightly, I glanced at the white house with green shutters, "next door."

Lifting the sheet off the floor, I clutched it to me and ran towards the hallway. I hesitated just a moment before heading directly to the door I knew had been my room. I pushed it open and stared around it. It had been pink. That much I remembered. Now, after over twenty years of having no one live in it, it was faded but still pink. I covered my mouth as tears ran down my face.

I couldn't breathe. It was all too much. My magik continued to rush throughout the house, repairing it all, restoring it to what it had once been. Instantly, my childhood bedroom filled with dolls, stuffed animals, a white canopy bed, everything I'd left in the storage units. It all had a place. It all belonged here. All except me.

I rushed down the hallway, taking the stairs at an alarming rate. When I hit the main level my entire stomach twisted. It was just as I remembered it being. I slowed as I approached the dining room, still able to remember the countless times I'd fallen asleep at RJ's feet, listening to he and my father go over plans, strategies, whatever it was that they did.

Unable to deal with it all, I ran towards the back door, needing to escape it all, needing to outrun a past I hadn't been looking for. I pushed the screen door open fast and found myself tripping over the end of the sheet. I held it tight to me and fell to my knees. I looked up at the sky, watching the sun set and let the tears continue to flow.

I hadn't come here looking to find the keys to my past. I'd come to protect Amber and the men in the unit. "Ohmygods, the team, it's Dad's…it's RJ's. No. I didn't come for him. No."

Strong, warm arms wrapped around me. "Come in the house, Kars. We'll talk about it there," Riston whispered. "I should have said something but I wanted to get to know you, Kars. I wanted to…"

"Where are my parents buried?"

"In the cemetery just outside of town." He hugged me tight and as much as I hated to admit it, it felt good. "I'll take you. I promise."

"Right after."

"What?"

I wiped my cheeks and leaned into his embrace. "I told you that I'd answer your question. You asked when it was that I thought of someone else. It was right after we were done. My fear of you being hurt is what prompted it. I didn't want him…umm," I let out a choked pathetic laugh, "to hurt you. That's why I wanted to make sure we would be fine with leaving it like that, Riston--RJ, whatever the hell it is you go by. I wasn't thinking of another man as in bringing him here to be with me. I was worried that he'd come here and find you. I didn't want anything to happen to you because I'd fallen for you. Are you happy now? Is that what you needed to hear? I fell for you the minute I laid eyes on you. Way to instantly assume the worst about me."

"Honey, look at me." He tugged on my shoulders gently.

"I'm not your honey. I'm not your anything, Riston, RJ." I threw my hands in the air. "I don't even know what to call you. Not that it matters. I could call your name for hours. You won't answer. What are you going to do now? Huh? Are you going to load me up and drop me off with strangers? Hey, why don't we make an appointment with the devil? I'm sure you could dump your burden off on his lap." I laughed. "Though, now, with what I'm becoming, I'd have way too much fun playing with him."

That did what I wanted it to do. It made him let go of me. I looked behind me to find I was alone. I hadn't heard Riston leave but I wasn't in the best of shape to trust my senses so I didn't pay a lot of attention to that.

Standing slowly, I wiped my eyes and clung to the sheet with my other hand. I didn't stop. I headed straight back into the house and went to what used to be my room. I sat on what used to be my bed and stared around the room.

"Are you planning to sit there and mope all night or are you going to embrace what you've been given, Legs?"

Legs? Only one person used that as a nickname for me.

"PJ?"

A white light flashed before me and a tiny woman with endless waves of dark curls stepped free from it. Her blue eyes seemed to sparkle as she winked at me. "I have to say, I was starting to think you'd never figure out who Riston is."

I stood quickly and hugged her to me, needing to be sure that she was really there.

PJ laughed. "I'm here, Karri. As much as you like to hide behind your eccentric behavior, you're not, nor have you ever been crazy. You also weren't able to communicate with me before either. I'm not on the front lines as a soldier like Tripp so I can't become corporeal for just anyone."

"Am I dreaming?" I asked, unsure what was going on but damn happy to see her.

She shook her head. "No, Karri, you're not dreaming."

"How is it that I can see you then?"

She sighed and lowered her gaze. "I think you already know the answer to that."

"Because I'm dying."

She nodded. "Have you told Amber yet?"

"Why? She doesn't need to know the truth. She can't stop it."

PJ shook her head. "I disagree. She should know that her time with you is limited. They should all be told that, Karri."

"I wouldn't change anything. I'd do it all the same, PJ."

"I didn't think you would change it, Karri. Without you healing Amber every time her illness overtook her, she'd have passed away eight years ago. I should have warned you not to heal the dead. I never anticipated that Amber would fall ill to the psychic attacks in addition to her own power eating at her. And I never thought that..."

I sighed. "I'd willingly take her death into me repeatedly. Yeah, well, if that didn't get me the darkness that seems to eat away at me would." I smiled. She didn't. "Does Tripp know, umm, now that he's on a higher plane does he know that I was keeping that from him? Does he know that's the reason I said no to adopting a baby-- an infant. I knew I wouldn't be alive to be there for it, for him."

"No. Your father has done a good job of hiding it from everyone, your mother included. He couldn't hide it from me because I felt it when I came to you eleven months ago, before I died."

"That's why you refused to let me heal you and why you tried to bind me," I said, finally understanding what she'd been talking about. She nodded. I hugged her again. "I am so sorry that I went against your wishes and let Hilary say goodbye. I just thought..."

"Shh," she pressed her tiny hand to my lips, "you were right to do that. I couldn't see it objectively. You let Riston say goodbye to me too. Eric as well. They needed that closure, Karri. But you already knew that they would."

I pulled back and held in my tears. "Hilary is beautiful and smart. She's perfect, PJ."

"Thank you. Eric, Riston and Amber have done a good job of raising her since I've been gone. She doesn't know it but when she dreams that she's playing with me, she really is. So, I get to spend her nights with her." PJ took my hand in hers and patted it. "Thank you for helping her hear me, Karri. When she tipped her head back on the front lawn, after flipping around, it was the first time since I had to go that she listened when I spoke to her in waking hours."

"Hey, cut the kid some slack. She gets her stubborn streak from her mom."

She laughed. "And her Uncle Riston and Aunt Karri."

That made me stop laughing. "I'm not Aunt anything. I can't be anything to your brother, PJ."

She tipped her head and gave me a puzzled look. "But you already are, Karri."

"No I'm not."

"Do not make me throw lettuce at you again." She grinned mischievously. "I miss our time together. It changed my life. Did you know that?"

"Yeah, right." I took a deep breath. "PJ, why am I not freaking out right now?"

"Because I've blanketed you with peace and serenity so I could talk with you openly, hon. Plus, I thought you could use a friend and a moment of downtime right now."

"I miss you."

"I know. I think about you all the time. The minute I sensed your energy around Hilary, holding her secure while you swung her around in the yard I couldn't have gotten there faster if I tried." She played with a strand of her long hair. "I knew they'd be okay now that they had you with them, Karri. Just like I was okay once I had you."

I snorted. The idea of me helping anyone was absurd. I was and had always been a mess.

"I'm serious, Karri. I was supposed to die nine and half years ago. See, I never told you that before I met you I'd been sinking into the darkness you now find yourself spiraling towards. I couldn't seem to find my way out and Riston couldn't figure out how to help me. It wasn't until I heard you screaming out for help that I felt like I had a purpose."

I shifted, pulling the sheet up more and listened to her go on. "Karri, I stopped Riston from hearing your cries for him. Amber was right. He would have come and he would have slaughtered them but he wouldn't have stopped there. He'd have kept killing, trying to work out his hate with himself for having left you there to begin with. And he wouldn't have been able to ever look at you again without the guilt of that weighing on him." She rubbed my arm lightly. "I came because I knew I could help you both. I could protect you and I could keep him from being lost to the darkness. I wanted you both to be happy, Karri."

I covered my mouth and shook my head. "PJ, I blamed him. I said the most horrible thing to him about not coming when I called. He left. I don't know where he went. He just..."

"Vanished?" she asked, not seeming the least bit surprised. "He can do that. So can the rest of the team. It's a trick your father taught them over a hundred years ago but you already know that. You just like to push details about him out of your mind."

My jaw dropped. "Riston is over a hundred years old?"

"Well, duh, who did you think the two-hundred-year-old pain in my ass was?"

I lifted the sheet high and went to head towards the master bedroom. "I need to get dressed and find him, PJ."

She snickered. "You don't honestly think that he'd just walk away and leave you for making a comment that hurt him, do you?"

I locked eyes with her. "He walked away and left me once before. I need to find him."

Taking hold of my arms, PJ held me steady. "Karri, listen to me. The man was confused. His life turned upside down that day too. Do you know what he used to do?"

I shook my head.

"He used to sit in his room, with the shades down and try to mentally see you, Karri. Just like he could see you when you danced for him while he was chained to the bed. That's why I put you in that get up. If he'd have seen you and recognized you as being his Karri-Lynn, he wouldn't have asked you to stay back. He'd have broken his chains and taken you." She gave me a rather serious look. "Riston would use that gift while he was alone and stay like that for hours, watching you as you grew up."

That couldn't be true. "He would have seen what..." I stopped in mid-sentence and closed my eyes tight. "I stopped him from seeing that, didn't I? I didn't mean to."

"No, you didn't. William did." She sighed. "His obsession with you being a demon came from what he tried so hard to deny, his own power."

I took a step back fast and hit the wall. "Ouch. Wait, you're saying that William wasn't human?"

"No. He wasn't. And he hated himself for that, Karri. That sick bastard took that fact out on you. There would be certain times of the day that Riston couldn't get to you mentally, no matter how hard he tried. He couldn't connect. After I passed, I learned why. William would sense him and block him from seeing you. That's why he was..."

"So, adamant that RJ cared, that RJ..."

She nodded. "RJ loved you and didn't trust his gut when it came to them. And that he would indeed try to come." PJ followed me as I headed into the master bedroom. While the walls looked like they used to, my bed and my dressers are what filled it. "Blame me if you have to blame someone because there were times that you were there that Riston had packed to go to you and I stopped him. I thought you were fine. I didn't know, Karri."

I stilled, letting her go on.

"All of us thought he was nuts when it came to you. We had to explain to him that it wasn't appropriate to just pop in and watch you grow up whenever he wanted. Don't get me wrong, he didn't have anything he shouldn't have had on his mind. It was impossible for him to think of you that way. But that didn't mean he couldn't worry about you, couldn't care for your well-being and happiness."

As I thought back to my time with William and Madge I could pick out moments, away from them, while I was at school or walking to or from, moments that I felt a certain something. I couldn't put my finger on it at the time but now it made sense. "That was him? The times when I'd sense something, someone watching me. Ohmygods, it was Riston." My breath hitched. "He was the only positive reinforcement and feeling of being loved that I had, PJ and I thought he was just my imagination--I thought he was..."

"A feeling that your mind created to keep you from going insane? Yeah, I know that now, honey." PJ put her arms out and looked every bit the part that she didn't have to play. She was the real deal. An honest to god angel. "On days that were good for you, days that you'd do something special at school and be happy, Riston would beam. But times that you were picked on, upset, even sick, it took all of us to control him. To keep him from rushing to you."

I thought about what she was saying. While part of it made sense, the rest didn't. "He didn't know me when he saw me in the front yard playing with Hilary. He had no idea who I was until I told him in the kitchen and he looked floored, like he couldn't believe that I'd actually grown up. And he's made comments about that since then. How could he have come to me all the time and not know me when he saw me? I haven't changed a bit since I was sixteen, PJ."

"Karri, William managed to completely lock Riston out by the time you hit high school. He went off the deep end, dragging his team and me out to look for you, positive that you'd been hurt. When I found you singing in a church choir you sounded so happy, so full of life that I told him you were fine and not to show himself to you because you were happy. We were all concerned that you'd recognize him and none of us were sure how you felt about him after he was forced to put you with someone other than himself." She shook her head. "After meeting you I realized that you're always happy when you're singing. It doesn't even matter what the song is. I am so sorry. Had I known, had I sensed your pain I wouldn't have stopped him. I'd have let him go in and take you."

Something brushed past me and I turned, expecting to find someone. No one was there. "I think my house is haunted. That or someone else I know that kicked it is toying with me."

PJ just laughed. That was never a good thing. I rolled my eyes, snickered and went to my dresser and pulled a gray thong out. PJ clapped for me and I rolled my eyes. "Yes, I am finally wearing underwear. Happy now?"

"Yes and no."

"What's that mean?" I asked, sliding the thong up and over my legs.

She grinned. "It means that I'm happy but if I know my brother he'll put an end to that very soon. It still amazes me how different you became the second the ritual was completed, Karri. You went from being shy about who you are and what you look like to being completely open and practically dripping sex." She laughed and shook her head. "When I ran into Victoria again, after I passed, it hit me then. You were made to be that way and had she lived you would have grown up being around her, seeing her natural ability to be sexy. And if you would have learned from her, it wouldn't have left you doing a one-eighty after the ritual."

"So, you're saying that you woke up my inner slut?" I asked, playfully.

The smile that spread over her face was a classic. One I missed seeing. "No. I'm saying that I simply unlocked the door that had to remain closed until you were of a proper age, Karri. And in doing so, I made it possible for you and Riston to be together. He couldn't have desired you sexually without it being done and you couldn't have wanted him that way either. I'm more than happy that it worked."

"PJ."

"Oh, don't give me that 'don't get so excited' tone. That man loves you and he is not one to take no for an answer."

A bubble of laugher erupted from me. "Riston does not love me. I think the air up there must be thin or something."

"Or thin around the five foot ten level down here," she said, not giving an inch. "Karri, he told you that he loves you."

"Eww, you were watching when I was with your brother? I, the one who normally has no stopping point, think that is wrong." I wrinkled my nose and shivered.

PJ flipped me off. "I was not watching you fuck my brother. Though I can only image his surprise when he figured out he had a bed partner like you for a mate."

"Hey, what the hell is that supposed to mean?"

"Hmm, let me see," she pressed a finger to her lip, "remember the human, the one who took your virginity?"

"Not really but Amber reminded me that his name was Dom. Does that sound bad?"

She chuckled. "No. I remember him. He lay in your bed for an entire day after you were done with him, staring wide-eyed, like he wasn't sure if he was dreaming or not. He was still pining after you long after I left and Amber arrived."

I pointed at her. "That was not my fault. You didn't tell me that my magik would flare up during intercourse. How was I to know that? And while we're on the subject of my virginity why in the hell did you go to all that trouble of sending me to Riston while he was chained to a bed and then not let him be my first?"

The look on her face surprised me. "So, you would have wanted RJ to be your first?"

"PJ, if he really is who everyone keeps telling me he is, my mate, then I wish he'd have been my only anyone," I said, meaning every word of it. "Don't take this the wrong way, I cared for Tripp more than I should have. I know that but..."

"You didn't love him like he loved you. I know that. So does he, Karri." She arched a brow as she noticed the bra I'd picked out--a tiny, barely cover me grey one. "Nice. Anyway, Tripp never pressed you to tell him that you loved him because he knew that he didn't own that last piece of your heart. The part you kept separate without even realizing it. The part that holds RJ in it, Karri."

Unsure if I was ready to deal with that fact or not, I changed the subject. "Why do the two of you have nicknames that no one but me uses?"

"Because Jack gave them to us and they stuck. Whenever we were around him we were PJ and RJ. To the rest of the world, we're just Paula and Riston." She laughed. "Gawd, for over a hundred years your father pissed Riston off by calling him RJ."

I smiled. "What changed that?"

"You did."

"Huh?" I asked, as the feeling of being touched returned to me.

This time I didn't bother looking around for the source. I just gave in and let it hold me.

PJ tipped her head and ran her fingers over the end of my bed. "I think you were around one when it happened. We thought you'd picked up a bug from a supernatural playgroup that your mother insisted you be part of. It was horrible. You ran high fevers, couldn't keep anything down and fussed non-stop." She stopped and stared at me as I finished zipping my jeans. "I wanted to help Victoria and let her get some sleep so I offered to take you and watch you for a few hours. Riston, Jack and the team had been gone on a week-long mission. When they came rushing into my house with Riston in their arms, unconscious with a high fever and the sweats I didn't know what the hell was going on."

I pulled a tiny navy cami-like top over my head and freed my hair from it. "Well, what was wrong with him?"

"He'd been ambushed by a series of *sparterous* demons. Their bites are poisonous to any form of shifter. When they told me what day he'd first been bitten I could hardly believe it. It was the same day you came down sick. Riston is six foot five and..."

"Two hundred and thirty-two pounds," I said, helping her out. "Oh, he wears a thirteen shoe size in case you needed to know. Don't ask. Carry on."

PJ snorted. "You started crying and screaming at the top of your lungs while they were there. I ran and got you and then ran back to try to help Jack and the guys figure out a way to heal Riston. I set you down long enough to grab a book Jack needed and you hobbled over to Riston, still walking only on your tiptoes. I watched you fall and tumble right into him. Something happened, you took his sickness into you, completely healing him. His eyes snapped open and he snatched you up just as you began to convulse."

She headed towards my closet. "You father went for you but Riston actually did a partial shift and put his clawed hand to your father's throat. He wouldn't let us have you. He encircled you with his power and healed you. You opened your eyes and said "RJ" clear as could be. It was then that we all knew that there was a bond bigger than we ever thought possible between you and Riston. It was also the day he stopped being pissed about being called RJ."

PJ turned and pitched my black, chunky heeled sandals at me. I caught them and blew her a kiss. "Ever the helpful fashion consultant."

"Well, death can't stop everything," she said, tossing her hair back and doing her best southern belle impersonation. "You know, I think Riston doesn't even know how much you've softened his rough edges, Karri."

"Huh?"

"Before you were born he was all about the next kill, the next party, the next easy fuck, the..." She bit her lip. "Umm, sorry. Don't be upset with him."

"PJ."

"Yeah?" she asked, looking concerned.

"The man was alive for centuries before I showed up. If he didn't screw other women I'd be worried about him. You don't have to worry. I'm not the jealous type." I thought about Riston sliding into another woman and instantly wanted to kill something. "Okay, I lied. I think I might be that type. Oh gods, what the hell is happening to me?"

She snickered. "It's natural, Karri. He's your mate. The need for monogamy is great when it comes to that. I expect that a lot will be different with him than with other men. But one may still prove to be an issue."

"Who, Tripp?"

PJ shook her head. "Jean-Paul. I understand why you did it, why you let him mark you but it..."

My stomach tightened. "I didn't understand what I was agreeing to, PJ. I swear it. All I knew was that I was losing the war with the darkness and had no anchor. When he offered to help me, I didn't know that it gave him certain powers over me."

She came towards me fast and put her hands in mine. "I know that, Karri. I know how innocent and trusting you were then, and I know that at the time Jean-Paul was in the height of trying to win your hand. His distaste for Riston is great. He thinks that any man who would not show up when his mate, especially you, was ready to accept him has no right to call himself your mate."

That was a good assumption on Jean-Paul's part. I could hardly blame him. "Wait, why didn't Riston come? I mean, after you left why didn't he ever come?"

"Because the moment I took you to him while he was chained to the bed you felt how powerful he was and it scared you. It scared you so much that I couldn't let you lose your virginity to him, Karri. He's a powerful alpha male. Even at his most gentle he would have hurt you unintentionally and I'm not sure you could have forgiven him for that, not with being so close to what had almost happened with William. It had only been about two months. If I'd let Riston free of those chains he wouldn't have been able to stop himself from taking you, not after I'd sent you in to tempt him--to get him thinking of his mate."

I laughed. "Didn't take him long to forget me."

"Yes, it did. He was still pissed about me sending 'some woman' to him with the scent of his mate on her a year ago. In fact, he'd make snide remarks about it often, reminding me just how much I'd played with his emotions." She winked. "He wanted you, Karri, not a woman with your scent. I never told him it was really you."

"Why didn't he ever come for me then? I mean, if he really did want me, why didn't he come? I can't believe you'd stop him again after having spent all that time with me."

She waved her hand in the air and an image of me appeared. It was when I was in the dark side garb, meaning I was playing for their side--or pretending to anyway. My hair was sleeked back from my face and wrapped in a tight bun. It looked so much darker than it was. My eyes were black as was my barely there outfit.

I watched, seeing myself in the middle of a fight with the good side, the side I was really working for but had to pretend not to be. The minute I spotted Riston in the image I gasped.

"What was he doing there?"

"Looking for you," she said, smiling, "you were so busy concentrating on staying in character, pretending to be evil but not hurting your own team that you let your natural guard, the one you erected the night you met him when he was chained to the bed, down. The instant it lifted he could sense you. The man rushed out of a picnic and went to you. But he couldn't find the Karri-Lynn he remembered and found himself being thrust out of there before he could register that you were you."

"Opps, I did the thrusting. Umm, think he'll forgive me?"

PJ snickered. "Well, you did save his life so I'm thinking that's a yes. Had he stayed he'd have been killed."

I thought about something that I didn't think would ever come up. "PJ, is there a spell I can do to keep him from claiming me?"

"Why?"

"Because I'm scared to death that I might take him with me when I go. My dad mentioned once that he'd follow my mother wherever she went and I got the feeling that it was already set up to be so. Tell me I'm wrong. Tell me that Riston will be fine regardless what happens to me."

She put her head down and sighed. "I can't, Karri. You're right. He'll follow because he can."

"What does that mean?"

"It means that once claimed, he can always find you in life or death, Legs. He no longer has to rely on you letting your guard down. He will forever be able to locate you."

My breathing quickened. "Give me something, anything that will prevent him from wanting to claim me. Anything. I'll leave tonight if I have to. Hell, I'll leave now. He was there, he knows about the attacks coming. I'll have Seger and Branson stay to get him up to speed on what we've found out." Pushing past, PJ, I went to the closet and snatched a bag out.

On my way past her, she grabbed my arm, bringing me to a fast stop. "PJ, you should be helping me not stopping me. He's your brother. Do you want something to happen to him? I know I don't."

"Karri." She held firm.

"No, don't take time to lecture me about fate. You and I both know how very close my body is to giving out. Even if it keeps going by some miracle, the darkness has spread to the point that I have little control over it, PJ. I refuse to let him suffer because of that."

"Why?"

My eyes widened. "What do you mean why?" I tried to break free but she kept a hold on me. For a little thing she was strong. I felt something else touching me then.

PJ tipped her head. "Tell me why you don't want Riston to suffer, Karri. And tell me the truth."

Taking a deep breath, I faced what I didn't want to. "Because I love him."

She smiled. "Karri, Riston has already claimed you. In the eyes of lycans and the majority of the supernatural world, he's your husband." I dropped the bag a second before I went down too. The room seemed to spin and I fought hard not to pass out. Somehow, I knew that I would fail.

"Riston, stop lurking and show yourself. Your wife just found out she's married and isn't taking it so well. Maybe you should have told her that by exchanging blood with her while you were making love to her and biting her meant you were claiming her. Ya think?"

I opened my eyes just in time to find Riston staring at PJ. He looked shocked. "She said she loves me."

"Yes, she did, dipshit. Now, pick her up and love her like you know you do."

"Riston?" He dropped down next to me fast, only making the dizzy, uneasy feeling I had worsen. I wasn't able to get anything else out before I gave in and closed my eyes.

Chapter Nine

"Are you sure you're ready for this?" Seger asked, adjusting my ear piece just so.

I glanced down at the costume dress I was wearing and shrugged. "Ready as I'll ever be. Hey," I touched his forearm lightly, "did Matty find anything about where Riston and his team are?" I'd woken to find myself alone when all I'd wanted was my husband. Amber had told me that he and Eric raced out of the house so I knew it was work related, I just didn't know where or exactly what he was doing.

"No, Karri. I know you're worried about him. If I turn anything up, I'll let you know. Now, you need to get into character, go out there and give your 'husband' a great performance for his new role as general to the underworld."

I pulled myself together and stood tall. I walked out onto the stage and took my place. Nodding to Seger, I let him know that I was ready. The music started and I followed the haunting chant with long fluid moves. My cover was that I was the wife of a now general and had once been an entertainer. The story was that he found me dancing in a club and claimed me for himself. They seemed to believe it so we went with it.

The lights hit me and the entire underground club went silent. The beat went on and I followed it, extending my arms, letting the straps of the silver gown I wore flow about in a tempting fashion. The upper portion was a silver corset that thrust my breasts up and almost out. I was made to look seductive to men and it worked well.

I skated along the edge of the stage, the lights bright, making it hard for me to make out the crowd. This was when I was at my most vulnerable. I trusted Seger, Branson and Jean-Paul to keep me safe through the stage portion of our act.

Seger had told me once that I looked like a dark temptress, beautiful yet untouchable when I was on stage playing this part. I wasn't so sure about the beautiful part but I had to admit that I enjoyed it. Too bad it was a production for the bad guys.

I dropped down, tipped my head and let my eyes narrow as I zeroed on where I knew Jean-Paul would be, center table right before the stage. When I spotted him sitting there dressed in a dark grey silk shirt, designer black pants and shoes I locked gazes with him. His chin-length black hair hung onto his pale face just enough to cover one of his blue eyes partially. He sat there with an ankle on his other leg. The famous legs crossed with several buttons undone on his shirt to show off his muscular, alabaster chest was a signature move for Jean-Paul. One that he'd not only perfected, but did just to tempt me.

I leaned down, off the stage just a bit and he put his hand out towards me as his jaw dropped slightly. Up until about three months ago I'd never been sure if he really did get off on my performances or he was just acting. Turns out, he really did get off on them.

I felt his pull on me and knew that the rest of the patrons did as well. It was a necessary part of the act. They needed to believe that I was his mate, his wife and that he maintained complete control over me. Keeping with my pre-choreographed routine, I stood quicker than a human could without assistance, knowing it made it appear that Jean-Paul had yanked me up like a puppet on a string.

The beat increased and I began to sway to it right before I interrupted the chants by singing out hard and loud, providing the perfect contrast to it all. The lyrics were dark, about immortal love and dying for it and I made sure to keep my voice at a level that suited the piece. A fallen angel, that's what Jean-Paul said it sounded like and in truth that was what it was. I let just enough of the darkness up to help it be different from my normal singing but keeping it darker, seductive, the voice of a siren.

It also provided a valuable gift to us. It let the men move about freely and read the others in the club to find out their intentions. It's how we'd been so good at remaining one step ahead of the enemy. It was also how I'd learned about the possible attacks on Riston's team. Often, the men who frequented the clubs of the underground would drink, loosening their natural defenses and then when they heard me, my call to them to pay attention, to respond, they'd slip tiny details.

I concentrated on Jean-Paul as I continued on. The lights dimmed a bit and I let my glance flicker over the others at the table with him. The minute I found Riston staring back at me my breath caught, stopping my singing in its tracks. A worried look moved over Jean-Paul as the patrons began a low hush of whispers.

Jean-Paul stood, in an elegant manner and came to me, stepping onto the stage in one fluid movement. "Lynn, my love," he said, loud enough for the patrons to hear him. "Does my new guard frighten you?"

Say yes.

I stared into his eyes as I heard his voice in my head. "Yes."

"Fear not, fair-haired one, he is here to assure you are not harmed. A creature of such beauty full of such a wicked little dark streak is sure to be something in high demand."

When a series of whistles, growls, snarls and howls sounded, Jean-Paul flashed his fangs and ran his hand down the front of me slowly, as he used his other hand to guide my head back enough that my neck was there, offered up to him on a platter. They stopped making noises instantly, knowing that Jean-Paul was powerful enough to kill them should he decide to do so.

As he leaned in to kiss it, he took a deep breath and locked gazes with me, looking confused. *You smell of another. Why?*

Having a fight over me smelling like another man wasn't what I wanted to do now. In fact, it was the absolute last thing I wanted to do. I touched his cool cheek and stared into his royal blue eyes. I didn't hesitate. No. I immediately began to sing again, this time to him. As much as I wanted it not to be aimed at him for real, I found that wasn't the case. Problem was, Jean-Paul knew it.

He took my hand in mine and held me at arms length. A sly smile played over his entirely too handsome face. I spun until I was wrapped tight to him, tipped my head back and finished the song so close to his face that if he wanted to kiss me, he could. The second I finished, he did. Normally, Jean-Paul kept it simple yet seductive. Not this time. No. Now he made sure to kiss me so that no one in the room could think I was anything but his.

As he pulled back the place erupted into applause. "I think you will all understand that I wish to have my wife to myself for a bit. She can return to entertain you after I have had my time."

No one argued at that. I didn't think they would. Jean-Paul took my hand and led me gracefully down the front of the stage towards the table. Carefully, I offered the men at the table a cool, sexy smile, never once breaking character. I skimmed past Riston's face fast, knowing that he alone held enough control over me to cause me to fuck up big time.

I took my seat, which was, of course, next to Riston's. Thankfully, it was angled towards the stage so my back would be facing him. Jean-Paul bent and kissed my cheek before moving to his own seat on the other side of me.

There I was, sandwiched between two men that meant the world to me. One for his commitment and his help for the last nine years of my life and the other for simply being him--being my mate.

Jean-Paul lifted a strand of my curled hair and smiled. "Mmm, I do so love it when you wear it this way, Lynn."

Different, thumping dance music began to play, drowning out the rest of the club. Jean-Paul turned to his right and gave Branson a questioning look. "Did someone forget to fill me in on all the details?"

Branson looked to me for help and I nodded slowly giving him permission to answer Jean-Paul. His eyes widened. "Well, I can hardly tell you what I don't know, asshole."

Jean-Paul cast him a sideways glance and smiled. "You are no longer under my direct command, Branson but do not let that fool you into a false sense of security." He looked at me. "My apologies for not briefing you on the matter of having company this fine evening, *ma chérie*, but as you know, things change at a moments notice."

Glancing around the room, I spotted Eric near one of the exits appearing as though he were engrossed in conversation with another. When I realized it was Seaton, the life in the fast lane guy, I knew that they were on a mission. Unfortunately, our missions crossed paths.

Jean-Paul leaned forward and caressed my cheek gently. "Ah, to have a quiet moment to ourselves, *ma chérie*. I wish to tell you exactly what it is that you did to me while you were up there."

I could take a hint. I threw my magik up and around us, locking our conversation in and all others out. "Talk, they can't hear you now."

"Who is he?"

"Who is who?" I asked, cupping my hand over his doing my best to keep up appearances for any one that may be suspicious and watching us.

Jean-Paul's temper began to rear it ugly head as his jaw tightened and his fangs showed. He did his best to hide them from me but I saw them there and knew how very pissed off he was. "It is common courtesy to inform your significant other that you are fucking other men, Karri, or do you not feel those small things apply to me."

"Correct me if I'm wrong but we," I leaned in and stroked his inner arm tenderly, "are not a couple, Jean-Paul."

"That is odd," he said, maintaining a smile. "I seem to recall finding you, unarmed and sitting in the center of a hotspot not caring who or what showed up to kill you, Karri. You were naked, shivering and in a mental place that even I could not reach."

Branson pushed his drink aside in disgust. "Christ, Jean-Paul, what the fuck does you finding Karri the day after Tripp was killed have to do with anything? It could have been anyone of us who found her naked. You cover her up and get her to safety. You don't throw it in her face eight fucking months later."

I knew exactly what Jean-Paul was telling me and at the moment, I hated him for it. I went to pull my hand away from his but he held tight. "Careful, Karri. One wrong move and you will put all of our lives in jeopardy. I am sensing at the moment that you would stake me yourself if given the chance but know that your precious little boys are here." He cast a sideways glance at Branson. "You would not wish harm to come to them. Do not forget that your Matty and Seger are among the crowd as well. They will not fade away if they sense you are upset. No. They would sacrifice all to assure your happiness. As would any of the men you call your own."

"Do you have a point or do you just like hearing yourself talk?" Branson asked, clearly disgusted with Jean-Paul.

The soft chuckled that came from the now livid vampire sent chills down my body. "My point is that if Karri simply bats her lashes any one of you would do anything she asked."

"And?"

"And now," Jean-Paul ran his fingernail over my wrist slowly, tracing each vein carefully, "it would seem that Karri has allowed the tables to be turned. She has given someone the power to simply bat his lashes and she will do whatever he asks."

"Oh, sort of like what you do to her? Gotcha, dead boy." Branson didn't back down and for once I was happy with that.

"Do I force you to do things you do not wish to do, *ma chérie*?" Jean-Paul asked, his French accent thickening as it often did when he was upset. "Do I make you come to me when you are at your most dire points? Did I force you to seek me out when you knew what would happen if you healed Amber, who was on her deathbed? Did I make you select me to entrust yourself with during the fourteen days that you lay lifeless because you took her death upon you? Did I make you select me to keep away the demons that surged forth to torment you mentally the entire time, tugging on your essence, your very soul, to claim it for their own?"

I didn't buckle. I sat there smiling at him with one that told him exactly how I felt at the moment--deadly. "No. You didn't. But don't sit there and pretend to be holier than thou, Jean-Paul. I distinctly remember having to sign my life away on a contract with the powers for a four year period to get the assistance that I came asking someone, who I thought was a friend, for. It's not like I didn't pay a high price for your help."

"That is neither here nor there, *ma chérie*. The fact of the matter is that you came to me. You did not call upon the assistance of the porcelain doll, PJ, and you did not call your pathetic excuse for a mate. You called me."

"Whew, I don't know about anyone else but I'm so happy that lecture had a point." I curled my lip slightly. "For a moment I was afraid you'd go on and on and begin mixing French and English because you're too pissed off to pick one or the other."

Branson laughed. I just smiled. Jean-Paul picked then to do just what I'd teased him about. "*Il y a quelau' un d'autre?*" He narrowed his blue gaze and let his eyes begin to swirl with flecks of black. "Are you, *ma chérie?*"

"What the fuck did he say? I hate trying to guess," Branson said, not helping Jean-Paul's mood.

"He wants to know if she's seeing someone else," Riston bit out.

I did my best not to focus on Riston but hearing him voice exactly what Jean-Paul asked only made what I had to do all the more difficult. I had to lie. "No."

"No?" Jean-Paul arched a brow just as I felt Riston's energy wrap around my waist.

I nodded. "You heard me right. I said no."

"*Ma chérie*, you smell of another man. You have been marked by him." He laughed. "More than marked. He has claimed you, taken you for his mate. It could not have been an easy feat since you are already powerful and bore my mark."

"Bore?"

He nodded. "You no longer seem to carry it. Whoever your bed partner is, he is quite powerful. To break another's hold is something only the most powerful of each species can do."

"Can you do it?" I asked, hope surging through me.

"Yes. Why do you ask?"

"Because I want his claim on me broken." It hurt to say the words but it was true. I needed Riston's hold severed. I refused to take him with me when I died. I loved him too much to do let him die too.

Riston's power clenched me tight and I could almost hear his protests in my head. He reminded silent to all around, no doubt knowing that we would end up under attack should we reveal who were really were.

"I thought it was your wish to be free of me." Jean-Paul picked up his glass of champagne and took a sip. "You made it so clear at our last meeting."

"Jean-Paul, don't. I'm offering you a chance to have what you want. Take it and don't question why."

A slow smile moved over his face. "And what is it I wish to have, *ma chérie*?"

Branson slammed his fist down. "Oh like fucking hell! I see where this is going and I will not let her hand herself over to the likes of you. And I'm not the only one," he glanced towards Riston, "I'm guessing that this husband of hers is not going to take having his bond with her broken lightly."

"He doesn't have a say in the matter, Branson!" I spat back.

Jean-Paul stiffened. "We may have a problem."

I followed his gaze and found Matty pushing some demon hard near the bar. I sighed. "I'll go fish him back in. And for the record, I have told you all not to let him have bar duty. He can't handle the temptation when some jackass of a demon makes a snide comment."

"I'll get him," Branson said, pushing his chair out.

Jean-Paul tossed his hand in the air. "*Non*, he is one of Karri's little boys. She will handle him. You will stay."

"Talk to one of them again like that and you'll find yourself on the pointed end of a stake."

He licked his lower lip. "Funny, I seem to recall you saying that very same thing when I first brought you down here some eight or so years ago. You warned that if I tried anything 'funny' that I would wake to find that very thing." He winked. "It is rather amusing that it was you who ended up on the end of my 'stake,' *ma chérie*."

"You slept with him?" Branson asked, not bothering to stay in his seat. His brow furrowed and then he stepped back fast. "Oh, I'm going to be sick. That's why you bought a new bed. You're always touching shit and knowing things about it. You got rid of the old one because…uhh…yep. I'm going to hurl."

Jean-Paul laughed. "I would assume that she did get a new bed since she set the other on fire. I do so hope that the next time she also ensures I am not in it at the time."

I wanted to lash out at him. I wanted to kick him in the head again. I didn't. Instead, I took a long calming breath and smiled. "Break the hold and," I swallowed hard, "I am yours. You have my word. I'll sign another contract if you want. I'll do anything, just promise that the bond will be erased, that he can't follow me wherever I go, Jean-Paul."

I didn't stay to hear his answer. I already knew what it would be. I dropped my magik and headed towards Matty who was now holding a demon in a headlock. As I neared, he turned and locked gazes with me. Instantly, he let go of the demon who then tried to attack him once more. I tossed a bit of magik at it and sent it flying in the other direction.

I gave Matty a cross look. He dropped his head down and came to me quickly. The demon stood fast. "That's it, coward. Run like the whipped puppy you are to your master's whore."

Matty stopped next to me, squared his shoulders and prepared to turn to fight again. Tossing my arms out, I let the dark power in me unleash. It caused a wind to sweep through the club. "I'm sorry, but you were saying?"

The people around began to move out of the way no doubt sensing my anger. The demon morphed into human form, his hair long, almost to his waist and as white as snow. His pale grey eyes found mine. I could see the fear, the question in them. Could I take him? He wasn't sure. I was.

"Mattyson, what seems to be the problem here?" I asked, keeping my eyes on the demon.

"My lady, there's no problem." He bit back a smile knowing how much I hated it when he called me my lady. "Please accept my apologies for drawing you away from the Master's celebration."

The master's? I wanted to vomit every time the men had to call Jean-Paul that while undercover.

"Ah, Lynn Dupre, I thought I sensed you," Drogo Lazarus said, appearing out of thin air. It didn't surprise me. He owned the joint. What did surprise me was the blood on his hand. Granted, vampires tended to like blood more than the average Joe but they didn't wear it around especially not when wearing a suit that easily cost over four grand.

Drogo followed my gaze and lifted his hand. "Ah, my apologies, Lynn. A spy was found among us and I was handling the situation."

"A spy?" I asked, watching as he withdrew a handkerchief from his breast pocket and began wiping the fresh blood from his hand. "And you've taken to torturing them yourself now? I am impressed."

The laugh that came from Drogo made the others around us back up more. "Ah, Jean-Paul, do share how it is you managed to find such a beautiful wife with such a taste for death."

Jean-Paul took another sip of his champagne and nodded. "I would say I was blessed however you have not had to deal with her when she is not happy. It is most unpleasant."

Various chuckles sounded from around the room. Drogo tossed the handkerchief into the air and it caught fire, burning up before it could fall to the ground. "She has brought me much pleasure, allowing me to listen to her voice while she performs only for you. I should like to return the favor."

He motioned towards the stage and a man appeared. He was tied to a chair, his shirt missing and was covered in blood. Two guards appeared next to him and lifted his head. The minute I saw green eyes staring out from the bruised face my chest tightened. They had Hansen. Images of Tripp and finding him slaughtered came at me fast. I clenched my fists, trying to push them from my mind.

Matty touched my shoulder lightly, offering me his strength to draw from. I did my best to stay in character. "Drogo, I know this man. He is no spy. Who told you these lies?"

"He was sent on an important mission. One that he could not fail. We should now have either the Dark Angel among our ranks or her head staked to the wall. We have neither. Nor do we have the shadow demons sent to clean up the mess. That tells me that he let her go." Drogo moved up next to me and ran his ice cold fingers over my bare shoulders. To my credit, I didn't shiver. "He is my gift to you, Lynn. I have heard many stories of your creative torture techniques. I wish to witness them for myself."

"Drogo, as gracious as this offer is, my wife does not make torturing men a habit while we are out. My work kept us apart for more than a week. I wish to spend the evening with her. Not with her and her pet whipping boy," Jean-Paul said, doing his best to keep this from going any further.

Drop lifted his hand. "Very well, kill him then."

I grabbed his arm and drew it to me, letting the back of his hand scrape over my cleavage. "Don't be so hasty, Drogo. I didn't get a say."

"No," he brought his face down close to mine and I wanted to gauge his eyes out, "you did not. I am sorry for that. Do you wish to accept my gift?"

"Of course, I never pass on an opportunity like this one."

He laughed from the gut. "Should you ever decide that a Frenchman is not who you want to share your bed with please keep me in mind, Lynn. There is something so incredibly tempting about you." He caressed the top of my breast lightly, clearly trying to keep Jean-Paul from seeing the action. "Now, please have your way with this one. I am sorry that I did not think to allow you to torture the one who shared his face."

I froze. Tripp. "There was another?"

"Indeed. Though, it perhaps is for the best that you were not able to attend his torture."

I fought to keep my breathing under control. "Why is that?"

"One of the enemies happened upon the group of men I sent. He managed to kill every one of them and then," Drogo touched my cheek lightly, "he lured an entire legion of my men to their deaths. I would not have wished to lose something as precious as you to that."

"That's most thoughtful of you, Drogo."

He raked his gaze over me, making me nauseous as he went. "Ah, Lynn, you would have enjoyed it. Before I lost communication with the men I had sent in, I had an open line with them, allowing me to hear all that went on." He smiled, licking his fang as he did. "The one they were sent to torture had a female who lived with him. I instructed my men to seek her out and destroy her. I also forced the knowledge that they would do this into his head."

I swallowed hard.

"He begged for her life, Lynn. A soldier for the other side's front line actually begged for the life of one he held dear. Is that not pathetic? It shows how weak they are, Lynn." He brushed his lips past mine and I tipped my head back. "Imagine how powerful we would be together," he whispered so soft that I barely heard it. "With Jean-Paul out of the way we would rule."

"Are you asking me to kill my husband?"

He chuckled. "I would never ask you to do that. In fact, I am saving you the heartache."

"What?" I asked, suddenly scared for Jean-Paul's life. I glanced over at him and watched as he lifted his glass of champagne to his lips. I knew then what was going on. I thrust power out, knocking the glass from his hand and tipping any more that were on our table over. All the men glanced my way. Well, all except Riston.

Drogo laughed. "I see that you truly are concerned for him but with the amount of poison that was in it, it matters not if he ingests anymore. Now, shall we start our reign?"

"No." I went to go to Jean-Paul but found Drogo holding me back.

Matty made a move and Drogo instantly had several of his guards surrounding him. I hated that the vampire had the power to make men materialize. Basically, I hated him and knew I would be the one to kill him.

"Let go of me."

"What does it matter if you go to him or not? He will be dead, or rather, deader than he already is, very soon. You cannot save him. You have not the ability to heal." Drogo pulled me close and tried to kiss my cheek. I jerked my head back. "Do not try to tell me that you actually love your husband."

I locked gazes with Jean-Paul just in time to see the color begin to fade from his. My heart thumped wildly. He was a major pain in my ass but he was also my friend. Glancing over, I found that Riston had turned to meet my gaze. As I stared at him I nodded. "I love my husband."

Riston tipped his head, seeming surprised by my public admission. I tugged harder to be free. "I love my husband, now let go of me."

Riston stood fast, followed by the rest of group. Jean-Paul attempted to stand but failed. I gave Riston a pleading look and he closed his eyes. I thought he'd tell me no, that he wouldn't help Jean-Paul but when he opened them, he nodded.

I mouthed the words "thank you" and watched him try to go to Jean-Paul only to find vampires and shifters materializing in his path. They all went at him at once. Something stopped them from actually touching Riston. Confused, I paused. So did Drogo.

Seizing the opportunity, I brought my elbow up fast, catching him in the throat. "Matty!"

He launched into action, pulling his weapon and firing it at the men who surrounded him. Seger came leaping out, his claws erect and took the remaining men away from Matty and me, leaving only Drogo standing. I jerked him hard, pulling him to me.

Putting my hand out, I let my power rise. "Stake." One appeared on demand, causing the crowd to whisper. The men surrounding Jean-Paul and Riston stared at me as though they weren't sure what to do.

"Back away from them, now," I said, lifting the stake high ready and itching to kill Drogo.

Drogo gasped. "Lynn, I do not understand. I sense that you want me yet you..."

"You sense I what?"

Seger cleared his throat. "You tend to ooze that sex magik when you sing. I think he took it as a sign that you, uhh, you know."

"What did you give Jean-Paul?" I glared at Drogo. The need to stake him was great. "Tell me what you gave him. I will not play games with you, Drogo." I glanced over my shoulder. "Matty, get

Hansen, we're taking him with us."

"He is a spy, Lynn, he will turn you over to the enemy." Drogo moved to embrace me and I thrust the stake into his stomach and yanked back fast. He held himself, clearly in pain. "You did not kill me?"

My breathing came in ragged intakes as I saw Jean-Paul's skin graying. "What did you give him and how can I fix it?"

"You cannot heal a vampire, Lynn. Even if you had the touch of healing you could not."

"Jean-Paul?"

He averted his gaze from me and sat there, slowly decaying before my eyes. "He is correct. I am technically already dead, *ma chérie*. To attempt to heal me would be to sign your own death warrant."

I jerked Drogo hard. "You fucking demon piece of…wait, demon, that's it." I handed Seger the stake. "If he so much as blinks, kill him. Do your best to keep him alive. I'd love to try some of my famous torture techniques on him."

"Lynn?"

Ignoring him, I ran at the men blocking Riston and the others. They turned, faced me and laughed. One stepped forward, thrust his chest out and had the nerve to sneer. "We fear no man's whore."

A flash of something across the room caught my attention. When I spotted Eric and Seaton moving up slowly I smiled. They nodded.

"So am I just a whore or do you dislike women in general?" I asked, not bothering to keep my darkness up as much as I normally would in this circumstance. "I think I should make it clear that I'm going to help him and none of you are going to stop me."

The man adjusted the bulge in his pants and laughed. "Babycakes, I love women but they're only good for one thing, well two if you count when they're on their knees. It's sick how Jean-Paul lets you lead him around. It's even sicker how Drogo is willing to risk the wrath of the council for you. You're just another piece of ass. Maybe," he undid his belt, "if you had a real man you'd know your place."

Snapping my fingers, the music began to play again, its haunting sound filled the air. I smiled before letting a laugh erupt from me. "And you think you're the man to do this? Whip it out. Come on. Let the room see."

The man looked confused. I snorted. "It's not that hard, opps," I covered my lips with my hand, "slip of the tongue. What I was trying to say before I accused you of impotence. Wait, do you have issues with that? I'm just asking. Most of the time when I meet a guy who wants to play macho bad ass and all women are inferior, he either has size issues or issues in general."

"She's stalling, kill them," another said. I locked gazes with him and let my eyes fill with black. "It can't be."

"Why you bitch. You want to see what I've got. Fine." He came charging towards me. I sensed Matty coming and put my hand up. The man was on me in an instant. He took hold of my hair, arching my head back. "Not so tough without your men standing between you and me are you?"

"Oh, yeah, you're a tough guy. Pulling hair is very manly. Often, when I'm thinking of what gets me hot, I think of big strong men who fight like girls."

I watched carefully as Eric and Seaton moved into place. Eric winked and I knew he was all set. The man holding me yanked me off my feet by my hair. I winced but didn't cry out. He brought his hand back and slapped me hard across the face.

"Oran, no!" Drogo yelled out. "You will not harm her."

Oran pressed his face to mine and licked my cheek. "Master, she tricks you, using her gifts. She's a siren. You listen to her voice and she works her way into your head. You can't see it but it's true. Just look at how she tries to save Jean-Paul."

"Psst, Oran, you hit like a girl too." I stilled and tipped my head a bit before bursting out into laughter. "I think I just brushed past your cock but it was rather small so it might have just been a wrinkle in your pants or something."

Oran brought his hand back again and I felt it, what I'd been waiting for, Drogo's power. It ripped Oran from me and seized hold of the other men, the ones standing between Jean-Paul and me. Eric and Seaton drew their weapons, watching Riston's six. I ran to Jean-Paul and caught him a moment before he went limp.

"Help me, please."

Seger was there in an instant, picking him up and putting him over his shoulder. Matty came rushing down from the stage with Hansen over his shoulder as well. I shook my head. "What the fuck went wrong? This was supposed to be an intelligence run not a blood bath."

They both pointed at Riston. "Their team showed up."

I glanced behind me to see Drogo battling it out with Oran and the others. "That will only hold them for a little bit. We need to get the hell out of here and get Hansen and Jean-Paul to safety." I followed behind Seger but stopped when I realized that Riston and the others weren't coming.

Branson tapped his arm. "Hey, big scary lycan magik guy, are you planning on leaving or not?"

"I think we'll stay a bit."

"Riston?"

Branson looked at me and shook his head. "No, get it out of your head. You can't stay too. Go home, put pearls on, cook dinner, umm, scratch that last comment and wait for your husband there. The shit's hitting the fan here and you aren't staying to play in it."

"Eww, you are nasty."

He grinned. "Thanks. Now, come on." As he reached for me, I pulled away.

"Riston, what's going on?"

"Go," he said, refusing to look at me.

Puzzled, I reached for him. "Riston?"

He growled and Eric pushed me back. "Take her and go," he said to Branson.

Branson took my arm and I reached for Riston. "I'm sorry."

He let out a soft laugh but didn't turn to face me. "Go see to your vampire, *Lynn*."

"Riston, please just look at me."

Eric shook his head lightly with a sad look on his face. "Go, I'll make sure he gets home."

"I'm sorry about everything. I shouldn't have blamed you. I know that you..."

Riston turned his head and glared out through pits of icy blue. His eyes were so light that they almost looked white. He curled his lip, revealing a set of teeth that were anything but human. "Go see to your vampire. As soon as he's feeling better he can break that bond for you."

"RJ."

"What?" he asked, snarling as he did.

"I wasn't lying."

"You weren't lying about what?"

"I really do love you." Not wanting to see his disgust for me, I turned quickly and went with Branson.

"You have no idea what love is, *Lynn*." He squared his shoulders. "Go back to your own life."

Chapter Ten

I pulled into my driveway and couldn't help but stare at Riston's house. There was no sign of him. I exhaled and decided it was safe to stop white-knuckling the steering wheel. As I opened my car door I sensed someone close by. Turning, I found Amber standing there, her face blank but her emotions raging enough on the inside that I could actually feel it. It didn't surprise me. I'd earned it.

"Here to stay or stopping in to pick of a few things before you disappear for another three and half months? Hey, why not go for seven years?"

"Hi, Amber."

"Hi Amber? That's all I get?" She put her hand on her jean-clad hip and folded her arms across her chest. The light blue sweater she wore looked great on her but I didn't think it was a good time to point that out. "You leave again, and that's all you have to say to me?"

"Aunt Karri!" Hilary shouted, running across the street with a ponytail bouncing madly as she came.

Amber stilled. "Go home, Hilary."

"No," she said, plain as day. "I told you that she's come back. I told you that she wouldn't miss my birthday party."

"Honey, I don't think Karri came back for that."

I winked at Hilary as I walked to the back of my car and opened the trunk. Reaching in, I pulled out a large wrapped box. It was heavier than I'd been lifting and had been placed in the trunk by Matty.

"Hey, let me help you with that." The sound of Eric's voice was music to my ears. He pushed in and took the present from me. "Geesh, tell me that you didn't get her a ton of bricks."

I laughed. "I didn't. I promise."

"Eric, don't stand there like nothing happened," Amber spat.

He glanced at me and then towards Amber. "It's not our business, Amber. It's between them. Leave it that way."

She shook her head. "No. You can't stand there and tell me that. Not when you're the one who has to convince Riston to come out of his house anymore. To bother to live. You're the one who has had to shoulder everything because she left him a wreck. How could you just leave, Karri?"

A slight breeze blew past reminding me that summer was nearing an end. I shivered and second guessed my decision to wear a long, gypsy-like red skirt. The long-sleeved white peasant blouse I wore was loose fitting and provided a bit of protection from the cool breeze.

Eric sighed. "She left because he told her to, Amber."

"Uncle Riston was being a bird head," Hilary said, shocking all of us.

"Hilary."

Eric laughed. "Well, she has a point." He nodded towards the bags in my trunk. "Let me take this over to the party and I'll help you in with all of that."

"Thank you."

"Eric." Amber stood rooted in place looking as though she wanted to spit fire.

Eric swallowed hard and cast me a wary glance. "This is going to leave me being yelled at for weeks but, Amber, knock the attitude off and spend some time with your best friend." He looked down at Hilary. "Come on, pumpkin, we need to get back to your party."

"But isn't Karri coming?"

I glanced at Amber. "I'll be over in a minute, sweetie."

"Are you here to stay?" she asked, touching her father's leg.

I held Amber's gaze. "That's not up to me anymore. But I'd like to stay."

Hilary smiled wide as she walked back across the street with Eric. Amber on the other hand, didn't crack even a slight smile. No. She gave me a hard look and for a minute I thought she'd yell. She didn't. Instead, she cried.

The instant I saw her tears I went to her and wrapped my arms around her tight. As she went to me, her hand brushed over my stomach and she let out a choked laugh. "I see you finally started eating. It's about time you..." She stopped and stared up at me through her tear filled eyes. "Karri, are you?"

I nodded and couldn't help but tear up a bit too. I lifted my blouse, revealing my slightly swollen abdomen and she squealed. "Holy shit! You really are. Oh God, you need to tell Riston. Come on."

Amber tried to pull me across the street but I stopped her. "Amber, no."

"No? Karri, he's the father, right?"

Shaking my head, I rolled my eyes. "Of course he's the father but wait a minute. I want to talk to him privately, not in front of all the birthday party guests. Okay?"

She nodded. "Sorry, I'm just excited. Gawd, I'm going to be an Aunt. You're going to be a mommy. I can't believe this."

"Yes you are. And you're also going to be a godmother."

Her eyes lit as she hugged me again. "Here I am yelling at you and…hey, you should have called and told me."

"I needed time to think. Time to get things in order." And heal, but I didn't tell her that.

Her brow furrowed. "Get things in order? Like what?"

"Like, quitting my job or rather, stepping down as team leader and handing it over to Seger." I smiled as she hugged me tighter. "You were right, I don't need to work and I refuse to put," I ran my hand over my stomach, "anyone else's life at risk."

"Are you really back for good?"

I shrugged. "That depends on you. If you'll let me back into your life, I'd like to stay."

"Karri, of course I will. In fact, I've never shut you out of my life." She gave me a good squeeze before she let go of me. "You know, Riston isn't doing so good."

My chest tightened at the mere mention of his name. "What do you mean?"

"I mean that he's worse than when Paula died, Karri. He shuts himself away for weeks at a time and no one can get through to him. He even stopped going on missions. Eric's concerned. We all are. I know he told you to go but the fact that he has fallen apart should tell you that he didn't want you to really leave."

I kept my head held high even though all I really wanted to do was hang it and cry. "We should get over to the party. I meant to be here an hour ago but traffic was heavy."

"You're changing the subject," Amber said, not cutting me any slack.

"And you're very perceptive."

I took her hand in mine and headed towards Eric's house. The sound of music and laughter filled the air the closer we got to the backyard. As we headed around the house, balloons and streamers seemed to be everywhere. Hilary spotted me and was running straight towards me before I could even get my bearings.

Amber stepped in front of me and caught her a second before she would have slammed into me. "Hey there, birthday girl, take it easy."

"Aunt Karri, come show my friend Mindy how you can flip around like me."

"Oh, umm, Aunt Karri can't do that now," Amber said, clearing her throat. "Go play with your friends. It's present time soon."

"But..." Hilary's smile fell.

I put my hand out and touched her cheek. "I missed you and I missed seeing you do your flips. Have you been practicing what I showed you?"

"Uh-huh."

"How about you head back and play with your friends and I'll come over in a little bit to see how good you are it at now?"

She beamed. "Okay."

Amber took my arm in hers. "I'm going to steal Karri to help me in the kitchen."

Hilary seemed to accept that excuse as she ran off to play with her friends. Amber led me towards the back porch. I glanced around the large yard and stopped dead in my tracks when I spotted Riston with his back to me, flipping hamburgers on the grill.

I watched as he stood there, a beer in one hand and spatula in the other. Any other man would look like he was doing something not too out of the ordinary but for Riston to be drinking beer it meant he wanted to sleep--wanted to forget.

"Uncle Riston, look at this," Hilary yelled as she and her friends did somersaults.

As he turned he head to watch her, I saw that he'd stopped shaving and had a full beard. He had also apparently given up cutting his hair because it was to his ears. While he didn't look bad, he didn't look like the Riston I'd last left.

"Good job, sweetie," he said, his voice lacking any real emotion.

It broke my heart to see him that way. I would have gone straight to him but I wasn't sure if he'd cause a scene or not. We'd parted on bad terms. So bad that he'd been partially shifted when he told me to get out of his life.

"Go to him," Amber whispered.

I shook my head. "I don't want to cause any problems, Amber. I'll talk to him after the party. Let's just go in and finish what needs to be done in the kitchen and I'll tell him I'm here in a little bit."

"Aunt Karri, Aunt Karri, are you coming to watch me flip now? I told everyone you'd come but they didn't believe me. Uncle Riston said that he didn't think you'd ever come back--ever. I told him he was wrong. I said you'd come and you did."

Amber snickered. "Or, Hilary could just announce that you're here now."

Riston stood tall and turned ever so slowly. Our eyes locked and for a moment, I couldn't breathe, couldn't even think. He didn't have his glasses on so there was nothing between his blue eyes and me. The way he stared at me left me feeling like he wasn't pleased to see me. I'm not sure what it was I'd expected him to do when he saw me again but just staring at me wasn't it.

"Go to him, Karri."

"He doesn't really look like he wants me to, Amber. I'm not about to piss him off in front of a backyard full of guests. It's fine. I'll, umm," the threat of tears hit me hard, "I think I'll head back across the street for a little bit. This was a bad idea. I..."

Amber touched my arm lightly. "Karri, go to him. You know you want to, don't you?"

"More than you'll ever know."

"Then go." She gave me a tiny push but I held my ground.

"Amber, he looks like he hates me. I can't..."

Hilary waved her hands madly. "Aunt Karri, come on!"

I backed up a bit. "Oh gods, Amber. What was I thinking? I can't do this. I can't face him and hear him tell me to go again. I just had to see him. I had to know he's okay. I..."

"You are forgetting that he's a lycan and can hear every word you're saying," Amber said, drawing me out of my mini-freak out. She was right.

Looking up, I found that Riston was no longer manning the grill, Seaton was. He wagged his brows at me and nodded his head. Confused, I scanned the yard for Riston but didn't find him. Instantly, my stomach churned and I had to take a deep, calming breath. "He left. Amber, I didn't mean to hurt him. I swear I didn't. I only asked Jean-Paul to break our bond because I didn't want Riston to die. I never did it because I didn't want him. That wasn't it at all. I swear to you that I love him and didn't mean to hurt him."

Amber seized hold of my arms. "What do you mean that you wanted your bond broke because you didn't want Riston to die? I thought he's immortal."

"He is." A sinking feeling came over me and I knew that I couldn't hold it together any longer. Turning to run, I slammed into something big and hard. Large arms wrapped around me as I went backwards, preventing me from falling. As I looked up I found myself staring into a pair of crisp blue eyes.

Riston stared down at me, his face neutral. "Are you okay?"

"I am now," I said, without thought.

"Aunt Karri!" Hillary called out.

Riston ran his hand down my arm slowly. "I tried to explain that you aren't her aunt but she doesn't want to hear that."

"Why am I not her aunt?" I asked, doing my best to keep from throwing myself into his arms.

A puzzled look came over his face. "Uhh, because you had your vampire friend, who, by the way, I heard made it thanks to your blood, break our bond, Karri. That means you divorced me the same day I took you as my wife."

"Who did you hear that I gave Jean-Paul blood from?"

He motioned towards Seaton. "I sent him to check on you, after I," he averted his gaze, "lost my temper and said things I didn't mean. Things I was too late to take back, Kars."

"So Seaton told you that I gave Jean-Paul blood, okay. I understand that because I did. William had spent so many years feeding me poisons that I was sure I'd been exposed and had overcame whatever Drogo gave Jean-Paul and I was right. But what makes you think I'm not Hilary's aunt?"

He sighed. "Come on, Karri, you know as well as I do that when you had Jean-Paul sever the bond between..."

I pressed my fingers to his lips, rendering him silent. "Riston, answer a question for me."

He nodded.

"Do you understand why I asked him to do that?"

As he closed his eyes and exhaled I could feel his pain. Oh, he knew. I was right. He'd been in the room the night PJ had visited. He'd heard everything. He nodded.

"Then you should be happy that I asked, right?"

Shaking his head, he took my hand from his mouth and held it to his now bearded cheek. "No, Kars. No part of me is glad you did it. I took you as my wife, to love for always, regardless how long or short that is."

"Is it possible for a mate to lay claim to his significant other a second time?"

He looked as though he was in actual pain and that made my chest hurt even more. "Not if his mate had the connection purposely severed of her own free will. If she did that then he can never take her as his wife again."

"Whew."

Amber and Riston stared at me like I'd lost my mind. I smiled wide. "Damn good thing I didn't let Jean-Paul go through with breaking your bond with me then."

The wide-eyed look I got from Amber told me exactly how shocked she was. As I directed my attention to Riston I realized that her reaction paled in comparison to his. "Riston, are you upset that I didn't have him do it?"

He lifted me high into the air so fast that my stomach felt like it dropped. "Are you serious? You didn't have him...We're not...You're still my...?"

Laughing, I stared down at him. "Yes, I'm serious. I didn't have him do it. We're not divorced and yes, I'm still your wife." I hesitated. "That is, I'm still your wife if you want me to be. I can understand completely if you're not willing to risk..."

Riston brought me down fast and held me tight to him as he captured my lips with his. Thrusting his tongue into my mouth, he covered me in his power sending the mystical threads that I'd never allowed to be broken into a frenzy. I wrapped my arms around his neck and returned his kiss with all that I had, letting my tongue trace his. My entire body responded to him. My nipples hardened, my inner thighs tingled and my pussy grew damp with each swipe of his tongue over mine. My heart beat madly, thumping wildly as I ran my fingers through his hair and his beard bit at my face.

"Umm, guys, kids are here and they are all watching the two of you," Amber said, laughing slightly under her breath.

Riston groaned. "Mmm," he kissed me again, "I don't want to stop. Tell them to go away."

Laughing, I cupped the sides of his scruffy, beard covered face and pulled back from him. "It's our niece's birthday."

He smiled wide. "Our niece. I like the sound of that, Kars."

"If you like the sound of that imagine how you'll like the sound of being called..." Amber paused as I shook my head. "Umm, being called a happy guy again. Boy o' boy for a while there we were just calling you hermit."

Smooth.

Something tugged on my skirt and I glanced down to find Hilary standing there. She smiled wide and I noticed that her front teeth were almost all the way in. "You looked like you really like kissing a lycan."

Reaching down, I ran my hand through her ponytail. "Well, birthday girl, I really like kissing your uncle so I guess that's a big yes."

"Will you come and show my friends how you flip?" she asked, this time sounding even more desperate.

"Honey, I'm wearing a skirt and this time I don't have shorts on under it so I'm going to have to pass right now. Plus, I haven't been doing much flipping around lately." I traced a line down her cheek and tapped the tip of her button nose.

"Why not?"

Riston cupped my hand in his as I answered, "Because I've been very tired lately and have to take it a little bit easier now. The doctor told me to cut down on my flipping for a little bit."

"Doctor?" Riston asked, concern lacing his voice. "Karri, no. We'll fix this. I know we can." He pulled me to him and hugged me tight.

I tried to pull back from him but he kept a death grip on me. I tapped on his arm. "Riston, you're cutting off my breathing."

"Oh," he loosened his hold, "sorry. Are you okay?"

"I'm just a little tired. I drove straight here." I put my hand out to Hilary. "How about we make a date to dance together in a little bit? How does that sound?"

"You can still dance?" Hilary asked.

"Yep. Can you?"

She giggled. "You're silly. No, you're crazy beautiful."

Bending down, I cupped her face and kissed her forehead. "You, my darling, are amazingly beautiful, just like your mommy."

"Really?" she asked, her eyes wide.

I nodded.

"Oh, Daddy said I could open presents. Will you watch me?"

"Yes," I laced my fingers tight with Riston's and lifted his hand, "we will, Hilary."

Hilary ran off towards her mound of presents just as Eric walked up to us. He glanced at our joined hands and smiled. "Looks like I have to move over and let the team leader have his spot back, huh?" He put his hands up fast. "I'm fine with that. More than fine with it to be exact."

A slow smile moved over Riston's face. "Good."

"Aren't you glad I forced you to get out of bed and shower today?"

Riston growled and hugged me to him. "Yes and I'm sure Karri is even happier about that considering I'm hanging on her at the moment."

I poked him in the stomach and realized just how much weight he'd lost. "Riston, when is the last time you ate something?"

He glanced at Amber. "Umm?"

Rolling her eyes, she put her hand on her hip. "Yesterday morning. I forced you to eat an apple."

"Great, I gain weight while my husband loses it. Wonderful, why is it I'm not liking this set up much?" I asked, running my hand up his side, under the black tee shirt he wore. By my guess, he'd lost at least ten pounds, maybe a bit more. He was still solid muscle he just wasn't taking care of himself like he should be.

Riston ran his hand over my hip and I waited for him to comment on my swollen abdomen but he stopped just shy of touching it. "You haven't gained any weight, Kars and you still need to."

Amber laughed so hard that she sounded like a seal barking and I joined her. Eric and Riston just stood there trying to figure out what was so funny. I met Riston's gaze and smiled. "Honey, you need to look a little harder or put your glasses back on."

"I'll have you know," his gaze fell to my breasts, "*hello*."

Amber and I only laughed harder.

"Kars, did you, umm, is it me or are your," he glanced at Eric, "chunga-chungas bigger?"

"On that note, I'm turning around to watch my daughter who is now ripping open the huge box that Karri brought and ignoring you." He chuckled. "Don't fall in, sweetheart. I don't think we'll find you again."

Hilary's mouth opened wide but no sound came out. She looked up at me and narrowed her gaze. Eric glanced back at me. "Why is my daughter giving you the evil eye?"

I didn't have to answer, Hilary did. "This better mean what I think it means."

"What did you get her?" Riston asked.

"*We* got her some new toys."

Hilary yanked on the side of box and I sent my magik out and over the yard to help her get it. It fell away and she stood there staring at two white wooden doll cradles, two matching highchairs, a doll stroller for two and another wrapped box."

Amber drew in a sharp breath and covered her mouth. Eric went to her side quickly. "Amber, what's wrong? Are you feeling okay?"

Nodding, she glanced at me and I smiled. Tears filled her eyes.

"What's in this one?" Hilary asked, lifting the smaller, still wrapped box.

"That's from Uncle Riston."

Riston ran his hand up my spine slowly. "It is?" he whispered in my ear.

"Mmmhmm."

"Funny, I could have sworn that I got her a bike."

Reaching up, I took hold of his chin and focused his attention on Hilary just as she finished opening the second box. She screamed and Eric jumped. Amber held tight to him and patted his hand.

Hilary held up one lifelike baby doll dressed in pink and another dressed in blue."

"Damn, Eric, we should have thought to get her dolls. She looks like she might pass out," Riston said, laughing softly.

A muffled cry came from Amber and Eric put his arm around her. "I think maybe we should avoid them. Amber looks like she might pass out too. I never knew a toy could cause such an uproar."

I stared out at Hilary and motioned to the small box. "There's one more thing in there."

Hilary bent down, cradling the dolls like a new mommy and gasped. She lifted a diaper bag and held it out for all to see. Embroidered on the side was 'World's Greatest Big Cousin.'

Eric chuckled. "Aww, Karri that was a great gift. She's been after Riston about getting cousins since she met you. The dolls will keep her happy. Thanks."

I didn't comment. Rather, I looked out at Hilary and smiled. She held the dolls close to her and hugged them tight. "Will you teach me how to change diapers, Aunt Karri?"

I snorted. "Sweetheart, we're going to need Amber to show us that. You need to practice being a big cousin and I need to practice being a mommy. We better hurry. We've only got about four months to get it right. They tell me that since I'm having twins they might come earlier than normal."

"Oh, shit," Eric said, turning to stare at Riston.

I did the same. Riston stood there like a statue, his breathing was sporadic at best. When he didn't move or comment I backed up a bit worried that he wasn't as excited as I was. I looked away and swallowed hard. "I'm going to rest for a bit. I'll stop back by later today."

"Karri, wait," Amber said, coming to me quickly. "Are you serious? Twins? A boy and a girl?"

I nodded. As I went to take a step I felt Riston's power wrap around me tight. He looked at me then stared at the sky. It was then I realized what he was doing--blinking back tears. He didn't want to cry in front of anyone let alone one of his men. It was the alpha in him.

Putting my hand out to him, I smiled. "RJ, I'm tired. Take me home for a little bit and sit with me just until I fall asleep. Please."

He nodded and drew in his lower lip. Eric glanced at me and winked. He knew what I was doing. Riston walked slowly, almost robot-like to me. He took my hand and followed me into the side yard. When we were far enough from the party to not be seen or heard, he stopped me and pulled me to him.

"Kars? We're…I'm…?"

"We're pregnant, Riston. Well, I'm pregnant anyway, but yes, we're having babies."

"Babies," he said, sounding as though he were trying to comprehend the entire thing. "I'm going to be a daddy." He stared at me and something moved over his face. Before I knew what was going on, he had me swept up in his arms and cradled to his chest.

"Riston, put me down. You're going to hurt yourself."

"Honey, talk to my niece. I've picked up a car for her. You're like holding a feather." The shit ass grin he gave me made me laugh. He turned us in a circle fast, leaving me clutching hold of him. "Karri."

Doing my best to suppress my newfound fit of the giggles, I stared up at him. "Yes?"

A lone tear fell down his cheek and my breath caught as I leaned up and kissed it away. "Are you happy, Riston? Please tell me that you're not upset."

"I just found out that my mate, the one and only woman I have ever loved in my life didn't divorce me and trade me in for a vampire. And that she not only still loves me after I was being the biggest jackass in the world but is carrying my babies in her--our babies. Happy doesn't even begin to cover it, Kars. No. It doesn't even scratch the surface."

Holding me even closer to him, Riston kissed my forehead. "Karri, I fell apart without you. I thought I could make it. I thought that since I only really had you as my mate a few days that I could go on. But I couldn't." He shook slightly and that made me cry for him. "I love you so much that it hurts inside. It fucking hurts, Kars. Why?"

"I don't know, Riston, but it hurts me to be without you too."

"Marry me," he said fast.

Confused, I arched a brow. "RJ, darling, umm, we are still married."

"I know that. I mean marry me like humans do. Walk down the aisle and meet me at the end. I want to write in the sky that you're my wife. I want the world to know."

"Great, my husband is crazier than me. Riston, we're already…"

He grinned. "You can dress like a ballerina. Just like you told me you wanted to when you were little."

"Sold. Okay, what's the date?" I asked, laughing softly.

"The sooner the better. Can I still write it in the sky?"

"Only if you promise to write RJ and Kars forever."

* * * *

"Riston?" I clung tight to him as he opened the door to his bedroom. I'd already spent most of the time goose necking around to see everything in his house. While it was still the house I remember him living in it had been updated over the years. I wanted to see more of it. Riston seemed to have other plans. "What are you doing?"

Instantly, his magik was around me, caressing me and making me feel as though he were touching me everywhere. It ran over nipples that were now extremely sensitive and I arched my back.

Riston stood me up and yanked his tee shirt over his head. The moment I spotted his bare upper body my pussy quivered. It wanted him as much as I did, maybe more. Denying it the pleasures that Riston offered had been difficult to say the least. As he began to remove his boots and then his jeans, I knew it wouldn't be long before I had him in me again.

He stilled, right before pushing his jeans all the way down. "Kars, I need you to tell me now if I can't make love to you. If it will hurt the babies at all, tell me now. I'll also need you to call Eric and your men if I can't," he said, his voice sounding strained.

"Why? I don't want a room full of men in here with us."

A thin sheen of sweat broke out on Riston's brow as he pushed his pants down and then off. He took hold of his cock and only stroked it once before it was hard. He gripped it tight and stared at me. "Kars, I'm serious. If I'll hurt you or the babies in any way I need to know. I'll need to be chained until the urge to be in you passes."

My eyes widened. I didn't hesitate. Pulling my blouse over my head, I exposed my naked breasts to him. My nipples had darkened slightly and they had been filling a D-cup easily. I watched as Riston licked his lips, fixated on my breasts. A tiny tick began in his jaw and it was then I knew what was going on. The alpha in him had been denied its mate--RJ had been denied me, someone created to love him and be able to handle his sexual appetite far too long.

A sickening thought occurred to me. He'd mentioned once that after his sexual buttons were turned back on by his mate that he required sex multiple times a day. I'd been gone for fourteen weeks, who or what had he done that entire time?

He came at me and I put my hand up stopping him. "Riston?"

"Kars, hon," he put his hands out to his sides and claws shot from them, "I can't hold back from a full shift if I have to wait much longer."

I stared down at his clawed hands and took a tiny step back.

"Riston, have you been with other women since I've been gone. I need to know."

"What? Why in the hell are you asking me that?" His eyes swirled to an ice blue and I couldn't help but gasp. "Have you been with other men? Is that it, Karri?"

He came at me fast, lifted me off my feet and had me lying on the bed before I could even blink. He clawed the skirt free of me, leaving it in tiny shreds. Hooking a finger nail under the thin scrape of red material I called panties, Riston cut them free of me. "Have you, Karri?"

Lifting my legs, he somehow managed to get them up high without so much as grazing me with his deadly claws. My heart beat madly in my chest as he climbed over me in all his naked glory. The ice blue eyes he stared out at me from were the wolf's. I knew that and accepted it.

"Have you?" he asked, pressing the head of his cock to my wet entrance. His eyes flickered and his body stiffened. "Karri," his voice suddenly sounded more like his own, "call for help."

Reaching up, I cupped his face and shook my head. "No, Riston. I won't call anyone to stop my husband from loving me. I won't break and the babies will be fine."

"Kar-ri, call for...help," he bit out.

Having enough of his attempts at saving me from himself, I let my magik rise fast. It sought his out. Closing my eyes, I concentrated on loosening the natural hold on my sexual power as well. The minute I felt it slip free, Riston thrust into me with a growl that seemed to shake the house.

His massive cock spread my channel taut and filled me to the brink of pain. No part of me cared or worried. I had the power over him. I knew that now. Even when the beast was sharing his command, I still had the reins because I controlled me--what he wanted. My greatest weapon with Riston like this was sex and I knew it.

Wrapping my legs around his waist, I clung to him as he began to drill into me with the strength of ten men. The sexual energy I was releasing began to run over us slowly, caressing, seeking out pleasure points and stimulating them. The moment it found my clit I cried out under Riston as I took all that he had to offer.

I felt it then, Riston's power creeping up and wrapping me in a coating of protection, paying extra attention to my womb. As far out of control as he appeared to be, my RJ was still in, still making sure the people he loved were safe.

"That's it. Right there, Riston. Right there." Tipping my head back, I gave in to the pleasure that was building, causing my toes to tingle and the sensation to move slowly up my legs. They quivered in its wake and the moment it moved through my abdomen I cried out. The orgasm was too strong, too powerful, too perfect. My pussy clenched Riston's cock in a death grip, pulling him back into me each time he tried to exit.

"I'm coming. Yes, there."

Our breathing was all over the place. Mine came in fast pants with each thrust he made. As his cock began to swell I felt the tension in his body easing. The added filling in my pussy of Riston now rubbing against my G-spot left me clawing at his back and gritting my teeth.

"Uhh, Karri," he whispered as cum shot forth from him, filling me. Riston held tight there, continuing to fill me. The longer his orgasm the more he seemed to regain control of himself.

I closed my eyes as yet another wave of pleasure washed over me. The minute I felt Riston's fingers tracing the side of my face I knew he was back. His claws were gone. "Mmm, thank you."

"Did I hurt you or the babies?"

Smiling, I peeked out to find him with nothing short of concern etched all over his face. "Riston, I'm fine. They're fine. It's safe for us to be together and I felt you making extra sure of that."

"Gods, Kars, I couldn't help myself. I've spent months trying to sleep every moment I can to control the urge but when I saw you..."

"You spent months denying that kind of pull?"

He let out a soft sigh. "It was that or show up on your doorstep and fuck the living hell out of you, honey. I didn't think you'd appreciate that too much."

"Why me? Why not some other woman?" I asked, staring up at him. "I woke up your sexual desires but when I left...I...I thought you were throwing me out of your life to find someone else to fill them, Riston."

"No, gods no. I didn't throw you out, Karri. I chased you away with my inability to keep my temper under control. I'd never felt anything like that before. Seeing *him* kiss you on that stage, even knowing it had to be done for effect, I couldn't handle it. Then to hear that the two of you...to hear that was too much. I couldn't deal with it and temporarily lost my mind. The minute you told me that you loved me I started to pull into myself." He kissed the tip of my nose. "Turns out, I'd challenged the entire fucking bar full of supernaturals to a fight to the death."

My eyes widened. "You did what?"

Riston blushed and I couldn't help but laugh. He nodded his head. "Yep. I went so crazy at the idea of you breaking our bond and leaving me that I decided to take on everything in there. I knew I couldn't live without you and I was hoping one of them would end it for me."

Hearing that hurt but I didn't comment. I knew what it was like to feel that desperate so I didn't have room to lecture. "So, what made you fight instead of taking what they could dish out? I get the feeling that the only way one of them was going to win was if you lay down and let them kill you."

His lips found mine and the kiss he gave me made my toes curl. The feel of his cock twitching within me made me smile, reminding me that we were one. "Mmm," he pulled back a bit, "I fought back because Eric reminded me that you are Jack and Victoria's daughter."

"And?" I asked, unsure how that would change his mind.

A sly grin moved over his face. "And, Jack was stubborn as hell but Victoria knew how to deal with him. Jack would piss her off but she'd always bring him back to his senses. No matter what dumbass, macho thing he did or said, she'd set him in his place and they'd be fine." He kissed me again. "Eric told me that you were genetically prone to dealing with someone like me and that while you too could be stubborn, you were in love with my sorry ass."

I cupped his ass cheeks and licked my lips. "Nothing sorry about this, baby."

Riston chuckled. "Eric also pointed out that you'd managed to forgive me for everything that had happened growing up and if you could do that then there was at least a snowball's chance in hell you'd forgive me again. I punched him in the face and told him that he didn't know his ass from a hole in the ground." He shrugged. "I guess I owe him an apology."

I laughed even though the nagging question of him being with other women was still weighing heavily on me.

I should have let them call him. I shouldn't have hid it all from him. I deserve to find out that he moved on without me. I deserve...

"Karri."

"Hmm?" I pulled myself out of my self-induced panic attack and focused on him.

"I can hear you, in my head when you let your guard down or concentrate on me." He shook his head and looked pained. "Honey, you are my mate. It doesn't matter if you keep me around or not, I cannot and would not ever betray that. You are the only woman I've been with since I met you, Karri-Lynn and considering I was there the day you born you should feel pretty damn good about that. Because that means I haven't been with another woman in twenty-nine years."

I couldn't stop the swell of joy that rose. Pulling on the back of his neck, I brought his head down and kissed him with all my love.

He drew back reluctantly. "Kars, what do you mean when you said you should have let them call me and shouldn't have hidden something from me. What?" I could almost see the wheels in his head churning. He gasped. "No, Karri. Tell me that you didn't leave and end up with Jean-Paul again. Tell me that you didn't let another man enter you. Please."

"Riston, Jean-Paul spent about three months sharing my bed."

His eyes flickered back and forth from their normal blue to ice. His jaw tightened. "I'm going to kill him."

I pressed my hand over his mouth as I stared up at him. "Oh, would you shut-up and keep your temper in check long enough to listen to me?"

He gave me a rather cold look and I took that as a sign to get to the point so I did. "Riston, he is the reason you're going to be a daddy."

Riston arched a brow and tipped his head, clearly not buying what I was telling him.

I kept my hand over his mouth. "I cut myself and forced my blood down his throat to save his, whatever he calls his vampire self. Anyway, during the time that he was still out, still recovering, I got sick, Riston. Very sick. I knew it was coming I just didn't realize it was going to happen so fast."

He stopped looking like he wanted to comment and started looking concerned. I took my hand away from his mouth. "What happened?"

I glanced away from him. "I died."

"You what?" He shook his head. "No. I would have felt it. I would have sensed your spirit trying to leave this plane, Kars."

"You couldn't sense what Jean-Paul wouldn't let go of."

"What?"

I ran my fingers over his full lips and offered him a small smile. "In his state of delirium, he still managed to sense what was happening in the next room. He held my spirit to this plane, Riston. He somehow managed to keep me from passing over while Seger and Matty fought to heal my body, make it strong enough to not only support me but the babies that Branson had instantly sensed."

"Oh my gods. You...I should have been there. I could have healed you."

"Riston, they worked around the clock for days until Jean-Paul recovered and guided my spirit back to my body. But that wasn't all he did, Riston."

He gave me questioning look.

"He held the babies' souls to this plane too. He held them to him just like he did me and refused to let anything harm them. He also helped them find their way back to my body, to grow and live. He did it all without being asked and asking nothing from me in return. He did it because whether or not he'll admit it, he is my friend and he does have a heart capable of caring--of loving." I cupped his face tight. "So, never let me hear you say you're going to kill him. He is the reason I'm here with you now. He's the reason..."

My stomach instantly felt as though it were full hundreds of butterflies. I stilled. It didn't. I felt something pushing against it, from the inside out. My breath caught as I seized hold of Riston's arm and guided his hand down the length of my body. Pressing his palm to my lower abdomen, I waited. It didn't take long. The movements began again, pressing and thumping against my stomach and his palm.

"Karri, is that..."

I nodded. "It's the babies."

He withdrew from me slowly, as if he were doing his best not to disturb them. It was cute so I didn't comment. When he moved down me with the speed of a supernatural to press his head to my stomach, as though he were listening to them, I gave in and giggled as I ran my hands through his hair. "I love you."

Riston stared up at me through dark lashes. "Karri-Lynn Wallace, I love you more than life itself, more than words can even describe. And," he pressed his lips to my stomach and kissed it gently, "I love our children and they aren't even here yet. Oh, I need to get a nursery set up and get their rooms ready."

I just bit my lip as I smiled.

His forehead creased. "Karri?"

"Yes," I said, amused with his behavior.

"Where are we going to live? I mean, technically, we don't live together--we're neighbors and I..."

"Riston, I trust you and love you. I'll follow wherever you go. Wherever you call home, I'll call home too. Though, you should know, Mr. Meticulous, that children make messes and ruin things."

A deep laugh tore free from him, catching me off guard.

"Riston?"

He kept laughing as he waved his hand in the air. His bedroom door slammed shut, startling me. He kissed my upper thigh and pointed towards the door. "Look closely at the wall."

I did and sat up so fast that I nearly knocked him off the bed. I couldn't believe my eyes, there, on the wall behind the door was a picture of the two of us. I could still remember the day that my father had been working on a project with Riston and I'd decided I'd do something nice for them. At the time, drawing a picture seemed like the perfect thing. I found a black marker on the table they were working at and used that.

I'd climbed the stairs, hunting for the perfect place to draw and when I found Riston's bedroom door standing open, I knew where I wanted to put--somewhere he'd be able to see it when he woke up everyday. It had been hard work, making a picture just right for him. I'd decided to make him something special so I drew a picture of his house and the family I just knew he'd have some day. Granted, the finished product looked more like several starved stick figures in front of a giant rectangle with flowers and a big tree but the point was made.

"Riston, you kept it?"

His entire face lit as he smiled wide. "You remember making it for me?"

I nodded. "Yes," I stood slowly, "I remember wanting to do something special for you because," I thought hard about it, "it was your birthday, but I knew you didn't tell anyone. I have no clue how I knew that. I just did."

I went to take a step towards it and found Riston sliding his hands around my waist and pulling me to him while he sat on the edge of the bed. He ran his hand over my slightly swollen belly and planted a kiss on it.

"You can tell you're pregnant when you stand up without your clothes on," he said, lightly.

Running my fingers through his hair, I snorted. "Gee, thanks for pointing that out to me, honey. I love knowing I'm getting fat."

"Kars, you're beautiful. This," he rubbed my stomach, "is one of the most beautiful things I have ever seen, next to you that is. Well, it's part of you so I think it still comes back to you being the..."

I laughed and pushed his forehead. "Okay, Romeo, you can stop laying it on so thick. You got me. I'm yours now, like it or not."

"Mmm, I love it." He kissed my arm, looking so happy that I never wanted the moment to end. "And I love you."

"I love you, too. Now, tell me why you kept that behind the door. You were," I glanced around his bedroom, "are, a neat freak. Gawd, I can still remember my father finding me doing it. He yelled so loud that I instantly began to cry. He told me that I had to go sit in the chair until it was time to go and apologize to you."

Cradling his head to my stomach, I caressed the back of it gently, savoring the feel of having Riston all to myself. "By the time my father was done lecturing me about how wrong it is to draw on someone's wall I wanted to crawl into a corner and hide instead of face you and tell you what I did. But you didn't yell. In fact, you asked me to tell you all about it--who each person was and so on. I can't remember much from there though."

He squeezed me tight. "You pointed to the figure that's me and told me that you drew me with glasses on because you thought they would help me see better since I would get headaches sometimes. You were right, Karri. Turns out that while my eyes are shifted, my vision is off the charts but in normal form, while it's still better than an average human's, it's not near what it is as a wolf. Most other shifters maintain one high level of great vision in both forms. Since mine varies so much, it tends to give me headaches."

"I love you," I said, feeling like it needed to be said every second of the rest of my life.

"I love you too, honey." Riston planted kisses over my stomach and squeezed me again. "Mmm, do you know what else you told me that day, Kars?"

I shook my head.

"You pointed at the figure of the woman and told me that was my wife. I commented on how she was very tall and you said she would have to be." He chuckled. "I asked why and you started on about how anyone shorter than her would need to stand on a chair to give me hugs or make me pick them up like I used to have to do with you. You also told me you were sorry you didn't have any other color marker to make my wife's hair blonde because you knew she would be."

A tiny laugh escaped from me as I listened to him talk.

"When I told you that I hoped my wife would have big beautiful brown eyes, you just giggled and told me not to be silly, not that many girls had hair that was as blonde as you knew my wife's would be and dark brown eyes." He gave me a look that told me just how amused with the entire event he was. "You also told me that when you found her, because you were sure you would, you'd bring her to me as a birthday present."

Riston stood slowly, sliding his arms around me snuggly as he went. "You did it, Kars. You did what you promised. You brought me my wife on my birthday. Somehow, you managed to time your arrival perfectly, blowing in like a tornado on my birthday. I watched you, when I spotted you in your front yard with Amber, I..."

My jaw dropped. "The day I came here was your birthday?" He nodded. I flicked his chest with my finger and laughed. "And you pulled that going invisible thing and lurked around didn't you?"

Putting his hand up, Riston did his best not to laugh. "Guilty as charged. I couldn't help myself. You're captivating, Kars. I had to be closer, hear your voice, find out anything I could about you. Hilary can sense me when I'm that way. She can do that to Eric too. That's why she came running out. But the second she saw you dancing with Amber she was captivated too."

He drew in a deep breath as he caressed my back. "Karri, you have no idea the havoc you caused on my system, on my senses. I couldn't think straight. I could only stand there staring at you, trying to figure out how my entire body could be reacting to a perfect stranger. The minute you told me who you were I knew then that you'd held true to your word. You brought my wife to me on my birthday--you brought you."

"Riston," I sighed, "I brought nothing but drama back into your life."

He balked. "Excuse me, sweetheart but did you happen to miss the fact I head a team that guards one of the biggest portals to the underworld around? Everyday is chaos for us. Remember the ice cream man you so artfully scared away by threatening commitment?"

I nodded.

"Yeah, that was a typical day, Kars. It's why we live in a tight cluster, separated from humans. It's why Eric keeps Amber so close. He's scared to death she'll be attacked because of her gifts and taken to serve as a mate for some evil thing that is anything but her true mate."

"Riston?"

He kissed the top of my head. "Yeah, Kars, I know there is something brewing between Eric and Amber. It makes sense. Paula wasn't his true mate. She knew it, so did he. She wasn't like you, Karri. She was able to have a family without hers. She was also able to love another fully. Most can. That's why Victoria apologized to you. She knew that it was different for us--we aren't the only ones like this. I don't have numbers or anything but I know they exist."

"Is Amber really Eric's mate?" I asked, doing my best to follow along.

Riston shrugged. "I honestly don't know. She might very well be but that's something only they can determine. I'm a little more concerned about who my niece's mate might be and who my daughter's will be."

Hearing him talk about his daughter made it all so real. "Why are you worried about her? She's not even here yet."

"Karri, I was in the room when you came into the world. I will never forget it. The second that you let out your first cry and I spotted you, everything changed for me. I stopped behaving the way I had been and suddenly became a workaholic. Paula already told you that we figured out why, when you were a little over the age of one."

I took a tiny step back from him. "Riston, nothing was wrong with the way things worked out for us. Nature keeps everything acceptable and I for one would love knowing that our daughter's mate is someone we know and trust. Why are you worried about it?"

"What if someone like Seaton or Branson ends up being her mate?"

I smiled. "Then I guess their days of living life in the fast track will end."

"Honey, you're missing my point."

Reaching down, I took hold of his cock and began to stroke it slowly. "No, I'm not. You know how you are sexually and you don't want to think about one of your friends or someone you know, who is as bad as you used to be, being with her when she's an adult."

"Exactly."

"Hypocrite."

He placed his hand over mine while I continued to stroke him. "Just tell me that we can lock her away from the world and never let any males see her and I'll be a happy man."

"What about your son?"

"Oh, well, we can only hope he gets out there and enjoys as many women as he can before he..."

I cupped him tight, almost too tight. "You were saying?"

"Uhh, oh, lock him away from the world too. Yep. Throw away the key."

I pressed my mouth to his and continued to stroke him. "RJ, make love to me now. Worry about being an overprotective father later."

"Yes, dear," he said, smiling as he inserted a finger into my pussy. "You're so wet and tight. You're going to have to stop being this way every time we're together, Kars or you might find yourself pinned under me upwards of six times a day."

"Promise?"

He growled out and looked upwards. "I'd like to say thanks to whoever made my mate. She may be more insatiable than I am."

"Riston, you do realize you're thanking my parents."

He cringed. "Damn, now I know how Jack must have felt. How the hell did he not kill me?"

Snickering, I continued to caresses him. "My guess is because he asked the gods to bring you as much happiness as he had. Sorry, buddy, but you got stuck with me. Now, make love to me before I flip you on your alpha ass and take advantage of you myself."

Riston picked me up and laid me on the bed quickly. "I think I can handle that. So, tell me, Kars. Do I have to worry about you going anywhere or turning into anything that scares even me?"

"If you don't fill me with you very soon you might." I laughed as he wagged his brows. "But, no. Seger has given me a clean bill of health and Jean-Paul swears that since I married you my darkness began shrinking away."

Riston slid his body over mine and settled between my spread legs. "Mmm, please know that I am going to take you every way imaginable, Karri. I can't get enough of you."

"You'll have to learn to share my time with the babies when they come."

A wicked grin spread over his face. "Then I guess I should work overtime on making love to you before they get here."

"And if I'm right and the portal opens again soon, with an ass load of demons in it, you'll have to share me too."

He stiffened. "No, I won't because you won't be anywhere near the fighting, honey. You, Amber and Hilary will be locked in this house with a protection spell dropped on it. I won't risk my family."

He captured my mouth with his and went to slide into me.

A white light filled the room and Riston drew back a bit. A white piece of paper fell from thin air. Riston used his power to grab it to him and sank his cock into me as he drew it near. I grabbed hold of his arms and held tight as he read it.

"What is it?"

He smiled as he kissed the tip of my nose. "This session is going to have to be a quickie, honey."

I made a pout face. "Mmm, no. I don't want this to end."

"Me either, but the idea of Jack walking in on me making love to my wife, uhh, his only daughter isn't sitting well with me. Your mother was nice enough to send a warning that he's coming to visit in an hour."

"He's what?" I asked, staring at Riston, waiting for him to tell me that he was joking. He didn't.

He lifted the note again and read out loud. "RJ, you have exactly one hour to finish rocking my daughter's world before her father shows up and rocks yours. Love, your mother-in-law, Victoria."

"See," Riston said, thrusting into me. "I need to," he kissed my lips sensually, "rock your world, honey."

"Oh, you are way past that, RJ. Way, way past it."

"I love you, Kars."

"I love you, too, Riston."

The End

Printed in the United States
59573LVS00001B/109-129

9 781586 087852